Dark Matter Ascension

Book 5

SerasStreams

Mango Media LLC

Book cover by White Horn. Typesetting by Miblart.

Dedication

To my parents: my mom, who fostered my love of reading by taking me to the library multiple times each week, and my dad, who supported the household and shared in my love for fantasy. You both supported me in my endeavors, gave me a place to regain my footing when my life fell apart, and have always been there for me. I hope I've made you proud.

Contents

Recap

Xera was satisfied. Not particularly happy, or excited, or pissed off—but just content. Her brother and the rest of her species were saved, and Jace was on his way to finish his task. The Grand Design of The Architects, to close the loop of life and death and make their Universe as it once was—before the meddling of The Ancients.

Laying down in her bed, she hooked up the feed and tapped the button to initiate the extraction and compression session. *This one is going to be a long one*, she thought as she sank into the soft mattress.

[Hello, Xera.]
[Welcome to you. Are you ready?]

"Yes," Xera replied with finality. "Hopefully for the last time."

[Confirmed. Engaging memory extraction and compression protocol . . .]
[Standby . . .]
[Initialized.]
[State your name and designation.]

"Xera'tal Pen'arkon, overseeing administrator for The Cosmic System."

[Confirmed identity.]
[Discuss events that you wish to withdraw and compress.]

Xera took a deep breath before beginning. "Jace headed into the Astral Verge."

Her Signer and the current strongest member of her faction, the Dark Between Stars. Her lone wolf operative and an asset that she viewed more and more like a child whom she needed to protect and yet had to exploit at the same time. It left her torn, and the memories of her manipulations of his mind were still fresh.

"He destroyed a whole bunch of Astral Demons, and we learned that they can come in sub–Potency 1 varieties." She had gained a ton of information about how Astral Demons advanced and quickly divulged that information: "Once they gain enough Souls, they are capable of advancing in levels. Then, upon hitting a higher Potency, they can choose a path of evolution. Monstrous or Refined. Stronger and more animalistic, or Psykinetically inclined and more humanoid. They can mix and match as they progress."

Xera recalled the logs from Jace's journey and continued. "He met a species called the Gyanv, who run an alliance of Universes that are dedicated to trying to maintain order and egality across the first Layer." *A foolish endeavor*, Xera thought, *since Astral Demons are endless and cannot be permanently killed save by Psykinetics or Void.*

She sighed and continued, "After that, he saved another Universe from assault. Turns out, that Universe was ruled by a singular empire of almost-humans calling their species Vanguard. He helped them, they demanded his 'tech' that wiped out the army—Void—and he . . . declined. After a brief skirmish, he shook them, and got to . . ." Xera swallowed and whispered, "The ship."

The Architects' ship. The vessel that all but she had taken into the Astral Verge to try and figure out how to fix their Universe and convert it to a closed cycle of Souls once more. Like how it was before The Ancients had arrived in The Nethershift and fucked it all up. All of the passengers had died after it crashed, and they were trapped inside its safe confines. Their consciousnesses had been backed up to their cortical stacks.

And Jace retrieved them. Brought them back to her. He had rescued Xera's brother. Her only remaining relative. Xero. The one who handled the magic side of The Cosmic System's design. Now, The Architects were within a neural framework, undergoing intensive therapy to deal with countless eons of being trapped inside a device within their corpses.

Xera continued, "After Jace discovered the ship and rescued my fellows, he detonated it. Then, he went on his way, trying to get to the next Layer of the Astral Verge. Through that he encountered a city of demons, and we learned that they are not all bad. Some only consume Souls that are condemned by judgement in the Nethershift and distributed up the Layers by The Ancients.

"The city came under attack, and Jace helped defend it—saving it. The demon residents then revealed the location of a Vault beneath their city. A location set up by The Ancients to test people and grant them Relics if they passed the trial within. Jace cleared the challenge and received a powerful weapon. After, he was hunted down by minions sent by a Demon Lord: one of that species who was powerful enough within their Potency rating to command the obedience of others in their classification.

"He allied with one of them who sought to turn upon his master to take his throne. Taking the fight to the Demon Lord, Jace was able to beat the monster and set his new, unlikely ally up as the new ruler of that specific demon-centric city. Jace then headed out on a Mission given by that Gyanv Alliance Coalition, obliterating an army of sub-Potency 1 demons with a handful of stronger ones helming the assault.

"Meanwhile, Shhiv-zal, Jace's companion, had been ushered through The Cosmic System and up to Tier 10 by using vast stores of Stardust to effectively skip her up to that ranking." *Although*, Xera thought, *I did not fully expect her to survive merging the System into her being. She has a strong will.* Xera continued aloud, "I introduced her to the Astral System and leveraged her Cosmic and Astral [Classes] to get her into Rune Carving."

Runes, the language of The Ancients and literal symbols that carried power when etched by a Rune-based [Class]. Demons seemed to be able to make lesser versions, but for the Dreamers—those who entered the Astral Verge from a Universe—they needed an appropriate [Class]. Xera continued, "Jace returned home for a visit, and during that, Shhiv augmented his gear with the new Runes, increasing his odds of survivability, as Psykinetics went right through his armor.

"He returned and found another Vault, this time fighting in an arena and having the opportunity to face off against a Potency 8 Astral Demon. One who seemed to be a . . . good Demon Lord. One who only ate damned Souls. In attendance for the fight were two Ancients. The Quiet One, and the Loud One."

She shuddered slightly as she recalled seeing the replay of Jace's death. His body had been all but turned to paste, and the difference in power between Potencies was on full display. Thankfully, The Ancients had ensured his survival—and Jace's NICIF, those wonderful nanites that were a slight fluke of The Cosmic System's inner machinations, they protected his brain from any damage.

Xera shook off the discomfort of seeing the feed and reading the damage readout. "We learned that every few eons, The Ancients seek out someone, or a group of people, even up to a civilization, to take on something they call the "Mantle of Burden." Tasked with killing off and annihilating the Demon Lords who had chosen to embrace Soul consumption regardless of their status of being judged as evil or good.

A task that led to more Vaults, which Jace conquered. That led to more Relics, powerful pieces of Gear that merged and replaced Jace's old Equipment.

"After meeting with The Ancients for the fifth time, Jace learned that the Vanguard species, that one he saved around the same time he arrived in The Astral Verge, had embraced Soul consumption, becoming Dreamer Demons and capable of leveling up with both Essence and Souls. The Vanguard Empire clashed with the Gyanv Alliance Coalition, and Jace brought their armada crashing down. But their leader, Highlord Tibalt, escaped into a city of demons and Jace lost him."

A threat, she thought, *if this Tibalt holds a grudge and has descended into the Layers in his pursuit of power*. But Xera knew Jace could handle the threat. What is one foe compared to what he has faced? Troxanir was Potency 8 and Tier 9, and Jace was able to take him on . . . granted, it was close, and he cannot use Void as liberally while in the Verge due to it destroying the Essence he needs from defeating demons to level up.

She sighed and continued, "Jace went down into Layer 2 and met the Demon Lord who he was charged with giving control to. He went off and killed his two rival lords and beat a Vault before descending to Layer 3. There, Jace killed yet more demons and ceded control of the Layer to another good ruler." She groaned. "It feels so weird saying 'demon' and 'good' in the same sentence."

[Please stay on track.]

"Yes, yes. Anyways, he destroyed Astral and Dreamer Demons alike and acquired enough Essence to go up a Potency. He descended to Layer 4—" Xera groaned once more. "He forgot about the Vault he could have cleared on Layer 3!"

She raised her wrist and tapped on her wristpad, sending off a quick message reminding Jace to go up to Layer 3 and defeat a Vault up there, as he could still acquire one Relic from that Layer. Letting her arm drop, she ignored the machine's admonishment and finished speaking.

"Now, he's on a Layer of the Verge that is a vast desert. More of the demons that chose the monstrous path of evolution. But there is a stronghold, run by the Demon Lord that he is going to be helping cede control of the Layer over to." She sighed. "Alright, I'm done. Complete process."

[Confirmed.]
[Data extraction of described events in process.
[Stand by . . .]

The familiar sense of weightlessness and isolation took hold of Xera as she floated in the inky void. *We are almost there*, she thought. *So close to being done.*

[All data extracted and compressed.]
[Confirm re-upload?]

Yes, she thought. Returned in a rush of warmth and heat, she came to in her body once more. *Soon enough*, she thought as she kicked out of bed and stood up, *I'll be able to die and get a real reset*.

That was one problem The Architect's discovered when it came to re-sleeving one's self: degradation of the persona. Over time. It was insidious, and could be staved off with the process that she had just subjected herself to, but eventually—maybe in another thousand years—Xera would fully succumb to it. Her psyche would fragment and fracture beyond repair.

She needed to die. For the Soul carried a person's truest consciousness. Glancing at the mirror, she briefly accessed the voidlight tether interface and drew on Jace's new prosthetics, checking her Karma Coefficient in the mirror.

[Karma Coefficient]
[–15]

"And there's that," she muttered to herself. "Once we install that Judgement Matrix that Jace is going to get from these Ancients . . . I need to experiment." She went to her battle station, sitting next to the console. Pulling up her Stardust reserves, she opened accounts for and set up a bunch of small donations to various entities. Mostly charitable organizations that the Star Council or Nebula Alliance operated.

And, as she did, she kept her focus on the small mirror above her monitors, keeping an eye on her Karma Coefficient for any change. It took hundreds of thousands of Stardust, but she finally saw the number flip one closer to zero.

Xera smiled. *Charity does the trick*, she thought. *Time to focus on artificially increasing my Karma*.

The plan was straightforward enough. Jace gets the Judgement Matrix, she installs it in the Penrose Sphere around Oblivion, it captures Souls and either annihilates them by throwing them into The Architect's Gate at the bottom of our singularity's funnel or puts them into a freshly cloned body.

She was not sure if she could manipulate the Matrix in any way and frankly did not want to mess with technology from a reality-traversing species. Better to let their arcane machinations tick away and just be happy that we got off so easily with them permitting my idea in the first place. Xera was sure that The Ancients could have shut down her ideas immediately, but instead they had been okay with it, and even proposed the "Soul-ship Courier" plan that Jace would be responsible for implementing.

Hopefully, she thought, *one of only three responsibilities he will have. Doing that Soul check-in with the Afterlives and any Souls originating from our Universe that want to return, occasionally helping The Ancients with their whole Burden thing by eliminating the evil demons in the Layers, and then being the watcher of the Wayfinders for our Universe.*

She sighed. *Jace . . . you've done so much for me. For us. Just a bit more. Then, you're free.*

Chapter One

Traversing the Desert

Ollie spoke in Jace's head after reading Xera's message aloud, *I scanned when we were up there, and even queried the Astral System—Layer 3 had no Vaults that were undefeated.* His voice shifted to one of pride, *I tried using your Holy Hunt Talent to track down the locations of any uncleared Vaults—but none showed up.*

Jace clicked his tongue. "Disappointing," he replied as he ran across the desert dunes. The glimmering, brown sand reflected the heat of the pure, white skies above along with their brightness. If not for Jace's prosthetic eyes, he would have been blinded long ago by the reflected rays. He could see the light blue of Souls scattering throughout the air, with some darting down into the sand, wiggling down before vanishing—percolating down to the next Layer.

Jace replied, "Send a message back to Xera, please. Let her know."

I will ask her to task a drone with keeping an active scan on the Layer. We have the stealth technology. I will then keep my eyes open for notifications once, or if, they . . . respawn? I do not know if they respawn, or refresh, or what they call it down here.

Jace shook his head as he kept running across the dunes. Every direction showed naught but expanding sands. Far, far off in the distance, he could see the faint outlines of buildings and structures in a few locations. "Do we have a map?" Jace asked.

Ollie pulled up the HUD before Jace and projected a two-dimensional image. *We came in at the center of the Layer, and the funnel for demon and Dreamer access to the next is to the east. In between us and it is the safe haven of Respite, run by Esmerelda. Then there are these eight locations which I think are cities of some type. Maybe ruins? I was not able to get much information.*

Jace looked at the total distance and knew he could traverse one thousand two hundred miles in a single cycle—just about twenty-four hours. Given the size of this Layer, he could go from the eastern edge to the west in about four cycles—just a little under. From north to south, a cycle and a half. *If I'm sent all over the place*, he thought, *it won't take me super long to travel. That's a plus.* He was thankful, once more, for the Augmentation to his prosthetics that came from his time on Nihilethelea that enabled him to walk atop surfaces that could support his weight.

An Astral System message flickered across Jace's vision. Pink text on a black box.

[Mission: Consolidate control over Layer 4 to Demon Lord Esmerelda.]
[Reward: Legendary (Essence Cache) Infusion.]
[Sender: The Ancients.]

"About time that popped," Jace muttered with slight annoyance. "It was faster on other Layers, wasn't it?"

Not really, Ollie replied. *You okay? You sound upset.*

Jace shook his head. "Just wanting to head back and visit Shhiv is all," he replied. He had been craving a home visit but did not want to risk it until Valcrinox's army was back in Layer 10 and would have even less of a chance of running into his voidlight tether. Jace did not want to risk anything when it came to his home and his safety.

The Demon Lord of Madness; Jace knew that he would have to topple that powerful entity that caused fear in other Demon Lords. One of the first of his kind. *But*, Jace thought as his resolve hardened, *I beat one of his fellow first-wave demons. I beat Troxanir. And once I'm Potency 10, I don't need to hold back with using Void.* He would not need Essence and could just obliterate his foes without concern for the empowering substance being lost in the process.

He continued his run across the dunes and could see a small geyser of sand off to his left. Pivoting to a stop and leaving a small fishtail, Jace drew his sword and activated several Talents. Psykinetics from the Astral System.

His Valiant Crusader's Might, which was always active, filled him with strength, ensured he could always strike around defenses, caused all his attacks with Psykinetics to leave a burn, and gave him a better chance to move foes with the force of his strikes. Plus, he activated [Vengeful], feeling a deep pain in his stomach as his weapon surged with golden flames to deliver an empowered blow.

His shield manifested on his left arm. A barrier of Psykinetic energy, a golden screen of light and divinity—a hero's defense. The small spikes covering the front flared up with flickering flames, ready to retaliate against Psykinetic Talents he blocked. His defenses, improved. His ability to be pushed around, reduced. And, as long as he stood within the slight, glowing circle barely visible in the sand, his defenses would continue to improve as his damage reduction built up and up.

An area thirty feet around Jace exploded to life. A sphere of flickering flames that would inflict suffering on all who Jace desired to afflict. The same aura would stack up a burning damage-over-time effect, and his defenses were even further improved. He was not nearly as defensively oriented as Greg, his fellow Dark Between Stars Signer, but Jace was a hard nut to crack.

Keeping an eye on his energy, Jace went through a suite of Skills from his innate Cosmic System. With a thought, he activated several: Dark Energy Mine (Rank 1), Dark Matter Mending (Rank 4) [Rending], Raging Cleave (Rank 10), Aura of Wrath (Rank 11). The surging purple flowed around him as a crackling crimson nebula flickered within the purple clouds—only visible to him.

The spray of sand got closer, and Jace readied himself to jump. He saw a small fin appear in the sand before him. His Edge's Intuition [Danger-Sense] kicked off, and he leaped skyward. Thirty feet straight up, propelled by his prosthetic legs.

Beneath him, where he had been standing, a pair of jaws appeared; gnashing and chomping at his prior location—the lure having been pulled away from the thing at the last second. Jace used that opportunity to take in the creature's form and throw his sword down at it. The carapace-covered hide was covered with countless tiny, sharp spikes that must have acted like flagella in helping the monstrous Astral Demon propel itself through the sand.

This thing really went hard down the monstrous route, Jace thought as the sword scored a hit on the interior of the jawline of the creature, a golden explosion of radiant flame flashing out from where the tip of the blade struck. Thanks to the weapon's (Returning) Augmentation, he was able to warp the weapon back to his grip as he dropped down.

The demon dropped slightly as well, but then submerged, and Jace's downward plunge struck naught but sand as the creature vanished. *Holy Hunt*, Jace thought as he felt the thing leave the radius of his [Danger-Sense]. A thin gold line shot out from him and across the sands before limning a form under the top layers. The Astral Demon's form outlined, Jace could make out the full scale of the creature's size: easily comparable to a truck, if not a bit thinner. More like an eel than a shark.

It turned and began to move at Jace again. *Might as well rinse and repeat*, Jace thought as he prepared to jump again.

It is an Astral Demon, Ollie advised. *It is not an animal or dumb creature. Maybe not as smart as a demon who went down the refined path of evolution, but I would not expect the same trick to work twice.*

Jace braced himself as the thing got closer—inside his [Danger-Sense] radius. Then, to the side! He leaped horizontally, going to his left, as the creature broke the surface and bit down on where he had just been standing. Jace was close enough to strike a blow with his sword, and he found to his dismay that the weapon skittered off of the scaled hide. It's tough—like that Vault with the lava creature.

Monstrous path does mean they get more combat-focused, Ollie reminded him.

The thing dove back into the sand. "No you don't!" Jace shouted as he fired Dark Matter Dart (Rank 4) [Exploding] into the now-vanishing tail of the monster. The darts shot forward, hit the hide, and exploded—purple shockwaves of Dark Matter sending ripples across the sand. But the darts also carried with them the brilliant gold of Jace's Psykinetic strength and left the lingering burn upon the creature—burns that would never go out.

Just a matter of time, Jace thought. But his [Danger-Sense] picked up movement behind him, and instinctively, Jace used Void Step (Rank 10) to warp fifty feet straight up. Another set of jaws emerged from where he had been standing—a similar-looking Astral Demon, but this one was not a pale, dirt color. Instead, it was bright pink, and the jaws opened once more before projecting a stream of glittering purple Psykinetic power at Jace. He interposed his shield, and the cascade splashed against the defense. The stream, being a Psykinetic Talent, activated the (Retaliating) feature of his Crusader's Bastion, and a golden spike of Jace's Psykinetic power launched back and burrowed into the throat of the creature.

It let out a roar, dipped beneath the sand, and burrowed away. Right as Jace landed, he felt the [Danger-Sense] go off again, and the dirt-colored one he had been tracking leapt up out of the sand, like a fish breaking the surface of the water, and barreled directly toward him.

Falling to his knees, Jace let the thing pass over him as he jammed his weapon up—but the blade skidded off the form, and the creature finished its pass before dipping into the sand again. *Annoying*, Jace thought as he got up.

Then, another [Danger-Sense] trigger. A third one. *Three Astral Demons*, Ollie warned him. *Better stop playing around.*

I'm not, Jace thought back. *This is me trying while conserving energy.*

All three forms of the creatures rushed forward, and Jace had an idea. He stood still, waiting. The one he had highlighted with Holy Hunt was coming in for another jump-strike from his side. The one below him was going to come straight up again—probably the pink one he had struck with the (Retaliating) Infusion. But the third demon, the one he had not seen yet, came at him from an upward angle.

Positioning himself as best he could, Jace counted out the beats of his thumping heart, and the second the first of the creatures breached the surface, he used a Void Step and got above the cluster.

All three emerged slightly after each other, missing their mark—they did not impact each other, which Jace would have liked to see, but that wasn't his plan. *Templar's Smite (Blast),* Jace thought as he poured his energy into the Talent. A geyser of golden flames surged out from his palms, coursing down across the sands, scorching it to glass, and consuming the Astral Demons that writhed and screeched in pain.

They were not defeated, but the surface being turned to glass meant they could not immediately burrow down again, and Jace used that opening to activate (Vengeful), feeling the deep pain in his chest as his weapon ignited with holy fury. Letting gravity pull him down, Jace unleashed a devastating slash through the mouth of the pink-scaled one that had shot the projectile of Psykinetic force at him.

The empowered strike was enough to slice clean through the head and leave behind a wriggling body that was quickly consumed by the golden flames. But Jace didn't stand there and wait; he reused the (Vengeful) Infusion, feeling that deep, throbbing pain in his chest like he was having a cardiac episode. Pushing past that, he sliced the brown colored one in two as well.

The last one, however, was different. It was . . . humanoid. Not fully monstrous. Bulky shoulders, a horn-covered head, coated in a smooth layer of defensive scales. Somehow familiar. It had made enough distance to get into the sand, and it vanished.

Holy Hunt, Jace thought as he activated the Talent, and saw the golden outline around the Astral Demon that went down deep into the sand. Jace was going to go after it, but an Astral System notification popped up in his vision.

[Wraith.]
[This is Esmerelda.]
[The sooner you get here, the better.]
[A more detailed area map will accompany this message.]

Jace sighed, “Well, I guess that demon gets away.” He sheathed the sword and let his Talents fade. “How much Essence from the two?”

One thousand, Ollie thought back.

Jace examined the map that was up in his HUD. “Well, this matches up with the map from earlier. It just has more information about a few areas.” His eyes wandered over to the ruins upon the exterior of the Layer’s layout. “Ruins? Why?”

The Astral Verge is created from the combined dreams, memories, and nightmares of every Soul that passes through it. Ruins are a constant across every Universe—civilizations rise and fall. Perhaps due to the weird percolation that Souls do on this Layer versus going in a singular stream like the other ones above we have passed through already.

“Makes just about as much sense as anything here,” Jace replied as he continued to run across the dunes towards Respite.

Chapter Two

Villains and Respite

Tibalt, former Highlord of the Vanguard Empire and now Dreamer Demon—was terrified. He had chased down Wraith after seeing the Mission pop up from Valcrinox. And unlike the more monstrous demons who did not keep their wits and just threw themselves at the Dreamer . . . Tibalt knew better.

He is still beyond my capabilities to defeat, Tibalt thought. *I need to grow stronger. Devour more.* He kept swimming through the sand, keeping his senses extended in all directions and dashing toward Souls that trickled down through the sands toward the next Layer below. But they had to go through a lot of sand to get there—and it gave Tibalt time to gobble them up.

The screaming mass in his chest was a constant comfort to him. A reminder that he was on a path to glory, an ascension to a throne. The first Dreamer Demon Emperor. Ruling all of the Layers of the Astral Verge and controlling everything. Bringing his justice to reality. His will. Imposing his structure upon all of it.

Snatching yet another Soul, he cupped it and felt the warmth between his now-clawed fingers. Shoving it into his gullet, he gulped it down to join the writhing mass within. *More . . . I need more!*

Valcrinox, the Endless Madness, ruler of the tenth Layer of the Astral Verge, sat upon his Relic throne. He awaited the return of his demonic horde, who had traveled to the first Layer to raid a Universe for its Universal Matter: building blocks of creation that he hoped to use to make a custom Universe. One that he could bring captured species of Dreamers into, to breed them, drive them mad, and then consume. An endless feast of flesh and gore.

Absentmindedly, he reached up, and a spike whipped out, lanced through the body of a Gyanv Dreamer on the ceiling who was impaled upon meat hooks, clacking their mandibles in pain. Valcrinox ripped them down and chomped down on the crunchy, juicy, sweet shell of meat as their rasps of agony reached his ears. Munching down on his snack of flesh and chitin, he consumed them wholly—Soul included.

And yet the snack did not comfort him, despite normally providing some modicum of relief. No, Valcrinox was afraid. He knew of a gold flame Psykinetic user—a heroic individual fueled by an Emotion Source that enabled them to inflict lasting harm to Astral Demons of a far higher Potency, bypassing a restriction placed upon the Astral System and its inhabitants. But worse than that, far worse, was that this person, this Wraith as he learned they were called—he carried the Mantle of Burden.

The Ancients . . . those fuckers, always meddling, Valcrinox thought. They had tried to "balance" the Layers of the Astral Verge many, many times before. Each time, all but Layer 10 had succumbed. Valcrinox was the oldest, and most definitely the strongest, Astral Demon within the entirety of that piece of reality. Many bearers of the Mantle of Burden—other heroic-Psykinetic users, entire armadas, civilizations—all had been bested.

But the golden flames got the closest to besting him. And Valcrinox had heard of Wraith's deeds from a Dreamer Demon with aspirations of growing in might. The very idea that Wraith had some form of technology that enabled him to obliterate matter at will was terrifying. Valcrinox had only one defense against something like that—his throne. The Relic that he acquired after clearing out the Vault on Layer 10. The only Vault that existed there.

He had to wait. Wait for his army to return. Hope that they brought back enough Universal Matter for him to flee and create his own Universe. Escape the Astral Verge permanently and the threat that The Ancients posed. *In some ways,* he thought, *I am a bit jealous of that wayward original demon.*

Valcrinox was thinking about the one of their species who felt called to a Universe, got himself lodged into a funnel, and gorged himself for countless eons. Troxanir, the Endless Hunger. The Astral Demon who had escaped the Astral System's machinations of demons fighting among themselves. Just him and a Universe for his consumption.

But Valcrinox learned from his wayward brethren's demise. Devouring a Universe just means that one would have to return back to the Astral Verge to repeat the process. *No, I desire my own, custom-made Universe. One that ensures my safety and supremacy. A Universe made after my own whims, where I create a System and am the sole user of it. None could challenge my authority ever again.*

He sent another lancing spike up to the ceiling, grabbed another Gyanv—they were so numerous, being insectoid Dreamers—and brought it to his glistening jaws to gobble up.

A demon will complete the Mission I set out. That bearer of the Mantle will be destroyed, and I will be safe.

Jace encountered another six Astral Demons along his journey. And he had figured out the best strategy after the second encounter. Stand still, jump at the last second, and then immediately throw his sword into the open mouth, followed up by Templar's Smite (Spear) that went right down the throat and detonated with golden flames within.

The more of those there are, he thought, *the easier time I'm going to have harvesting Essence. How much are we up to?*

Ollie replied in his mind. *Those six gave you another 3,000 Essence, putting you at 7,000 total. Enough for one level, but if you hold out for another 1,000 Essence, then we can do two levels in one go!*

Then we hold off, Jace thought as they reached their destination. A walled settlement—the walls easily a hundred feet high and made of a deep, grey stone. A singular, titanic slab formed and shaped into a large, square wall surrounding Respite.

Jace did not see any openings for a gate or doorway, but did see a set of small notches along one wall. Almost perfect handholds. *Good thing I don't need that*, he thought as he activated Void Stalker and ascended with his Soul Tether, the invisible, undetectable, and noninteractable grapple line enabling his ascent into the sky without a fixed point to grapple to.

Cresting the wall, he saw a series of large, grey buildings that were arranged in small pods. One such section had a grey landing pad at the center, where a few starships were sitting. There was another section with a small market in the center. And lastly, another pod next to the main feature of this place.

A huge oasis. A bubbling pool of fresh, clean water that was clear as could be, revealing the smooth, white stone at the bottom. Jace did not see any defenders upon the walls, and he used his Soul Tether to descend into the settlement. Glancing back, he saw the massive Runes upon the walls. [Forbidden] [Restricted] [Dreamer] [Refined] [Fortified].

Scanning . . . Coordinating notes with Shhiv . . .

Shhiv's voice came over the comms. "Hey, honey!"

Jace smiled at hearing his wife's voice. "Hey there. What's up with these Runes?"

"Looks like it means that only pure Dreamers, and Astral Demons who have chosen the path of refinement exclusively, can go within the radius of the walls. It's a safe place."

"Up to what Potency?" Jace asked.

Shhiv made an unsure noise. "Umm . . . can't say. That information isn't in the Runes."

Jace felt gratitude wash over him. "Thanks, love. You're the best."

"I know it," Shhiv replied haughtily. "When you coming home?"

"Once those Potency 10 demons head back to their deep Layer," Jace replied.

Quinn's voice came over the comms, "Xera's probes have been tracking them. Right now, they are plundering a Universe. I'd guess a few more days—erm, cycles."

Shhiv whined, "Aww."

Jace replied, "It'll be fine. You just wait; that time will pass super quickly."

"Okay. Love you! Gotta go!" Shhiv replied.

Quinn's voice came back, "Also, you had a visitor. Your mom came by. Dropped off a letter for you. Want me to send it your way?"

Jace shook his head. "No, I'll read it when I'm back." He cut off the communication line and used his Holy Hunt to track down Esmerelda, the Demon Lord who had contacted him. The line shot off toward the small starship port, and Jace headed over there, letting his Void Stalker drop.

The handful of Astral Demons that were sitting under awnings looked up at the sudden appearance of a Dreamer among them—one decked out in Relics from a variety of Vaults. Jace strode past them and took a good, hard look at the starships. They were all of designs he was unfamiliar with, save for the one that was slightly bulbous—a Gyanv vessel. Looking around, he did not see them. In fact, he saw no Dreamers outside.

Must just be resting up, or maybe trading wares, or something like that, Jace thought as he followed the golden line to a building with a firm stone door. Rapping his fist on it a few times, he took a step back from the threshold and waited, one hand on the hilt of his weapon sheathed in the extradimensional space next to him.

The door opened up, and the Astral Demon woman he had seen up on Layer 3 talking to Malphitria stood before him, limned in a golden outline of his Holy Hunt. He let it fade as she spoke. "Ah . . . Wraith, I believe. Please, come in."

Jace did not enter, looking back at the ships. "Where are the crew?" he asked.

She pointed to one of the buildings across the ship landing area. "We have something akin to a . . . I believe your kind would call it . . . a tavern? A bar? Something along those lines."

Jace nodded and walked into the building. The scent of some type of perfume hit him instantly, and he took in the surroundings briefly. A well-appointed chamber with cushions, silklike cloth hanging from the ceiling to make different partitioned areas, and a large bed. She gestured to one of the cushions and sat on the one opposite.

As he sat, she spoke, "You should have a Mission from The Ancients, yes?"

Jace nodded. "Consolidate control of Layer 4 over to you."

". . . Good," Esmerelda replied softly. "You may have noticed our lack of population on this Layer, here in Respite. That is because most who follow the path of refinement tend to not survive on this Layer." She pointed up to the ceiling. "Hence why Layer 3 is filled with them. It takes a brave demon to come down here, venture through the desert, and make it to safety."

Jace sank back into the cushion, feeling quite comfortable as he put his hands behind his head to prop it up and maintain eye contact—though to her, she only saw his gleaming visor of the helm. "Tell me what I need to do to get you the control you want."

She raised her hand and began manipulating an Astral System screen. A map appeared floating between the two, and she spoke. "There are eight Ruins which have other Demon Lords, the strongest who pursued a mix of mostly monstrous evolutions, with a dip of refinement. They are sort of like pack leaders. Kill them, and you will grant me control over the Layer." She smiled. "Plus, they have Infusions. And each Ruin is also the location of a Vault."

"Tell me a bit about that," Jace said. "I know on Layer 3 all of the Vaults were beaten already. Do they . . . respawn?"

She nodded. "It can take a varying number of cycles. But it is worthwhile to do one Vault per Layer for the Relic it awards." She looked past the screens at him. "Which I believe you know well enough about, given your attire." She cleared her throat. "Any Astral Demon you see that is refined and not on their way from the funnel to Respite here, you can consider as one worthy of slaying."

"Can you give me names?" Jace asked. "Or descriptions? Something I can use to track them?"

She cracked a smile. "I wish. I do not know their names." She dismissed all of the System screens and looked at Jace with a hard, piercing glare. All friendliness dropped from her voice. "Once you defeat all eight, then the demons who were under their control will be loose. Ideally . . . you wipe out every Astral Demon on this Layer who is monstrous by any degree."

"How many is that?" Jace asked.

" . . . I do not know," she replied.

"Seems like a big task. Any way I can get them all together?" Jace inquired.

"Perhaps . . . force each of the eight Demon Lords in each Ruin, get them to recall their minions, and then slaughter them. That should do the trick."

Jace stood up. "I better get to it, then. But before I go—any chance you have a thousand Essence sitting around?"

She smiled, and the lightness came back to her voice. "I suppose I could give you a bit of a signing bonus." She stood up, walked over to a jar sitting on a countertop, and came back to him holding it. "This has Essence in it. Take it. It is yours."

Jace took the jar and opened it, seeing the white, liquid-smokey Essence within. Reaching a hand in, it coalesced around him before sucking up into him, sending a warm rush up his forearm before that sensation faded. *How much, Ollie?*

5,000 Essence! Enough for three levels. We should do that before heading out.

Jace looked to her and handed the jar back. "Thank you. That should help a ton."

She accepted the object and put it back on the counter. "Perhaps you could strike deals with the other Dreamers here. Some of them are Potency three or four. They might be able to help."

Jace shook his head and opened the door, the slab of stone grinding into the wall as he pulled it aside. "I work better alone." He shut the door behind him and used his Soul Tether grapple line to pull himself up into the sky, intent on reaching the easternmost Ruins. *Then, I can go clockwise, and end up nearly back where I started—just south of the entrance to the next Layer going down.*

He activated Void Stalker and descended to the sand dunes on the outside of Respite, running off toward his first objective.

Chapter Three

The First Ruin

Jace ran across the desert dunes. The white light of the sky—well, the curved ceiling of the Layer above—was constantly emitting the bright glow that illuminated the entire Layer. Despite being in a desert, the heat was not that bad. Jace knew it was partially due to the armor he wore and the various Augmentations to his Gear carried over from his Cosmic System Equipment, but still, he was thankful for the reprieve from the expected heat.

"Let's get those two levels," Jace said.

Okay! Let us do it! Ollie replied. *Purifier is damage-focused, so I would suggest Specialization to either Templar's Smite, Hero's Arena, or Valiant Crusader's Might.*

"I actually wanted something new, and a Specialization with the new Talent. Something that lets me empower my weapon so that those harder-to-crack shells and defenses can be more easily dealt with."

Hmm. I think I have something here.

[You have leveled up!]
[You have chosen New Talent!]
[Talent Name: Purifying Edge.]
[Effect: The user's weapon temporarily sunders defensive Talents, shutting them off.]

[You have leveled up!]
[You have chosen Specialization of Existing Talent!]
[Talent Name: Purifying Edge.]
[Specialization Name: Cleansing.]
[Effect: In addition to defensive Talents, the user's weapon temporarily sunders support Talents, shutting them off.]

Name: Jace Seren (Potency 4)
Emotion [Class Level]: Valiant [Purifier 33]
Talent [Specialization]: Astral Adaptation, Astral Translation, Valiant Crusader's Might [Burning] [Vengeful] [Poised] [Unstoppable] [Bracing], Crusader's Bastion [Retaliating] [Reinforcing] [Grounding] [Redoubt] [Spiked], Hero's Arena [Aura] [Incinerating] [Vexing] [Bolstering], Indomitable Will [Zealous] [Intimidating] [Inviolable] [Enduring], Templar's Smite [Spear] [Blast] [Lingering] [Challenging], Holy Hunt [Marked] [Bursting] [Authoritative] [Provoking], Purifying Edge [Cleansing]
Essence: 0
Infusions: x2 Epic (Essence Cache), Legendary (Specialization), Legendary (Gear)
Gear: <TPSB>, (Convergent Edge) [Ruination 1] Hero's Blade, (Explorer's Embrace / Beacon) Paragon Armor, (Prosthetic Savant) Astral Appendages, (Draconic Sovereign) Arbiter's Sight, (Anathema) Astral Sleeve, (Flexible) Adamantine Skeleton, (Reactive) NICIF, (Restoring) Flame of Valor

"It's sort of like having my [Astral Annihilator] back from my Swordmage Stance," Jace commented.

Sort of. That still works, but it is Cosmic System–specific. I took that concept, looked through the list of Talents, and then discovered something neat! I can take your innate Cosmic System, and we can choose Talents that are either closely aligned with them, or, nudge those Talents available to function more like what you have previously utilized! Ollie sounded quite excited at the revelation. *Plus, I found out that once you reach Potency 5, so the next one up, you get something else for your advancement. I do not know exactly what it is, but I will keep working on it!*

"What would I do without you," Jace commented.

Probably not a lot!

Xera sighed with relief, sitting in the same grove within Xero's digital construct world. He was progressing with therapy well, and he was going to hopefully be rehabilitated within a few months.

She was leaning her head against his shoulder, just enjoying being with her dear brother, when he spoke. "You should reconsider."

"Reconsider what?" Xera asked.

"Death." Xero turned to her, his face full of understanding but with a pained expression. "We might know how to trap Souls, and have this Karma Matrix you spoke of to ensure the bad ones are filtered out . . . but I don't want to risk losing my little sister just after finding out she survived." He had some tears in the corners of his eyes.

Xera reached up and wiped them away, feeling a bit of moisture in her own eyes within the digital construct's space. "Don't worry," she whispered. "I have done a lot of research on how Souls and death work. I'll die, and be back as I've always been. Just . . . not . . . well . . ." She trailed off, having seen the symptoms occur ever more frequently.

Xero gulped. "I . . . I understand." He squeezed her close in a hug. "Don't leave me," he whispered. "I just got you back."

She returned the hug, and just stayed there for some time. How long, she did not know. But eventually, her Wayfinders prodded her. "I need to leave," she said softly. "System needs."

Xero reluctantly let her go. "Visit again soon?" he asked with sorrowful eyes.

"Of course," Xera replied as she activated her interface and ejected herself from the neural network, returning fully to her body. Ripping the tube out of the base of her skull, she looked at the blob-form Wayfinder. "What did you need?"

"The Vault on Layer 3 has refreshed. Well, one of them. There are more we are tracking."

"Good. Use Dark Matter to seal off the entrance." Xera had outfitted all of her drones with Dark Matter shielding, weaponry, and cloaking—they were practically undetectable, very hard to destroy, and could block access to the Vault until Jace got there. Unfortunately, Void was still an Ascended Power so potent that only someone ingrained in The Cosmic System could use it.

And drones, sadly, were not eligible as they were not conscious beings. There was no way Xera was going down that path of synthetic life forms. She had seen firsthand how that worked out on some worlds that reached the threshold for Cosmogenic Merging.

"Notify Jace and Ollie," she said as she stood up and stretched. "Send them the coordinates."

Jace received a Cosmic System notification—gold text on a black background. Xera's heads-up that the Vault on Layer 3 was available. "I think our game plan," Jace began as he saw the ruins in the distance growing ever closer, "is to do this Vault, then go clockwise until we hit the northernmost one that is closest to the Layer 3 funnel, head south quickly to do the Vault up on Layer 3, then drop down and resume our journey."

Sounds like a plan! Ollie replied. *And we have to make sure we do every Vault at each of these ruins. Even if we only get a Relic from the first one, having the extra Essence is going to help for sure!*

Jace continued his journey, and to his surprise, the Astral Demon attacks had ceased. *Maybe it is because I'm using Void Stalker*, Jace thought, *and all of them are the same Potency. None higher who stuck around.*

Logical to think that, Ollie replied.

Jace reached the outskirts of the ruins and took them in fully. A series of black pillars sunken into the ground, with some shifted down at angles that caused them to interweave like a chaotic lattice from certain viewpoints. As if towers were dropped into the sand and let to fall where they may lay. He could make out the outline of doors just like the ones he had seen in Respite. *Okay . . . Holy Hunt*, he thought as he activated the Talent, focusing his intent on the closest Demon Lord.

The gold line shot off to his right, and he drew his sword, activating all of his go-to Talents and Skills. As his blade cleared the extradimensional sheath, he could see a flickering, white flame interspersed among the gold. *Must be the Purifying Edge Talent*, he thought as he continued to walk down the narrow, zigzag corridors, following the golden line.

His journey through the ominous, silent city of spires was only punctuated by the howling of wind through the twisting towers. It was unnerving. *Something is off*, he thought.

His [Danger-Sense] went off, and he ran forward as one of the towers crashed down to the ground right where he had been standing. Then, another notification from the Skill. Another tower descending down to him, attempting to crush him into the sand below. Jace kept sprinting forward as the tower, almost like a chain reaction, toppled behind him.

This could be a way to try and get us to a specific location for an ambush, Ollie advised. *I would take to the sky.*

Jace nodded and used Void Step (Rank 17) to warp straight up eighty-five feet, grappling in place using his Soul Tether. That's when he spotted them—Astral Demons, monstrous ones, who were all forms of amalgamated masses of flesh, chitin, muscle, horn, and claw. Almost all had gnashing teeth and crackled with Psykinetic power.

How did they know I was here? Jace asked Ollie as he saw the thin, gold line shooting off into the distance to a partially submerged pyramid.

Ollie was silent for a few seconds before speaking. *The only thing that makes sense is that one of those demons, or several, or the Demon Lord, have either a Talent that contests with or even supersedes your Void Stalker. It is either that, or they have a higher Potency demon present.*

Jace did not like the sound of that at all, despite having fought above his Potency before. He quickly counted the demons below, coming to a total of thirty. They had not seemed to notice his new location, and he swung toward the pyramid as they continued to topple the towers below him along the path he would have traversed.

Reaching a point where he was above the pyramid, dangling from his grapple line affixed to a point in space, Jace considered his options. *I could destroy all the demons out here, but they might overwhelm me. But, if that happened, I'd suffer enough damage for Shattered Limits, which would absolutely allow me to wreck them all. Thoughts, Ollie?*

Time to destroy some buildings!

Jace grinned and activated Ruination Razor (Rank 3) [Wrecking], which enabled his next three weapon swings that impacted structures to destroy the target struck beyond repair. It only worked on buildings or similar constructions, but that was all he needed. Throwing his sword down at the pyramid, the blade cut into the top like a hot knife through soft butter, slipping inside the building. He recalled the blade to his hand and waited.

The pyramid's exterior fractured, and then it sunk in on itself slightly. Jace kept his eyes peeled, watching for any sign of movement in the rocks and watching the golden line that went from him to his prey.

Void Stalker dropped.

Shit! Jace turned and barely got his sword up in time to strike one of the towers that had been launched up at him—a huge projectile crumbling to rubble as his weapon's second of three empowered strikes shattered the structure. But the rocks and rubble provided the ideal screen. Using Void Stalker once more, Jace dropped down among the rubble, landing on the sand below.

He heard the shuffling of stones and cursing. Looking over to his right, he saw the Demon Lord he was hunting. They looked like the Astral Demons who had followed the path of refinement for their evolution but mixed with monstrous characteristics, much like the one that Jace had fought earlier that cycle along with the two worm-eel looking demons.

Jace used Void Step, warping behind them, and held the blade just under their chin. "Move and you die."

The figure froze, and growled. "What do you want with me?"

"All of your Astral Demons. Every one of them under your control—recall them here. Now."

The Demon Lord barely nodded and raised a clawed hand out in front of their torso. They snapped, the fingers and claws making a clacking noise as the sound reverberated out. The Astral Demons that had been toppling towers onto Jace rushed over but came to a halt thirty feet in front of him and his hostage.

"How many more?" Jace asked.

"Just the thirty," the Demon Lord growled back.

With a quick pull, Jace sliced through the Demon Lord's head, the golden flames of the Psykinetics burning bright. *I guess they keep their friends close*, Jace thought as he readied himself for the assault of the other Astral Demons.

They rushed forward as a group, wild hounds let off the leash, and Jace ran forward to meet them. Keeping his shield on his left, he hacked repeatedly with his right, the sword exploding with golden flames and tinged with pure, white heat. He sliced clean through the armored carapace of one Astral Demon.

But their numbers were significant, and he was only able to keep his footing for so long before he had to back up and find something to put his back against. The ripping teeth and razor claws would wend past his defenses and score hits. Some of them were able to cut through his armor and actually hit him—and the pain cut deep. One lucky strike lacerated something important in his shoulder, and the arm went limp for a split-second before the NICIF inside his body repaired the damage.

All part of the plan, Jace thought as he gritted his teeth through the pain and saw his HUD with the layout of damage accumulated across his body and overall vitality drop down lower and lower. Finally, after an agonizing thirty minutes of fighting against the things, he hit the threshold.

[Shattered Limits enabled.]

Jace activated the Skill, and at its maximum Rank 19, it amplified his physical, sensory, and cognitive traits by x100. With a swift slash, he dispatched four demons with a single blow. The golden flames exploded out from his strike, and he moved past all of the Astral Demons, getting behind them, and carved straight through one's forelegs. It was sent tumbling to the sand, and he followed up with a stab before rushing around the exterior of the pack—still trying to track him but unable to thanks to his blinding speed increase.

He picked them off, one at a time, his energy slowly draining all the while. As it hit twenty percent remaining and he had killed all but five, he shut off the Skill so he would not need to tap into his Emergency Battery.

The Astral Demons moved in, and Jace grinned, confident in his abilities.

The ground shook beneath him, and his [Danger-Sense] screamed at him that something was coming from directly underneath. Jace used his Void Step and warped straight up as the sand beneath exploded in a massive geyser.

Chapter Four

Layer 4, Vault 1

The fuck?! Jace thought as he glanced down, extending his Soul Tether to stay up in the air. Beneath him, a massive explosion surged up toward him, and using another Void Step, he got out of the way of the geyser. At first glance, it was sand that surged up in a massive pillar. But on closer inspection, he saw it was full of abrasive particles that would have torn and ripped into him.

Jace looked back down to the five Astral Demons, who looked equally as confused. *What caused it?* he thought.

Another geyser shot up toward him, and Jace used another Void Step to get out of the way. *Holy Hunt,* he thought as he activated the Talent to hone in on the source of the projectiles. The line shot off to his left, and looking over that way, he could see a humanoid figure in armor, hiding behind a pillar but poking their head out. Their hands flashed briefly with brown light before another geyser shot up.

Jace chained two Void Steps together and appeared behind the person, stabbing them through the chest and lifting them up with the force of his thrust. They let out a gasp of pain as the blade pierced their lungs. A shockwave surged out from them, and Jace felt himself slightly pushed back—but thanks to his Crusader's Bastion (Grounding) Infusion, he was resistant to forced movement and barely budged.

Jace brought his shield to bear and used the (Spiked) front to slam into the Dreamer Demon's back, as he had determined that the alien was not a true Astral Demon given its appearance. A similar appearance. Like one of the Gyanv insectoid-people from above. But a bit bulkier, with horns and spikes poking up from their shell and armor that was futuristic in design. He saw a pistol on their hip and left his sword in them as they dropped down. Retrieving the firearm, Jace saw it ignite with golden flames as his Valiant Crusader's Might imbued the item.

Mentally summoning the Hero's Blade back to the dimensional sheath near his hip, Jace instinctively deactivated the safety on the weapon, thanks to his Edge of Possibility Skill making him a master of the plasma pistol. A globule of green shot out as he thumbed the trigger, tinged with golden flames as it consumed the back of the creature he had stabbed—ending their pain.

Jace looked around the pillar and saw the five Astral Demons approaching at speed. With a grin, he raised the pistol and fired—each shot igniting the air around it as the globules raced out, slammed into the demons, and scored wounds upon them that burned and seared. But the pistol ran out of charges after six shots, and Jace threw it aside as he drew his sword once more. Raising it, he launched it in an overhand throw.

The blade sank into the forehead of the leading Astral Demon, dropping it mid-charge as it tumbled into the sand before the golden flames of his Psykinetics consumed them. Recalling the weapon, Jace was able to get off one more throw—but the demon dodged it. *Four remaining*, he thought as he raised his shield.

The one who had taken the lead tried to slam into him. But Jace turned at the last moment, performing a backhand slash across the legs of the demon as it went by. The second demon, also charging him, got into arm's reach, and Jace used Void Step to warp out of the way—appearing directly above and in front of the creature. He slashed down as it passed beneath him, slicing it cleanly in half before landing.

The third one stood a short distance away, and a bead of purple Psykinetic energy coalesced before blasting out at him. Jace got his shield in the way, but he felt the searing pain around the edges as the blast had some amount of overflow damage. *Dark Matter Mending (Rank 4) [Vampiric]*, Jace thought. The soothing warmth of Dark Matter surged through his body and mended him entirely, but his energy was dangerously close to zero and tapping into the Emergency Battery.

Something he wanted to reserve in case of emergency. Cocking his arm back, he threw the weapon. It surged through the stream of Psykinetic force, slamming into the demon's head and dropping it.

Summoning the sword back and with vision no longer obscured by the torrent of Psykinetic power, Jace scanned for the last demon. *Holy Hunt*, he thought.

The line extended out to his left, and sprinting across the sand, he spotted the demon trying to run away. With a swift throw of his sword, Jace ended that escape attempt. He was breathing heavily as he summoned his weapon back to his hand. "That's all of them, yeah?"

Yup! Ollie replied. *Good job.*

Jace ensured he gathered up all of the Essence, knowing that he had to get close to the demon corpses to absorb it. *Another 3,000*, he thought. *Puts me at 18,500.* Going to the Dreamer Demon, he removed their armor, weapons, and other gear. "Ollie, anything we can salvage here? Or use in some way?"

Ollie illuminated and outlined a small pouch along the figure's hip that Jace had removed. *More ammunition if you want to keep the pistol.*

Jace grabbed the plasma pistol and ammunition. *Two reloads' worth*, he thought as he swapped out the empty cartridge. "Shouldn't we also get something like his Infusions?"

Ollie sounded slightly sad, *They did not have any. I think that you are one of the few that hordes Infusions.*

"For a good cause," Jace replied. "I want that Divine rarity."

That will take a while. You need five Legendary for one Mythic, and five Mythic for a Divine. Ollie sighed, *I suppose we could look into some type of Astral Marketplace on Layer 3 when we visit. Maybe Demon Lord Malphitria could facilitate transactions.*

"We don't have anything to sell," Jace replied as he used his Templar's Smite to burn away the corpse of the Dreamer Demon. "Now, Holy Hunt." The path to the Vault illuminated just before him, and he began walking along the outline. Back to the rubble of the pyramid. "Of course," he muttered, "I would have buried it." Sighing, he began moving chunks of rocks out of the way.

It took a good ten minutes, but after clearing the rubble, he found a compartment—some type of basement—with a large trap door made of stone. Hauling it to the side, he revealed a familiar-looking stone tunnel leading down. Descending, Jace came upon a Vault door just like the ones on higher Layers. "Here we go," he said as he touched the door and got sucked through it.

The chamber was like the others, and like the Vault he had defeated on Layer 2, a glowing crystal hovered above the dais. An Astral System message appeared above him, and he quickly read it.

[Vault Challenge—Activated.]
[Win the race.]
[Special Parameters: No movement Skills, Talents, or Gear Infusions are allowed. Three attempts permitted.]
[Score to beat: 2 minutes.]

The world shifted around Jace, and he found himself standing on a shockingly familiar street. He was back on Earth, back on the docks where he had picked up the CIF. A bag was sitting on a glowing pedestal—just like the messenger bag he had that was climate controlled all those months ago. *Vaults can scan my memories?* he asked.

Seems like it, Ollie replied.

Jace saw a map appear above him. It was the exact same city, the exact same layout—but he only saw a destination. The drop point that he would have delivered the package to. Immediately, his mind went to the different routes he could take. Way back when he had his Runner's Replacement prosthetics, his fastest time to that location would have been fifteen minutes.

But now, with all of his enhancements, he could probably make the run in two minutes. Probably.

Well, I get three tries. Let's try the bridge first. Jace took a deep breath to steady himself, made sure all of his Gear was stowed in the TPSB—armor, weapons, everything—just leaving himself in his casual clothing he wore under the armor. Taking a few small hops to hype himself up, Jace went into his stretch routine that he used to do, mentally preparing to run.

You will do fine, Ollie thought to him. *You got this!*

Jace grinned and broke into a dead sprint, grabbing the bag off the pedestal. The moment it left and he slung it over his shoulder, he heard the blare of a siren and saw a small timer appear in his HUD—counting up from one, with milliseconds ticking up rapidly. Jace surged forward, reaching the wall that he had jumped over so long ago.

Tensing his legs, he launched himself skyward and cleared the wall by ten feet, somersaulting and landing on the opposite side—thankfully, with no gang to hunt him down. Sprinting through the alley, he had to jump over the barricade at the end as well—and kicking off the walls was easy enough as he did the routine bit of parkour he had mastered before his Edge [Class] made him so skilled at everything he tried.

Reaching the river, he rapidly considered his options. Go with the bridge as the plan, or try to jump the river. He made up his mind without breaking stride and went right for the expanse of water. Easily two-hundred feet across, he doubted he would be able to clear it in a single jump. But there were pylons standing upright in the water, spaced every fifty feet or so.

Putting a foot on a railing overlooking the water, he leapt forward, aiming at the pylon fifty feet away. He landed and immediately realized his mistake—the pylons had a rounded top. His foot slipped off to the side, and he went tumbling into the water.

But he was a swimmer, and loved swimming. Kicking into freestyle, he covered the remaining distance in the river as the timer slowly ticked up. Getting to the other side, there were no ladders—but he used his raw strength and his prosthetics to carve out small handholds with his fingertips, giving himself just enough of a small ledge to get the traction necessary to hoist himself up. Moving his toes to the gaps he had made with his fingers, he was able to leverage his weight forward and jump to the top of the rail.

Bringing himself over, he knew he would be cutting it close. Continuing his sprint, he went down another set of alleys full of cars that were in the process of being chopped apart or customized. Kicking off the walls, he made it through to the neighborhood on the other side and hustled across the open street, making it to the building on the other side.

The delivery spot was up in the executive suites, and he went right to the elevator, ripping the doors open with his arms before going inside, punching the access panel above him, and ascending via the cable—hand over hand as he muscled his way up. Getting to the correct floor, he ripped that set of elevator doors open.

A shimmering, silver pedestal sat in the center of a room, and Jace slammed down the bag containing the package.

One minute twenty seconds. Really fast! Ollie said.

Jace was panting and sucking in air. He couldn't help but feel proud of himself. He had come so far. That journey would have taken him so long back before The Cosmic System. And now? He had just cleared the distance at speeds that he would never have dreamed of.

The Astral System screen appeared in front of him.

> [You have cleared a Vault.]
> [Reward: Relic.]
> [Open the Reliquary to claim your Relic.]
> [Optional: Earn an Infusion by beating your time.]

Jace grinned and spoke. "Let's go again and try to beat my score!"

Tibalt gorged himself on every Soul he could find. Dreamer Demons that were up on the surface, he dragged beneath the sand and consumed, eating flesh, bone, sinew and cartilage. And yet the hunger was never sated. The screaming, swirling mass of Souls within him demanded freedom, but he craved more.

Time to level, he thought as he used every soul to level up. Picking Talents that would increase his offensive capabilities and movement speed, his body became slicker, less monstrous, and a bit more refined. Reaching the Potency 5 threshold, he grinned as he knew he could take on Wraith.

Now just to find the fucker, he thought as he coursed his way through the desert dunes, seeking out his prey. The entity whose death would bring him closer to his goal. He grinned as he tore across the great expanse, searching the Astral System's interface as he went for any sightings, any notifications, any information on where his hated foe was.

Chapter Five

Talking and Stalking

Jace was teleported back to the start of the challenge. The same bag appeared on the pedestal, and this time, he saw the timer in his HUD start at his prior completion time, and instinctively knew it would count down. "Okay. Any advice? Analysis?" he asked.

Ollie hummed. *Hmm. I would say that the improvement would be to intentionally dive into the river, build up speed, and then rocket out of the water to avoid the climb. As for the building, you should climb the outside. It had long, horizontal lines you could grip and launch yourself up.*

Jace nodded and backed up several feet down the docks so he could achieve top speed. Planting his fingers, he felt the tension build up in his thighs and calves, bracing for an explosive start. "Ollie, can you play music?"

Sure. What did you want?

Jace grinned. "My mentor . . . sorry. Dad's favorite song."

Got it!

Jace heard the familiar bass beat in his ears, followed by the strumming of an electric guitar. He tried to time his breathing to the beat of the music, closing his eyes briefly. Then, as the introduction faded and the guitar solo began, he took off. His feet dug into the ground with such force that they carved grooves into the cement. He dashed, grabbed the bag, and slipped it around him as he tore across the docks.

Reaching the wall, he easily jumped it, and the increased speed from a longer running start enabled him to clear not just the wall, but get enough height to land on one of the roofs—saving him valuable time as he did not have to kick off the walls to dodge debris. Sprinting along the rooftops, he vaulted the edges and went over the small, interconnecting side alleys as he reached the edge of the buildings on the opposite side.

Jumping with as much force as he could muster, he cleared the whole street and dove into the river. The cold met him and was refreshing, welcoming, in a way, as he kept his arms pointed in front of him and kicked with his feet in perfect timing, like a pair of fins. He knifed through the water, losing only a tiny bit of speed compared to his full-on sprint. Angling his arms up, he propelled himself through the cool liquid and exploded upward.

His speed carried him well above the railing—but he reached out to grab it and pull himself forward. The roll he had to perform to help reorient his trajectory was slightly awkward, but he got back into a full sprint and kicked off the walls down the full-of-cars alley. He cleared it, got to the business square across another street, and began scaling the building. Each fingertip found a spot to grip, each toe snaked its way into the crevices, and he scaled up the side.

Reaching the delivery level, he slammed his fist through the window and swung himself inside, planting the bag on the pedestal with only two seconds to spare. He was sucking in air as the System message appeared above him.

[Optional condition met.]
[Reward: Epic (Essence Cache) Infusion.]

The Vault reappeared around Jace, and the floating crystal on the pedestal hovered there, waiting to be claimed. But next to the dais was a figure. A familiar one. The Loud Ancient, who waved and smiled, still looking very human, but Jace knew that was just to put him at ease, as he doubted his mind could comprehend this entity's true form.

"Hey there!" the Loud One said. "First Vault on this Layer, done. You skipped Layer 3 though."

Jace walked over and let his helmet recede, crossing his arms. "Yeah, well, they were all done. But we have our eyes on one that is being held for me."

The Loud One nodded. "Great! Happy to hear it. Well, you are doing pretty well, all things considered. This Layer is going to probably take you a bit of time, given how many rival Demon Lords exist here."

"I don't think it'll be that bad," Jace replied. "I mean, I took out fifty demons pretty easily. Plus their Demon Lord, and a Dreamer Demon."

"I saw," The Ancient replied. "Well, just a word of warning. Valcrinox has dozens if not hundreds of Missions out for information about you and high-rarity rewards for those who actually manage to kill you. Expect to be hunted."

Jace frowned. "Anything you can do to help out with that?" he asked.

"Nope! I can't interfere like that."

Annoying, Ollie thought, *being these dispassionate arbiters.*

"Well . . . I'm just going to keep doing what I'm doing," Jace replied. "Speaking of, if you don't have anything else—"

"Oh, I do!" The Ancient smiled. "We have been keeping tabs on you. And we appreciate you not using that Void power from your Universe. At least in an offensive or defensive capacity—movement is still fine. That warp is a nifty trick!"

"It's saved me a number of times," Jace replied. "Why can't I use it, aside from not getting the Essence from a kill?"

The Ancient frowned slightly. "It is the opposite of creation. Of existence itself. Void can destroy Essence, which means it can destroy Souls—"

"I've never done that!" Jace replied.

"I know," The Ancient said as the frown vanished to be replaced by a neutral expression. "But it could, and if your innate Cosmic System got into another person's hands . . . "

Jace narrowed his eyes. "What is it you want to do?"

"Nothing. Just notifying you. Should you perish, my partner and I will ensure that you are instantly annihilated. Nothing will remain. We cannot risk your System being taken by others."

Can Astral Demons do that? Ollie asked. His voice emanated from the armor as if a low hum.

"It is sort of like Gear," The Ancient replied. "The problem is this—you die, and we annihilate you, your Soul is getting destroyed also. It's intricately entwined with your Cosmic System."

Jace shook his head. "I don't plan on dying. I won't die. I've got a job to finish . . . and past deeds to redeem."

The Ancient smiled. "Fair enough. Well, enjoy! You probably won't hear from my partner or I unless something . . . interesting develops." They vanished with a glimmer of bright pink energy.

Jace walked to the pedestal and grabbed the crystal. It settled into his hand—an elongated, two-sided pyramid with a long shaft in the center.

[You have acquired a Relic of the Ancients.]
[The Astral System has detected another System present.]
[Do you wish to integrate Relic with existing {Equipment}?]

"Yes," Jace replied. He saw the shard split into two, leaving him to hold the tube-shaped central piece. The two pyramids circled him, their flat side facing him. They spun, faster and faster, creating a small, pink lattice that wrapped around him like a cocoon before soaking through his armor, into his body—and causing horrible tickling sensations. Jace lost it as he giggled and cackled, rolling on the ground as he let out laughter from feeling his insides tickle.

[Relic Equipped.]
[Psycrystal Lattice.]

[Amplifies depth of emotion related to the Valiance Emotion Source. The user's limbs bones cannot be broken, fractured, or cracked.]

[Effects from merged {Equipment}:]
[Flexible—Causes the skeleton to become malleable and bendable as the user dictates, enabling for greater dexterity, flexibility, and reduced harm to the skeletal structure.
[Effects merged to new designation: Reinforced.]
[Future alterations will be merged into new designation.]

The tickling faded, and Jace was able to take a few deep breaths before he was ejected from the Vault, sent skidding along the tunnel for a brief moment before he stopped on the dirt floor. "That . . . that was weird. I've never felt a tickle inside my body."

It was quite odd, Ollie replied. *Now up and on your feet! We have another Demon Lord to kill, and another Vault to plunder!*

"But no more Relics for this Layer," Jace replied as he got up and made his way up to the surface.

He's close, Tibalt thought as he raced through the sand. Thanks to the Specialization he had picked up by using an Infusion claimed from a Dreamer Demon he had slain, he could locate any Dreamer within a distance based on his Potency. And he knew that if a Dreamer wasn't in Respite, that walled city that he could not enter, or coming down from Layer 3 above, it had to be Wraith.

He coursed through the sand, following the man as he ran across the desert sands. *How is he on the surface?* Tibalt thought as he kept a decent distance from the Dreamer. *Deep Analysis.* He activated a Talent meant to find any flaws or weaknesses in his foe. It would take time, and he would just have to keep a distance from Wraith.

Tibalt knew that Wraith had some means of detecting anything that came within a certain radius from beneath or beside—his encounter with the Astral Demons back toward the dunes near the Layer 3 entrance having shown that in spades.

Just stay close, learn everything about every capability, and bide time.

Tibalt itched for the reward. Enough Souls to hit Potency 10 once he slew Wraith. Then, he could serve this Valcrinox for a while, building up his familiarity with his Talents before overthrowing the tyrant and usurping his place.

Jace sprinted across the sands. Traveling with Void Stalker active, his plan was still on track. Go around the perimeter of the Layer, hitting every single Demon Lord in their Ruins and clearing the Vaults for the Essence Cache rewards he would get now that he had claimed a Relic on this Layer.

"We have six levels' worth of Essence?" Jace asked.

Yup! Ollie replied. *Leaving you with 500 Essence left over.*

Jace smiled. "All into Specializations." He'd done some theory crafting as he ran, with Ollie checking some variables in The Astral System's database. What he concluded was that having a new Talent was good and could help fill a missing need, but Specializations were extremely potent because they all stacked, unlike The Cosmic System, which only enabled one application of a Skill Evolution at a time.

In other words, the same energy expenditure for more effects on the same Talent.

[You have leveled up!]
[You have chosen Specialization of Existing Talent!]
[Talent Name: Purifying Edge.]
[Specialization Name: Searing.]
[Effect: When the linked Talent is used on a target, they take damage from your Psykinetics.]
[Talent Name: Purifying Edge.]
[Specialization Name: Purging.]
[Effect: When the linked Talent is used on a target, temporarily sunder offensive Talents, shutting them off.]
[Talent Name: Purifying Edge.]
[Specialization Name: Sanctifying.]
[Effect: When a Talent is shut off, reactivating it costs double the energy unless five seconds pass in the interim.]
[Talent Name: Holy Hunt.]
[Specialization Name: Inciting.]
[Effect: The user gains a movement speed boost when moving toward their target.]
[Talent Name: Templar's Smite.]
[Specialization Name: Inferno.]
[Effect: When the linked Talent is used on a target, they continue to suffer from the lingering flame of Psykinetic energy. Stacks with (Burning) from Valiant Crusader's Might and (Lingering) from Templar's Smite.]
[Talent Name: Hero's Arena.]
[Specialization Name: Suppressing.]
[Effect: Those in the Hero's Arena who suffer damage must spend twice the energy as normal to activate Talents.]

Name: Jace Seren (Potency 4)
Emotion [Class Level]: Valiant [Purifier 39]
Talent [Specialization]: Astral Adaptation, Astral Translation, Valiant Crusader's Might [Burning] [Vengeful] [Poised] [Unstoppable] [Bracing], Crusader's Bastion [Retaliating] [Reinforcing] [Grounding] [Redoubt] [Spiked], Hero's Arena [Aura] [Incinerating] [Vexing] [Bolstering] [Suppressing], Indomitable Will [Zealous] [Intimi-

dating] [Inviolable] [Enduring], Templar's Smite [Spear] [Blast] [Lingering] [Challenging] [Inferno], Holy Hunt [Marked] [Bursting] [Authoritative] [Provoking] [Inciting], Purifying Edge [Cleansing] [Searing] [Purging] [Sanctifying]
Essence: 500
Infusions: x3 Epic (Essence Cache), Legendary (Specialization), Legendary (Gear)
Gear: <TPSB>, (Convergent Edge) [Ruination 1] Hero's Blade, (Explorer's Embrace / Beacon) Paragon Armor, (Prosthetic Savant) Astral Appendages, (Draconic Sovereign) Arbiter's Sight, (Anathema) Astral Sleeve, (Reinforced) Psycrystal Lattice, (Reactive) NICIF, (Restoring) Flame of Valor

"Two more levels to the next Potency," Jace muttered as he continued his run across the dunes.

But the Essence cost is going to go up. And we might have a situation like Layer 3 where we were short on the leveling currency. I would advise we just continue to use Essence and level up, even if we go well above the Potency requirement for the next Layer down.

Jace saw the outline of the Ruins in the distance. Not circular towers, sunk into the ground like the last location. Huge, ossified, bulbous shapes were tilting at slight angles. Jace slowed slightly and used his Soul Tether to pull himself up into the sky to get a better view from above. He spotted another pyramid structure, far in the center of the clusters.

Oh! Ollie said with recognition, *the buildings are fossilized mushrooms! Probably hollowed out and capable to be lived in. Fascinating. Our Universe doesn't have fungal architecture, or any species created from fungal spores—though there are plenty of parasitic types on certain worlds!*

Jace only half-listened to Ollie as he was more intent on scanning for Astral Demons. But he did not see any. *Holy Hunt*, he thought as he focused on his target—the Demon Lord in the Ruins. The small line shot out, charting a course to one of the fungal structures. *There you are.*

Tibalt saw Wraith raise his arm and fly up into the sky as if he was pulled aloft by a tether. Keeping his distance, he kept burrowing and concluded his Talent's scans.

What he had learned terrified him further.

Wraith had some sort of innate technology—lots of cybernetics. Including an artificial intelligence housed within his form. *That explains how he can move so fast*, Tibalt thought. *He is not controlling his body—the AI is guiding his actions at faster processing speeds.*

It made Tibalt envious. That, and the plethora of Relics that Wraith was carrying that contributed to his longing to have what his foe held. *I should go and conquer a Vault or two of my own*, he thought as he used a Talent to place a "tag" on Wraith that would allow Tibalt to focus his attention to him through an Astral System HUD at any time.

Then, Tibalt burrowed away. South, to the closest Vault to his location. *A few Relics for me.*

He did feel the call of the next Layer. The desire to sink deeper into the Astral Verge from his demon side. But he could stave it off. Long enough, he hoped, to clear the Vault and claim a Relic to augment his Psykinetics.

My only hope is a surprise attack, from range, in a location with very little maneuverability so he cannot dodge. I shall bide my time and wait for the opportune moment to strike.

Chapter Six

Layer 4, Vault 2

Jace descended the Soul Tether and headed to the huge, bulbous, slightly tilted mushroom-design building. The sand beneath his feet started to crunch a bit, and he looked down to see a web of mycelia that was dry and brittle. Drawing his sword, he activated all of his Talents and Skills that he usually did.

The building did not have doors of any type. Instead, an open cylinder that once perhaps held some type of aperture of the root structure had cracked and remained permanently open. Going inside, he could smell the oddly fruity scent of something in the distance. Following the golden line leading to his objective was simple enough, and Jace was standing next to another one of the circular aperture doorways. Poking his head through, he spotted quite an odd sight.

The figure he was looking for was outlined in gold, and Jace could tell the individual was mostly monstrous, but not like any Astral Demon he had seen before. The figure was seemingly crusted into the wall, with fungal plates growing around them. A hideous blob of pulsating mushrooms that glowed with a visceral, green hue. Raising his hand, Jace prepared to use a Templar's Smite.

But his [Danger-Sense] went off as something approached from everywhere. His senses were screaming at him to dodge, and instinctively, he dipped to his left. But it was a fruitless attempt, as the entire building squished inward in an attempt to crush him. *Void Step (Rank 17)*, Jace thought as he focused on the entrance not too far away.

Warping outside, he saw the enormous, fallen-over mushroom building compressed in on itself. The same sickly green glow that had surrounded the Astral Demon fused to the building interior and spread across the whole structure, and it pulled itself out of the ground. *Shit*, Jace thought, *I was going to try and use the Demon Lord to lure the ones under its control over here.*

Focus up! Ollie reprimanded. *And beat this thing.*

Jace threw his sword. It flew true, striking what he envisioned was the trunk of the mushroom building. The weapon embedded itself, spreading its golden flames—but the Psykinetic power went out nearly instantaneously. Summoning the sword back to his grip, he frowned under his helmet. *Annoying. It's just a building; I need to get to the core.*

Luckily, he had something for that. Ruination Razor (Rank 3) [Wrecking]. His weapon surged with crimson light as the nebula clouds dripped off of it, and cocking back his arm once more, he threw the weapon at the now-thirty-foot-tall mushroom building that slowly moved toward him. But the sword sank into the building exterior, vanishing within and impacting something deeper inside.

Recalling the blade, Jace quickly threw it twice more at slightly different angles but along the same general throwing path. The weapon sank into the structure on both strikes, but the building did not collapse. In fact, it was as if [Wrecking], which should have destroyed the structure beyond repair, did absolutely nothing.

Oooh, Ollie whispered. *It is a living creature, so your Ruination Razor cannot work on it.*

Annoying, Jace thought as he backed away from the mushroom building now slowly shuffling toward him. The green energy surrounding it began to swell, glowing brighter and brighter. *Any thoughts on how to deal with this?*

Void Beam the building to get line of sight to the Astral Demon, then throw your sword. Purifying Edge with the Specializations you have applied to it should cancel out whatever defensive Talent is allowing them to encase themselves.

Jace raised his hand, pointing it just above where the Demon Lord was. *Void Beam (Rank 1) [Piercing]*, he thought. The white-grey beam of energy surged out, boring a hole clean through the entire mushroom structure, and revealed his target. Rapidly throwing the sword through the gap, the weapon struck the Demon Lord, who let out a shriek of pain and anger. The mushroom building stopped moving as all of the green coloration vanished.

Templar's Smite (Spear), Jace thought as he launched the bolt of blazing fury. The golden fire smote the creature, applying the three different damage-over-time effects from his various Specializations, three distinct shades of golden flames intermingling and waving in between each other. It was a mesmerizing sight to look at, and Jace let his sword stay planted in the Demon Lord as he waited for it to expire.

His [Danger-Sense] warned him once more of something coming at him from behind, and wheeling around to face the threat, he was taken aback by what he saw. The other buildings had begun to glow as well and were moving toward him. One in particular was getting very close, but they moved ponderously.

Jace simply used his Soul Tether to draw himself up to the sky and out of range. A rush of Essence flew up to him from where the sword had been embedded in the Demon Lord, and recalling his blade, Jace looked down at the handful of moving buildings. "More Astral Demons who took after their associated Demon Lord."

Seems reasonable to assume, Ollie replied. *And it is not all of the buildings down there that are moving—just some of them. Implying that they also host Astral Demons. But finding them and getting to them may be difficult.*

Jace swung himself to his left as a cloud of Psykinetic energy shot up at him from one of the slow-moving mushrooms. "I'm not going to spend who knows how long here trying to get at the demon controlling the building. The one I just killed, I had an idea of where it was located. These ones? No clue."

Try Holy Hunt?

"I mean . . . I guess. Holy Hunt," Jace replied as he focused on the mushroom building below him and the demon controlling it.

But his Talent did not activate. "Um . . . not Astral Demons."

Ollie groaned. *Try using it again, on that Demon Lord.*

Jace did so and saw the golden line appear before forking off and showing a course to every one of the mobile buildings. "Oh."

Yup. I thought so. The Demon Lord had some Talent, that most likely grew these mushrooms. Then, it stayed dormant. But when you threatened it, it . . . hive minded out its consciousness? Best way I can describe it.

"But I got the Essence!" Jace complained as he swung out of the way of another potshot Psykinetic blast.

Maybe . . . just a thought, but it could be that you killed one of its bodies. We do not know of any of the demons serving it.

"It's all of them," Jace reasoned. "The Demon Lord was able to hive-mind the other demons into its mushroom network thing. So all of them are the target."

Seems logical. Guess there's nothing for it now. You just have to use Psykinetics in a big area.

"Or I say 'fuck this' and do it my way." Jace swung on his Soul Tether, refiring it as needed until he reached a short distance from the ruins. Turning back to face them, he cupped his hands. "Void Beam (Rank 1) [Horizon-Splitter]." The blast of white-grey energy surged out and tore across the landscape, fully draining his energy. But he did not fall unconscious thanks to the [Enduring] Infusion and chose not to use the Emergency Battery, instead relying on his natural regeneration rate.

The sand, the mushrooms, the pyramid—everything was gone for a half mile in a cone before him. "And done," he said as he sat down on the sand behind him.

No Essence, though, Ollie commented.

"Time versus effort," Jace replied in between panting breaths, watching his energy trickle up again. "Only five hundred per demon at this Potency on this Layer. We don't need the Essence right here, right now. And honestly? I'd rather just do this."

I cannot fault you for wanting to save time.

Jace stood up as his energy ticked back up. "Onto the Vault," he stated as he began walking toward the pyramid's location.

The Quiet Ancient looked at his alerts and frowned. *Void*, he thought. Standing up, he went to his partner's room. "Did you tell Wraith not to use Void?"

"Hmm?" The Loud One looked back at him from his chair. "Kind of? I was a bit noncommittal about it, to be honest."

The Quiet One sighed. "Send him a message. Tell him no more Void. Except the movement ability, and the one that protects his Soul. He has just damaged Layer 4. Severely."

The Loud One frowned. "Okay, my bad. I'll send it now!"

Good, the Quiet One thought as he returned to his room and sat down at his console. *Hopefully that's the last time Wraith uses Void in such a manner while in the Verge. If he keeps it up . . . I'll have to admin-lock his Astral System until he knocks it off.*

Jace received a System message and quickly read it. "Damn. Ollie, you see this?"

Yes. Seems like The Ancients really do not want you utilizing Void. Makes me wonder if even they are scared of its power.

That idea struck Jace as slightly odd. "A trans-reality species that cannot do what Xera's species did? That doesn't seem likely."

Think about it. They arrived in the Nethershift, not in a Universe. For all we know, their home reality does not have matter by default. It may not have Void by default. Nothingness is a tricky concept.

"I'm not going to use it against them, if that's the concern," Jace muttered as he reached where the pyramid used to be. The entire top had been blown away with his earlier Void Beam, and the passageway down into the depths was clearly visible from the now-smooth surface of solid rock Jace walked upon.

Descending into the passage, he saw the familiar sight of a Vault door. He took a seat opposite the door and waited for his energy to refill. While he sat there, he pondered what Ollie had proposed. *If Void is something that The Ancients know of but do not know how to use, then why not just . . . rip the information from me? They are obviously powerful, tech or otherwise.*

Ollie replied, *They have that weird pact where they cannot directly intervene and require intermediaries like us. Otherwise, I would say that we offer them knowledge of how to use Void, and they could deal with the Demon Lords who did not follow their plans themselves.*

Jace sat on that thought until his energy refilled, and once it was full, he stood up. "Time to get to work." Reaching up and touching the Vault door he was sucked inside and found himself once more inside a chamber with a crystal hovering above a dais.

[Vault Challenge—Activated.]
[Hold out for five minutes against the attackers.]

The entire world shifted around Jace, and he drew his sword as he activated his suite of Talents and Skills. He found himself atop a building uniform with others nearby. Extremely familiar buildings. Ones that he had fought Black Hole Conclave Signers at, and which he had led nanite-infused zombies to.

It looks like the Vaults are starting to draw upon your past, Ollie stated.

Jace turned to face the entrance to the roof and stomped over to it, ripping the door open and off its hinges. He could hear the screeching and clamoring of the horde of rampaging, animalistic, raging creatures on the approach. And the glow of energy down the stairs informed him that they had energy infusing them. *Probably Psykinetics*, he reasoned. *Otherwise they couldn't hurt me, and this wouldn't be a challenge.*

The horde got up the stairs, and he saw the familiar upright corpses rushing toward him. Readying his shield, Jace held firm as they flung themselves upon the barrier made of Psykinetics. *Just hold out for five minutes*, he thought. *Let them congest up the stairs, and I can just hold in place.*

The horde continued to come, and the press of bodies built—but Jace stood firm. Keeping his whole body behind the tower shield, he had to turn slightly to brace in the doorway. The Psykinetic-empowered claws of the creatures raked across and tried to get past his shield, but it was a fruitless effort. And the whole time, Jace's Hero's Arena continued to burn them, to incite them to move close and try to consume him. The ones closest to Jace burned to ashes, only to be replaced by more as the stairwell continued to fill up; bodies clawed over each other, and all sought Jace's demise.

However, something stirred in Jace. A desire to purge this obviously diseased-by-magitech group of creatures. Just how his <Wrathblade> Expansion once pushed him on to violence, he felt that near-alien presence pushing against his psyche. Driving him to purify. To cleanse and wash clean with righteous fury.

Fuck it, Jace thought as he heaved with his whole body, shoving the crowd of Velenian zombies back as he whipped his sword around. The golden flames exploded from the strike, and giving into his [Purifier] Class seemed to resonate with his Emotion Source as the Hero's Arena expanded to its maximum radius, scorching the next three floors down the flights of stairs.

Slice, slash, carve, cut; every blow slaughtered one of the nanite-driven zombies. Every strike led to another death, and Jace slowly made his way down the stairs through the press of bodies as ash continued to pile up, only to be swept away by his movement further down. The press was endless, and Jace reveled in the feeling of his superiority. The overwhelming might he had over these creatures from his past.

It was almost a shock when the room returned to normal around him, and he saw the floating crystal above the dais shift and pixelate before being replaced with a capsule the size of his fist. Walking over, still ablaze with shining glory, Jace grabbed it.

[You have cleared a Vault.]
[Reward: Epic (Essence Cache).]

One more of those and we can upgrade the five to a Legendary!

Jace was sucked out of the Vault door and landed back in the tunnel, the clear, white sky above him shining down thanks to the upper structure having been obliterated. Jumping up and using his Soul Tether, he could see the sands were slowly returning, pushed by some invisible force, as he had not felt any wind up thus far. "Onto the next Demon Lord," Jace stated as he began moving to the next location.

Hold up! Ollie said, and Jace stopped. *You should head to Layer 3. We can cut down and at a southwestern angle to reach it, and then when we return here, it's a straight-north shot to the next location.*

"Sounds good," Jace replied as he altered course slightly and picked up his pace.

Chapter Seven

Going Up!

It took Jace two cycles to run the distance back to the entrance leading up to Layer 3. During that run, he was not accosted by any Astral Demons thanks to his Void Stalker Skill, and he spent most of that time just letting his body autopilot in its sprint under a program Ollie ran through his prosthetics.

That gave Jace the opportunity to focus on an "internal simulation" that Ollie had rigged up using his innate Cosmic System. Effectively, Jace was able to project his consciousness into a video-game-esque environment where he could practice Skills—and now, thanks to the Astral System, Talents.

Those two cycles of travel were not wasted time, as Jace was able to drill himself over and over, again and again. Pulling up old fights with foes long-since gone but catalogued thanks to Ollie's presence. Well, except for the few fights where Jace was inside a location that was disconnected from The Cosmic System.

The one he spent the most time studying, replaying, and re-fighting was the fight against Troxanir. Fighting on the incomplete Penrose Ring around Oblivion, Jace could see himself in stark contrast against the black hole in the background. Troxanir was dangerous, and Jace didn't notice at the time, but there were small trails of gold flames that raced after his blows—indicative of his Valiant Emotion Source being tapped into.

A dangerous fight, to be sure . . . but Jace was able to battle him despite the massive difference in Potency. Jace at Potency 1 should have stood no chance at all against Troxanir at Potency 8.

When he brought it up with Ollie, the Wayfinder appeared in the virtual space next to him, swimming through small nebula clouds. "Well," he said as he paused the combat and waved his paws. The world shifted and became the inner, deeper parts of The Cosmic System, where Troxanir was pinned in and locked to. "He was not able to access all of his power. I did some researching, and it looks like Troxanir came up one of the first Universe funnels to appear. He must not have known how to fully bring his Astral System Talents into our reality, to manifest them properly. And by the time he learned, he was already too late—The Cosmic System was shackling him."

Jace walked over to the pink blob shape, surrounded by Dee, Priam, and Greg—all frozen in place in a recapture of their beatdown of his forces and the final defeat of the dread entity. Jace squatted and looked at the pink, pulsating sack of the Astral Demon's bound body. "I'm a bit confused. I thought that The Astral System was . . . stronger than the Cosmic one."

Ollie floated over to Jace and shook his head. "Nope. They operate on different layers of reality. Equal, yet not equal. Troxanir could not fully manifest his Psykinetics—including all of his passive benefits of being Potency 8 compared to your Potency 1."

Jace stood up. "I got lucky, then."

"Not really," Ollie replied. "Just a happy coincidence!" He clapped his paws. "We're here, by the way."

Jace nodded and closed his eyes, feeling his body once more as he came out of the inner virtual reality turned training ground. He was standing in a depression underneath the film that led up to Layer 3. The open space was still slowly trickling full of sand—evidence of his prior removal of the substance when he first arrived. Firing off his Soul Tether, he ascended up through the film. It clung to him briefly before he passed through, and he clambered over the edge of the ledge in the basement of the tower.

Standing up, he headed outside. The city was bustling with life—Astral Demons that had seemed to choose the path of refinement roamed about, chatting and moving from place to place. Hearing a loud roar of thrusters, Jace looked up to see a ship exit through the film leading to Layer 2 up above. *Good to see that the trade is still happening down here.*

<u>*Depends on what they are trading*</u>, Ollie thought back. <u>*Those could be Dreamer Demons and not just Dreamers.*</u>

Jace frowned at that thought and returned his attention to the ground floor. *Okay. Holy Hunt.* He activated the Talent as he focused on finding the Vault that Xera had closed off. The golden line shot off to Jace's right, and he followed the path.

Tibalt gasped for breath as his organs finished regenerating. The viscous, blue blood that had coated his torso slowly soaked back into his body. "Come on!" he screamed in rage as he faced down the foe before him. A massive mech, wielding a wicked blade that thrummed with vibration to increase its cutting power. A reminder of where he came from: the war-torn worlds of his glorious Vanguard Empire. The civil war he had fought in that had helped him elevate to the level of Highlord.

Tibalt ran forward with a howl of fury, brandishing his claws that hummed with the crackling Psykinetic energy that fluctuated around his form, his anger fueling his power as he tapped into that Emotion Source that he held so dear. Wrath. Pure, simple, and without bias. The crackling purple energy coursed over the tips of his clawed fingertips, and he dodged the swipe of the mech's sword before planting his claw into the knee and ripping sideways—tearing out a servo as black goop surged out.

The mech fell over, and Tibalt jumped on it, yanking away the canopy and tearing into the pilot within. *Die, rebel scum!* he thought with glee as he replayed the vision of the fight in his mind. Him in his power armor, on the ground, against a twenty-foot-tall mech, the metallic claws of his armor's integrated weaponry covered with the thick, goopy blood of a nanite-enhanced soldier.

And then, the world vanished around Tibalt, and he was returned to the Vault. Going to the dais, he grabbed the crystal and activated the Relic. The object fractured into a spiral lattice that surged into him. Tibalt fell to the ground, writhing in agony as the Relic augmented something he had long forgotten about.

The nanites coursed through his body. The potent, empowering, repairing, and miraculous nanotechnology kept him at the peak of health despite his hundreds of years of life. And now, with this Relic upgrade to the substance in him, he had no doubt that he could defeat Wraith. His muscles bulged with power; he knew his healing capabilities were on par with the fastest regeneration that rivaled that of the Tarraxor Apex Predators back in his Universe, whose wounds would seal instantly.

I can kill him, Tibalt thought as he was unexpectedly sucked backward, flying down the small corridor and landing on his feet. *Oh, interesting. You are forced out when you defeat it.* Tibalt shrugged and went up the small, spiral staircase, emerging into the pyramid interior. He spared a brief glance at the Demon Lord's throne nearby. Unoccupied. Tibalt grinned, went over, and slammed it with his fist, crumbling the backrest to fragments that exploded outward with a bang.

You should have just let me go into the Vault and not been in my way, Tibalt thought as he reminisced on feeling the blood gushing over him as he ripped that Demon Lord asunder. *Now, where are you, Wraith?* Tibalt accessed his Astral System and saw that he was somewhere in Layer 3—sadly, the Talent only showed exact locations on the same Layer, otherwise it would just notify him of where his hated foe was.

He will return, doubtless. The longing for the next Layer drew on Tibalt all the more fiercely, and he resigned himself to the call. *I will descend, defeat another Vault, gain more Potency . . . and then, I will hunt him.*

Jace made it to the building in which the Vault was located. The interior was completely clear of all furniture—just a big, empty, vertical box of several floors. Jace followed the golden line to the stairwell in the back but paused as he saw something glistening in the dark, covered in the purple of Dark Matter whose color instantly stood out to him. "Ollie?" he asked cautiously.

Oh, just one of the drones. It's been blocking the path. Ollie sounded quite pleased. *And it's now ours.*

"Come again?"

Xera's voice came over the comms. "I'm tasking this drone to be your personal one. It will follow you at a preset height, but Ollie can interface with it and have it scout for you. I can only spare the one, since I'm working hard on establishing an intelligence perimeter of drones coated in Dark Matter beneath our Universe. An early warning system, of sorts. Plus getting them established and set up in the different Layers."

Jace felt gratitude toward Xera, and spoke softly. "Thank you."

Quinn's voice cut in, "Good news on the Stardust front. We've made a big trade deal as part of a merger and acquis—you know what, you probably don't care about the specifics. The long and short of it is that the Dark Between Stars is very stocked up."

"And the Stardust set aside for Chroma?" Jace asked.

Quinn replied, "Still there. The numbers are a bit different, though, because Xera is shifting the progression of The Cosmic System for Stardust costs. Effectively, for non–Dark Between Stars Signers, leveling up is going to take a lot longer. A miniature overhaul."

Jace frowned. "But that is going to just incentivize—"

"No, people will lose their levels if they go against the faction and leave it."

Jace was slightly irked. "I wasn't going to talk about that. But . . . is it just you and me on the line?"

"Mm-hmm," Quinn replied.

"Do you really want Xera to have a ton of high–Tier Ascendants at her command?"

Quinn laughed lightly. "Who do you think is going to run the Dark Between Stars? Not Xera. It's going to be the current Signers for the faction. Xera has already declared her intent to step down and have you be the overseeing administrator for the whole Cosmic System. The rest of us who are current Signers will be like sub-admins under you. The Dark Between Stars, keeping an eye on the whole Cosmic System from the shadows." She cackled with glee.

Jace wasn't quite sure how to feel about that. Greg he trusted. Priam, he trusted. Dee was trustable but also a bit of a loose cannon. And Quinn was obviously out for herself. *But if I'm going to be over the rest,* Jace thought, *then I could always revoke their access if they tried something horrible. And Shhiv is going to be at the same admin status as the rest of them.* He nodded. "Okay. Ollie? Task this drone with keeping an eye on the outside."

The drone, a sphere with four fins sticking out of it that silently thrummed with vibrations keeping it aloft, seemed to wink its small, purple lens that Jace imagined was the camera aperture. The drone shrank down in size, compressing from the size of a door down to that of a cosmoscreen, and it flicked past him and out the door. Jace could see the camera feed appear in the top-left corner of his HUD.

Okay, another Vault, another Relic. Jace headed down the stairs, drawing his weapon and activating his Skills and Talents as he went. Five flights of stairs and Jace was in a familiar, stone-carved hall with the Vault door standing before him. Reaching up with his shield hand, Jace touched it and was sucked through the stone, landing inside the familiar chamber. What's the challenge?

Chapter Eight

Facing the Past

Jace waited for the Astral System message to appear. But it did not. He tapped his foot impatiently, waiting . . . but nothing happened. “What’s going on?”

[Still calculating worst regret.]
[Stand by . . .]

Worst regret? Jace thought as he felt a pit form in his gut. *I . . . I have to face off against the worst thing I regret?*

Ollie spoke in his mind. *I have narrowed it down to three possible events. Either your sister’s demise, your killing of the workers at Pheracorp Industries back on Earth, or your tear of destruction on Deckard’s home world of Teresii.*

Jace frowned. “I don’t regret what I did at Teresii. Deckard deserved it, and I spared those who surrendered and fled.”

I am just calculating based upon the Astral System’s likely parameters.

[Vault Challenge—Activated.]
[Stop the <Wrathblade>’s rampage.]

Jace saw the world warp around him, and he was in the factory hellscape of South America at Pheracorp Industries. He could hear the sounds of combat in a nearby building; ones that were familiar to him. He heard the helo overhead and saw the combat mechs drop down on ropes before they landed with a thud, disconnected their lines, and rushed inside.

Stop myself? Easy enough. Jace began to move after the mechs, following them inside. The sight that greeted him was gorier than he remembered—corpses dismembered and blood slick upon the floors. Machinery, cut through and torn to bits. The mechs were in the process of being destroyed, and Jace saw his past self.

Wrath incarnate. Crackling, crimson nebula clouds pouring off of his past self, Nethaldrim held firmly in one hand as the Dark Matter pulsed along the edge, making it invisible to all except for Jace and past-Jace. Bringing Hero's Edge to bear, Jace intercepted the next blow from his past self, deflecting the swing away from the mech and the pilot within.

Past-him looked feral and wild. Unhinged and out of control. *Arbiter's Anathema*, Jace thought as he used the Skill granted by his still-Augmented skin. But that only shut off the Dark Matter effect on the sword—the effects of Wrath's Embrace were still upon past-him, and the cruel smile was aimed at Jace. The voice that came out of that mouth was unmistakably his own, but there was a sinister edge to it. "More corpo-scum? You'll die like the rest."

Jace backed off and instinctively wrapped himself in his Void Shield as the world exploded around them. Everything was annihilated within a fifty-square-mile radius as past-him used the Archmage Pyromancy to obliterate everything that Pheracorp owned. It left Jace and past-him standing on a cracked and broken earth.

[Scenario failure.]

The scene vanished, and Jace was back in the Relic chamber of the Vault. "What was that?" he asked aloud.

<u>*Seems like you did not stop your past self in time.*</u>

Jace sighed, "Okay, let's try again."

The Astral System seemed to hear him as the world warped once more, and Jace was standing back on the building, watching the mechs slowly descend. But he wasted no time, instead using Void Step to warp down to the building, behind past-him, and instantly decapitated his old self.

[Scenario failure.]

Jace was back in the Vault. "Motherfucker," he growled, getting really pissed off.

Maybe you should focus on calmly stopping your past self.

"Again!" Jace shouted. Once more, the Vault seemed to hear him, and he appeared back on the building's roof. Using Void Step, he got behind past-him. *Void Counter,* Jace thought as he deactivated past-him's Skills. Using the Skill over and over, Jace stripped the past him of all Skills, leaving a partially prosthetic-filled cybernetic swordsman.

The mechs arrived and filled past-him with bullets, and the body sagged down. *You're not dead,* Jace thought as he grabbed past-him and ran. He slashed through the door at the rear of the facility and sprinted out to the edges of Campinas, reaching where the jungle began to re-emerge from the cracked asphalt and concrete of the construction that decimated much of its holding on the region.

Jace set his past self against a tree and stood up, sheathing his weapon and waiting for past-him to heal. "I know the NICIF kept your brain intact," he stated to his past self.

A minute passed, and the bullets slowly schlorped out of his old self's body, clattering down in a pile next to him. The eyes slowly fluttered open, and Jace knelt as he removed his helmet, staring at the old-him. "You need to calm down," he said firmly.

Past-him tried to grab him, but Jace just slapped the attempt away and pinned old-him to the tree with his hands. "Calm. Down."

"You don't understand!" past-Jace said as the crimson began to crackle around him. "They all need to die! Everyone who sold themselves to the corporations! They betrayed everything they stand for!"

Jace used a Void Counter to deactivate the Wrath's Embrace that was building up, making old-him gasp in shock. "This isn't us. This isn't you. It's our mentor—no, it's our dad's indoctrination. He made us hate the megacorporations. But those people? They aren't the cause. They aren't the CEOs and the people at the top. They are just trying to support their families and survive."

"Survive . . ."

Jace grabbed past-him by the back of the neck and pulled him close, whispering, "We always survive. For her."

Past-him tensed briefly. "How do you—"

"I am you," Jace replied. He felt that remorse still. That shame at what he had done. "I know what happens if you go down that path. If we just rampage and destroy it all. Trust me, it's not worth it. And I'm still trying to fix that mistake."

Past-him was quiet, but nodded ever-so-slightly. "I hate it," he whispered. "I hate being manipulated."

Jace felt that resonate on a deeper level than he cared to admit. His whole life, he had been manipulated by others. His dad, Xera, even Shhiv to a small extent, though he was okay with why Shhiv did it and had forgiven her. *My whole life, I've been manipulated*, he thought. And whispering back to past-him, he said, "The best life we had was when it was just us and Chroma. No other responsibilities." His voice hardened, and he raised it from the whisper. "We'll survive. I'll get everyone back that we killed in a rage. And then we'll have our life, fully under our control."

Past-him shifted, and the face distorted slightly before becoming the face he recognized of his past self up on Layer 1 of the Astral Verge. "But we will always be at The Ancient's call, to be their bearer of the Mantle of Burden."

Jace struggled with that for a brief moment before his resolve reasserted itself. "I . . . no. We . . . I—I'll always choose to do that. To balance the scales. Nothing is forcing us to do that after we finish this gig. It's something we can do . . . and I want to do it. I want to help out others when I can, and it will be easy and safe, given my power."

Old-him chuckled, "Just us, Shhiv, Chroma, and our friends. No responsibilities except for keeping a handle on The Cosmic System."

[Scenario success.]

The world returned to normal around Jace, and he was in the Relic chamber once more. Ollie spoke in his mind, calm and sincere. *I can also take over a whole bunch of The Cosmic System responsibilities for you as overseer of other Wayfinders. I will never go rampant thanks to you reaching Tier 10 and keeping me around. You can have even less responsibility!*

Jace smiled. "Thanks for that, buddy." He walked over to the floating crystal and grabbed it.

[You have acquired a Relic of the Ancients.]
[The Astral System has detected another System present.]
[Do you wish to integrate Relic with existing {Equipment}?]

[Relic Equipped.]
[Nanite-Infused Cyberconnect Integration Fluid Enhanced by Psykinetics.]
[Amplifies depth of emotion related to the Valiance Emotion Source as with NICIF's baseline abilities, but also grants them the ability to warp back to the user within limited range.]

[Effects from merged {Equipment}:]
[Reactive—causes the NICIF to (1) replicate more quickly to replace lost mass, and (2) move to an impact site in less than one zeptosecond to reinforce the flesh and/or prosthetic, reducing total damage re-

ceived. Additionally, can normalize the skin coloration and/or pattern of the host.]
[Effects merged to new designation: Pinnacle.]
[Future alterations will be merged into new designation.]

Jace did not feel different. "Uhm . . . NICIF? You there?"

[Here, boss!]
[We feel great!]
[This is a pretty neat upgrade.]
[Also, all your Equipment has been turned into Gear now, except the tent, the TPSB, and the bedroll.]
[Super excited to keep you alive, and now we can just warp to the site of an injury instead of having to travel.]

Jace was launched out of the Vault and landed in the stairwell, his back slamming into the wall with a little bump thanks to how heavy-duty the armor he wore now was. "Good to know," he said in reply to NICIF's response.

They are peppy and really enthused, Ollie said joyfully. *And their intelligence has been enhanced a bit, so I can task them with a few more subroutines and processes to keep your body operating at peak efficiency.*

Jace ascended the stairs and headed outside. The drone that was keeping an eye on the doorway shifted position, floating a good five feet above him, and as he activated Void Stalker, he headed to the entrance leading back down to Layer 4.

Quinn finished her second drink and laughed at Shhiv's joke. The two had become fast friends in the past few weeks, and Quinn really valued the woman's friendship.

After calming down, Shhiv used the fabricator to manifest another bottle of champagne. The Stardust cost was very low, and she popped the cork with glee before pouring another glass for each of them. "Ah, yeah. Being a kid was interesting."

Quinn crossed her legs and smiled. "Any thoughts on how you will deal with Chroma when Jace brings her back?"

Shhiv stopped mid-pour for a split-second before catching herself and moving the bottle to the table nearby. "Well . . . I imagine she is going to be like a little sister to me. She'll be going to school through The Eternal City's standardized upbringing program, but I would bet she'll spend a lot of her time here at the apartments. What age do humans start to get more independent?"

Quinn grinned. "Their teenage years. If Jace brings her back and she's the same age—no clue how that works with the whole Soul-in-new-body deal—then I would say four to five years before she gets her rebellious phase."

Shhiv nodded. "As long as we can rely on Auntie Quinn—"

"No. Nononono." Quinn shook her head. "I'm not good with kids. I can ask my parents if they'd be interested in helping babysit here and there, and I bet Priam would be great with kids."

"Good point. I bet Priam would be a great surrogate uncle." Shhiv took a sip of the champagne and smiled. "As long as I get my alone time with Jace, then I don't mind."

Quinn nodded. "I am sure that is doable. We'll figure something out. I will help by spoiling that girl rotten."

"Why?" Shhiv asked.

Quinn sighed. "I had a good childhood for a street kid. But it is nothing compared to what is available here in Khrox."

"I didn't know humans could get rotten."

Quinn let out a barking laugh. "Not literally rotting. It's a turn of phrase."

"Ah." Shhiv swirled her drink before taking another sip. "I am curious, though, Jace's mom left a letter for him. I wonder if it has anything to do with Chroma?"

Quinn frowned. "I fucking hate what Felicity did to Jace. So many parents did that—put their kids into the megacorps' boarding schools and then work up the ranks. They hope for a better life for their kids, but what they end up doing is putting their child into an indoctrination camp."

Shhiv grunted. "Disgusting behavior. Too bad Cosmogenic Merging didn't happen earlier."

Quinn stood up and drained the rest of her drink. "Gotta go. See ya, girl." She headed out of the room and went to the elevator, going back to her room and closing the doors. *It's none of my business*, she thought.

Chapter Nine

Going Down!

Jace headed back to the tower. But on the way, he spotted the various Astral Demons running indoors and taking shelter. "What's happening?" he muttered.

Not sure, Ollie replied.

Jace then heard it. A screeching. Sounds of triumph. Noises of celebration that ripped at his ears and caused an intense, pulsating headache that made his vision go white. He heard laughing, and it took a second for him to realize that he was the one laughing. *What's happening?* He tried to think. All of his Talents were disabled, and he could do nothing but feel his thoughts fade with the searing headache.

Astral Demons from Layer 10. They are all Potency 10, so even your Indomitable Will Talent is not keeping their Talent's effect suppressed. Ollie's voice switched to panic. *Get inside! Now!*

Jace tried to get up, tried to stagger to the building nearby—but he couldn't and instead lay there on the ground, cackling madly as his thoughts fizzled into a puddle of nothing. Something grabbed him and dragged him to an open doorway, and then the door slammed shut behind him.

Once the door shut, the world began to focus around him again. The Astral Demon, dressed in a casual business suit with a blazer thrown over one shoulder, let him go. "That was close," he whispered. "Keep quiet, keep still."

Jace did as he was told, staying put. He could hear the howling and laughter outside, but the effect seemed to not take hold as long as he was under cover. Or perhaps it was the city itself that was resistant in some way. Jace wasn't sure, but he was thankful.

Then, the noise faded. The Astral Demon that had dragged him to safety let out a sigh of relief. "They are gone."

Jace got to his feet, and his vision swam as he staggered upright. "Thanks for saving me." He reached into his TPSB and grabbed one of the blood-infused vials of holy water that Priam had given him so long ago to deal with undead. "This is all I can pay you with," he said as he handed the Astral Demon the liquid.

The male figure looked at the vial, shook the contents, and then glanced back at Jace. "I suppose I could sell it for some soul coins."

Jace went to the door and opened it, but glanced back before leaving. "Those Astral Demons . . . do they melt everyone's minds?"

He nodded in return, pocketing the vial. "Dreamers, yes. Dreamer Demons? A little. Astral Demons? No."

"Why help me out?" Jace asked with genuine curiosity.

The Astral Demon shrugged. "It . . . it felt . . . right. I can't tell you anything more than that, because I really don't know." The demon chuckled. "I recently got to this Layer. I'm hoping to get to Potency 10 and see if there's any truth to taking the path of refinement all the way down."

"I'm headed down to Layer 4 if you want to come along," Jace said. "I can at least get you to Respite, the safe place on the Layer."

The Astral Demon shook his head. "Thanks for the offer, stranger, but there's Missions out against you. And I don't want to be near you." He tapped a few invisible-to-Jace screens, and then the screens became visible. Jace could see hundreds of Missions that were given by Valcrinox, the Endless Madness, to track down Wraith. The Astral Demon closed the screens. "Don't worry, I'm not going to try and go against you. Something tells me . . . I don't know, a gut feeling . . . that if I try to take a shortcut, I'll miss out on something important."

Jace nodded tersely. "I hope you achieve your goal."

"Hey, you do what you did up on Layer 2 and on this one, and my trip becomes a lot safer. Word has spread based on those Missions—the Mantle of Burden's bearer has been destroying Demon Lords who don't only consume judged Souls." The figure pulled on his jacket. "Now, please, go finish off all those evil Demon Lords so I can have a safer journey. That's how you can repay me. Pave the way for me to . . . try and be more than this."

"Will do." Jace turned and reactivated Void Stalker, leaving the temporary refuge and going to the tower at the center of the city. He went into the basement and looked up at the drone. "Go through and show me what's down there."

The drone buzzed past him and through the film leading to the next Layer down. Jace could see the camera feed in his HUD—and thankfully, the Astral Demons from the tenth Layer were gone. Jace jumped down through the film and used his Soul Tether to lower himself to the sand below. The drone hovered above him a good fifteen feet. "Ollie, what's the range on this thing?"

Limitless, Ollie replied. *It functions off of its own voidlight tether.*

Jace nodded and checked his map. "Straight up north, and then on our counterclockwise path. We have six more to go." He began running across the desert, the drone following him and keeping pace.

Tibalt sank into Layer 5. The sight that greeted him as he went through the film was awe-inspiring and also irritating. Not open desert, with easy-to-traverse terrain, but instead rocky mountains with towering cliff faces and narrow valleys that promised the only safe route of travel. Snow topped several of the ranges in the distance, and he flapped his wings there for a few minutes, just taking in the environment. *Another Layer that I will eventually rule*, he thought.

He could see the Souls that percolated from above, gently drifting along with the snow before piling up and forming a near-constant light-blue stream that flowed like a river. And right there, easy feeding again. He licked his lips and let out a chuckle of gluttonous delight as he knew going up in Potency was about to be a lot easier.

He felt a weird sensation of pressure against his temples, and flapping down toward the ground, he looked up. He saw an army of Astral Demons—a small regiment, maybe a hundred if he had to guess numbers—pour out of the film and fly across the Layer, vanishing into the distance past some of the peaks. *Valcrinox's forces*, he thought as he innately sensed their incredible Potency compared to his. *Double my Potency. First things first—Vault, and then Souls. Now . . . how to find the Vault . . .*

Jace reached the northernmost location on the map and stopped a short distance away from the ruined buildings. The buildings that sagged and were jutting out at various angles were all curly in design—intricate lattices that were wound together in clumps and elegant, meandering-with-a-purpose vines that extended out to connect the different buildings. The nature inspiration was all around, entwined with the architecture.

He drew his sword and activated his suite of Talents and the handful of Skills he was allowed to use. His [Danger-Sense] almost instantly notified him of incoming projectiles, and he raised his shield as he blocked a flurry of Psykinetic-empowered thorns. They slammed into the barrier, and then, thanks to the (Retaliating) Infusion, golden spikes shot back at the veiled attackers.

Astral Demons who had clung to the walls and blended into the vines moved—and their movement was enough for Jace to identify them as targets and throw his sword. Striking a blow that exploded with the golden flames, a porcupine-esque demon let out a squeal of rage before flopping down to the sand and charging him on foot.

Jace detected another barrage coming from his left, and he moved his shield over to block as he threw his sword with his right hand, scoring a hit on the porcupine-demon charging him. The blade sank into the thing's forehead, and the horse-sized creature tumbled to the sand before burning away in the radiant inferno—the strands of white Essence coalescing and shooting to Jace, filling him with warmth.

"Ollie, task the drone with recon from above. Highlight targets."

On it! The drone lifted off and began flying high up, and Jace saw his HUD overlaid with a series of small, red rectangles that showed targets. Dozens of them—all moving around the various buildings and heading to assault Jace. They released thousands of thorns imbued with Psykinetics, and Jace simply used his Void Step to avoid the assault and warp out of line of sight.

To his surprise, the projectiles seemed to track his movement and follow him, as they turned in air abruptly and shot right toward his new location. *Irritating*, he thought as he brought his shield up to intercept the now-combined storm of shards. But they split off, arcing around his shield and slamming into him. He could feel the spikes pierce his body with intense pain as the needles stabbed deep. A dull ache set in a moment later as some type of poison began to spread through him—only to be nullified by the NICIF. But Jace's stomach rumbled as they burned through his excess calories to regenerate the damage.

Dark Matter Mending (Rank 4) [Vampiric], Jace thought as he used his Soul Tether to pull himself up to the top of one of the towers. Thanks to the drone, he knew exactly where the foes were located—and he used a Void Step to get behind one as he chopped clean through it with a massive swing. The corpse, sundered, fell into glistening golden flecks as the Essence unwound from the corpse and surged up to Jace. He also felt his wounds heal over as the Dark Matter Mending kicked in.

More shots were fired his way, and knowing their tracking capabilities, Jace kept on the move, running, using Void Step to warp, and learning that they eventually fell down and became inert. Since the Astral Demons seemed to have followed a similar evolution path, they did not have any variety, and he could easily dispatch them in the same efficient manner.

Holy Hunt, he thought, focusing on the Demon Lord's location. Sprinting along the path of gold, he checked the drone camera to confirm that it did not see the line like he did. "Ollie, bring the drone back to tether on me." The device hovered over his head, and Jace kept pushing forward, finding the pyramid structure.

And it was covered in bristling spines. The golden outline covered the whole structure, and that was when Jace realized that the whole entire building was the Demon Lord. The entity reacted to his presence and fired off hundreds of the barbs, covered in Psykinetic energy. All arcing to follow Jace.

Templar's Smite (Blast), Jace thought as he unleashed a torrent of golden flame. But the projectiles kept coming, unimpeded, even though the blast hit the Demon Lord and inflicted the three different burning effects. Jace got his shield in the way of some of the darts, but more surged around his shield and into him. He let out a yelp of pain as the spines dug into his body and tried to wriggle further, but Jace poured his energy into the Templar's Smite, the damage fueling his [Vampiric] Dark Matter Mending even further as he outpaced the injury he was suffering from with the healing he was receiving.

But his energy was draining, and by the time the Astral Demon Lord succumbed to the riotous flames, Jace was at ten percent of his maximum energy. He was sucking in deep breaths as he let the Talents and Skills fade. "And . . . another one . . . down."

Great job, Ollie said. *I'll have the drone scout the pyramid.* The drone shot forward and vanished into the pyramid interior. Jace watched as it went through the building, down through the tunnels, and arrived at the Vault door. *Nothing down there*, Ollie commented as the drone flew back up and took up a station above the pyramid, slowly spinning to provide overview of the area. *Ready for a vault?*

"A little breather," Jace replied as he walked into the pyramid and sat down on the small, raised pedestal. "It's kind of interesting, how we've found these pyramids in the middle of every set of ruins."

Must be part of the Layer's original design, Ollie replied. *When The Ancients created the place.*

Jace nodded and leaned forward, elbows resting on knees. "This Vault, and then we can go up the voidlight tether and visit home for a bit." He was craving being with Shhiv, feeling her warm caress.

I will tell her to have her schedule clear!

Chapter Ten

Layer 4, Vault 3

His energy full, Jace descended the steps and placed is hand on the Vault door. The worn stone surface sucked him in, and he ended up on the other side. Skills and Talents ready to go, he waited for the notification message to appear.

And he was not waiting long, as only a few seconds passed before the message flared to life in front of him.

[Vault Challenge—Activated.]
[Defend yourself.]

The room shifted and faded around him, and he was standing on a small, wooden pedestal with a railing rising up around him. Chains appeared around his wrists and bound him to the structure as a bench with three figures, shrouded in shadow, sat in silent judgement.

Jace pulled against the chain, but it cut into his armor, crunching it down as it squeezed tight, and he felt the pain course through him.

Looks like a courtroom, Ollie observed. *And I would bet they are going to ask questions.*

True to Ollie's prediction, the central figure spoke. "Wraith, aka Jace Seren. You stand here to defend yourself. You are charged with the killing of millions of sentient creatures." They tapped a floating screen before them, and Jace saw the fight between himself and the Nebula-powered megacorp asset who he had fought on Velenar Prime. "First was this woman, whom you slew."

"It was self-defense," Jace replied confidently. "She attacked me first."

The one on the left spoke. "While true that she attacked first, you killed her instead of incapacitating. Why?"

Jace felt that kernel of anger in his stomach as he replied, "She wouldn't have shown me any mercy, either."

The leftmost judge spoke as the screen shifted and showed the large dog-person alien that Jace killed. "And what about this one?"

Jace almost barked out a reply. "He tried to kill me, too. Self-defense."

The central figure spoke. "Would you say that you tend to attract people who seek to harm you?"

That put Jace back for a moment. *I don't think so? I mean, back on Earth, pre-Cosmogenic Merging, I never went out of my way to find trouble, and it rarely found me. It was only after joining up with Xera that it became a problem.* But he shook his head. "No."

Again the screen shifted, showing the cat-person back on Nihilethelea, and then flickering through all of the Aspirants he had slain. "And these?"

"They came after me, too," Jace replied. "All of them were promised something to capture or kill me—I just kept myself safe."

This same process repeated; images of people Jace had killed would be put on the screen, in groupings based upon where the incidents occurred, and almost every one of them was Jace replying in some manner of self-defense.

But then came Earth. The image of Campinas, the earthquake-stricken city that caused the deaths of hundreds of thousands. "And what do you say to this?"

"Guilty," Jace replied. "I did it. I'm not proud of it, and at the time, I was blinded by hatred and rage. But I know what I did was wrong, and I'm trying to make amends. I will get them back to our Universe and make things right."

The central judge stood up. "You have admitted to the killing of innocents."

Jace felt that familiar anger in him, but it was more of a righteous anger. "I've also saved billions! Trillions, possibly, by killing Troxanir. Just look at my Karma Coefficient. If it's positive, then in the end, I'm not a bad person, am I?"

The other two judges stood. "Congratulations. You have passed the test," the one on the left said.

The one on the right then spoke. "This challenge was to determine if you could see past your morality for singular events to examine the overall effects of cumulative actions."

The room vanished, and Jace was back in the Vault—with the Quiet Ancient standing next to the floating crystal that shifted and warped in shape, turning into a capsule. Jace walked up and grabbed the object, adding another Epic (Essence Cache) to his inventory. *Ollie, convert those five we have to a Legendary.*

You got it! That puts us at one Legendary of each type: Essence Cache, Specialization, and Gear.

The Quiet Ancient spoke, "The Vaults have been giving you . . . intriguing challenges." His voice was quiet and subdued.

Jace faced him, sheathing his sword. "You don't set them up?"

"Vaults are meant to challenge any number of aspects. We Ancients set them up, but we do not control what goes on within. The Relics are created by the Vaults after a set time, and when they detect someone such as you, who has many Relics already, they know to swap the reward." The eyes of The Ancient narrowed. "You have had quite a few encounters with morals and ethics of your past actions. I have seen your past. And I have also seen your grappling with the idea of doing something for the greater good versus individual acts of morality."

"Yeah, well, I don't want to do bad things for a greater good," Jace replied. "My boss did that, and it got her a negative Karma Coefficient."

"Yours would be, too, if you had not slain Troxanir and freed the Souls trapped within."

Those words struck Jace like a blow, but he quickly recovered his composure as he already knew he would be making up for his past mistakes. "Yeah, well, I'm on my way to fix that."

The Quiet Ancient stared at him for a few moments before nodding tersely. "Best of luck on your continuing travel." He vanished with a slight burst of pixelated, purple sparks.

Jace turned to the Vault door as he was sucked outside and landed on the smooth stone surface. Trekking back up, the probe flew down to float above him, and he kept traveling along the outside edge of the Layer. "Ollie, current Essence?"

We are at 9,000. Enough to hit level 41, and Potency 5.

"We'll head back home first." Jace took off into a sprint, gaining some distance from the ruins as he activated Void Stalker to keep himself concealed. Once he had gained a good twenty miles of distance, he looked at the drone. "Can we task this thing with staying here, watching where I'll come back? Should keep us apprised of surprises."

Tasking drone now.

The drone lifted up a good two-hundred feet to provide a wide overview. Then, Jace reached out to the voidlight tether that had been silently following him, a constant presence that could only be interacted with when he chose to do so. Gripping it, he activated the recall protocol. His form compressed down and traveled up the voidlight tether, popping him out in the Penrose Sphere. Looking out the window overlooking Oblivion from this small command center, Jace could see millions of tiny voidlight tethers extending down into the black hole.

Ollie separated from his head, and Jace quickly used Dark Matter Mending to stop the wicked headache. "Sorry about that," Ollie said. "No way to get around it, sadly. AI extraction is always going to be painful!"

Jace waved the comment off as he stared down to Oblivion. The black hole with the white-grey and purple mesh covering it. "She has a lot of drones down there."

"Yup! Shhiv has been busy Rune Carving." Ollie clapped his paws. "So, you have two levels. What do you want to spend them on?"

"I want to get more Purifier Specializations for existing Talents."

[You have leveled up!]
[You have chosen Specialization of Existing Talent!]
[Talent Name: Indomitable Will.]
[Specialization Name: Ameliorating.]
[Effect: The user cannot be incapacitated by mental or emotional effects.]
[Talent Name: Purifying Edge.]
[Specialization Name: Terminating.]
[Effect: In addition to defensive Talents, the user's weapon temporarily sunders offensive Talents, shutting them off.]

Name: Jace Seren (Potency 5)
Emotion [Class Level]: Valiant [Purifier 41]
Talent [Specialization]: Astral Adaptation, Astral Translation, Valiant Crusader's Might [Burning] [Vengeful] [Poised] [Unstoppable] [Bracing], Crusader's Bastion [Retaliating] [Reinforcing] [Grounding] [Redoubt] [Spiked], Hero's Arena [Aura] [Incinerating] [Vexing] [Bolstering] [Suppressing], Indomitable Will [Zealous] [Intimidating] [Inviolable] [Enduring] [Ameliorating], Templar's Smite [Spear] [Blast] [Lingering] [Challenging] [Inferno], Holy Hunt [Marked] [Bursting] [Authoritative] [Provoking] [Inciting], Purifying Edge [Cleansing] [Searing] [Purging] [Sanctifying] [Terminating]
Essence: 0

Infusions: Legendary (Essence Cache), Legendary (Specialization), Legendary (Gear)
Gear: <TPSB>, (Convergent Edge) [Ruination 1] Hero's Blade, (Explorer's Embrace / Beacon) Paragon Armor, (Prosthetic Savant) Astral Appendages, (Draconic Sovereign) Arbiter's Sight, (Anathema) Astral Sleeve, (Reinforced) Psycrystal Lattice, (Pinnacle) NICIF-EP, (Restoring) Flame of Valor

As the Essence was utilized, Jace felt the all-too-familiar pain of his Potency going up. He doubled over, mouth forming into a silent scream. The worst cramping pain that he had felt before amplified to an immeasurable degree as the same cramping traveled all over his body, his muscles—even the prosthetic limbs and their approximation of muscles—contorting with agony.

And then, as quickly as it began, it faded. The world seemed just a little clearer to Jace, crisper and in focus.

"Neat," Ollie said. "Weapons can now shut down all Talents of targets you strike. Temporarily, at least."

"And," Jace replied as he stood up, "double energy cost when they try to reactivate them before ten seconds pass. Really close to [Astral Annihilator]."

"Too bad it will not work on those whose Potency is above yours," Ollie stated as he swam in small circles.

"That wasn't in any description," Jace replied.

"Part of the Astral System—despite heroic-Emotion Source types being able to harm those who are far higher Potency than them. It is sort of like your Void Counter and Arbiter's Anathema—you can only disable Psykinetics of someone your Potency or lower."

Irritating, Jace thought as he put all of his gear into the TPSB. "Warp me to the apartment." The world shifted around the duo, and Jace was standing in the living room. Stripping down, he went over to the hygiene station and then dressed in casual clothes. Emerging, he did not see Ollie. *Must have gone to visit Josie*, he thought.

Pulling up his innate Cosmic System, he messaged Shhiv. The comms immediately opened up once he sent the message. "Hey! I'll be home soon. Just going to finish up this lunch outing with Dee and Ree."

Jace smiled. "See you soon, then." He walked over to the living room and sat on the couch, sinking into the soft cushions.

Ollie appeared with a pop, holding a letter. "Your mom dropped this off," he said.

Jace immediately felt uneasy, and he snatched the letter, ripping open the paper sleeve and pulling out the neat, legal-pad-yellow message within.

To Jace,

I am still sorry and want to try and reconnect with you. I would bet you want nothing to do with me, given what happened, and I would understand if you elected to ask me to remain at a distance. I only ever worked for the megacorp to try and give you a better life and would have given up my work in a heartbeat if I had known you were being abused at the boarding school. I have only ever wanted the best for you.

I'll admit, I never really knew Chroma, and I know you cared for her deeply, while you think I just viewed her as a tool. I won't deny, that was one of the intents I had for her.

But this isn't about her. This is about you and me. You are my son. I love you, and always will.

Felicity Seren

Jace crumpled the letter and let the golden flames of his Psykinetics surge up, incinerating it. *Chroma is going to be part of my life, and you have no place in it.* Jace did, however, feel a slight pang of guilt, and he opened up a System message to the woman.

[I am going to bring dad back.]

[I am going to bring Chroma back.]
[Chroma will decide if she wants to know you or not, I won't take that choice from her.]
[But she is going to be my responsibility, and I will take care of her.]
[If, and this is a big if, you and dad reconnect and get back together—maybe we could give trying to be friendly a go.]
[But that is a long way off from now.]
[I will reach out, don't contact me again without my permission.]

He sent off the message and then leaned back into the couch with a deep sigh, letting his eyes shut as he knew he made the best decision for him and his sister.

Chapter Eleven

Back again

Shhiv warped through Khrox, back to the apartment, and quietly walked into the living room. She peeked around the corner and saw Jace, comfortably snoozing on the couch. *Oh, I know what I can do!* She went over to the food fabricator and paid a bit of Stardust for the extra expensive food that she knew Jace had fallen in love with. The table filled up with a plethora of seafood—primarily crab and shrimp—all perfectly prepared with plenty of steaming tubs of melted butter ready for dipping.

She carefully went around to the other side of the couch, and lightly tapped him on the nose. His eyes snapped open instantly. "Wake up, sleepy," she said with a smile.

He reached up and cupped her chin, scratching it ever so slightly. "Hey, sweetness. Something smells great." He stood up and hugged her, then looked back to the table and his eyes lit up with delight. "Mmm. Looks tasty."

Shhiv pulled him around the couch and to the table, forcing him into his seat by his shoulders as she pulled a chair up alongside him. They dove into the meal, and in between eating and cracking shells of more delicious crustacean meat, Jace shared his experiences from the traveling. Shhiv listened to him, not enthralled, but enjoying the recount of the past.

It gave her time to eat. Not that she was hungry, but who would pass up a delicious feast? *I need to work out extra today*, she thought as she overate and felt her stomach hurting a bit.

Jace continued to put away plate after plate, and when they were finally done eating, he slapped the button on the table that cleared it. Looking over at Shhiv, he grabbed her hand gently and gave it a squeeze. "What about you? What have you been up to?"

"We went on a few girls' night out events," Shhiv replied. "Dee and Ree are a riot when they get intoxicated. Quinn and I mostly babysat them, but it was hilarious." She pulled him up, "Come on, down to the gym."

"I don't need to work out," Jace began to protest.

Shhiv dragged him to the elevator regardless. "I want you to work out with me. Then, tonight, we are going to a night club to dance."

He cracked a smile and kissed her cheek once they got into the elevator and the doors shut. "Whatever you want."

Jace's few days of downtime were spent going out with Shhiv and doing all types of activities he had never even thought as recreational or really enjoyable. They visited a different club every night—often on unique worlds connected to The Cosmic Corridor, and sometimes accompanied by their friends.

Different sports, as well. Jace had an unfair advantage thanks to his Edge of Possibility, and it was only after he asked Ollie to turn that Skill off that the events became fun. Especially throwing axes—something that seemed really dangerous but was quite fun.

That also revealed how bad Jace was with weapons. Which made sense—he had never trained, his Swordmage Stance ensuring he was able to fight well, and then Edge of Possibility taking over to an even greater degree. It was humbling, especially as Shhiv scored bullseye after bullseye.

But he enjoyed himself, and the week of enjoyment and leisure eventually came to a conclusion. Of course, every night after going out clubbing, they would return home and absolutely ravish each other.

Jace was running his hands through Shhiv's hair in the morning, his fingers tracing along the fin atop her head. "I should probably head out today," he muttered. "Not that I want to. Just that I don't think The Ancients are good waiting for too long."

Shhiv turned around in the water-cube bed floating in the replica of the Starlit Sea. "Well . . . just be safe, and come back to me."

"You know I will," Jace replied. He gave her another kiss, then made his way to the edge of the water cube, stepped on the platform that instantly dried him off, and equipped his gear from the TPSB. "Ollie? Ready to go?"

Ollie appeared with a pop. He was all smiles. "Yup! Ready when you are."

Jace looked back to Shhiv, who gave him a longing wave that he returned as Ollie warped him to the voidlight tether observatory. Jace sighed and looked at Ollie. "Okay, Verge Protocol time."

Ollie flew into his head, and the cool rush that was all too familiar washed over Jace. *Ready to go!*

Jace grabbed the voidlight tether and traveled down to his departure point on Layer 4, appearing just under the drone, which quickly zipped down to hover five feet overhead. He began running along the edge of the Layer toward the next set of ruins. *Five more to go*, he thought.

Actually, Ollie interrupted, *seems like someone else took out a Demon Lord near Respite. Also looks like they cleared the Vault, at least if this Layer report is anything to go by. Think of it like a newsletter that sends updates.*

Jace frowned. "One less Vault for me, but ultimately, that's not a huge deal." He kept pushing onward, sprinting across the desert with Void Stalker active—and knowing he was not really going to be threatened anymore on this Layer, given that the Astral Demons who were Potency 5 were already on the next Layer down. This would be almost routine—get to the Demon Lord of each set of ruins, use them to get their associated demon minions closer, destroy them all, clear the Vault. Rinse and repeat.

Jace saw the next set of buildings ahead and used Holy Hunt to lock onto the Demon Lord. These buildings were all square and did not look wrecked, or tilted, or otherwise run-down. In fact, the whole location was well-organized, with patrolling Dreamers.

That ground him to a halt. *A Demon Lord is definitely here, but they also have Dreamers working for them? Or are they Dreamer Demons?*

Cannot tell, Ollie replied. *Their armor obscures their physical form, so we cannot determine.*

Jace frowned, knowing that one of these Dreamer Demons could be of his Potency or even higher—which meant his whole stealth strategy was put into question. *I guess there is nothing for it*, he thought as he unsheathed his sword and drew the plasma pistol with his other hand. Both weapons flared with the golden flames of his Psykinetics. He moved toward the compound and could make out the thin lattice of a fence topped with slightly glowing cords. Using his Soul Tether, he grappled into midair well over the fortification and got above the area, spotting the building that the golden line led to.

Swinging down and dropping into the facility, he had not been noticed. The door was made of stone, and was ajar. Peering into it, Jace saw a Dreamer Demon—one of the Gyanv with demonic features—interfacing with some type of holographic console. *Dreamer Demons can become Demon Lords. Huh. Interesting.*

Very interesting, Ollie replied. *I would wager that they are Potency 4, considering they have not spotted you and they are still on this Layer.*

Jace walked into the building and right up behind the figure. Putting the sword against their neck, he dropped Void Stalker and said, "Move and you die."

The figure spoke, their mandibles clicking and the translation in Jace's ears. "What do you want?"

"Bring all of your minions over. Line them up in formation for inspection. Come on." Jace grabbed them by the shoulder and moved the Demon Lord in front of him, sword still on their shoulder in between a jutting horn and the neck, ready to kill. *Void Stalker*, he thought as he vanished once more.

The figure did as he was told, reaching over to his wrist and tapping a bracer that blinked with lights before speaking aloud. "This is Commander Mikhcha. All troops report to formation grounds. Now!"

Ollie, send the drone up.

The drone went skyward, and Jace could see from the high-up view that the entire fortification, all of the Gyanv Dreamer Demons, were rushing over to the formation ground, an open space cleared of sand with small barricades pushing the invasive substance back. It took a few minutes, but soon enough, the force of just under two-hundred stood there.

Jace ruthlessly decapitated the commander right in front of their men, before releasing a Templar's Smite (Blast) that consumed the entire regiment in a single, torrential burst of righteous fire. The bodies burned away, light-blue Souls ascending skyward before drifting in all directions and slowly moving through the sand on their journey to deeper Layers.

The Essence escaped from the Dreamer Demons and floated over to Jace, infusing him. *How much?* he asked Ollie as the drone descended down to their level.

A nice chunk of 4,000, Ollie replied. *Dreamer Demons are not worth nearly as much Essence.*

On the plus side, Jace thought as he went between the piles of gear now on the ground, *we can loot them*. Going through their various pieces of gear, he found the fare he was expecting—laser weaponry in the form of firearms, ammunition packs which were just pre-charged batteries that could easily be swapped out, and a near-uniform type of armor.

Might have been a splinter faction of Gyanv, Ollie remarked.

Jace put all of the gear into his TPSB and fired off a message through the voidlight tether to Xera in regard to the other-Universe tech. *Now, to find the Vault. Holy Hunt.* The line shot back into the complex, and Jace jogged over to find the well-concealed pyramid, hidden underneath several tarps. Descending down, he grimaced as he saw the cracked façade. *Damn. Already done.* Just to be sure, he put his hand on the stone door—but nothing happened. *Okay, well, three more to go.*

Tibalt had it easy. The easiest he ever had life. Finding a nice, secluded stream of Souls rolling down in a rivulet, he simply parked himself at a narrow gap and shoved his face into the streams, gulping down Souls.

He had been doing this for days, and the supply never seemed to end as he continued to glut himself. The screaming, swirling torrent filled him with glee, and the yells of beings trapped in agony were like a beautiful song to his ears.

Already on the cusp of Potency 6, the Dreamer Demon couldn't help but wonder, *Why doesn't every demon do this? This is so easy!* He would have cackled with delight at the thought of how simple this whole process was. *Every demon should do this to get to a higher Potency. I wonder why they don't.*

The flood was sweet and intoxicating, and he found himself growing only hungrier as the time passed forward. Eventually, the stream faded to a trickle, and he backed away, manifesting his wings and flying up as he went to find the next one to suck dry.

Esmerelda, Demon Lord of Layer 4, scanned through the Astral Verge reports for the cycle. Plans were progressing nicely, as Wraith had destroyed many of the rival Demon Lords and was almost done with his task. Someone else had dealt with one of them, but she did not care all too much. What mattered to her was that her control was about to be cemented.

An Astral System message appeared. *Ah, it has been a while since I have heard from you.*

[Esmerelda, I see from the reports that this Wraith is on the move and almost done with your Layer.]
[When you see him next, tell him that there is a trap waiting for him on Layer 5.]
[The Demon Lord who is in contest for that Layer is lying in wait.]

She smiled, sending a message back to the Demon Lord. *And send*, she thought as the message went to the recipient. Sitting back in the shade under one of the ship wings, she saw another Dreamer vessel land, and pilots exited before beginning to unload cargo. Her little Respite was safe, and would be all the safer soon.

Wraith would kill off the Demon Lords and most of the threats so that more of the Astral Demons who had fully followed the path of evolutionary refinement could come down and begin sharing in the bounty of judged souls.

Chapter Twelve

Repulsive and Reviled

Jace sprinted along the edge of the Layer, following the line charted out by his Holy Hunt talent that showed a clear path to his target off in the distant ruins. *Another target to kill.*

Quinn's voice came over the comms. "I just got a whole bunch of gear from Xera dumped for research and diagnostic."

"I'm helping!" Shhiv added over the line.

"The hell did you do down there?" Quinn asked.

"Killed Dreamer Demons," Jace replied bluntly as he breathed smoothly.

Shhiv squeed with delight. "Oooh! They had miniature micro-wormhole generators to power their subsystems inside the armor!"

"I didn't know you were that knowledgeable about tech," Jace quipped.

"Oh, I'm not," Shhiv replied. "But Skills are fantastic at filling the gaps. And I'm the best crafter in the whole System now!"

Quinn sounded slightly frustrated. "Put that down, I don't want micro-whatsits showing up in my apartment."

Jace chuckled. "Alright, ladies. Any other reason for the wonderful call?"

"Nope!" Shhiv said. "Love you, hon."

Quinn sighed. “Just wondering where you got it all. Xera didn’t pass on message. She must be busy.”

“Check in on her,” Jace requested. “She’s still the System Admin, and we can’t have her going off the deep end until she cedes control over to me.”

“Will do,” Quinn replied as the comms went silent.

Jace picked up the pace, not sure what was going on with Xera but knowing that the sooner he completed his task for The Ancients, rescued the Souls using the new starship that Shhiv had put together, and returned them to a closed loop in their Universe—the sooner he could take the System Admin role from an unstable individual. Someone who he only trusted because she was bound by a System-made contract to be honest with him in all her dealings.

The next set of buildings dipped into and out of view as Jace raced across the dunes. Tall, upright rectangles with shining, shattered, and scattered glass windows. Just like some of the skyscrapers he saw in New York or Japan. The massive metal and concrete edifices stood upright, not tilted, but still obviously in a state of major disrepair. He drew his sword and activated the Skills and Talents he relied upon and kept sprinting after the line.

Ollie sent the drone up high, and it began to scan the area with its camera, and several red targets were painted in Jace’s HUD—movement inside of buildings up above him. “Task the drone with looking into the buildings. Let me see what I’m up against.”

<u>*On it!*</u> The drone’s camera view in the top corner of Jace’s HUD shifted, and he could see the vile form of the demon on the floor. It was lying flat, having thrown itself down as its body rose and fell with wheezing, wet breaths. The body was covered with pulsating pustules that looked absolutely putrid, filled with some pernicious pus.

Jace pushed on to the pyramid structure, rushing inside and finding another of the creatures, but this one was a slightly more hale and healthy color. *I’m not getting close to that for threatening it*, Jace thought as he simply pointed his hand. *Templar's Smite.* He focused the column of golden flames to encompass the creature.

The powerful Psykinetics flicked out of his hand, surged into the ground, and then exploded up. The fire splashed against the ceiling before scattering out in all directions. The Astral Demon shuffled its mass, moving to face Jace with one huge, orange eyeball. And the golden flame of Psykinetic might seemed to harm the thing; as Jace shut off the Talent, the creature was still there—very much alive.

It reared back slightly, and one of the pustules on its back burst—propelling the mass forward. Jace quickly used a Void Step to dodge the creature's mass, warping himself outside. The demon followed him out, and Jace quickly chopped down into it—his weapon sticking into the fleshy hide, drawing blood that smelled absolutely rank and almost made him vomit right there.

Hopping back, Jace raised his shield as another pustule on the creature burst, sending a vile burst of some ichor at the shield. *Ew!* Jace thought with revulsion as the goop coated his shield and the smell amplified even further. *Ollie, turn off my sense of smell.*

On it! his Wayfinder replied. Jace's olfactory senses were shut off, and he was able to refocus on the creature as it moved closer to him, the large, fleshy mass just surging forward as it was propelled by another burst pustule on the back that functioned like some horrific thruster. It slammed its bulk into Jace's shield, and he slammed the shield into it, using the (Spiked) Infusion to deal a counterstrike.

And, thanks to Purifying Edge along with its various Specializations, all of its Talents were briefly deactivated. The creature reactivated them rapidly before Jace could even get a swing with his sword in—but just as the new applications of the Talents popped on, Jace's weapon hit and shut them off again.

And then he discovered the issue with Purifying Edge. His energy drastically dipped when he struck a blow with both his shield and sword.

Ollie seemed to have the answer. *It costs energy each time you turn off a Talent.*

Can we turn the Talent off? Jace thought. As if responding to his will, the slight flickering of white flames on his blade vanished, and only the golden blaze remained. His question answered, Jace swung down into the creature again, striking another blow on the Astral Demon Lord as he managed to slice off a chunk of pulsating flesh.

Flesh that was consumed in golden fury. The blob slammed its bulk into Jace again—and he was actually pushed back a few feet in the sand. His [Danger-Sense] detected something fast coming at him, and Jace used Void Step to warp out of the projectile's path. Where he had been standing, a ball of pulsating pus had landed, exploded, and spread in a miasmic fog that hugged the ground. The sand it touched was disintegrating as the substance ate away at the ground.

Jace was not just disgusted, but also infuriated. These unclean abominations were spreading their vile filth. His [Purifier] Class drew on him, calling on him to purge such corruption and horrible, gross Talent users. With a swift stab, Jace planted his sword deep into the Demon Lord's back, activating (Fulmination) as he got down to the hilt. The explosion of gold flames detonated the thing from within, and flaming chunks scattered around—including coating Jace—before burning away to ash and dust. The light-blue of Souls escaped into the sky, and Jace turned to spot another projectile coming his way.

Well, now I know how to kill these ones despite their higher defenses. Jace warped using Void Step up a building side and used his Soul Tether to rise the rest of the way. He spotted a smaller but just as disgusting-looking one of the Astral Demons, and stabbing his blade deep into the head, he poured his Psykinetic power into the weapon, draining his energy as he amplified the (Burning) effect of his Valiant Crusader's Might.

The creature melted from within, and Jace soaked up the Essence before moving to the next building, the next target, and slaughtering it. Within minutes, he had destroyed all ten of the Astral Demons in the area and soaked up their Essence. *Along with the Demon Lord*, Ollie said, *we are at 5,500 Essence. Enough for one level and 500 left over.*

Jace moved to the pyramid structure on the ground, and the drone took up its observation position above the building. Glancing up, Jace also saw Quinn's Celestial Observer and felt a slight reassurance that, when needed, she could use her Stratagems to help even the odds should he struggle in a fight. "Sure, let's level up. I'm still a [Purifier], so either a Specialization or Talent that builds on that."

How about something that lets you purge effects on yourself?

"It's an offensive [Class], I thought," Jace replied as he went down the stairs toward the Vault door.

Self-support is not off limits to the [Class], Ollie replied.

"But the NICIF can filter any toxins or poisons," Jace added.

True . . . maybe we hold off on leveling up until the next Layer, when the new Class Transmutation becomes available.

"Just what I was thinking," Jace replied. "What is the next [Class] if I keep going up the damage route?"

Justiciar, Ollie replied. *Looks like it has Talents that help in amplifying damage against a struck target. More single-target focus, effectively.*

Jace nodded and placed his hand on the Vault door, finding himself sucked in once more and standing in the open chamber. "Start looking up different Talents in that [Class]," Jace instructed as he waited for the Astral System message to appear.

Tibalt gorged himself upon another stream, reveling in the power humming within. *Almost at the next Potency*, he thought. He cast his gaze toward the entrance to the prior Layer and frowned. He saw the trap that had been set by Valcrinox. Or rather put into motion by the entity.

A Potency 10 Astral Demon, waiting for Wraith. Sitting on the small mount underneath the passage to the Layer. Tibalt knew he could not challenge such an entity, but also knew that Wraith was not going to be easy to deal with. *But*, he thought as he supped upon more Souls from another stream that ran in a rivulet down the mountainside, *I can wait for the perfect, opportune moment and strike the killing blow. Get credit, immediately go to Valcrinox.*

Astral Demons could only descend the Layers if they had the correct Potency. Dreamers had no such limitation. And so once he had Wraith's corpse, or at least recorded proof thanks to the Astral System, Tibalt could leapfrog his way up very, very quickly. Reaching his goal. Potency 10, and his Vanguard Empire that would cover every Layer of the Astral Verge.

Yroshnak, the Demon Lord of Blood, stood at the entrance to the huge hall that marked his stronghold. He could see the expansive lakes that covered the Layer, including the whirlpool that led down to the next Layer below and the entrance above that originated near a waterfall that fed the massive lagoon on the edge of the territory.

He had already gained control over his Layer but knew he could not go deeper on his own. Stockpiling Souls, Universal Matter when he could get his hands on it—he had enough banked to instantly achieve Potency 10. He needed help, though, to topple Valcrinox and take the throne at the deepest Layer of their reality.

Wraith, he thought as he composed an Astral System message to Esmerelda to pass on, *needs to be careful. Extremely careful. One of Valcrinox's minions. I am going to send along an Infusion—give it to Wraith. He'll need it.* "Send."

Yroshnak sighed and went back into his hall, going to his large chair and taking a seat as he pondered strategy with the assumption that Wraith would succeed, but also making secondary plans in case Wraith perished. He spoke softly to the hooded figure nearby, "You have other bearers of the Mantle ready?"

The Ancient, who always remained cloaked and shrouded, spoke softly but with firm resolve. "I have been preparing alternative bearers. We will achieve our peaceful end and the return of only judged Souls being consumed." He sighed. "Except for Layer 1."

"Still no progress on that?" Yroshnak asked.

"Nothing to be done about it," The Ancient replied.

Another voice emanated from the space right in front of Yroshnak, and he rose to his feet as he pulled out his massive war axe. A female voice spoke. "Well now, there is plenty I could do about it."

The Ancient seemed to relax. "Ah, Xera'tal." His hood moved to look at Yroshnak, "Lower your weapon, friend."

A small metal orb appeared above the two, about eye level with Yroshnak's towering form, with small wings spreading out from it. "Yes, hello there, ruler of Layer 8. I am Xera'tal Pen'arkon. Wraith is one of my assets. And, I have a means to protect all Souls on Layer 1. A permanent end to the rise of Astral Demons who consume innocent Souls." She sounded quite confident.

Yroshnak sneered. "But at what cost?"

"Simple," she replied with a smug sound to her tone. "My Universe is off-limits. As the soon-to-be strongest Astral Demon—my asset will see to your ascension to Valcrinox's throne—you would be able to enforce your will on every Layer above, yes?"

"To an extent," Yroshnak replied with genuine curiosity. "My orders get less and less effective the higher up the Layers one goes."

"But you can travel up there," Xera replied.

"Yes," he said again.

Xera made a satisfied noise. "Then it is simple. You will make it so that every Astral Demon ignores Universe 348."

He looked over to The Ancient, who spoke softly but sounded neutral, as if he was just a passive observer and not an interested party in the ongoing conversation. "Easy enough. The one with the mesh covering it—you've heard of it."

Yroshnak had heard of it before. It had been around for dozens of cycles—some type of protective encasement that protected a Universe entirely. "I can do that."

"And one more thing," the voice said. The floating metal sphere moved to The Ancient, "I need you to begin making the inroads necessary for Wraith to recover all of the Souls from the Afterlives."

The Ancient dipped his head. "It is already being done. Messages have been sent, received, and willing Souls are being advised of their decision. Are we still on-pace to have an every-decade revisit from Wraith?"

"Yes," Xera replied.

The Ancient shrugged. "Then all is as it was before." He looked to Yroshnak. "Do what you can to help this asset. While I do have backup bearers of the Mantle ready to go . . . I would rather not have to use them."

The metal orb vanished from existence, and Yroshnak trudged over to the entrance, trying to spot where it went to. But the orb had completely blinked out of existence. *What type of species has technology that rivals the teleportation capabilities of The Ancients?* he thought.

Xera let out a deep breath of relief. She took a sip of tea, hoping it would calm her nerves. Her probes had traveled deep, all throughout the Astral Verge's lower Layers—although the one sent to Layer 10 was instantly destroyed. But she had a good map of each location to forward to Ollie and Jace.

The relief slowly faded as she felt a sense of completion. A task well done. A mission accomplished. *Right, now that that's done*, she thought as she warped herself using the subspace teleportation network to the Penrose Sphere. Walking through several automatic doors on the space station surrounding Oblivion, she entered the first chamber dedicated to cloning.

She went to a machine and began fiddling with a few switches, double-checking her prior triple-checked to-do list.

The programs should be set, the subroutines a-go . . . nothing for it but to test. She did not look forward to this part, with knowledge that Karma Coefficients existed. But, she had maxed hers out at +5. Charitable donations was all it took. *A very easy system to break*, she thought.

Going to a higher Karma Coefficient would require more altruistic acts—and she was only concerned with keeping herself above zero and in the positive range. Well, what's one murder of a convicted serial rapist and killer. She held up her wristpad and warped one such convicted individual who was already sentenced to death in a court. One of the Yittka species from Graskorn.

The figure appeared, bound to a metal slab by chains, and looked around, bewildered. "What is this?" he shouted.

Xera pulled out a laser scalpel, burying it in his temple and instantly killing him. "Soul capture apparatus, engage."

The light-blue Soul, only visible to her because she had tuned her eyes to be able to see in that spectrum of reality, was sucked into Oblivion. She watched through the window as it traveled back up from the bottom, through one of the tubes, and into the machine in the embryonic chamber. The computer interface showed the genome matrix cycling through various genetic patterns before it sent the list of required components.

The synthesizer utilized raw Stardust to create a new body with the exact specifications, with a few alterations. *Let's see what he chose*, she thought.

The tube bubbled and hissed as a Yittka body was grown in seconds to full size. Five years old, the threshold of being middle-aged for the species. The light-blue Soul traveled down a tube to its assigned body, and the fluid drained as the figure's hand hit the glass containing it. The panel lifted, and the figure looked at Xera with bewilderment.

She sat down on a floating stool and began taking notes. "Okay, tell me what happened."

Chapter Thirteen

Layer 4, Vault 4

[Vault Challenge—Activated.]
[Clear the infestation.]

The world warbled, and Jace was standing in the central plaza of a huge space station. The arcing reinforced glass above him showed the stars far off in the distance, and the constant thrum of noise surrounded him, indicative of some type of power source. He was not floating, but was grounded against the decks below.

Looking around, he could see people—humans—who were dressed extremely well. People who had never known a day of labor in their life as small robots and other maintenance machines buzzed around the floor, cleaning up after them. They did not seem to notice Jace at all.

I guess we have to find the infestation, Jace thought as he tasked his Holy Hunt to finding the location of the threat. But the Talent did not seem to work—it malfunctioned. The line began to move away from him, then stopped, receded back to him, and moved toward another direction before stopping and repeating the unsure process.

Seems like the infestation is all around, Ollie stated.

Jace frowned and walked over to one of the people who were sitting outside of a small boutique store, drinking beverages that he could never imagine affording back on Earth. The scent of the roasted coffee, the luxurious spices, they were intoxicating. Neither person seemed to notice him as they continued a conversation about fashion trends.

Maybe inside the buildings? Jace went into the boutique and moved past the rows of shelves and mannequins, past the countertop with the automated cashier mounted to the surface next to a cash register and scan-reader, into the back room, where he found boxes upon crates of more inventory.

Odd. Maybe down into the station itself? Ollie reasoned.

Jace looked around the storage room for any type of access leading into the bowels of the station. Finding nothing, he went outside and down the corridor between several buildings that were in this main atrium shopping center. Finding a maintenance cover, he wedged his fingers into the gap and pried it open, finding a small crawlspace that cut sideways before leading to a ladder.

Descending, he heard the thrumming machinery even louder. The mechanical heartbeat of the station, keeping itself alive and ensuring the survival of the residents. Into a maintenance crawlspace, he shuffled forward in a low squat, but could not find anything of note. *Nothing underneath,* he thought, *and no other maintenance tunnels.* Going out another hatch, he was back in the shopping atrium. *What are we missing?* he asked.

Ollie replied, sounding frustrated, *Maybe the infestation are the people?*

Jace stood stock-still, upright. He looked up through the glass ceiling and focused his attention on the slightly spinning stars. He spotted what he was looking for. Orion's Belt. *Fuck,* he thought, *we're on one of the orbitals above Earth.* He looked back at the people moving around, trying to see any indication of their affiliation with one of the megacorps.

But he saw none.

This is just a construction made by a Vault, Ollie stated. *They are not real people.*

Jace swallowed and nodded as he walked over to one of the men chatting with someone else under an awning. Bringing his blade up, he quickly slashed through the person's neck—but the blade phased through harmlessly. *Nope, that's not it.*

Ollie sighed with exasperation. *Let us check out other parts of the station, then.*

Jace headed down one of the corridors and entered an airlock. It cycled him through, and he emerged in a hallway with several locations marked via arrow. *Maybe hydroponics? If it's an organic infestation of some type.* He began moving to that section of the station.

The thrumming and humming of machinery grew louder, and he stopped once more. *Wait, Ollie. What if the infestation is in the station? Like, the mechanics? The circuitry?*

Oh! Neat idea! Find an interface port, Ollie replied. *It will look like a small socket you could stick a drive into.*

Jace scanned the walls, finding one such port near a doorway. Holding up his hand, the NICIF pulled his armor back and shifted his fingertip into the appropriate type to interface with the station's system. Slotting his finger in, Jace felt a thrum of electricity buzz up his hand and tingle his arm.

Accessing… nope, not seeing any type of infestation. There is something weird going on with the hydroponics bay, though. A report of clogged air filters.

Jace pulled his hand back, and the finger resumed its normal appearance as the armor re-emerged from the wrist and encompassed his limb once more. *Then we move that way.* Swiftly pushing on, he reached the hydroponics bay and cycled through the airlock.

Inside, botanists were moving about in between vertical planters, checking all manners of display showing humidity inside enclosed containers, water levels, sulfur content, and more plant jargon that Jace didn't care to really delve into. Instead, he looked up to the ceiling and tried to find the air filter Ollie had mentioned.

It didn't take long, and using his Soul Tether, he pulled himself up to the ceiling to inspect a slightly damp vent. Digging his fingers into the edges, he ripped the metal panel off and revealed a small patch of a brown fungus or mold. *This is it?* He raised his hand and placed it on the mass, willing his Psykinetics through his palm to incinerate the substance.

But the thing moved—it fled deeper into the vents. *That is not good*, Ollie remarked.

Jace used a Templar's Smite (Blast), channeling the flame down the small shaft, hoping that the searing energy would incinerate the substance. But he had no way to tell. *Well, maybe Holy Hunt will work now.* To his satisfaction, Jace saw the golden line shoot off down the air shaft—only to stop and return to him. *What?*

Something grabbed his leg, and looking down, he saw one of the botanists, eyes a deep green, that yanked on him. "The heck are you doing?" Jace asked.

The person wordlessly continued to pull, and Jace allowed himself down. Ollie spoke in his mind. *I would wager that the mold or fungus—whatever it was—infected the food stores and the people in here. It may be a hive-mind type of situation, where all of the components are part of the same whole.*

Jace grabbed the botanist and saw others coming over with the same purple look in their eyes. *Well, they are infected, and I need to stop the infection.* He reached up and grabbed the man's neck, trying to snap it with one swift movement. But his hands passed through them. *That's not fair*, Jace thought as he felt frustration build up. *He can touch me but I can't touch back? How can I clear the infestation, then?*

Maybe only substance of this place can harm them. Try picking up that tool.

Jace reached over for a metal rod sitting nearby, a tool meant to interact with the plants on higher shelves, and brought it across the botanist's head in a crushing blow. But the implement phased through them. *Okay. Fuck this. Void Step.* Jace warped out of the man's grip and back to the hallway on the other side of the hydroponics bay airlock.

Going to the window that showed out into space, he slammed his fist into the hardened, damage-resistant glass. It fractured then shattered, sucking him out into space. A few of the people in the hallway were also dragged toward the aperture, but an emergency shutter slammed over the broken glass.

Jace used his Soul Tether to keep himself from floating off into open space and looked at the station from the outside. He could see Earth beneath them, and the push-pin shape of the station reminded him of when he used to long for the stars, leaving Earth behind and going up among the rich with Chroma in tow.

Now . . . how to destroy the station.

That would stop the infestation and presumably clear it, Ollie replied.

It would burn up in orbit. I just have to disable its correction boosters. Using his Soul Tether, he pulled himself down to the base of the structure, near the bottom, where he presumed a thruster would be located. He spotted a series of cylinders along the underside of the main, circular habitat and, moving closer with the Soul Tether, saw the small bursts of gas that corrected the orbit of the structure.

Pulling out his sword, he slashed through the structure. *I might not have been able to interact with the people*, he thought, *but I can interact with the structure*. Slicing through the thruster, he moved to the next one in the circle. It was a swift process, disabling the propulsion system, and the object began to lose height and slowly drift down toward the Earth.

It would take a while, though. *Hmm . . . any way we can speed it up?* Jace thought.

A big impact from above?

Jace used his Soul Tether to gain distance and then turned around. He made sure to stop his momentum fully and then used the grapple line once more to move through space, getting to as fast of a speed as he could manage before launching himself into the station's domed roof. It cracked slightly under the weight of his impact. *Not heavy enough*, he thought.

We can just wait it out. You don't need to breathe thanks to the NICIF.

Jace would have sighed if he could. *Seems boring. There has to be something I can do to speed this up.* He had nothing in his inventory, and as he looked at his TPSB's storage, he shook his head. *Nothing. I don't have a way to generate more thrust or give myself more weight.*

He wished that the Paragon Armor had kept the integrated Sliver Arc, which did create a propulsion effect to travel fast. *Oh! Maybe I can try something like that!* He began looking around.

Like what? Ollie asked.

There's lots of space debris, Jace thought back. *I just need enough big chunks of it that I can use cold welding to make a huge mass of matter—and then propel that along with me using the Soul Tether to make a bigger impact!*

Sounds feasible. Scan the environment with your sight—I will tag debris that is of the same metal composition for such a feat.

Jace began searching the space around them and below the station. Ollie highlighted thousands of bits and chunks of debris that were all about the size of a cardboard box. Jace used his Soul Tether, traveling from one to the other and holding them to each other—fusing the metal almost instantly. Going from debris chunk to chunk, he amassed a large amount of metal in a single cluster—easily the size of a large delivery van. Moving back behind the station with his payload, he got some distance, and then used his legs to grip onto the bulk of matter.

Here we go! Jace used his Soul Tether to generate momentum as he gained speed with his payload. He launched the chunk of metal with his legs, generating a bit of extra force as the strike slammed into the station, crushing the top dome and causing the atmosphere inside to vent outward—creating even more propulsion that caused the station to fall deeper into Earth's gravity well, where it accelerated further.

Jace watched with satisfaction as the edges of the station turned a cherry red then white as it fell into orbit and through the atmosphere that superheated it from the descent. The walls of the Vault returned around him, and the crystal floating above the pedestal shifted into a capsule shape.

Jace walked up and grabbed it, acquiring another Epic (Essence Cache) Boon. Then, he was sucked out of the Vault and back into the hallway. Dusting himself off, he headed up topside, and the drone that was holding above the pyramid flew to station-keeping overhead. *How many left?*

Three more Demon Lords, three more Vaults, Ollie said. *Let us go and clear them out!*

Jace began sprinting over the dunes along the edge of the Layer.

Chapter Fourteen

Beat Me to It

Tibalt had stopped himself just shy of reaching Potency 6. He did not want to feel the call of the next Layer and instead wanted to lie in wait. Watching the Potency 10 Astral Demon who lay in wait at the entrance to the layer, he was struck by the sheer difference between them and their relative power.

Thankfully, he had found a stream of Souls that was rolling down the mountain in a small river, and he had been quaffing greedily and hungrily to mass up a supply so that he could level up in an instant if he needed a new Talent to help him turn the tides.

Taking stock of his newfound capabilities, he verified that he was prepared offensively, defensively, and could self-mend. Plus, he could hide very well—his new Talent enabling him to blend into the environment with unmatched efficacy.

The perfectly balanced predator.

The thought of tearing Wraith apart and devouring his Soul was so intoxicating that Tibalt spent cycles upon cycles just drinking the river of Souls, feeling the screaming masses inside him, and imagining keeping Wraith's Soul just to play with. To keep trapped within him, forever, to torture at his whim for ending his dreams of a Vanguard Empire.

No, Tibalt admonished himself. *He only temporarily set me back. I will have my Verge-spanning Empire.*

Jace reached the next Relic Ruins within less than a cycle, but he had Void Stalker up and made sure the drone was well-cloaked in its Dark Matter shell as he approached. A starship was hovering above the tilting-sideways, near-crystalline structure. And he saw Dreamers walking around the pyramid at the center, directly underneath the ship, which projected a light-green tube of light that seemed to facilitate entry to and from the ship as a person drifted up the column of light.

Demons, or not? Jace asked.

They do not seem to appear as Dreamer Demons, Ollie thought back. *But they are wearing armor.*

Heavy armor at that. These aliens—some type of hulking species with a pair of horns that extended from the top of the suit—were carrying heavy-duty firearms: weaponry that was massive. The species was easily double Jace's height, and their firearms were as big as he was.

Well, we approach cautiously, but I don't want to fight them if they don't have ill intentions. Jace dropped the Void Stalker Skill and shouted out as he waved, "Hey! Are you Dreamers, or Dreamer Demons?"

Dozens of guns were brought to bear on him, but none pulled the trigger. "Dreamers! What are you?!" one of them shouted back in a deep, gruff voice.

"Dreamer also," Jace replied as he let his helmet recede. "See? No demon body stuff."

One of the aliens took their helmet off, and Jace could tell they were somehow related to the species that he had saved—the cow-bull people from when he rescued their Universe stronghold mountain on a mission for the Gyanv Alliance Coalition. "We call those corrupted features," the gruff voice said. "Weapons down!"

The Dreamers lowered their weapons and went back to their business—which seemed to be recovering weapons and gear from fallen allies and setting up a defensive perimeter around the pyramid holding the Vault. Jace jogged over. "I'm Wraith."

The figure raised an eyebrow. "And that is supposed to mean something?"

"Maybe not to you," Jace said. "Are you related to . . . what was their name . . ."

Oxknowl.

"The Oxknowl species?" Jace asked.

The bull-man's eyes narrowed. "Yes, distantly, but yes. Before they forsook technology and embraced magic fully. We were exiled for our desire to stick to the old ways."

"Ah. I saved that Universe from an Astral Demon army."

The man snorted. "Good for you." His voice was dull and bored-sounding. "What are you doing here?"

"Esmerelda, the Demon Lord running Respite, sent me to go kill all the Astral Demons in the Ruins. I've dealt with all of them to the east and north—now I'm on my way counterclockwise."

"Imagine that," the man said with a chuckle, his voice lightening a bit. "We're out here clearing Vaults. Trying to get a Relic for each one of our members."

Jace nodded. "I know there is this one and then another two before all have been claimed."

The bull-man shook his head. "The ones on this Layer refresh frequently. Only a few dozen cycles. We will stay at Respite in the meantime." He looked back to the pyramid. "Once we secure the perimeter, we send a squad in to clear the Vault. Our success rate is high." He looked back to

Jace, scanning him up and down. "You've cleared quite a few if your gear is anything to judge it by."

"How can you tell?" Jace asked.

"Ancient Gear all has telltale signs," the bull-man replied. "Smooth, with only a few accents. Functional, but with a bit of flare."

"Maybe you can help me out," Jace said. "I'm the bearer of the Mantle of Burden for The Ancients. They've tasked me with killing off all of the evil Demon Lords on every Layer."

"Oh . . ." The bull-man's expression softened slightly. "You're that person. I knew someone had received the Burden, but not their name. Wraith, you said?" Jace nodded. "Well, Wraith, I am Voor." He looked over to the pyramid. "I do not speak for my whole unit, but I can run the idea by them. Taking out Astral Demons is always good for morale."

Jace followed Voor over to where the others of his species were setting up a perimeter. "Hey!" the bull-man shouted. "This Dreamer is the bearer of the Mantle. Do we want to help him out?"

There was some conversation over comms embedded in their armor that Jace didn't pick up, but it sounded like a quick, intense debate. Voor frowned and looked over to him. "Sorry, they don't want to risk getting tangled up with Valcrinox or his ilk."

"Fair enough," Jace replied. "I'll leave you all to this Vault, then, since you more than earned it by taking out a Demon Lord."

"I can help in one way," Voor said. "You only have a blade and a blaster?"

Jace nodded. "Yeah. One is a Relic, the other is just something I took from a Dreamer Demon."

The bull-man snorted and gestured to the ship up above. "Come on up. I can at least give you a proper blaster with some ammunition." He walked into the beam of light, which began to pull him skyward.

Jace followed and felt a tingling wash over his body as he stepped into the green beam and floated upward. He could see a slightly off-green hue of a parallel beam that had been hidden from his line of sight thanks to being behind the one to ascend. He floated up into the belly of the ship, and the beam gently held him in place. Reaching out to a nearby guide rail, he grabbed it and pulled himself out, gently hitting the deck.

Voor waved him over to a massive rack of futuristic-looking, high-tech weapons. "Swap out that piece of garbage for something really useful."

Jace quickly discarded the blaster and the ammunition into a small crate that was marked with a label reading "Disposal." He looked across all of the neat, well-maintained racks. "You're all very organized," he commented.

Voor chuckled. "Yeah, well, when you are the last of your species to use specific types of tech, you get used to organizing. It's not like we have endless means to reproduce this stuff. Just repair it."

Jace glanced at him. "You sure you want me to have one then? If they're that valuable, I don't want to take them from you."

"We only have sixty crew left," Voor replied. "And a few are keeping an eye toward retiring in the next few hundred cycles. Lots of places on Layer 1 that could be a nice, safe haven. I heard Richter's Repose is a solid city to settle down in, and word reached me that Kirkhold is under new management."

"Yeah, I helped with that," Jace commented as he selected what to this species was probably a small rifle but to him was the equivalent to a shoulder-mounted, massive assault rifle. "I think I'll take this."

"Good choice. A Retribution Carbine. Fires condensed beams of photons that have an effective range of a thousand feet before the damage falls off considerably." He scratched his slightly extended chin. "It can take Psykinetics since its handheld, so Talents will augment it. Don't forget replacement batteries." He reached into a locker and pulled out three cylinders. "One battery can keep it going for twenty shots."

Jace tapped his wrist to the trio of cylinders, and they vanished into his TPSB. "Thanks."

"Where'd they go?"

"Ah, extradimensional storage solution," Jace replied.

"Neat tech. Mind sharing?"

Maybe. Ollie?

<u>*TPS is well-known. Just tell him it operates on shrinkspace.*</u>

"It operates on shrinkspace," Jace stated.

Voor clicked his tongue. "Too much energy for our ship to handle. Well, I hope the weapon helps you with your Mission from The Ancients." He clasped his fist to his chest and dipped his head. "I wish you luck in clearing out all of the evil Demon Lords."

"Thanks," Jace replied as he held out a hand to shake. Voor looked at it questioningly for a moment before shaking his head and Jace lowered the hand. "Right, should've figured gestures don't always carry over."

Voor chuckled and walked over to the slightly off-green beam, stepping into it. "Let's go, Wraith. I've got a Vault to help defend, and you have Demon Lords to kill."

Jace hopped into the beam and quickly cycled through the weapon's settings, configuring them to his liking as if it was second nature, which it sort of was, thanks to the Edge of Possibility Skill. As they reached the bottom, he grabbed a pole that had been planted in the sand to pull himself out of the beam.

Voor clapped him on the back, and the big palm would have toppled Jace if not for his (Grounding) Infusion. "Take care out there, Wraith."

"You too, Voor. Safe travels, and good luck on the Vault!" Jace stored the Carbine in his TPSB and activated Void Stalker as he began moving along the outside edge of the Layer, heading to the second-to-last Demon Lord and Vault. *I'm getting closer, Shhiv. Almost done with this Layer. Hopefully the other ones don't have as many evil Demon Lords to wipe out, and we can speed this up a bit.*

Voor watched as Wraith vanished from view. He shook his head. *Interesting guy*, he thought as he headed to the pyramid and checked in with the survey team. "We good to go on this one?" he asked.

"Yeah! Just about ready to send in the first squad," one of his companions replied.

"Good," Voor replied as he made sure the defensive perimeter was set up and well-established. A message appeared in his vision, and he frowned, because it was not something he had ever seen before. Not the pink-on-black of the Astral System. No, this was gold-on-black. *Ah, what the heck.* He opened the message.

> [I am X.]
> [Wraith is my asset.]
> [Thank you for assisting him.]
> [I interfaced with your ship logs while my asset was on board your vessel—no offense intended, but I needed to know more about your species before deciding on this offer.]
> [I wish to hire your expertise and services.]
> [Report to these coordinates if you want a hefty reward.]

Voor looked at the set of Astral Verge coordinates up from Layer 1. *Hmm . . .* He looked over the other aspects of the job offer, and a smile spread across his face under his helmet. *I think this could be very beneficial.*

It was a straightforward deal. They would head to the location and answer some questions about tactics they had used against Astral Demons. In exchange, they would receive portable shrinkspace tech like what Wraith had demonstrated. Normally, shrinkspace tech required massive energy reserves—but X promised a miniaturized version.

Perfect for a group of Dreamers on the move.

Voor quickly shared the details to the squad members who had set up the perimeter, and after conferring, they agreed to sharing expertise and doing some simple interviews in exchange for that type of technology.

He responded, and a contract appeared. Double-checking the terms, he signed and sent it over, receiving a confirmation. *After this Vault*, he thought as he looked after where Wraith had run to. *Good luck, stranger.*

Chapter Fifteen

Layer 4, Vault 5

Jace raced across the sands. The feeling of reaching his top speed and going full-out, faster than he had ever imagined back in his courier days on Earth, was exhilarating, and he just enjoyed the runner's high that he achieved each time he went for a long stretch. But he could also sink his consciousness back and let the program Ollie had rigged take over the physical act of running while he entered that inner virtual reality and trained.

Most of the training time was spent facing off against constructs that replicated his fight against the strongest Astral Demon he had faced thus far—Yroshnak. The one who he had fought in the Vault arena encounter. The Potency 8 Astral Demon who he had barely kept up with, even with his Shattered Limits active.

His focus was instead studying how his foe had fought. What were his patterns? What types of strikes did he rely on? What were the best routes to approach the fighting style that Yroshnak had utilized?

Figuring out the best route to counter such a brutal fighting style was not easy, but Jace had ultimately figured out an idea that could work. And he practiced it against the construct. Over and over, throwing his virtual avatar into the AI reconstruction of the Demon Lord. The best course of action was to rely on his range and speed, trying to stay away while throwing his weapon over and over.

But he also tried incorporating throwing knives—imbued with his Psykinetics—which he would fling at the same time as his sword. The tactic worked brilliantly as the weapons found their mark while the figure focused on blocking the sword over anything else.

I will ask Quinn to put some throwing knives into your TPSB, Ollie said. *Your body is at the outskirts of the ruins.*

Jace returned to his conscious body and took control from the program as his vision focused. He could see what looked like a bombed and blasted-out suburbia from back on Earth. Pulling the Carbine from his TPSB, Jace funneled his Psykinetics into the barrel, the weapon flickering with golden flames as he placed the weapon on his shoulder and shifted the sights down to the left side of the barrel.

Tasking drone, Ollie said as the camera view on the corner of Jace's HUD shifted—the drone lifting off to go and tag targets in the blown-up and ruined remnants. Several targets were highlighted—enormous, shaggy Astral Demons who were curled up in balls inside the houses, covered in bristling fur and thrumming with Psykinetic energy. Dormant, but very much present.

The Pyramid at the center was different than the rest of them Jace had encountered. The top had been peeled off, and a massive Astral Demon who looked like the bear creatures lay on top of the tunnel that led down to the Vault entrance.

This will be easy enough, Jace thought as he moved to an angle where he could get line of sight into one of the wrecked houses. *(Burning) from Valiant' Crusader's Might should apply, as well as (Searing) from Purifying Edge.* Jace targeted the creature through the aiming reticle and squeezed the trigger.

A beam of bright, crimson light shot forward—golden flames trailing after it. The shot hit the creature and then exploded in a golden inferno thanks to Jace's Flame of Valor causing a small area-of-effect detonation. The creature let out a terrifying, earth-shaking roar as it stood up.

Jace fired shot after shot, not having to wait between them. It took five to bring the beast down, and the others were rousing to the call of a pained cry. Jace targeted the next one that stepped into the main avenue of the streets and fired the weapon another five times, slaughtering the creature with the Psykinetic-imbued weapon. *This is too easy*, he thought as he turned to another and killed it with five more trigger squeezes—the red beam causing a glittering, gold explosion each time it struck a target.

Then, Psykinetic barriers were erected around the creatures, and Jace saw one of his bolts bounce off them. *Guess it's time to swap*, he thought as he stored the weapon in the TPSB and drew his sword. Manifesting his Crusader's Bastion, Jace sprinted forward to meet the charge of the bears. A quick Void Step took him behind the rearmost one, and he sliced into its back leg—but his weapon caught on the middle of the bone.

The creature wheeled about, slamming a Psykinetic-empowered claw into Jace that he caught on his shield—but the impact sent him tumbling sideways—the force so great that even his (Bracing) Infusion hardly helped. He landed with a grunt and rolled to his feet as the bear-demons began to move in on him, bodies lit up with crackling, blue Psykinetic energy.

<u>*This has turned rather quickly*</u>, Ollie commented.

Not serious enough for Shattered Limits to activate, Jace thought back as he raised his shield, blocking a strike, and used Void Step to get to the other side of the mass of demons, using Raging Cleave (Rank 10) [Echoing Cleave] to strike all of them. The golden line of arcing energy tinged with crimson nebula clouds created a razor-thin line across the mob before him before detonating with golden flames.

Which only seemed to irritate the creatures, as they moved forward almost as a singular mass and threatened to overrun Jace. But a quick Void Step up into the sky got him out of the way. While his foes scanned for where he had warped to, he unleashed a Templar's Smite, pouring forty percent of his energy reserves into the enormous blast that sent a pillar of golden flame skyward.

The Astral Demons roared their pain, and Jace landed among them, deftly swinging his sword left, then right as he cut into the creature's hides and then sprinted—still fueling the Templar's Smite, which now functioned as a golden smokescreen of pure flame that concealed him. Chopping through limbs and necks alike, Jace was down to twenty percent energy by the time he had finished off the mob and let his Talent fade.

And as the corpses vanished, light-blue Souls scattering in all directions and white-grey Essence flooding into Jace—the Demon Lord approached. A massive, bearlike monstrosity that was covered with spines and horns, whipping tendrils with spikes all darting toward Jace as the charge continued in earnest.

Jace used a Void Step, got behind the thing, and unleashed a Templar's Smite (Spear), the golden flame streaking out and slamming into the monstrosity before exploding into the flames that sparkled in contrast to the dull desert dunes. The creature wheeled around and charged him, and Jace just repeated the process. Void Step, Templar's Smite (Spear), and repeat. He tapped his energy down to near-empty, but finally, the foe fell, Souls escaping and Essence being absorbed.

Another 5,000 total. Want to keep banking it?

"Yes," Jace replied as he headed to the pyramid, taking deep breaths as the exhaustion weighed heavily on him. He descended the steps but stayed a distance from the Vault door, waiting for his energy to recover as he sat on the stairs.

Quinn has put forty throwing knives into your TPSB, Ollie advised. *Doing okay?*

Jace nodded and leaned back against the stairs. "Doing just fine," he replied.

You do not want to talk about that whole space station Vault encounter? I would have figured you would want to talk about it.

Jace shrugged. "It was a constructed challenge. Those weren't real people. And if they were able to be interacted with, I would have incapacitated them until we figured out a way to cure them, or remove them from the ship and then blow it up, or something like that. I'm good, I promise."

Sounds good to me!

Jace waited on his energy and, in the meantime, reached into his TPSB and pulled out a throwing knife, playing with it by flipping it, balancing it on his fingertip to perfect stillness, and eventually juggling four of them—just to keep his hands occupied as he waited for his energy to refill. Putting them away after a few minutes, he pulled the Carbine out of the TPSB and checked the battery's charge. *Still the same*, he thought.

It needs to be ejected to be refueled, Ollie commented.

Jace reached into his storage once more and pulled out a battery, swapping the full charge for the partial one. Putting the partially powered one back in the TPSB, he ensured the weapon was at full charge before storing that as well.

Finally, his energy was full, and Jace stood up as he redrew his sword and walked to the Vault. Placing his hand on the door, he was sucked in and almost immediately greeted by a System message.

[Vault Challenge—Activated.]
[Defeat the heretics.]

Space warbled and shifted, and Jace found himself standing in the midst of an army on a distant planetoid, judging by the curve of the horizon far in the distance. Enormous, skyscraper-sized mechs that looked like supersized versions of armored soldiers slowly trudged through the battlefield, and craning his eyes up, Jace could see the massive cannons easily the size of a whole building firing devastating lasers at the other mega mechs.

Humanoid creatures whose features were indiscernible rushed around Jace, and they were dressed in superheavy power armor, just like Greg's. They were holding a variety of slug-throwing weapons, flamethrowers, and other projected energy weapons. They were charging forward into a line of defenders, others who were wearing similar armor, but theirs was covered in skulls and painted a deep crimson.

"For the Exarch!" a battle cry sounded from the side that Jace had warped to.

"Kill the nonbelievers!" from the other side.

Jace used a Void Step to get up above the fray and his Soul Tether to stay up there. *Some type of hyper-tech civil war*, he thought as the towering mechs continued to unleash fury upon each other. In the distance, Jace could see artillery batteries firing cascading clouds of shrapnel that descended onto the charging forces. *This is chaotic.*

No kidding. How are we supposed to defeat all of that? Ollie replied. *Just look at the size of those mega mechs!*

Jace frowned, but then an idea struck him. Sheathing his sword, he drew throwing knives from his TPSB. *What do you want to bet that those giant mechs are not used to zero gravity?* He applied Dark Energy Mine on the knives—one apiece—and, with a quick toss, threw each of them—one at each huge mech. Reaching into the TPSB for even more throwing knives and using his Soul Tether to travel up and down the line of combat—which thankfully did have some type of predefined edges, as he encountered an invisible barrier that stopped further progress—he went through a total of twenty of his throwables.

And . . . detonate.

Thanks to Dark Energy Mine only needing to affect a portion of the object to affect the whole thing, each of the hostile mechs on the "heretic" side was afflicted with thirty seconds of zero-gravity. They slowly lifted and began moving into the air above, several tilting on their sides as they tried some type of recovery maneuver.

Up, up they went, and Jace watched with a morbid fascination as he saw them continue to ascend. Then, the timer faded, and gravity reasserted itself.

Crash! The mechs all slammed to the ground, and they were most definitely not built for being slammed on their side, as the support structures within groaned, whined, and snapped—the entire mega-sized mech force crumpling before him.

Good job! Ollie said in his mind. *Now how about the rest?*

Jace drew his sword and used his Soul Tether to head toward the mortar and artillery teams. *I clear the path for the ground forces.* He had to dodge several stray shots that were sent up his way, but the armies seemed intent on each other and not the looming threat that was advancing toward them.

A bright glow caught Jace's attention from behind, and he saw one of the friendly mega mechs unleash a blast of pure, destructive force as a torrential green beam hit a huge cluster of the heretic troops, turning them to naught but ash.

I don't think I could survive a straight hit from that, he thought.

I doubt you would.

This type of tech exists?

Somewhere, I am sure. In some Universe.

Jace just shook his head in bewilderment. *Absolutely insane.*

He got to the mortar and artillery crews, and instead of using his throwing knives, he threw his sword—scoring critical hits on the weapon emplacements that disabled them permanently. This did draw attention up to him, and he had to drop down to reduce the incoming shots. Landing on the ground and bringing his Crusader's Bastion to bear, he rushed through the backlines of the army.

He suffered hits, metal slugs that slammed into his shield, the slight hue of Psykinetics upon the bullets before a (Retaliating) spike of golden flame returned fire and scored impacts. But these foes were tough, and Jace found himself quickly surrounded from all sides—suffering hits to his back that his armor staved off but still bruised underneath.

But he was successful in disabling all of the distance-based weaponry. However, he could see his energy almost depleted. *I need to get away*, he thought. *Find some place to hole up while the friendly forces mop things up.* Using a series of chained-together Void Steps, he was able to flee from the hostile backline and back into the comparative safety of the friendly forces.

Able to stand back, he watched as the heretic legions were dismantled systematically and brutally. As a flag was raised, the world warped around Jace, and he found himself back in the Relic chamber. The crystal above the altar shifted to the capsule shape, and Jace grabbed the Epic (Essence Cache) Infusion. *One more to go*, he thought as he was sucked out the Vault and headed up the stairs.

Chapter Sixteen

Layer 4, Vault 6

Sprinting across the dunes, Jace couldn't help but ponder the sheer scale of the battle that had been going on in, to him, the background of his sabotage mission. *Those mechs were huge! And they were able to obliterate huge groups with single hits!*

You fought things of similar size, Ollie commented. *Back in our Universe. The big dinosaurs back on Graskorn, the Leviathan that was literally the size of a planet on Harkon Secundus? You have fought monstrosities that would have terrified most.*

But I had The Cosmic System and could freely use Void, which really evened out the scales, Jace thought back with concern. *How do species without a System deal with that?*

Our Universe is not the only one with a System, Ollie replied. *There are many Systems across multiple Universes. Some are more esoteric and less sensible than ours.*

Jace shook his head. *I am happy I ended up in our Universe instead of wherever else I could've ended up.*

He continued onward, conversing back and forth with Ollie, and the Wayfinder informed him that even Earth ran on Systems. He explained that the rules of reality—physics, chemical reactions, and how the underpinnings of the Universe's constant functions were really just a System all of their own.

The Cosmic System is really just a creation that slightly bends and tweaks the already existing "rules", or System, of our Universe's reality, Ollie concluded.

Jace had soaked in the explanation, and thanks to Xera's information-download chair he had made use of to acquire learning he did not get on the streets, most of it made sense. *I have one lingering question.*

Go ahead.

The Cosmic System lays over everything, but doesn't really upset the function—how? People are throwing around Cosmic Power.

It is a balancing act, hence the need for local administrators in the form of Ascendants, Factions, deities, or Wayfinders. It is why back on Earth I told you that you could not use your Archmage Skills so frequently—it literally disrupted the underpinning laws of reality.

Jace nodded as they reached the last set of ruins. Sending the drone up into the sky, he took in the terrain. More sandy dunes, as expected, but the ruins appeared to be the remains of a medieval-esque settlement, much like how Nihilethelea had the single primary capital city. One- and two-story tall buildings constructed of stone, some of the blocks having toppled over, were intermixed with small wooden constructions that had long since rotted away. None of the buildings had roofs.

His drone tagged yet more Astral Demons. *They were a bigger threat up on Layer 1*, Jace thought. *Especially the Demon Lords. Why are they so much easier here?*

You are one Potency above them, Ollie replied. *There is an offset because of that.*

Jace nodded and pulled out the Carbine, mounting it on his shoulder. A small display appeared on the viewfinder, and he felt an odd wheel along the thumb. "The heck?" he muttered.

Quinn's voice came over the comms. "Oh, that's us. Shhiv and I. She upgraded it. You can load up multiple shots into a single, larger burst—up to a full battery's worth. Just flick the dial, and the range finder will update."

"Thanks," Jace said. "You two ladies keep watching out for me."

"Always have my Observer on you. If I see you really struggling, I'll turn on the Stratagems. Just remember, it takes a long time before I can reapply it unless you come back home."

"Noted," Jace said as he cranked the dial to its maximum setting. Taking aim at the Astral Demon that was just barely within line of sight, he squeezed the trigger. The beam of energy that shot out, imbued with his golden Psykinetics, was much hotter—and he could feel the burst of heat on his face as he watched the lancing energy pierce the Astral Demon and immediately destroy it, the golden flames of the Psykinetics burning the corpse away to nothingness.

He quickly swapped out batteries and pivoted as the Astral Demons began to move out of the buildings. They were hybrids of the Gyanv species from Layer 1 and had heavily gone down the path of monstrous evolution as they were misshapen forms, covered in chitinous plates and writhing tentacles.

Tentacles that glowed with a deep, umbral purple light as beams shot out at Jace. He deftly dodged and returned fire, obliterating another one of them with the laser. Reloading quickly, he used the last shot to take out a third, then popped the battery out, stored it in the TPSB along with the Carbine, and drew his sword. Bringing his shield to bear, he placed the Crusader's Bastion in front of him, the beams of Psykinetic energy biting into the defensive redoubt before producing a (Retaliating) bolt of golden flame that lanced back to them.

He watched his energy slowly trickle away, and then become more of a dribble as even further shots joined in—his foes redoubling their efforts. But Jace was fine with the exchange—he was not taking injury, they were, and he was just going through energy slowly.

Still, he kept moving forward, an inexorable force that was unstoppable and unshakeable in his resolve. *Just the last one*, he thought as he got into range for his Templar's Smite and unleashed a cataclysm upon his foes. A torrent of golden light burst from beneath, scorching them all and burning them into crispy corpses that quickly evaporated into the air with the Souls they were holding onto. The Essence surged into him.

Puts us at 16,000! Ollie said excitedly.

Jace kept moving forward, keeping an eye on the probe camera to spot any further hostiles. Seeing none, he used Holy Hunt to try and find the last Demon Lord.

But the golden line did nothing.

Must have been in the group you incinerated, Ollie commented. Jace was going to respond, but an Astral System screen popped into his vision;

> [Mission: Consolidate control over Layer 4 to Demon Lord Esmerelda.]
> [Reward: Legendary (Essence Cache) Infusion.]
> [Sender: The Ancients.]

We have four Legendary Infusions we could use, Ollie stated.

I still want to save up, Jace thought back. *We are doing just fine as is.* He moved to the pyramid structure and descended. Entering the Vault, he was left waiting as the Astral System must have been scanning him. *This means we'll be doing something involving my past.*

Jace received his answer shortly after.

> [Vault Challenge—Activated.]
> [Reconcile.]

The world warped around Jace, and he was caught off guard as he was standing in Xera's living room. The Architect was sitting on the couch, holding a steaming hot cup of tea. She looked up to him, those purple eyes boring into Jace. "Well? What did you want to say?" she asked innocently.

What type of challenge is this? Jace thought. *Reconcile? This isn't her. It's some construct.*

Maybe it is like an exercise to prepare you for the real thing. Just be honest, Ollie said with a tone of encouragement.

Jace sat down opposite Xera, sheathing his weapon and dismissing his Talents as the quiet set in. "I . . . I want to know why you manipulated me. The exact reason."

She shrugged. "I manipulate everyone. It is how I have lived my life. I manipulated my beloved brother so that I didn't have to figure out magic and could focus on technology. I manipulated factions against each other to ensure optimal outcomes for The Cosmic System." Her eyes narrowed and her voice went cold. "I manipulated you because you were a possible asset. Something I could take a small risk on, but would provide an excellent outcome from."

Jace nodded. "I figured that much out. But . . . why keep it going? Why not just come clean with me and tell me everything—about the Astral Verge, Troxanir's true identity . . . all of that stuff that we only learned over time? That you drip-fed to us?"

Xera frowned and sighed, her voice becoming slightly apologetic in tone. "I would have told you if I thought you could handle it. But let's be real, here; you were not smart enough—book smart, I mean. A lot of it would have gone right over your head. And assets are best when they are focused."

The reasoning made sense to Jace; not having to worry about bigger issues did make his tasks a lot easier to deal with and removed any unnecessary overthinking that would have gone into his actions if he knew about Souls and the fact that something waited beyond death. "I never forgave you," Jace muttered. "And I don't know if I can forgive you for all that you've done. You need to pay for what you've done." He looked down at his armored hands. "I need to pay for what I've done," he whispered.

"Don't drown in guilt," Xera said nonchalantly before taking another sip of her tea. "It does nothing to help you. Guilt is a deep well that you could drown in. Don't. Just acknowledge that you did something bad, but the greater good that will come of it will be more than worth the cost." She stood up and walked to her window. "Our Universe, safe forever, from everything. Every Soul, safe forever, as it was before The Ancients arrived in our reality." She turned to face him. "That is worth being damned to annihilation."

Jace stood up. "I . . ." He took a deep breath, then let it out. "I forgive you. I don't like your tactics, but it led to where we are now."

"You are so close," Xera said softly as she walked over, her shorter stature forcing her to look up into his eyes. She seemed so small in that moment, so . . . pathetic. Despite her phenomenal technology and magitech, possible even full-on magic at her disposal . . . Xera looked weak and hollow. A shell of what once might have been a powerful woman, brought to the edge of her existence because of time and actions that she had to take.

"So close," she continued, "to completing the Grand Design. Just a bit farther. Five more Layers. A few more Demons Lords . . . and then you are free."

Jace nodded. "I'm ready for it."

The Vault returned around Jace, and he quickly snatched the last Epic (Essence Cache) from the pedestal. The Vault sucked him outside, and reactivating Void Stalker, he made for Respite, hoping to get some extra reward from Esmerelda before heading down to Layer 5.

Xera finished her ten thousandth trial. There were quite a few murderers and others guilty of more heinous crimes that had been sentenced to death, and her replacing them with a clone before pulling their real body to the Penrose Sphere for testing had gone unnoticed.

Thankfully, the experiments were showing success. The process was almost flawless. Just a few adjustments, a few more tweaks, and she would have the

Soul-to-body apparatus complete. Ready to receive Souls, process them into new bodies, and let them pick up from where they left off.

They get to choose all aspects of their new body, she thought, having removed the idea of forcing them to remain static, as they once were. *Everyone gets to choose their ideal physique, age, species . . . everything. Sure, it might cause a little bit of tumult outside of Khrox, but that is their choice. Local administrators can deal with it.*

She was not doing this on a whim. She had run the idea past Xero and the Wayfinders—all of whom agreed that locking people into bodies they might not be comfortable with, or were not the idealized form they envisioned for themselves, would be cruel. In a worst-case scenario, they might commit suicide to get another chance in the machine.

No, Xera knew this was the better path to take. And now, she had the template and could increase production. Thanks to TPSB, she could actually compress thousands of the machines into every square foot of space on the Penrose Sphere.

The place that not only protected their Universe from threats in the Astral Verge but would also serve as the new origin of all who died.

And then that brings up the last bit of research, she thought as she leaned back and crossed her arms. *How do Souls just . . . appear? At what point of the process is a Soul formed?*

It was driving her mad—figuratively speaking—and she wanted to hold off on asking Xero what he thought until she had exhausted all possible options. Once they had that bit of data, they could ensure that The Cosmic System would improve the process, making it the most effective each time.

Now, she thought as she looked out the window and into Oblivion, *we just need the Karma Judgement Matrix. Hurry up, Jace. I'm running out of time.*

Chapter Seventeen

Preparing for an Ambush

Respite only took a few cycles to reach, and Jace used his Soul Tether to pull himself up and over the wall before heading over to the small spaceport. He used Holy Hunt to track down Esmerelda, finding her talking to one of the Dreamers who had seemingly just arrived with a shipment of cargo.

She turned to face him as he dropped Void Stalker, his booted footsteps clacking on the stone landing pad. "Ah, Wraith. I saw the notification—you have completed my task." She bowed slightly. "Thank you. I can work on instilling control over this Layer, and hopefully open it up to new refined-path demons who were hiding in Layer 3."

Jace dipped his head. "Happy to do it. I got my reward, just checking in to see if there is anything you could tell me about Layer 5."

She frowned, and turned to the Dreamer. "I'll be back. Go make yourself comfortable in the bar." She pointed the armored figure toward a building, then walked over to Jace. "We should speak in private." Her eyes darted around. "Can never be too careful."

Jace followed her into the building she seemed to call home, and once she shut the door, she spoke softly and urgently. "Valcrinox has left a minion on the other side of the entrance. Potency 10."

Jace felt a chill run through him. "You sure?"

She nodded, a grimace on her face. "It has been confirmed by a mutual ally. I believe you have met him before. Yroshnak, Demon Lord of Blood."

The memory of the arena encounter flitted through Jace's mind. "Yeah, Potency 8?"

"Yes. But he intends to assist you in your Mission from The Ancients. He asked me to pass this along to you." She held up her hand, and a small, bright-pink capsule floated above it. "An Infusion. A Mythic one. For a Specialization."

Ollie spoke in Jace's mind. *That is just one rarity rank below Divine!*

Jace reached his hand out and accepted the Infusion, gripping it as it was added to his status screen and inventory of Infusions that briefly flashed across his HUD. "Thank you. Do you have communication with Yroshnak?"

"I do."

"Why can't I correspond directly?" he asked. "I don't think I've had direct contact with any Astral Demon through the System."

"Some ancient decree. Only Dreamers can correspond with Dreamers. I suppose you could try to correspond via the public forum—anyone can talk there—but your conversation would be out in the open." She tapped her forehead. "I can contact Yroshnak directly. Would you like me to pass something along?"

"Just let him know that I'm on my way," Jace replied.

She squinted, her lips tightened for a few seconds, and then she smiled softly. "Done. Anything else?"

"What can you tell me about Layer 5?"

She sighed and crossed her arms. "It is covered in mountains, snow-capped ones. Souls trickle down through the desert here and condense into something akin to the water in the oasis."

"I've been meaning to ask—why is water here? It's not like Astral Demons need it."

"The Ancients' doing, I believe. When the Layers were created. Dreamers, almost all of them except for lithoids—rock-eaters—require sustenance." She raised a quizzical brow. "I might be saying 'water' to you, but I assure you, the word is being autotranslated to the substance most analogous to it in your language."

Ah, that makes sense, Ollie commented in Jace's head. *I should have figured that out way earlier.*

Jace nodded. "So the Souls collect into a stream and flow?"

"Like rivers and streams, down the mountains until they eventually get to the lowest point of the Layer, where the entrance to Layer 6 is." She raised her hand. "I can share a map, if you like."

We are good! I have one from Xera's probes.

"I'm good," Jace replied. "Any other information?"

"No," Esmerelda replied. "I am sorry. I wish I knew more."

"Last thing. Are you willing to give me any Infusions? Or trade for them?"

She laughed lightly. "Not me. I don't keep Infusions, I use them—much like most." She raised that quizzical eyebrow again. "Are you . . . holding onto them?"

"Yes," Jace replied. "I want to get a Divine Infusion."

Her eyes went wide at that. "You . . . oh, Ancients below . . . " She took a deep breath and let it out slowly. "Well, good luck. I've never heard of someone holding onto their Infusions long enough to combine them into a Divine rarity. I have no clue what it could be capable of."

"Hopefully something that lets me destroy Valcrinox with ease," Jace replied. "Thanks for everything." He turned to leave, but she spoke once more.

"Ask at the bar. Dreamers sometimes hold onto them for trade, but only briefly. And you need something good to trade them."

I have a whole bunch of stuff in the TPSB we can trade! Rare minerals, for example, Ollie said.

"I will," Jace replied as he left the building and went to the bar. Opening the door, he saw Dreamers of all different species and differing types of armor—not hundreds, but a few dozen. Not nearly as populous as the Layer above. A handful looked toward him, but most kept conversing as they ate and drank.

No sense in wasting time, Jace thought as he cleared his throat. "I'm here to trade for Infusions. Anyone have some?"

Some people looked his way, but no one spoke. Shrugging, Jace turned to leave—but one voice came up behind him. "I have a few I can sell." Turning, Jace saw the source of the noise was a squat insectoid creature—some type of slug with arms that was inside a suit that kept it fully encased. "I'm Leto," they said.

"Wraith," Jace replied. "What you want for Infusions?"

"What do you have?"

Ollie, can you give me a—

Sales inventory. Got it! Ollie broadcast a screen inside Jace's HUD, and Jace began reading off the list of various rare metals and elements—some of which he had never heard of.

The figure stopped him when he reached something called Iridium. "Yes! I can use that! How much do you have?"

"Ten thousand pounds," Jace replied. *We have a lot in there*, he thought to Ollie.

Your TPSB is accessing the larger TPS that Xera owns, Ollie explained. *You have your personal one, but I can also utilize Quinn to access Xera's overall stores.*

Leto sounded quite enthusiastic. "I'll make a deal for all you got! If you can give me a few cycles, I can round up quite a few Infusions from some others in my trade conglomerate. Can you give me two cycles?"

"How many are we talking about?" Jace asked as he crossed his arms.

"Well, easily a hundred Common rarity. Maybe some Rare and Epic. Let's say a thousand pounds per Epic I can manage to scrounge together—how's that sound?"

Is that all that Xera has in her inventory? Jace asked in his mind.

Nope. But she is currently unavailable, and we cannot just access the TPS at a whole—only a selection.

"Sounds like a deal," Jace replied. "I can be here for two cycles."

The worm person scooted off to a vessel that looked like a long, thick log with several bumpy protrusions akin to severed branches along the sides. They entered a small aperture, which sealed behind them, and then took off into the skies.

Jace sighed and looked around. "Might as well just relax a bit."

Xero saw how frazzled Xera was from the moment she pixelated and entered his virtual reality. "Hey, what's going on?" he asked her.

He could see the tears streaming from her face and the slight fuzz along her eyes that was indicative of a glitch in her cybernetic brain's processing. "I'm . . . I'm running out of time," she said with panic and fear filling her voice.

"You have the Soul capture device figured out?" he asked.

She nodded. "Yes. But I figured it out . . . Souls are spontaneously created and hosted in a creature shortly after conception." She shook her head. "But I figured out something worse. I know why degradation of a Soul happens in containment. It's because of this!" She raised her hand, and a screen appeared next to both of them. Xero saw them both and could see a set of numbers above each of their heads.

Xera's was at positive five, but slowly ticked down. She frantically scrabbled at her wrist pad, and the number ticked back up. Xero's was at negative fifty. "What's that mean?" he asked her.

"Our Karma Coefficients," Xera replied. "I'm staving off my negative deeds by paying Stardust to various good causes." She sounded incredibly stressed and spoke rapidly, as she did when she was in such a state, which he had not observed in her since before The Architects left. "Morality exists and is measured. It's not a matter of 'might makes right' anymore. There are parameters I don't know."

Xero put a hand on her shoulder and squeezed. "Soul degradation happens because of a negative Karma Coefficient?" he asked, trying to redirect her focus.

She nodded. "Yes. The Soul begins to punish itself for its misdeeds, slowly withering itself away. That's why Soul Capture technology always failed us! Because we had no way to filter out the good and the bad." She looked at him, and a manic smile spread across her face. "And I'm almost out of time!" She was on the verge of a full-blown meltdown.

Xero just grabbed his sister and hugged her tightly, feeling so incredibly torn inside. He brushed her hair gently with one pair of hands while the other held her close. "You have done incredible work, sis. You've told me of this Karma Judgement Matrix. I'm sure once we have it, we can rig it to filter Souls—"

"And what happens to ones like mine?!" she shouted, muffled, into his chest.

"Speed up the process of extraction to cloned body," Xero replied. "We had a closed loop before The Ancients fucked up our Universe. We can fix it." *We have to*, he added in his thoughts. Speaking aloud once more, he whispered to her, "If anyone can figure it out, it's you. And with me? Nothing lies beyond our reach. Reconfiguring some device? We'll do it. Together." He sighed, "Doctor Restra—great therapist, by the way—has told me I am almost done with my treatment." He pulled back and lifted Xera's chin slightly. "Go make my body—"

"It's been done!" Xera replied excitedly, but with tears still flowing. "It's been done for weeks. I've just . . . I need you back, brother."

Again, Xero was thrown back to when they were children. Two prodigies, taken to their civilization's highest place of learning. Taken from their parents to chase their academic pursuits of technologic ascendance. The nights that she cried, hugging him in bed, at being torn away from their family. He hugged her again. "I'll be in reality soon," he whispered. "Just a few more sessions. I still have a bit to unpack."

A beeping noise caught both of their attention, and Xera straightened up, pulling a screen up in midair. It showed an inventory log of some sort. "Damnit, Quinn! Taking my iridium? What could she possibly need it for?" She opened up some comm network on her wrist pad. "Quinn, the heck is going on with my iridium supply?"

A female voice came back over the comms. "Jace needed it."

"For what?!"

"Ten Epic Infusions of varying types," Leto the slug-person stated. "Pleasure doing business."

"Likewise," Jace replied. He turned to the wall at the eastern side of Respite and used his Soul Tether to get up over it. Sprinting across the desert with Void Stalker active, he spoke to Ollie. "Convert them all up."

On it! Ten Epic turn into two Legendary, and we can combine those with your other three Legendary to get a Mythic!

Do it, Jace thought back.

Done. We have two Epic (Essence Cache), and two Mythic (Specialization).

Let's use the Essence Cache ones.

Doing it now! Puts you at 26,000 Essence total. Five levels' worth, with 1,000 left over.

We need to save it, Jace thought, *until we get into the next Layer, I choose my next Class Transmutation, and I can get access to those neat Talents and Specializations.* Ollie had been doing his research, and Justiciar—continuing down the damage route—was the best out of the options available.

We do have the Potency 10 Demon ambush, Ollie said with slight worry.

"But we have Quinn," Jace said aloud. "Got those Stratagems ready?" he asked.

Her voice came over the comms. "Just got yelled at by Xera because of you," she replied with a slightly dour expression. "But, yes. I have Stratagems at Rank 63 ready to go on you. Twenty-seven-minute duration."

"List of effects? It's been a while."

She sighed, then spoke rapidly. "Double movement speed, double damage output, halved damage taken, no forced movement, not subject to mind-altering effects, your damage output is altered to a target's weakest resistance, you will have illusory duplicates that make you harder to hit, be hard to detect—not that that matters—will be able to do a one-time, one-hundred-foot teleport"—she took a breath—"and lastly, you can lock yourself into a temporary stasis of invulnerability; no moving or interacting with anything outside of you and your body, though."

Jace smiled. "So we have you pop all of those with the trigger of my entering the next Layer. Ollie, you have Shattered Limits with [Single-Minded Fury] ready to go the moment we get into a fight."

"And," Quinn said, "I will have Tactician's Orders active the moment you see a hostile with the objective to end the threat—which means you will have increased . . . well, a lot of stuff. Plus, Grand Tactics will give you another times-ten multiplier to everything you can do. And Coordinator's Critical Gaze gives your first weak-spot hit another ten-times multiplier. Plus, improved reaction times from Coordinator's Warning System."

Jace had forgotten just how much Quinn had loaded up into her Skill layout to be able to support others from a distance. "How often can we do this?"

"With you down the Layers? There is some type of Astral System interference the deeper you go. I use it on you here, and you are locked out from receiving—not me using, you receiving—the buffs for a whole fifty cycles. Sorry, fifty days. It's formulaic, ten days per Layer." She sighed, "Plus, it'll give me a wicked headache."

"Well, I appreciate you taking the hit to keep me alive," Jace replied as he continued his trek.

"Happy to do it," she replied. "Go kick whoever-it-is's ass."

The comms went silent, and Jace saw the circle in the distance. A low depression in the sandy dunes that was nonetheless kept clear of all sand by some unknowable energy surging out from the portal leading down. *Okay,* Jace thought as he readied himself. *Skills and Talents.* Crusader's Bastion, Holy Hunt, Dark Energy Mine (Rank 1), Dark Matter Mending (Rank 4) [Vampiric], Raging Cleave (Rank 10) [Echoing Cleave], Aura of Wrath (Rank 11).

His body blazed with golden, glorious flames as the shield manifested in his grip and his sword in his other hand. The slight dot of Dark Matter planted on his chest thrummed with a constant purple hue only visible to him. The golden line shot out from his feet and into the film before him—the gelatinous, opaque surface barely moving and placid. His weapon surged with crimson light as arcing red lightning cascaded around his form.

“Here we go,” he whispered breathlessly as he dove in.

Chapter Eighteen

Tier 10 Versus Potency 10

Jace fell through the film and emerged in the sky. Mountains stretched high up around him in all directions, with a small, rocky promontory directly below. At the base of that mound was a stream of light-blue-colored Souls, moving rapidly to the west. In all directions, snowcapped mountains—with the light blue of Souls cascading down to coalesce together. The sky above was a solid, light purple, dotted with Souls like wafting snow coming through the surface.

Jace had no time to take in the view, however, as his [Danger-Sense] activated, The Cosmic System message appearing in his vision.

> [Foe that is vastly superior detected.]
> [Shattered Limits enabled.]

Activating! Ollie shouted. *And detonating!*

Time slowed to Jace's perspective, weightlessness took him, and the impossible-to-see blurb of black that had been dashing up toward him moved like a regular person to his now-sped-up, enhanced form. Quinn's Stratagems all activated in tandem, and Jace could see a deep, bronze glowing spot on the Astral Demon's chest.

This one was not all refined, not all monstrous. It was an odd mix of both; humanoid with hulking features—broad shoulders, a massive chest—both covered in some type of metal plate. Six wings extended from their back, and in one hand, they held a large axe, the other, a shield, wreathed in bright orange flames that forced Jace to wince despite his prosthetics. The waist down was a mass of writhing tentacles and flesh that squelched upon itself as the tendrils writhed around the center of the figure. Each tentacle, coated with the same Psykinetic energy of orange fury.

The head was covered by a spiked helmet with a crown of fragments splintering off from it. And the voice that came from behind the helmet was incomprehensible. Just a scream of raw, primal savagery. The axe came sweeping in from Jace's left, and he raised his shield to block—but the figure tilted their angle just slightly enough that Jace was forced to use a Void Step to warp out of the way, behind the figure.

He chopped down, the phantasmal extension of his weapon arcing out and carving through the wings—but the appendages regenerated instantly, reforming a bond with the severed portion, and the figure wheeled around, delivering a wicked chop that Jace barely caught on his shield. The orange flames of the creature's Psykinetics were oppressive, and Jace had to turn his face away from the incredible heat. He pushed the strike away with his shield and chopped with his sword—but the Astral Demon caught the blade on its own shield, the blade embedding itself into the surface and sticking as orange flames clashed against gold.

Void Step, Jace thought as he warped directly backward. He summoned his sword back to his sheath, reached into his TPSB, and drew out eight throwing knives—one between each finger at the knuckles. Rapidly reusing Dark Energy Mine on each, he threw the first four.

The Astral Demon surged toward him through the sky and dodged or blocked the knives. *Detonate*, Jace thought with a smirk as the thing stopped in midair, which was the perfect opening for him to throw the other four knives, which sank into the torso before also detonating—golden flames surging out and causing the demon to howl in pain.

Jace drew his sword again and was about to move forward when every instinct, and then [Danger-Sense], screamed at him to dodge. Using another

Void Step, he dodged up and, glancing down, saw a massive torrent of writhing, orange flame surge out where he had just been.

And the flaming pillar chased him, angling up like a writhing serpent climbing through the sky. *Void Step*, Jace thought again as he warped directly behind the Astral Demon, summoning his weapon to his hand and chopping again.

But those tendrils whipped up and caught his arm, holding his strike back, and the demon's whole torso shifted in place as he chopped into Jace's ribs with the axe, the orange flames exploding against Jace's armor, which took the brunt of the blow. But Jace still had the wind knocked out of him, and Dark Matter Mending set to work healing the damage.

Void Step, he thought—but he could not move.

Higher Potency with some Talent to prevent warping, Ollie said with panic. *Incoming!*

Reflexively, Jace did what The Ancients told him not to do. *Void Shield (Rank 6) [Reflecting]*. The grey-white barrier surged into place around him, annihilating the Astral Demon's axe as the voice from the helmet sounded confused—still garbled and incoherent. The torrent of flames that was chasing Jace reached him and would have incinerated him—but thanks to [Reflecting], the entire blast was repeated back upon his attacker, and they screeched in pain.

Jace shoved the remnant of the axe out of the way and stabbed the thing through the torso with his sword, feeling the golden flame surge through his body, licking around the grey-white of Void encompassing his body, and something odd happened. The white-grey of Void, the purple of Dark Matter oozing out of Jace's wounds as it healed him, and the golden flames all mingled together.

The hue started to shift between gold and a deep, dark green. Jace ripped the sword out of the Astral Demon, kicking him back and relying on the null-gravity effect of Dark Energy Mine to push the foe further.

The orange flames licked around the demon's body, healing it rapidly, and the remnants of the axe ignited with more of the powerful Psykinetic strength. Finally, the guttural noises became somewhat legible. "I'll pay you back for that."

The voice sent chills down Jace's spine, and the figure warped—not teleported, warped, just how he had with Void Step. The figure slammed the axe down onto Jace, the white-grey barrier of void rejecting and replicating the harm that would have been inflicted back onto the attacker, eliciting another howl of anger.

Jace stabbed up, skewering the Astral Demon through the head; and yet, the body continued to fight on, tentacles and tendrils stabbing up at him to no avail as his Void Shield deflected all.

Tibalt was ready to fight. He had seen Wraith fall down, the Astral Demon serving Valcrinox fly up to intercept . . . and then he lost track of the fight.

Aside from a few fragments of seconds where the two were separated, their movements were complete blurs that stupefied Tibalt.

And now, seeing Wraith just floating there as an Astral Demon slammed weapons into him over and over . . . he knew he stood no chance.

Not yet.

Tibalt snuck his way down the valley, following the stream of Souls. *I must get stronger to face him.*

Jace continued attacking the Astral Demon, watching as his energy continued to deplete. Strike after strike, blow after blow, continuing to use the (Vengeful) Specialization to empower his strikes at the cost of his own well-being, stacking burning Psykinetic effects upon themselves. Hero's Arena, the golden flames licking and searing, continued to impact and harm the foe he faced off against.

But this Astral Demon was Potency 10 and must have had massive reserves of energy of its own. Dozens upon dozens of Talents and Specializations—all centered around combat, it seemed, as even though Jace struck what should have been devastating blows, the wounds continued to heal, and his strikes did not seem to do as much harm as they should have. Even hitting the weak spot highlighted by Quinn resulted in very little actual, permanent harm.

The demon had continued to try and break through Jace's grey-white barrier of Void, which only Jace could actually see. And Jace's energy kept going down from the constant drain on resources. *At least I have the Emergency Battery still*, he thought as he continued to exchange blows with this foe, chopping off tentacles and wings that would grow back again.

Then, his Dark Energy Mine ran out, and he used a Void Step before impacting the ground to warp to safety. The demon above shrieked and screamed, "You will perish!" Raising its hands above its head, it manifested an enormous sphere of orange flame that crackled so brightly and with such intensity that Jace was forced to squint.

I already used Void when the Ancients said not to. A bit more won't hurt. Void Counter (Rank 10) [Storing]. He tried to use a Skill that would have stopped the Talent that was about to be unleashed.

But the Skill did nothing, and Ollie rapidly reminded him, *Only your Potency or lower for Void Counter and Arbiter's Anathema.*

Jace kicked himself for not remembering and just stood there as the blast continued to build above him. *I've got Void Shield active. No need to move. And this thing has to be worth a lot of Essence, so I don't want to use Void Skills to destroy it.*

And then his Void Shield vanished. The white-grey protecting him disappeared. And the blast from the creature shot down toward him. Jace couldn't dodge, he couldn't get past the torrent.

But Ollie was an Artificial Intelligence with processing power tied to Jace's improvements from all of his layered Skills and Talents, Quinn's Stratagems and enhancements, and his own refinements done behind the scenes. *Void Step (Rank 17).*

Jace's body warped out of the way of the blast—and it angled toward him in midair, tracking his move. But it bought Jace time that he needed. First, he tried Void Shield, only to receive a Cosmic System message.

[Error: Skill deactivated.]
[Time until lockdown expires: 9.78 seconds.]

Jace put the Crusader's Bastion between himself and the blast, willing it to its maximum size that would cover his whole body. He poured all of his energy into Dark Matter Mending, knowing that he was about to be seriously injured.

And he was right. The flames exploded into him, crashing into the shield, which, thanks to the (Retaliating) Specialization, caused a series of golden flame spikes to shoot up at the Astral Demon. But Jace did not see the harm inflicted, as he was left breathless while the flames sucked all oxygen from around him, the torrent of orange Psykinetic power surging into him and burning up his insides—the NICIF working overtime with Dark Matter Mending to keep him from dying on the spot.

The pain wasn't bad, but Jace assumed that was because either his nerves were already shot or Ollie had turned off his pain receptors. In any event, he saw the armor singeing and cracking, his sword heating up, and he could feel darkness press in as his energy drained ever closer to zero.

[Emergency Battery, activated!]

Jace's energy filled to full, and he continued to pour his power into Dark Matter Mending. Now, it was a matter of who had more energy. Him, or this Astral Demon.

I've got one more trick, Jace thought. *Counter this! Mountains, crush this fucker; Archmage's Admixture!*

Jace activated the spell-like Skill, granted to him by the Nethal, a magic-focused species whose World Pillars had graced him with their power. Magic that was funneled through The Cosmic System but was part of the building blocks of creation on the world of Nihilethelea. The mountains responded to Jace's Skill, and they moved—rocks flying from cliff faces, limned with the golden flames of his Psykinetics—and slammed into the creature from all sides.

But that's when Jace saw it. The white-grey of Void surrounded the Astral Demon. *How?!*

A message from The Ancients flicked across his vision.

[I warned you about using Void.]
[This is why.]
[This Astral Demon has a Talent that enables them to replicate anything they see.]
[Thankfully, once they disengage with you, they lose that capability.]
[We cannot have that anymore, can we?]
[Requesting permission to merge your innate Astral and Cosmic Systems.]

Jace felt the flames amplify, and his Dark Matter Mending with the NICIF were not able to keep up anymore. His energy was depleting faster than his foe's energy. *Yes!* Jace thought as he sent off the message back to The Ancient. He assumed the Quiet One.

Chapter Nineteen

Integration and Improvement

Jace saw the gold flames flicker, tinged with a deep, green light that flared outward and seemed to reinforce his shield. He could see the same gold-green flames licking out of his wounds as Dark Matter Mending redoubled, and he felt stronger. Reinvigorated.

Timer's up! Ollie shouted.

Void Shield (Rank 6) [Reflecting], Jace thought as he saw the white-grey of Void reappear around him and stop all harm—but at the edges of the white-grey, he saw the same mellow green color. *Dark Energy Mine (Rank 1). Detonate.* He became weightless and used his Soul Tether grapple line to ascend to the Astral Demon still raining down orange flame on him.

Ollie? How do we counter Void Shield? he thought to his Wayfinder.

Void clashing with Void might do it!

Jace briefly channeled Void Blade (Rank 17) [Rending], and in addition to the white-grey of Void, green flames licked along the blade as the crimson nebula clouds dripped. He slashed, watching with satisfaction as the Void Shield around his foe vanished and the blade cut deep. The figure's torrent of flames shut off, and it shrieked as it tried to attack Jace.

The Void Shield seemed to take damage, and Jace was shocked as he saw his energy depleted as the shield suffered impacts. With the torrent gone, however, he felt comfortable enough disabling the Void Shield—and despite the thrashing tendrils and tentacles slamming into him, Jace knew he had the upper hand. He let Void Blade deactivate, and the green flames on his blade vanished as they were replaced by only the golden glow of his Valiant Psykinetics.

The Astral Demon manifested more blades and tendrils, stabbing with wild abandon. Jace blocked about half of the strikes while the others slammed into him—his armor taking the brunt of the blows. But some hits slipped past his defenses or inside crevices in his armor—still cracked in places from the earlier flaming assault. He felt the pain from those strikes, and his energy dipped ever more constantly.

Yet still his foe kept fighting on. *Okay. Fuck this. I'm not losing here. Void Beam (Rank 1) [Limited Range].* Jace saw the tiny white-grey dot appear next to him, then it shifted a deep green color—and a torrent of green flames shot out, washing over the Astral Demon and causing it to shriek. *The fuck is going on?*

I am trying to figure it out! Ollie shouted. *Just keep going! We have him on the ropes!*

Jace slashed again, from the shoulder down into the center of the chest. With a scream of rage that briefly ignited the crimson nebula clouds to crackle around him, he sliced through the torso entirely. The Astral Demon tried to heal the wound, but Jace shoved his fist into the thing's chest and gripped its now-reconnected spine. *Templar's Smite!* He focused the column into a single point that would consume the creature.

The pillar of golden flame surged up from below, and Jace held his foe in the stream as they clawed at his armor, trying to get away. But Jace held firm, despite the blows raining on him from the tendrils and tentacles. He saw his energy depleting rapidly and knew that if he did not kill this thing with this Talent, he would have to retreat.

The Astral Demon persisted and continued to attack Jace, and he saw his energy drop lower and lower. But it was slowing, tiring. *Just a bit more!* Jace thought as he continued to funnel his energy into the Templar's Smite. *Come on!*

The demon stopped moving mid-attack and crumbled to dust and ash. An explosion of light-blue Souls enveloped Jace before shooting down to join the flow below, and the white-grey Essence left overflowed into him. He let his Skills and Talents all fade as he hung there, Soul Tether keeping him aloft, sucking in breaths.

Good job, Ollie said.

Thanks for covering me, Jace thought back.

A shimmering, pixelized aura appeared next to Jace, and the Quiet Ancient floated in air, fully shrouded by their cloak. "I warned you, did I not?"

"You . . . you did," Jace said, still out of breath.

The Ancient sighed, "I have updated your innate Cosmic System into the Astral System framework."

What does that mean? Ollie asked, his voice emanating from the armor.

"Effectively, Void still exists—but I have retextured it, to use a more familiar term. It is visible now. And all Void Skill uses cost you energy—even Void Shield, which normally costs a set amount of energy per second—instead, it functions like your past Dark Matter Shield that encompassed your whole form."

"Energy for each hit," Jace stated.

"That is right. This retexture will enable you to use Void without destroying the Astral Demon's form with nothingness."

Can we disable the green flame retexture? Ollie asked.

"I will disable it when I sign over your Astral System upon completion of our Mission," The Ancient replied. "I want you to understand this, Wraith . . . Void is potent. So much so that even The Ancients rarely meddled with it despite having a full comprehension of it. We cannot let knowledge of its manipulation become widespread."

"Thanks for giving me the means to still use all my Skills," Jace replied, feeling some genuine gratitude. "I'm not limited in my loadout anymore."

"True. In your Universe, this function will automatically disable." There was some amount of regret in the voice. "I know you have struggled with being manipulated in the past, and I apologize that I had to manipulate your innate Cosmic System like this—but the risk is too great. You saw what an Astral Demon who could duplicate your Skill was capable of . . . imagine if every demon could use Void?"

The idea sent a chill through Jace, and he nodded. "I understand."

"Good." The Ancient gestured to the mountains surrounding them. "A Layer filled with ancient barrows and tunnels leading to grand halls. Here, let me give you the Mission for this Layer . . ."

[Mission: Consolidate control over Layer 5 to Demon Lord Kalec.]
[Reward: Mythic (Gear) Infusion.]
[Sender: The Ancients.]

Jace felt slightly confused and spoke rapidly. "Why go up to Mythic now?"

The Ancient shrugged. "Why not? I have heard your conversations with your internal AI."

I have a name, you know. It is Oliver! The Wayfinder sounded quite nettled.

"Sorry. Oliver. To answer your question more succinctly, I know you seek to acquire a Divine rarity Infusion . . . and I am curious to see what that will look like when utilized by you. You have two Mythic already, and Infusions being held onto by Astral Demons is already rare." The Ancient waved a hand. "Farewell." He vanished into a pixelated cloud.

Jace lowered himself to the ground and could hear the slight, rushing sighs of the stream of Souls flowing next to him. Then, a whole rush of Astral System messages, seemingly suppressed, came flooding to him.

[Congratulations on entering a new Layer!]
[You may choose to specialize your Class by performing a Class Transmutation!]
[Base Class = Purifier.]

[Options available:]
[Justiciar—expand upon your offensive capabilities. Leads to further offensive Transmutations.]
[Bastion—expand upon your defensive capabilities. Leads to further defensive Transmutations.]
[Lightbringer—expand upon your support capabilities. Leads to further support Transmutations.]

"Justiciar," Jace stated with confidence at choosing a damaging path of progression.

[Class Transmutation confirmed.]

Jace looked around. "Well, time to find this Kalec. Holy Hunt." The golden line shot off to his left, down the small berm, joining the river of Souls. Jace began trudging along the path, wanting to go slow to let his energy refill—not looking for any fight anytime soon.

We have 30,000 Essence now, after killing that Astral Demon, Ollie commented.

"That's what, six levels?"

Yup!

"Then I guess it's time to level up. Let's do it. What we had discussed." He smiled. "But since we can use Void now . . . let's see if we can get a Specialization or two that incorporate The Cosmic System into the Astral System.

I will do my best. Here we go!

[You have leveled up!]
[You have chosen Specialization of Existing Talent!]
[Talent Name: Valiant Crusader's Might.]
[Specialization Name: Voidbound.]
[Effect: Incorporates the user's {Void Blade} at maximum {Rank} and with all {Skill Evolutions} applied.]

[Talent Name: Crusader's Bastion.]
[Specialization Name: Resonating.]
[Effect: The linked Talent causes a temporary stunning effect to apply to those who strike the shield.]
[Talent Name: Hero's Arena.]
[Specialization Name: Wrathbound.]
[Effect: Incorporates the user's {Aura of Wrath} at maximum {Rank}, extending the radius to match that of the linked Talent, and with all {Skill Evolutions} applied.]
[Talent Name: Holy Hunt.]
[Specialization Name: Branding.]
[Effect: Incorporates the user's {Void Brand} at maximum {Rank}, applying the {Skill} to the marked target.]
[Talent Name: Indomitable Will.]
[Specialization Name: Dark Matter Binding.]
[Effect: Warning: Not linked to Talent by default, must be manually activated alongside Talent. Incorporates the user's {Dark Matter Mending} at maximum {Rank}, and with all {Skill Evolutions} applied.]
[Talent Name: Templar's Smite.]
[Specialization Name: Cosmic.]
[Effect: Warning: Not linked to Talent by default, must be manually activated alongside Talent. Enables the user to infuse their Templar's Smite with {Void Beam}, and apply any singular {Skill Evolution}.]

Name: Jace Seren (Potency 5)
Emotion [Class Level]: Valiant [Justiciar 47]
Talent [Specialization]: Astral Adaptation, Astral Translation, Valiant Crusader's Might [Burning] [Vengeful] [Poised] [Unstoppable] [Bracing] [Voidbound], Crusader's Bastion [Retaliating] [Reinforcing] [Grounding] [Redoubt] [Spiked] [Resonating], Hero's Arena [Aura] [Incinerating] [Vexing] [Bolstering] [Suppressing] [Wrathbound], Indomitable Will [Zealous] [Intimidating] [Inviolable] [Enduring] [Ameliorating] [Dark Matter Binding], Templar's Smite [Spear] [Blast] [Lingering] [Challenging] [Inferno] [Cosmic], Holy Hunt [Marked] [Bursting] [Authoritative] [Provoking] [Inciting]

[Branding], Purifying Edge [Cleansing] [Searing] [Purging] [Sanctifying] [Terminating]
Essence: 0
Infusions: x2 Mythic (Specialization)
Gear: <TPSB>, (Convergent Edge) [Ruination 1] Hero's Blade, (Explorer's Embrace / Beacon) Paragon Armor, (Prosthetic Savant) Astral Appendages, (Draconic Sovereign) Arbiter's Sight, (Anathema) Astral Sleeve, (Reinforced) Psycrystal Lattice, (Pinnacle) NICIF-EP, (Restoring) Flame of Valor, Retribution Carbine (20 shots / battery)

Jace could see the constantly active Hero's Arena take on a slight green tinge as it billowed around him like a cloak, crackling crimson nebula clouds storming within the flames of gold. *That is pretty neat,* he thought. *Always having Aura of Wrath active with (Voidflame Vestment).* He felt confident despite his close brush with a harsh combat just a few minutes before.

It seems like they are throwing their eggs into our basket, Ollie commented.

I mean, I am the person they chose to have kill off evil Demon Lords. I don't blame them for wanting to kit me out. Jace smiled under the helm as he continued his trek along the stream of Souls.

Valcrinox felt it. The pulsating through the Layers at the death of a powerful Astral Demon. One of his, as confirmed by the notification message he received through the Astral System.

And now I have one less among my ranks, he thought with a bitter smile on his face. The smile was not of satisfaction, or joy, but rather a panic response. *A Potency 10 demon, defeated by this Dreamer?*

And Valcrinox did not have enough Universal Matter to do what he desired. His forces were unable to bring him what he required. *I thought that one of my minions would be enough*, he thought as he stay put on his throne. "I need volunteers," he stated as he tapped the armrests of his chair.

Several Astral Demons stepped forth. All Potency 10. All capable of great and terrifying deeds.

"Wraith slew our brother. One was not enough. How many wish to go after him and seek his demise?"

Howls and screams answered Valcrinox, and he felt a giddy sensation rise up in him that washed away the panic. *I have nothing to worry about. Wraith handled one Potency 10 demon. But what about ten? Fifty?* He gestured to the film leading to the Layer above, some distance away from his citadel of madness. "Go up, and fight Wraith. Kill this Dreamer."

His minions flew off, and Valcrinox watched them depart . . . then his smile soured as several began to ascend, only to falter and come back down. He slammed his fist on the arm rest. "Damnit!" he shouted. *It is too soon; the call of the depths is too great. I need to call in favors, get others to slow Wraith until my brethren are able to shake off the call and rise up once more.*

Chapter Twenty

Hall of the Demon Lord

Jace followed the rivulet of Souls until it became a massive, torrential river—coursing its way down the mountain in a huge rush. Far off in the distance, down the massive, sloping mountains, he could see the far-off film of the next Layer.

But the golden line of his Holy Hunt led him into a crevice in the mountains. He went down the corridor, keeping his Crusader's Bastion active and sword in hand. The blade flickered with gold and green flame as crimson nebula clouds dripped from the [Rending] Skill Evolution. It felt good, not being impeded anymore.

Why do you think The Ancients waited so long to implement this change?

I have a bit of information on that in the background here, Ollie stated. *Seems that the innate Cosmic System was capable of doing it, but your body would not have survived the alteration. Potency 5 was just what you needed to reach.*

They could've done it before I went down to Layer 5 and fought that thing, Jace thought.

Perhaps they were gauging if it was necessary or not, Ollie replied. *It seemed like something they were loath to do.*

Fair enough, Jace thought back as they reached the end of a ravine. The golden line shot to his left, into the mouth of a cave that was slightly taller than him. Thankfully, he could see just fine, and entered the dark interior, his sword illuminating the path before him. Stalactites and stalagmites pushed up and down, respectively, from the stone of the mountain, a deep basalt grey color that was punctuated with occasional black streaks.

Following the line of Holy Hunt, he continued deeper and deeper, walking for hours as he followed the winding caverns. The air began to get hotter, and he could see a faint, orange glow off in the distance around the bend of a corner. Going around that curve, he was hit with a rush of hot air and saw a massive lake of lava. It reminded him of the volcano tile he was on in Nihilethelea, the oppressive heat sapping all moisture from the air and making his breaths come shallowly.

The golden line shot off across a large bridge that led over the lava; otherwise, the chamber was empty. Just a pool of liquid flame and bubbling magma and the stone span across it, with a single pillar holding up the center. Jace cautiously walked forward, placing a Dark Energy Mine on his chest just in case the floor suddenly collapsed from some trap.

A voice shook the room. It came from a tunnel on the opposite side of the bridge. A deep, rumbling bass. "You are the Wraith?" it inquired.

"Just Wraith," Jace replied. "Mind if I come in?"

"By all means. Please, come into the sanctum."

Jace walked forward over the rest of the magma chamber and into the deeper tunnel. After a short series of turns, the room opened up, and he was standing at the threshold of a huge, hollow space. He could see all the way up to a small circle, a pinprick in the roof of the mountain above. All around the outside, dozens of buildings were carved into the stonework.

Astral Demons were up on the concentric carved rings of the inside-a-mountain city, all of whom looked even more distinctly humanoid than Esmerelda on the Layer above. Jace assumed it was because they had followed the path of refinement further.

At the center of the area, he saw another small ship landing pad—but no Dreamers or their ships were present. *Must be because of the Astral Demon that was waiting to ambush me*, he thought. Following the golden line, he continued through the massive cavern—garnering stares from the demons up above. Ignoring their gazes, he walked up to a colossal pair of stone doors—just hinged slightly ajar.

The room that greeted him was not something he expected. A long, brazier-filled hallway, the flames flickering with a deep, umbral black that still lit the surrounding environment. Chandeliers, carved from the stone on the ceiling, hung down—suspended and filled with the same black flames to provide illumination from above.

At the far end, seated on a massive dais, was something he had seen before. Or rather, it looked like something he had seen before. Similar to the dragon he had encountered on Nihilethelea but mixed with the Leviathans from Harkon Secundus. A winding, sinuous tail that coiled around the base of the dais, a pair of massive wings furled against the back, and a head the size of a semitruck, resting. A single huge red eye gazed at Jace.

"Well now. You are about what I expected. You look the part of a Bearer of the Mantle of Burden."

"I assume you're Kalec?" Jace asked.

The figure chuckled, and the deep bass resonated through the entire room, shaking Jace's bones. "Yes. I am Kalec, the Demon Lord who rules here, a haven and refuge for those who chose the path of refinement."

"But you didn't choose that path," Jace commented.

The figure shook their head. "No. I meddled in both sides of the evolutionary path for my kind. We were visited, eons upon eons ago, by a creature that looked like this. Called itself a star dragon, from a Universe—punched its way right through the first Layer. It was a powerful Dreamer, and I was inspired by its form." Kalec made a pleased sound. "Now, you are here to deal with the other Demon Lords on this Layer."

"Yes," Jace replied as he walked toward the figure and pointed to a corner of the dais. "Mind if I sit?"

"By all means."

Jace plopped himself down, reached into his TPSB, and pulled out some survival rations and his canteen. "So," he said as he ripped open one of the pouches and his helmet receded. "Tell me about this Layer."

"You came down from the Layer above, at the farthest east end of the Layer. It runs some distance to the west, where the hole leading to the Layer below lies. Souls coalesce from the Layer above, drift down akin to snow, and then rush in a streaming river to their next step of the journey to the Nethershift." He rumbled out as he spoke, shifting his bulk slightly. "There are many mountain strongholds, much like mine."

"This place got a name?" Jace asked in between bites.

"Kalec's Hall." Kalec laughed a haughty laugh. "Now, there are three other Demon Lords on this Layer. They are located to the north, west, and south. I will give you a map." Kalec lifted a massive talon into the air, and Jace saw a series of screens appear above them.

Got the localized map, Ollie stated as he pulled up the screen in front of Jace. *Three-thousand miles across from east to west, fifteen-hundred from top to bottom. We won't be traveling as fast thanks to the terrain.*

"Koris is to the north, Vremiv to the west, and Daksha south of the next Layer's entrance."

Jace nodded. "What are they like?"

Kalec sighed. "They were part of the second wave of Astral Demons, like myself, behind Valcrinox and his ilk." He eyed Jace warily. "Which, you should be aware, demons on this Layer are seeking to claim the multiple bounties placed upon you."

"I can handle them," Jace replied quickly. "Now, the Demon Lords?"

"They, too, took inspiration from that star dragon in their path of evolution. I cannot give you much information aside from that, as their Talent progression is a mystery to me. We demons do not often give out that information."

Jace finished off a few survival meals and put the trash into the TPSB. He also quickly checked his inventory to ensure he had all of his Equipment ready to go. "Thanks for the intel. I'll be off."

"One more thing," Kalec commented. "Before you go. There is a Vault, here, behind my dais. You are welcome to attempt to clear it. I am sure a Relic will assist you in your endeavors."

Jace grinned and willed his helmet to re-emerge and cover his head. "Thank you for your hospitality."

"The least I can do for the one who will be dealing with my brethren."

Tibalt had scarfed, scraped, devoured, and hid from other Astral Demons. *Other demons?* he thought in a single moment of clarity. *I no longer consider myself a Dreamer Demon? Pah.* He did not care for labels. He was strong, and yet not strong enough.

He had seen a Potency 10 demon on equal footing with Wraith, who could not have reached Potency 10 with only Essence fueling his ascension. No, there was something else. Some hidden technology or other means of empowerment that Wraith had access to that let him bypass the limitations of his form.

I just keep consuming, keep devouring. Until I reach Potency 10. Then, I get into this Valcrinox's army. Work my way up his chain of command. Show my ruthlessness. When Wraith gets there, I can let him weaken Valcrinox. Kill the survivor. Take my place as the strongest Demon Lord ever!

"Ah, Tibalt, such a shame."

He wheeled about, looking for the source of the noise as he rooted around in the river of Souls. "Who is there?" he growled.

"You have fallen far," a hooded figure said from nearby. "You have pursued your goal greedily and with evil in your heart. Your Karma Coefficient is not looking good."

Tibalt ran toward the figure, only to be stopped by a wall of invisible energy that he bounced from. "Who are you?" he sneered.

"An interested party," the male voice replied. "There is a reason why Astral Demons do not gorge themselves as you have. Pushing your evolution too quickly, before your body has a chance to adjust, can cause drastic and severe consequences."

Tibalt snarled, "What do you know of it?"

The figure laughed. "I helped design your Astral System. I know it inside and out. You are a Dreamer Demon, so the effects are not as apparent . . . but if you keep this pace up, then it will happen."

"Why do you care?" Tibalt growled out as his hunched-over form heaved with anger and a desire to rip this figure apart.

The entity shrugged. "I am just letting you know. You are not beyond salvation, yet. You can redeem yourself by doing something for me."

Tibalt let out a barking laugh. "Oh? What's that?"

"Help the Bearer of the Mantle of Burden."

Tibalt frowned. "Who?"

"Wraith, as you call him."

"Never!" Tibalt screamed in fury. "He cost me my empire!"

"Suit yourself."

"I will become a Demon Lord like no other! A Dreamer Demon Lord. No, an emperor! The first one! Every Layer will fall under my will!"

The figure shrugged. "I gave you an offer, you rejected it. So be it. Your fate is your own." The figure vanished in a cloud of grey mist.

Tibalt roared out in fury and dove back into the river of Souls, gobbling them up as he consumed them down into his roiling gullet, feeling them scream and beg for release. *I need more!*

The Loud Ancient walked into his partner's room. "How did it go?"

"Well enough," the Quiet Ancient replied. "He rejected the offer, as expected. I do not think there is anything else we can do without violating our oaths. Wraith is on his own now."

The Loud One leaned against the wall. "Why did you choose to alter Wraith's functionality of Void? Why not just lock it off entirely?"

"We want him to succeed," the Quiet Ancient muttered. "Locking away his Cosmic System Skills would not be conducive to that goal."

"And you don't think that was meddling too much? Too much direct interference?"

"No," the Quiet Ancient replied. "If it was, the Council would have punished me already for merely having the thought in my mind."

"Why green?"

"My favorite color. Plus, it contrasts nicely with gold."

Chapter Twenty-One

A Foreign Goddess

Jace smiled. "Thanks. I'll do that." He headed past the platform and down the small passage behind it. Descending the stairs, he found a Vault door in a tunnel like all the rest he had encountered. Touching the stone, he was sucked through and landed on his feet in another all-too-familiar Relic chamber.

Drawing his sword, he smiled as the weapon ignited automatically with Void—manifesting as a green flame, the crimson nebula clouds of the [Rending] damage-over-time effect, and the golden flames of his Psykinetic power. Channeling a slight amount of energy, he manifested his Crusader's Bastion, and at that moment, the Astral System message appeared that denoted the start of the challenge.

> [Vault Challenge—Activated.]
> [Defeat another Universe's strongest being.]

Sorry, what? Jace thought as the world warped and shifted around him. He was standing on a vast, grassy plain. Before him, a woman stood. A woman with deep, black armor that encompassed her form, save for the helmet; that was gone, and instead, a shock of silvery-white hair cascaded down her back. A pair of elegant horns grew out of her head, and her sword looked like a laser sword—but ablaze with blue lava.

She shouted something in a language that he did not understand, and Ollie commented, *I wonder if she was summoned here, or if this is a shade of her like that version of Yroshnak we fought?*

Jace lowered his weapon and activated Templar's Smite, with the (Cosmic) Infusion. A geyser of gold and green flames erupted from under the woman—but she was surrounded by a glittering sphere of opalescent energy that fluctuated, striating.

Finally, his translation kicked in. "Magic? Fight with a blade, coward!" She ran forward—at a speed that rivaled Jace's own—but his Shattered Limits did trigger, so he knew she was on his footing. Her sword slammed into his shield, and the lava exploded with a liquid fury as Jace felt the ground buckle under him—the dirt and stone blowing away as the grassland was flattened from the force of the strike.

She danced backward and held her sword out to her side—the weapon shifting shape into a spear that she clutched before whirling around in a flourish to point at him. "Show me your might! Show your worth to a goddess!"

Goddess? I've killed gods. Jace rushed forward and slashed down with his Hero's Blade, a vertical chop that she deflected with the haft of her spear, performing a quick spin-kick with a clawed, draconic foot that Jace caught on his shield. The impact sent him back a foot, but he kept a strong stance and shoved back with the shield before slashing again with his sword. The woman deflected the strike once more, but Jace's weapon caught the edge of her forearm, nicking it—that was enough for the gold and green flames to begin spreading as the crimson nebula of miasmic bleeding crept its way along her arm.

She backed off for a brief moment, a green aura appearing around her before the flames vanished. "Impressive. No holding back, then." She chanted something at a speed that Jace could barely keep up with, but every instinct screamed at him to move. *Void Step*, he thought.

And not a second too soon, as he warped behind her, the landscape he had been standing on erupted in a cataclysmic inferno of bright blue lava that surged skyward before falling down in a goopy, devouring flood. She whipped around and grinned, her blue spear shifting to a deep black, covered with sparkles. The weapon altered shape as well—a short sword and shield.

Jace wasted no time; he moved in and slashed at her. She blocked, and struck back. Jace blocked, and attacked as well. The two exchanged blows back and forth—Jace not suffering harm, but each blocked hit of hers dealing damage back to her with the (Redoubt) and (Resonating) Infusions. She was slowing down while Jace was still good on his energy; he couldn't help but shake the feeling she wasn't close to being done.

His feeling was justified a split second later as his [Danger-Sense] screamed at him to move. Using a Void Step, he retreated a short distance.

Reality in front of him vanished. Just as if Void was used—a thirty-foot cube in front of this woman vanished. Air, flames from Jace's Hero's Arena, dirt—total annihilation. She held the sword up and smiled as it shifted shape once more into a massive war hammer. "This is destruction. This is annihilation." She sprouted wings from her back—big, scaled wings tipped with white spikes—and rushed forward across the opening.

You think that's impressive? Jace used a Void Beam (Rank 1) [Limited Range], watching the torrent of white-grey shift to green fire from his palm as it surged out and slammed into the woman—but it did nothing to her, and she continued to fly toward him. Time seemed to slow as Jace dodged to his left—getting his shield in the way.

Her weapon cut through the shield like it wasn't there and into his armor, then his shoulder. He could feel a dry sensation and, glancing down, saw his body actively disintegrating—sending his mind into a moment of panic as he was being destroyed atom by atom from the wound.

Indomitable Will (Dark Matter Binding). Jace's arm began to return as a surge of green flames geyser out of the wound, mending the injury. But he had to use another Void Step to dodge another swing from the annihilating edge. Standing now eighty feet away, he had a moment to catch his breath.

On the plus side, Ollie said, *thanks to Eidolon's Persistence, you will suffer fifty percent less harm from that effect.*

The thought didn't bring Jace any comfort, and he reactivated his Crusader's Bastion, also activating Void Shield (Rank 6) [Reflecting] and channeling a (Vengeful) strike into his arms.

The woman sprinted across the grass at him, wings flapping behind her to grant more speed. Jace rushed forward to meet her on equal footing, slamming his shield forward. She put the base of her hammer's shaft into the center of the shield, then used the impact to vault over him. He swiped up with a slice from his sword and neatly cut her across the stomach—viscous blue blood dropping onto his shield, sizzling.

She stumbled on the opposite side of him and her eyes glimmered with a pure, black darkness. "Nimble, aren't you? Then no more holding back!" She vanished from sight.

Jace looked around for her but couldn't find her. That's when he saw it—she was on the horizon—massive in stature, holding a bow with an arrow of pure, condensed blackness, covered with shining sparkles of some ancient elegance that once graced the tapestry of creation. She loosed the arrow at him, and Jace used another Void Shield, this time with the (Wall) infusion, creating a barrier in front of him.

What happens when annihilation meets Void? he thought as he kept his Crusader's Bastion planted directly in front of him. He could hear a roaring in his ears, see the projectile coming for the barrier—and it slammed directly into the fortification. Both forces zapped each other out of existence, and her silhouette vanished from the horizon.

Jace's [Danger Sense] kicked off directly behind him, and he dodged to his left, parrying a second stab after avoiding the first. The woman was now holding a pair of daggers, and she circled him like a predator. "Impressive," she muttered with an elegant-yet-gruff high-pitched voice. "You survived annihilation—few can claim that honor. Where are you from?"

Jace didn't answer, not wanting to say a thing to this construct, or person, or whoever it was that would possibly jeopardize his Universe. Instead, he responded with a series of hacking slices, battering her meager defenses as she barely got the dagger in the way of parrying the strikes.

Dismissing the Bastion, he reached into his TPSB and pulled out four throwing knives, instilling them with Dark Energy Mine and detonating them. Weightlessness overtook both of them, and Jace used a Void Step to get under her, prone on the ground. He kicked up—propelling her into the sky, and then he planted his feet and jumped up after her, slashing over and over again while she was off footing and fighting in unfamiliar terrain—zero-gravity.

He scored several hits across her body, the armor catching his sword but allowing for enough of an impact to impart the damage-over-time effects of the three different Psykinetic flames, the green flames of shrouded Void, and the [Rending] nebula. She muttered something and vanished in a glimmer of blue.

Turning around in midair, Jace brought his shield around, blocking the massive hammer swing that sent him flying up into the sky. *Dismiss*, he thought as he disabled the dark energy mine and used his Soul Tether to remain up in the air.

She had somehow moved behind him and swung at him like a batter, now flapping her wings. Her voice rang out to him, "You do know how to fight. I always wondered what types of threats other Universes would bring to my reality." Her weapon vanished, and she landed on the ground. "I do not concede, as that would end this encounter . . . instead, let us talk."

Jace used a Void Step to return to the ground but did not put his weapon away nor deactivate Skills or Talents. "Who are you?"

She smiled. "A goddess. I rule a world in an alternate Universe. One that was sealed off from the Astral Verge by my power." She held up her hand, and a glittering orb of prismatic light appeared. "These Vaults sometimes invite people from different Universes." She closed her hand, and the orb vanished. "Tell me; in your Universe, how do you rank against others in power?"

"I'm at the top," Jace replied. "Tier 10."

She giggled. "A ranking system? How quaint. Also, very video-game-esque." She sighed, "You are the top in power of your Universe, and I am the top of mine. Two equals, in a sense."

"Does your Universe use a System?" Jace asked. "Like that in the Astral Verge?"

"No," she replied with a cool, calm collectedness. "We have magic. A whole Universe full of mana, actually—think of that as fuel to a vehicle, but replace the vehicle with spells." Her eyes narrowed ever-so-slightly. "Astral System, where do you rank?"

No harm in telling another Universe's strongest power if they are sealed off from the Verge otherwise, Ollie thought to him.

"Potency 5. Halfway to the top."

She whistled slightly. "Impressive. And to think I was only barely holding back against you. Maybe I should reconsider my Universe being connected to the Layers."

"Don't," Jace replied with vehement hatred. "Just don't. It's not worth it. Souls eaten by Astral Demons?" He shook his head. "I'd give up this power in an instant if it meant that my Universe was fully closed off and a closed loop again, like before The Ancients arrived."

She nodded. "I will take your warning to heart, then. Now." She walked up to him, grabbed his flaming blade with seemingly no issue, and set it against her neck. "I concede, worthy foe. Thank you for letting me test my mettle."

"I'm Wraith," Jace said.

She smiled. "Call me Lyn—"

She was cut off as she vanished in a glimmer of sparks, and the room returned around Jace. The crystal representing the Relic floated above the pedestal, and Jace also saw an Ancient standing next to it. The Loud One, judging by the voice. "Hi! Well, you just met someone from another Universe!"

"Who was she?" Jace asked as he sheathed his sword and let his Skills and Talents fade.

"A goddess that controls her whole Universe," he replied. "Now! Enough of that. You have a task to complete."

"I'll be on my way once I get that Relic," Jace replied as he walked over and made to grab the Relic.

But the Ancient put a hand on his forearm. "A word of caution," he said cheerfully but with a hint of malice. "We cannot interfere much more. We are already pushing the limits of what we are permitted to do as is when it comes to being involved. Expect us to be silent until your task is complete."

"I understand," Jace said as he grabbed the Relic crystal. It was a circular shape that felt comfortable in his palm and was easily gripped by wrapping his fingers around the outside edges. "Thanks for the heads-up." The Ancient dipped his head and vanished in a cloud of pixels. Jace held the Relic up. "I don't think I have any Equipment that can be merged."

The object unraveled in his hand, like a diamond being cut, and began to slowly shrink in size and grow in refinement, leaving him with a small crystal in his palm.

[You have acquired a Relic of the Ancients.]
[Relic Capacity Detected.]
[Relic converted to Relic Upgrade Matrix.]

Jace frowned. "What? We have a cap?"

Try pushing it against one of your existing Relics, Ollie suggested.

Jace drew his sword with the other hand and touched the crystal to the hilt. He saw it sink into the weapon, and the sword blazed with violet light before it crystallized, extended slightly in length, and then refocused to a longer, more elegant version of his prior weapon.

[Relic Equipped.]
[Divine Revenge.]
[Amplifies depth of emotion related to the Valiance Emotion Source. While holding the blade, the user treats their Emotion Source as active at the maximum level, enabling Psykinetic use even when not acting appropriately to the emotion.]

Almost instantly, all of Jace's passive Talents surged to their highest degree of Emotion Source empowerment. The Hero's Arena expanded the full thirty feet, filled with crackling gold and green flames along with pops of crimson nebula clouds. *That is quite useful*, Jace thought as he recalled several encounters thus far where his Hero's Arena had been less effective because he was not acting in a way aligned to his Emotion Source or [Class] identity.

That is pretty good, Ollie said with excitement.

Jace was about to reply, but he was sucked out of the Vault and landed on his feet. Sheathing the sword, he headed up the stairs. *Now we have to move onto the hunt*, he thought to his Wayfinder.

Just means more Essence.

Xero gasped as he woke up in a bed. Not a virtual reality; an actual bed. He tried accessing the interface for the artificial reality, but nothing happened. *Okay . . . let's try The Cosmic System.*

As soon as the words crossed his mind, the black and gold interface appeared. He felt ecstatic, and remembered what had happened. Doctor Restra had confirmed his completion of therapy. He felt down his torso and smiled. *Yeah, this is real. My body. My real body. Or a sleeve, at least.*

He stood up, testing his legs and feeling them fresh and well-rested. "Xera?" he asked aloud as he took in the space. He was in a room surrounded by windows with a small kitchen on the far end and a hallway leading to a series of computer banks and holographic screens. Xero saw the gelatinous mass of Wayfinders, floating about and making adjustments to various holographic panels.

Xera walked around a corner in that hallway, a smile plastered across her face. She ran forward and hugged him. "Welcome to Khrox!"

Xero laughed aloud. "You named it after our pet?"

She nodded enthusiastically. "The one we snuck into academy." She winced, and gripped her temples. "Ouch," she muttered.

Xero frowned. "It's progressing that rapidly."

Xera nodded. "It hurts . . . but I'll manage. Jace will go fast." She lowered her voice, and he barely picked up her whispering, "He has to. I don't want to be judged and annihilated."

Xero sighed, "Why not another sleeve swap?"

"Done it," Xera replied. "Over and over again. I get the same result. You know we can only do that a certain number of times before it becomes untenable."

I do, Xero thought. Then, an idea popped into his head. "I'm conscious. Let's put you on ice. Total stasis field. Prevent any further degradation."

"Then . . . I wouldn't be able to help my Signers."

Xero smirked. "Introduce me to them. I'll take over while this Jace gets what we need."

Chapter Twenty-Two

Meet the New Boss

Xero finished the last few touches on updating the penthouse apartment in Khrox. The topmost tower. Xera was next to him, her body twitching every few seconds as her degradation showed ever more drastically.

Xero looked over to the stasis pod nearby. *I've already set it up*, he thought. *Once the handoff is done, Xera goes in, and she'll be safe until we get this whole Soul judging device sorted.*

Xera looked at him with a smile, her voice slightly glitching with staggered words. "Y-you r-ready to meet th-them?"

"Yes," Xero replied as he pulled up the interface. Xera reached over him and, with shaky hands, touched a panel, assigning Tech Support status and the current overseeing admin credentials to Xero. Then, she pulled her hand back.

Xero cleared his throat. "Personal redirect. Access Code E56745-XY-5R3." The console before him shifted and showed the entire display for the topmost access of The Cosmic System. He pulled up the contact list and information for Quinn Cipher. "Commlink open," he muttered.

There was a brief crackle, then he heard a woman's voice. "Xera. What do you need?"

Xera spoke, "Br-bring ever-every-o-one on . . . a call."

Quinn's voice immediately shifted to one of panic. "Fuck. Okay, yeah, give me a second."

Xero watched as Quinn's Cosmic System, the one innate to her being, reached out and accessed the various nodes that would enable connection with the voidlight tether, and observed her skillful manipulation of the subspace relay to contact other Dark Between Stars Signers within the Universe.

"We're all here," Quinn said.

"What's this about?" Greg asked.

Xera spoke quickly, her voice stilling from its stutters and malfunctions for a brief moment. "I'm going into stasis. My brother is taking my place. Meet Xero."

"You okay, Xera?" Priam asked.

"No, she is not," Xero replied, his voice cutting through all others. "I am Xero'tal Pen'arkon, co-creator of The Cosmic System's framework. Xera . . . well . . . " He looked over at his sister and smiled softly and with warmth to reassure her. "She is having problems with her brain and re-sleeving. She has to go into stasis until the Grand Design is completed."

Jace spoke, and his voice sounded neutral and disinterested in Xera's plight. "Quinn, the contract you facilitated between Xera and me—that listed her, or the overseeing administrator?"

"The admin," Quinn replied.

Jace sounded satisfied. "Good. Then the deal is still in place. Don't get comfy, Xero. I'll be back with the Karma Judgement Matrix soon enough."

Xero sighed. "Good. I was never management material." He chuckled. "Let's just get this loop closed. Your deal is still in place, the contract stands. Don't worry about me trying to take things over." He looked over to Xera once more. "I just want my sister to be okay."

There was an underlying tone of sympathy when Jace replied, "I understand."

Dee's voice came over the comms, "Does this mean we are going to be getting more missions to blow stuff up?"

Xera spoke, and her voice was clear and had stopped glitching. "No. Not in our Universe. However, mercenaries that Jace encountered are going to be visiting the mountain below our Universe. All my available Signers—Greg, Missy, Dee, Ree, Priam—"

Greg interrupted, "When did Dee's sister become an Aspirant?"

"Recently," Dee said.

Xera continued as if uninterrupted, "You five will be heading down to talk to them. Gather intel from them. And we will be extending The Architect's Gate to encompass the whole mountain, multiple webs within each other. On Jace's next visit, we'll establish those." She let out a grunt of pain and gripped Xero's arm, her voice glitching out again. "I—I—I n-n-need t-to—"

Xero got up and grabbed her, firm but gentle, guiding her over to the stasis pod, and lifted her up before setting her into the device. "Sleep, sister. I will handle things." He shut the lid and let his hand linger on the top as the device initiated—freezing Xera in a single, isolated point of spacetime. A true stasis, keeping her locked in that singular moment. He went back to the console and sighed, "Xera is sleeping."

Missy spoke, "Hope she gets better!"

"She will," Xero replied. "But she needs to die. No one has re-sleeved as much as she has. Back when we had a closed-loop Universe, it wasn't an issue. But now?" He sighed. "Jace, status update?"

"Heading to kill some Astral Demon Lords on this Layer," he replied.

Shhiv spoke, "Anything I'll need to do, Xero? More stuff to Rune Carve?"

Xero looked at the massive to-do list Xera had left behind. *Little Miss Lists*, he thought as he recalled the name he used to call her at academy. "Yes," he said softly. "We have work to do."

Jace continued his trek through the mountains. It was oddly peaceful, the stream of Souls sighing alongside him almost like a rush of actual water. That peace was shattered as he heard the sound of something headed toward him—something large, and lumbering. Several of them.

Drawing his sword, he activated Crusader's Bastion and waited patiently for the foe to show themselves. [Danger-Sense] activated, and he knelt as he angled his shield at an upward angle. A massive boulder, coated with a shimmering, blue Psykinetic power, slammed into the shield before ricocheting up and to the side. Jace barely registered the impact, and he stood up. "Seriously? Rocks?" he asked aloud.

Another boulder came at him from the opposite side, and he simply side-stepped the massive rock as it went sailing by him. "Ollie, task the drone with overwatch."

<u>*On it*</u>, his Wayfinder replied. <u>*Sending it up.*</u>

Jace saw the small camera feed on his HUD expand as the drone that had been quietly following him ascended. In the crags on either side of the stream, the drone tagged Astral Demons. They were easily the size of that Yroshnak Demon Lord he had fought in the arena Vault encounter—twelve feet high at the shoulder, massive sets of arms going down either side of the torso, and a single pair of legs.

Huh. Almost like trolls from some magic worlds. We fought something like them on Nihilethelea, on the glacier tile.

Jace ran up the slope to his side, dodging more boulders flung his way. When he got to the top, he could see the demon with his eyes, and the body glimmered with blue Psykinetic power, a shroud around its form. The thing lifted a massive rock and slammed it forward.

Jace caught the blow on his shield, pushing the strike aside as he returned with a sword swing of his own. The gold and green flame, along with the crimson miasmic nebula clouds, began to spread from the wound. And the blue Psykinetics of the creature seemed to hold it at bay, preventing the spread.

Oh look! Regeneration Talent.

Purifying Edge should have disabled all of their Talents on hit, Jace thought as he brought his shield back up and blocked another blow, this time from a large mace that slammed into his bulwark and transferred some force through to his body. [Danger-Sense] went off from behind, and he used a Void Step to get behind the astral demon as another rock came in from across the small ravine, slamming into the foe he was fighting as the friendly fire made a tremendous impact that cratered part of the demon's face.

Perhaps the demon reactivated its Talent immediately, Ollie theorized.

Jace slashed at the demon he was now behind, cutting deep through the muscle and bone of the calves. The demon went careening forward, arms spread to catch itself. And Jace just sliced down the spine, hoping to sever something important. He cut through the spine and saw the blue Psykinetic power fade for a moment before blazing back. *Yup, the demon is reactivating its regeneration Talent.*

[Danger-Sense] went off again—this time from above and behind him. Jace glanced back and used Void Step as a chunk of the mountain was sheared off and went slamming down to where he just was. He had warped straight up and used his Soul Tether to stay aloft. The source of the sudden rockslide was another Astral Demon just like these two he had been dealing with—but they were dressed in actual armor and held a massive hammer in two hands while their other smaller arms descending down the torso held nails and spikes.

Interesting. They had an ambush set up. Must be going after your bounty.

Jace used two successive Void Steps to get right up behind the thing and unleashed a vicious swing at the neck. He barely got a quarter of the way through before he had to let the sword go and drop down, summoning the blade back to his grip as the figure wheeled around with the hammer and would have smashed him. *Irritating*, Jace thought as he slashed at its wrist, severing something in the arm that caused the limb to go limp and the hammer to fall.

The thing roared at him, "You'll pay for that, Wraith!" And the scream was laden with Psykinetic power that washed over Jace like a wave. A sonic-based, Psykinetic-laced scream that hurt his insides as the vibrations spread through his body.

(Dark Matter Binding), Jace thought as he activated the Specialization for Indomitable Will. The damage to his insides was healed as the green flames lit up within him. Keeping his sword at the ready, he dismissed his Bulwark and activated Void Shield. The green flames sprung up around his body, encompassing his whole form, as he two-handed the sword. *(Vengeful)*, he thought as he used the Infusion for Valiant Crusader's Might to empower his next strike.

Then, finally, *Void Step*, as he warped ten feet above the thing and swung down at the top of the skull with all the force he could muster from the two-handed maneuver. His insides burned with pain as the (Vengeful) Infusion empowered his weapon with even brighter gold and green flame. The mighty chop sank through the top of the skull, down through the jaw, into the neck, and halfway down the torso before an explosion of gold and green flame surged up along the path Jace had fallen.

The demon crumpled, turning to ash as Souls escaped its form, and the white-grey Essence soaked into Jace's body. Looking down the slope, he saw the demon who had been covered by rubble slowly digging their way out. Jace sprinted down the slope, using the momentum to build up another strike, empowered with (Vengeful) once more. His energy was slowly draining, but he knew he had plenty left. With a mighty swing, he cleaved through the upper torso of the demon, chopping it in half just under the arms in a horizontal bisection. As he skidded to a halt at the bottom of the ravine, the Souls escaped, and he felt the warmth of Essence pour into him once more.

Glancing at the drone camera view in his HUD, he saw the other demon running down a small crevice up the slope. Sprinting up the incline, leaving a trail of lingering flames, Jace got over the slight rise and dropped in front of the thing. He raised the sword up to eye level. "Try it," Jace said.

To his surprise, the demon fell to its knees. "I surrender!"

The call, Tibalt thought as he felt a longing in his chest. A desire to descend. He was full up on Souls, feeling close to bursting as the screams and lamentations of wailing sorrow resonated within his chest. *I need . . . I need to go deeper.*

He had hoped to stay here, on Layer 5, supping on this easy-to-access river of Souls. But the call of the next Layer was too strong. *Why doesn't every demon do this?* he thought. *This is the easiest way to gain Souls.* He gobbled them up, continuing to devour them, gorging himself.

And he heard a tremendous roar behind him. Wheeling about, he saw a massive Astral Demon. One whose bulk defied his comprehension. A dread creature out of a nightmare. "You have had enough," it growled.

Tibalt growled back, "Why?"

The entity lowered its massive head to look directly at him, the eye the size of Tibalt's whole body. "You are a Dreamer Demon."

"What of it?" Tibalt said in retort.

"You type, not knowing your place. Only chasing power." The figure lifted their head and licked its maw. "Astral Demons know their place, as to Dreamers. You are done here. Go. Descend."

"Why?" Tibalt said. "Answer my fucking questions!"

"Astral Demons who advance too rapidly lose themselves. Their body needs time to adjust. And your presence here disgusts me."

I've heard that from the cloaked figure, he thought. *But I feel fine. Better than fine. Perfect.* He scowled. "Mind your business." He turned back to the stream of Souls and began to drink from it once more.

But a massive claw grabbed him from behind, and he struggled to break free as it crushed down on him. Faster than he could react, he was plunged through the film covering the hole that led down, deeper into the Astral Verge. Sinking into the film, he descended to Layer 6.

The claw released him, and he plopped down—sucked out of the sky, his wings force-deactivated as he landed face-first in a goopy swamp, the Souls flowing down from above in a stream before sinking into the miasmic muck beneath him. Looking up, he tried to use his Demon Wing Talent, but could not. He was grounded. *No!* he screamed internally as he let out a roar. *My easy Souls!* He tried to ascend, but could not.

I . . . I need more power. It must be that I need enough Potency to be able to go deeper, to bypass whatever limitation applies to my current Potency 6 form. He got to his feet and began scrambling to catch the Souls that spread as they fell.

Chapter Twenty-Three

Upgrades

Jace looked at the Astral Demon quizzically. "You . . . surrender?"

"Look," it said, it's voice deep and weak. "Mission on your head, instantly getting enough Souls and Universal Matter to hit Potency 10? Only a fool wouldn't try."

As Jace looked at the thing, he felt a brief moment of connection with it. It was trying to get power as quickly as it could, just like Jace was. But it was only a brief, faint instance of connection as he quickly stepped forward and killed the demon—a clean stab through the head followed by a decapitation and then a vertical slice down the neck stump and into the torso. The creature dropped without a word further, and Jace felt the Essence suffuse his body. "How much are we at?" he asked as he turned to keep following the golden trail leading him toward the first Demon Lord he had to kill—Koris.

2,100, Ollie replied. *And it is 5,000 per level right now, so we need 15,000 for level 50, and then another 6,000 to break into Potency 6.*

"Almost halfway there," Jace replied as he continued his trek along the mountain trail. A trek that was very short-lived, as he heard a colossal roar from above and looked skyward to spot a massive catlike Astral Demon on a ledge above him. The fur bristled and stood on end, alight with a deep, crimson glow of Psykinetic power. Thankfully, Jace still had Void Shield active, and the thing leaped on him only to bounce off the barrier and land neatly on its feet—the green and gold flames licking at its form.

Jace saw his energy bar dip down from the sudden attack. *Right. It's like the old Dark Matter Shield (Rank 3). Every hit costs energy now.* Keeping his sword in two hands, he moved forward and sliced across horizontally. The cat danced back and opened its mouth, releasing a blast of crimson lightning that slammed into Jace's Void Shield, draining his energy but resulting in no damage inflicted. He kept moving forward, slashing over and over, scoring hits on the thing that continued to spread the golden flames, the green fire licking along its form, crimson nebula clouds surging around its body.

And that wasn't including Hero's Arena, which was still in effect all around him. The crackling crimson bolts of lightning from his now-included Aura of Wrath were flickering with the green fire of [Voidflame Vestment], and the golden power of his Psykinetics continued to pop and sear, burning the Astral Demon.

[Danger-Sense] went off, and he used a Void Step to warp further back from the cat-demon creature. Another one landed right where he had been standing, and an explosion of red lightning arced out from the landing. "You'll die, Wraith," it growled.

The one behind it made to move but collapsed and turned to Essence that floated to Jace and suffused his body with warmth. The demon that had just landed in front of Jace ran forward, and he raised his forearm, letting the thing chomp down on it and the Void Shield that surrounded his body. Energy drained heavily, but Jace had a clear shot into the torso of the creature and stabbed up into the ribs over and over, gripping the edge of the jaw with his hand as the thing tried to let go to get away.

[Danger-Sense], once again, warned him of impending attacks, and he used a Void Step to move further down the slight ravine. Two blasts of red lightning impacted where he had been standing, and glancing up, he saw two more of the cat-demons standing above. The drone view in his HUD showed him another six descending the heights.

We do not have our Emergency Battery, Ollie warned. *And energy is getting low!*

Jace let Void Shield fade and re-manifested his Crusader's Bastion. *No more Void Steps unless absolutely necessary.* He saw a crevice in the mountain through his drone's camera and made a sprint for it—going down the slight trail that ran above the ravine along the cliff overhead.

The cat-demons chased him, firing more lightning bolts that he blocked with the Bastion, causing a (Retaliating) flame of golden fury to shoot up and impact them—but the damage inflicted was minor. Jace just kept running, kept trying to get further and further toward the crevice that would let him take these things on one at a time.

More lightning bolts joined in, and he knew from the drone's overhead view that the other cat-demons were on the heights above him. They continued launching their assault, and his shield could not block all of them. Pain coursed through him as his body locked up for a brief moment, causing him to stumble. But he turned that stumble into a roll, recovering and making it to the crevice.

It had just enough room for him to stand in with his stance bladed, sword extended. But he sheathed the sword and held the shield in front of him—the spikes on the front a more than good enough weapon. The HUD camera from the drone showed that the cats were surrounding the entrance, waiting for him. Jace shouted, "I'm not coming out there! You'll have to come get me!" At the same time, he activated his Paragon Armor's (Beacon) Infusion, shedding a bright, white light.

The promise of a Soul that would be delicious was enough to begin to bait the cat-demons in. The first one descended and tried to claw at Jace, but he just shoved the shield forward, stabbing them with the spikes on the front. This had the added benefit of counting as a weapon, and so it imparted (Burning), (Voidbound), and Purifying Edge's various Infusions. The thing recoiled in pain as the three different burning effects, along with the rending power of Void, the crimson bleed of [Rending], and its Talents, were shut off.

It crumpled and burned to nothingness. The next one came in, clawing and biting, and Jace just slammed it with the shield as well. The same process, the same result. The demons might have had some level of intelligence, but the (Beacon) still seemed to lure them in. And once they got close enough, Hero's Arena, thanks to its (Vexing) Infusion, made them move ever closer to him.

One by one, they fell to his repeated shield bashes. His energy dipped down, and he felt tiredness drag on him, but Jace continued his slaughter of the demons—not stopping until all were dead and his drone showed a clear exterior.

Nice job! Ollie said. *You got 7,000 Essence from that whole ordeal. 16,100 currently sitting around.*

Three levels, Jace thought as he dismissed the Bulwark. Glancing down the length of the crevice, he saw, to his satisfaction, that it ended in a dead-end. Going to it, he sat down and watched as his energy slowly regenerated; his (Dark Matter Binding) activated as he cured himself of his few minor injuries and burns inflicted by the lightning. *Let's level up. All three. You know what we discussed.*

On it!

[You have leveled up!]
[You have chosen New Talent!]
[Talent Name: Justice's Rebuke.]
[Effect: When the user is struck and suffers harm, their weapons and Talents deal additional damage.]
[You have chosen Specialization of Existing Talent!]
[Talent Name: Justice's Rebuke.]
[Specialization Name: Flaming.]
[Effect: When the linked Talent is activated, the additional damage inflicted is in the form of a damage-over-time effect. Stacks with (Burning) from Valiant Crusader's Might, (Lingering) from Templar's Smite, and (Inferno) from Templar's Smite.]
[Talent Name: Purifying Edge.]
[Specialization Name: Judging.]
[Effect: When the linked Talent is used on a target, they take additional damage equal to the number of unjudged Souls they have.]

Name: Jace Seren (Potency 5)
Emotion [Class Level]: Valiant [Justiciar 50]
Talent [Specialization]: Astral Adaptation, Astral Translation, Valiant Crusader's Might [Burning] [Vengeful] [Poised] [Unstoppable] [Bracing] [Voidbound], Crusader's Bastion [Retaliating] [Reinforcing] [Grounding] [Redoubt] [Spiked] [Resonating], Hero's Arena [Aura] [Incinerating] [Vexing] [Bolstering] [Suppressing] [Wrathbound], Indomitable Will [Zealous] [Intimidating] [Inviolable] [Enduring] [Ameliorating] [Dark Matter Binding], Templar's Smite [Spear] [Blast] [Lingering] [Challenging] [Inferno] [Cosmic], Holy Hunt [Marked] [Bursting] [Authoritative] [Provoking] [Inciting] [Branding], Purifying Edge [Cleansing] [Searing] [Purging] [Sanctifying] [Terminating] [Judging], Justice's Rebuke [Flaming]
Essence: 1,100
Infusions: x2 Mythic (Specialization)
Gear: <TPSB>, (Convergent Edge) [Ruination 1] Divine Revenge, (Explorer's Embrace / Beacon) Paragon Armor, (Prosthetic Savant) Astral Appendages, (Draconic Sovereign) Arbiter's Sight, (Anathema) Astral Sleeve, (Reinforced) Psycrystal Lattice, (Pinnacle) NICIF-EP, (Restoring) Flame of Valor, Retribution Carbine (20 shots / battery)

Jace smiled as he sat there, letting his energy refill. *Now, when I do get hurt, I can play further into the <Eidolon> Skills for Eidolon's Persistence and Power Through. Get even more damage output from suffering harm.* He didn't like the idea of having to get hurt for power, but he already had the Skills and figured that the best option would be to just lean into the already-existing Skill set he had.

I'm almost there, Jace thought. *Halfway to level 100. Halfway through the Layers. I'll get you back, Chroma.*

Shhiv was hard at work in the workshop, one of the hangar bays inside the Penrose Sphere, which housed dozens of starships. The first one that Xera had designed for Jace was still Shhiv's baby; she had poured so much effort into building it, adding little customizations just for him and layering Runes upon Runes to keep him as safe as possible. That vessel was in a separate hanger near the voidlight tethers.

These other ones were of a similar design, but Shhiv wasn't quite sure why they were building so many. Her several messages to Xera had gone unanswered.

"Excuse me," a male voice said behind her.

Shhiv turned around from her perch atop the starfighter she was working on and saw a male version of Xera standing there. "Oh, you must be Xero," she said with a slight smile.

"Yes, apologies for the late response. I am still getting caught up on all that Xera left me." He walked over to the ship and ran a hand alongside the hull. "Excellent craftsmanship."

"You are welcome," Shhiv said proudly.

Xero looked at her, and their eyes locked for a brief moment before he averted his gaze—not an unusual response to seeing a predator's eyes. He calmly spoke as he looked across the rows upon rows over starfighters. "Did she tell you the plan?"

"Not a lot," Shhiv replied. "Something about extending the Void net thing."

Xero sighed with relief. "Good. Yes, the plan is to effectively turn the edges of our singularity's funnel into Void and Dark Matter walls; a pillar, of sorts, encompassing the mountain on the first Layer as well. A pillar, invisible and undetectable, in the middle of the Astral Verge. Protecting us and providing for further layers of defense." He rapped his knuckles on the hull of the vehicle Shhiv was atop, and he chuckled. "These things are going to keep you and me safe as we work on this expansion project."

Shhiv felt a bit of fear in her stomach. "I don't want to go into the Astral Verge. It's dangerous."

Xero waved his hand dismissively. "You won't have to immediately. I'll take these ships—once I upload the software to slave the command console to the Wayfinder I'm putting in charge of the expansion project."

Shhiv slid off the vessel and landed on the ground, crossing her arms as she faced Xero. "We aren't trying to take over the whole Astral Verge, right?"

"Correct—"

"Promise. Do that pact thingy," Shhiv demanded.

Xero nodded as his mouth went tight. "I do not expect your trust so soon, so I will allow this. Let me contact Quinn . . ." His eyes went black for a brief moment before the deep purple lit back up. A golden contract appeared, floating, in between the two. "Here you go. She set out the terms."

Shhiv pulled out her cosmopanel and called Quinn. "Hey! Got a contract. All on the up and up?"

"Yes," Quinn replied, slightly annoyed. "Sorry, I'm busy right now. Got a big merger and acquisition deal going on to try and get some better relations between Star Council and Nebula Alliance." She hung up.

Shhiv signed the pact and saw it vanish as her Wayfinder, Josie, popped into existence next to her. "Oh, hi, Xero!"

"Hello, Wayfinder," he replied. "Sorry, there's a lot of you, and I'm still working on names."

"Josie," she replied.

"Oh! You were Xera's personal Wayfinder for a while," Xero replied with a grin.

"Yup! But I got on with Shhiv here so I can be with her husband's Wayfinder, Ollie."

Xero nodded. "That is wonderful. Wish you the best." He looked to Shhiv, meeting her gaze and not turning away. "Now, to answer your question—no, expansion is not planned except for this fortification. Taking the outside edge of our singularity's funnel, expanding it down via Void and Dark Matter. That's step one. Step two is I'll have you help me out with creating a megastructure."

"What's that?" Shhiv asked.

"Just really big structures," Josie replied.

"Correct," Xero said as he rubbed two of his hands together in eager anticipation. "We're going to have the Void and Dark Matter on the outermost edge, then inside, we are building a huge Starheart Steel tower that encompasses the whole mountain. The inside will be layers upon layers of turrets and defenses, with a central core."

"Just more defenses then," Shhiv said bluntly.

"Yes," Xero replied as his voice softened. "I've seen some terrible things on the first Layer. I can only imagine what can come up from deeper." He shook his head, and his voice brightened. "Anyways, we will be improving upon that for some time, I am sure. The ultimate goal is a self-sustaining and Wayfinder-controlled pylon in the middle of the Astral Verge. And, since the outside will be covered in non-visible objects . . ." He trailed off with a grin, waiting for Shhiv to finish the sentence.

But Josie finished it instead. "No one will know the defenses are there!"

"Correct," Xero said. "It will be as if the funnel exists as is—despite our supreme defenses." He gestured to the rows and rows of starfighters. "Thus the need for these. To keep us safe while we build the defenses, just in case."

"Okay," Shhiv said cautiously. "But we aren't doing some weird expansion of trying to take over the Astral Verge, right?"

"Would never dream of it," Xero said. "It is endless. Well, Layer 1 is, at least. I support what this Gyanv Alliance Coalition is doing—but it is a fruitless effort. We should all just keep to ourselves." He shrugged. "Isolation of each Universe is a fever dream. But our own? We can do that." He looked around. "You . . . uh . . . got extra tools on hand? Oh, wait! Never mind." He tapped his wrist pad and a set of mechanic's tools appeared in his hands. "Let's get to work!"

Chapter Twenty-Four

Demon Dragon Slayer

Jace got out of the narrow cave and continued to follow the golden trail. A few cycles passed as he was not able to move quickly through the dense mountains. The trails were constricting, and he felt hemmed in from all sides. Void Stalker was ever active, but he knew it would not help much as the Astral Demons on this Layer were his Potency or higher—but the ones who were that higher Potency felt that call of the depths he had heard mentioned many times, and so he wasn't concerned about being outmatched.

The concern came from how enclosed everything felt. And he was reticent to use his Soul Tether and travel across the sky because he would be far more visible while aloft. So, for now, he stuck to the ground. A slow, continuous trudge as he navigated cliffs, narrow ravines, and the ever-present streams, rivers, and tributaries of Souls that came from the mountain tops. Again the region reminded him somewhat of the rocky cliffs on the mountain tiles on Nihilethelea, but there were interwoven components of different mountainscapes he had seen on his travels across the Universe with Shhiv during their honeymoon.

Not only were there familiar patterns in the rock and the cliffs, but the sky was not a singular hue like he had seen on prior Layers and first thought this place would have. It slowly shifted across multiple hues, ending on a deep, burnt orange color when the cycle concluded.

He kept his Bastion active and sword drawn as he traveled through the rocky crags. The golden line of Holy Hunt kept providing a path to follow, and Jace finally reached what must have been the lair of this Demon Lord Koris. A large, carved archway—some massive claw having scooped out and excavated a tunnel that led deep into the mountain—the golden line leading Jace right toward the mouth of the cave.

In front of it was a large stone fortification—a wall covered with metal spikes that jutted outward. Astral Demons were atop the walls—Jace knew that's what they were because they lacked a Karma Coefficient hovering above their heads. They were not as monstrous and animalistic as others he had seen, with most being primarily refined and humanoid. They wore armor and wielded ranged weaponry, though he spotted spears and maces leaning against the wall they stood behind.

I can't use Void Stalker, Jace thought. *But maybe I can just use good, old-fashioned sneaking around.* He willed all of his Skills and Talents to stop functioning, meaning that it was just him, with no visual alterations, in his armor that felt like a second skin on his body. Going back down the ravine, he used his Soul Tether to gain height before crossing the mountain face in a similar fashion and getting both above and behind the arrayed defenders.

There, Jace reactivated his Talents and Skills. *Templar's Smite (Cosmic)(Blast).* Instead of a bead of golden flames forming in his hands, Jace saw the white-grey of Void that was quickly overcome by the green fires. He saw the bead get larger and larger.

Crack! Fwoosh! The enormous cone exploded out from his hands, green and gold fire intermingled as the retextured Void and his Psykinetic fury poured down from above—a holy judging from on high—that utterly destroyed the unaware Astral Demons, who were attacked from behind.

Jace dropped down and landed in front of the cave entrance, turning to face the few Astral Demons who were lounging about inside and quickly went to arms upon seeing a foe drop right in front of them. Hero's Arena began to sear and incinerate them—and they were drawn toward Jace.

A quick shield block for a spear strike was answered with a horizontal slash. Jace scored a hit on the foe, and they backed off slightly. Two more attackers came in simultaneously, and Jace was able to reorient his shield horizontally to deflect the two attacks with a single, upward motion that tipped his attackers off balance. He used that opening to slice horizontally, ensuring to end his swing with a throw that sent the sword sailing into the one he had initially struck, the gold and green flames exploding and consuming the Astral Demons.

Summoning the sword back to his grip, Jace strode down the cavern with confidence. He encountered a few other Astral Demons—all of whom launched various Psykinetic attacks or rushed at him with melee intent. Each attack was blocked, and the singular foes were quickly dispatched. He suffered minor injuries, and his energy dipped down as he healed through the harm.

Thankfully, a few cycles had passed, and the Emergency Battery had recharged. The stone halls were the same—carved out by some titanic claws that bored a hole. Uneven grooves ran along the walls, floor, and ceiling, and the only other distinctions were the striations of varying types of stones from all across the Universes connected to Layer 1. Stones of all types of colors and hues. It would have been beautiful, Jace imagined, if he was not so on-edge, following the golden line of Holy Hunt.

The line led him through a mazelike warren of compartments and quarters. No more Astral Demons came at him, though he sensed them with [Danger-Sense] rushing behind him and fleeing down the tunnel. He didn't give those ones any notice—they weren't a threat to him.

That bit got you 7,000 Essence, putting you at 8,100. Want to level up and hit Potency 6? Ollie asked.

Not yet, Jace thought back. *Going up in Potency momentarily incapacitates me—and we are in hostile territory.*

He entered a massive chamber. A natural cave, similar to Kalec's Hall he had met the Demon Lord inside of. The ceiling had several stalactites that hung down, ominous teeth within the enormous mouth of the hollowed-out mountain.

"Well, now," a voice said from above. Jace followed the golden line and saw it going up, behind one of the large pillars. "You are a pest, aren't you?"

Jace did not respond, instead reaching into his TPSB and pulling out a throwing knife. *Dark Energy Mine,* he thought as he attached the Skill to the knife.

"Wraith, is it? You will make—"

Jace threw the knife and it hit the stalactite. *Detonate,* he thought as the shockwave of purple only visible to him emanated outward.

"—What the—"

Jace launched a bevy of Dark Matter Darts with [Exploding] up behind the stalactite and above the source of the noise. The shockwaves surged out, tinged with golden flames, and the pressure that the expanding Dark Matter exerted upon the Demon Lord forced it down from its cover behind the stalactite.

A dragon, Jace thought, *just like that Kalec guy. Wonder if this one was inspired by a star dragon also?*

<u>*No clue. But should be a challenging fight*</u>, Ollie said.

Jace scoffed internally. *Yeah. Sure.* He threw his sword—which sailed skyward and hit the Astral Demon Lord, who let out a roar of pain, before summoning the blade back to his grip.

"You insolent whelp!" The thing righted itself in air and flapped its mighty wings, surging up into the heights of the cavern. It ripped a massive claw through one stalactite after another, sending them down to plummet onto Jace.

He just grinned under the helmet. *I want this entire cavern to be bare and smooth stone, infused with my Psykinetics. Archmage's Admixture.*

The entire cavern flattened instantly. The walls were rendered smooth. All of the stalactites vanished in an instant. The whole of the mountain interior flared with a golden glow, and the Astral Demon seemed incredulous, judging by the voice. "What is this?"

Jace used his Soul Tether to ascend, combining it with a Dark Energy Mine to quickly get up to the still-floating and maneuvering-via-wings Demon Lord. He hacked into it—but the weapon bounced off of the Psykinetic-empowered scales. However, thanks to Purifying Edge and its multitude of Specializations, the scales lost their amber glow, and Jace's second strike sank deep into the hide, spreading gold and green flames along with the seeping crimson nebula clouds of [Rending].

The thing spun in air, slamming its tail into Jace—who blocked with his Crusader's Bastion—and he used his Soul Tether to pull himself back into range to deliver a wicked stab, deep into the shoulder. He felt the blade grind against the bone inside and poured energy into the weapon as he activated the stored-until-now damage of (Fulmination). The weapon exploded with gold flames as the Demon Lord let out a roar of pain.

The thing was large compared to Jace, massive in its bulk, and he saw the scales get larger as the thing somehow grew. "I will not let an insect like you defeat me! Even if I have to use my Souls and Universal Matter and go up in Potency!"

Shit, Jace thought as the thing's hide exploded with amber light that formed tiny hooks and blades—shooting out and thudding into his armor. The small projectiles did not pierce the armor itself, but his movement was restricted thanks to the multitudinous hooks and lines that connected him to the thing's bulk.

It brought its mouth around, jaws brimming with amber light, and Jace used a Void Step to warp to the other side of its mouth. He stabbed into the crook between the thing's jaw and neck, ripping the weapon out as it whipped its head back and slammed into him. The rapid strike sent Jace sailing toward the wall, and he quickly used his Soul Tether to keep himself from hitting the hard surface.

The thing opened its jaws, and a beam of amber light streaked out, slamming into Jace. His shield was in the way, and the pressure from the strike rammed him back into the wall. He felt himself being driven backward into the mountain and the hole his body was quickly digging out from the sheer pressure applied from the frontal assault.

He tilted the shield a tiny bit. *Ollie, turn off my pain receptors.*

I can only tune them down to about ninety percent reduction, Ollie replied.

Jace nodded and let the beam slip past the shield. He felt a dull pain that spread through his body from the impacting point and kept a steady eye on his HUD as he saw the readout of his body suffering damage flicker from green to orange.

Eidolon's Persistence is active now, Jace thought, as he knew Talents like the one striking him would only deal half as much harm. Power Through was also amplifying him thanks to the percentage of his energy and health he was missing. But more important than that was his health readout on the HUD flashing fifty percent.

Shattered Limits (Rank 19) [Single-Minded Fury], Jace thought. He pushed back against the beam, bringing his bulwark fully to bear as he pushed his way out of the hole that the Psykinetic assault had pushed him into. Slowly, he made his way forward.

Why not Void Step away? Ollie asked.

Every instance of this Psykinetic Talent hitting my shield is triggering (Retaliating), Jace thought back, as he knew the golden flames were striking the creature despite his eyes not being able to verify the hits. *And we get to test out Justice's Rebuke.*

He reached the edge of the hole and, at that moment, used a series of chained-together Void Steps to get out of the beam, next to the still-firing Astral Demon, and brought his sword down—empowering it with the (Vengeful) Infusion as he felt the dull pain deep in his guts.

The weapon sliced clean through the Astral Demon's extended neck—not quite long enough to cut all the way through, but cutting half of it in two. The gold and green flames exploded in an immolating cloud that spread outward from the site of the impact, and the Psykinetic stream of the laser-like weapon was snuffed out.

The Astral Demon Lord, however, seemed to have some Talents to counteract damage-over-time Psykinetics; as Jace fell due to gravity, the thing's body sealed over. The crimson miasma of [Rending] was pushed back to the sites of the initial injuries, as were the golden flames. But Void was not able to be suppressed in such a fashion, so the green flames continued to spread.

The thing stared down at Jace as it flapped its wings to stay aloft. "Clever," it growled. "I'll actually try now." The thing raised its claws, and hundreds of bolts of amber Psykinetic energy formed in the air above it. With a gesture, a flick of the claw, the bolts descended to pound into Jace.

Dark Energy Mine. Detonate. Jace felt gravity cease its control on him, and he used his Soul Tether to ascend. *Void Shield (Reflecting)*, he thought as the green flames manifested around him.

Each bolt that redirected course and slammed into him precipitously drained his energy—but an equally sized spike of green flame raced up to slam into the Astral Demon, who manifested an amber-colored screen of Psykinetic energy before them like a shield.

Emergency Battery going off! Ollie shouted in his mind, and Jace saw his near-empty energy refill to max.

The bolt assault continued, and the damage continued to reflect as the amber barrier of the Astral Demon Lord cracked, fragmented, and scattered to nothingness. Jace used another Soul Tether and yanked on the line, surging up into the sky of the mountainous cavern. He slammed into the thing's torso, blade tip first, gouging deep into it.

Downside of being big, he thought as he summoned his sword back to his sheath and shoved his arms into the gap, *is you can be attacked from inside!* Jace squirmed his way into the wound, reached into his TPSB to draw two of the knives, and as they lit up with the golden flames, he began carving his way deeper into the mass of flesh and muscle. Blood, deep blue in coloration, poured onto and around him—but he did not need to breathe thanks to the NICIF recycling air in his body and filtering the atmosphere.

Very faintly, he could hear the roar of the creature and felt the walls squeeze in on him as the body tried to flex down to crush him—but his Void Shield held firm and even returned the squeezing as a painful cramp upon the

Demon Lord. Jace could barely hear what sounded like pleading, but he just continued to carve his way deeper into the thing—surrounded by flesh to stab and cut away at, golden and green flames, and dripping crimson nebula clouds.

You are about at the center, Ollie said.

Perfect, Jace thought back as he put the knives back into the TPSB. *Templar's Smite (Blast)*, he thought.

The golden flames surged out from his hands, devouring the inside of the creature with greedy abandon. He felt gravity assert its control, and the corpse withered away to nothingness as Essence flooded into him. Using his Soul Tether, Jace arrested his fall and took several deep breaths, letting Skills and Talents fade.

Demon Lord down! Ollie said excitedly. *Good job. That one was Koris. Two more to go on this Layer!*

And how much Essence? Jace thought as he descended down to the floor.

Only 900, which puts you at 9,000 total. 6,000 of that to gets you to Potency 6.

Jace looked back to the tunnel he had come from and the now-dull stone around him, as the Archmage's Admixture had faded after thirty seconds—the golden flames no longer imbuing the surfaces. *If you think it is safe enough.*

Tasking the drone to scout the whole complex quickly!

Jace sat down at the tunnel entrance, watching the camera on the drone. The whole facility was cleared, and Ollie re-tasked the drone with keeping a watch outside. *Okay then. Let's go. Potency 6, level 51.*

Chapter Twenty-Five

Buying Some Time

Jace braced himself for the pain he knew he would end up feeling from the Potency upgrade. *Here we go.*

[You have leveled up!]
[You have chosen Specialization of Existing Talent!]
[Talent Name: Justice's Rebuke.]
[Specialization Name: Bashing.]
[Effect: When the linked Talent is activated, the user's weapons and Talents gain the ability to blow foes back with concussive force.]

Jace screamed. His insides felt like they were melting and liquifying; a horrific convulsion overtook his body as he writhed on the ground, body spasming beyond his control as his form contorted. Then, the melting pain faded, only to be replaced with a crackling, tingling surge that was just like when he had been electrocuted on Poltor Six.

Survive, he thought as he gritted his teeth through the pain, the convulsions and spasms fading as he was left huffing on the ground.

Why did they make it painful, I wonder? Ollie pondered.

No clue, Jace thought as he pushed himself to his feet and checked the HUD camera for the drone and saw that the timestamp only read a few seconds having passed. *Good. Now. Holy Hunt.* The golden line shot off toward his next target. Heading out of the cave structure, he got outside, and the drone took its position above his head again.

There were a few refined Astral Demons hiding in the rocks above. Jace just looked up to them and spoke firmly. "Go to Demon Lord Kalec if you want to live. And shape up, no more unjudged Souls." The Astral Demons fled, and Jace kept following the golden path.

Why not just end them and get the Essence? Ollie asked.

We met that one refined demon up a few Layers. Call me an optimist, but I hope that they can reach Potency 10 and get a chance to live life with a Soul. No clue what that changes for them . . . but I don't need to kill them. I'm already above other demons' Potency on this Layer.

Fair enough, Ollie's voice said, softly. *You have a good heart.*

Jace smiled and activated Void Stalker, moving undetected across the mountainous landscape.

Valcrinox read the various reports coming to him through the Astral System. He had no word of Wraith, and his Potency 10 army was still under the siren call of the depths, forcing them to remain on Layer 10.

The Demon Lord of Madness had not left his throne since. Too afraid of leaving the beacon that amplified its power. Afraid of being annihilated. The strongest demon in existence, cowed into submission and hiding in his home by a Dreamer.

It infuriated him. *I should not be here*, he thought, seething. *We are so close.* He pulled up the meter in his Astral System interface, representing an ancient function that allowed for The Ancients to create new realities—new Universes.

[Universe Creation Progression: 97%]

Just a little more! he screamed in his mind, and the world around him shook and trembled with his thoughts alone, the now-still corpses on the ceiling and walls vibrating ever-so-slightly. *We are so close. Just a bit more.*

There was no Infusion for gathering Universal Matter. Nothing for it save to plunder the first Layer and the various Universes, ripping them apart, and not using that substance to level up. As he was Potency 10, and his minions were as well, Valcrinox had no need for the substance save for this defining moment. A Universe, dedicated to him and his cohort of demons.

He felt a flutter in his stomach as one of his demons entered the room. "Demon Lord!"

"What is it?" Valcrinox muttered.

"Three are ready!"

"Yes!" Valcrinox shouted as he almost made to stand up—but kept himself seated in his place of power. "Send them. Now! Two to fight Wraith, and one to get the last bit of Universal Matter we need!"

"Your will be done, Mad One," the demon replied as they hurried out of the building.

Valcrinox laughed. A long, deep laugh. *Three are already recovered; that means the others won't be far behind.*

Yroshnak felt something . . . off. He glanced up and saw one of the odd metal flying contraptions hovering in the corner of the room. "I see you," he rumbled.

"Wasn't cloaking it," a male voice replied. The accent was familiar, and the masculine voice continued. "I'm X. Well, X's brother, but taking over for her. I have probes down on deeper Layers—wasn't able to get one onto Layer 10, but Layer 9 for sure!"

"Spit out what you want to say," Yroshnak said with irritation.

"Potency 10. Three of them. Heading up."

Fuck. Yroshnak snarled, "Have you warned your asset?"

"Wraith is being informed right now," X replied. "I just figured you should know, since they're coming through your territory."

I could maybe fight two, Yroshnak thought. *But three? I would be hard pressed. I have minions, though.* He cleared his throat, stood up, and grabbed his massive axe that leaned against his seat. "I will defeat them. But if three are ready to ascend the Layers . . . the rest of Valcrinox's forces will be ready, soon."

"I know," X replied with a slightly panicked voice. "But I have a plan!"

Jace listened to Ollie rattle off the report, and he frowned. "We have to pick up the pace, then," he said.

"Well, actually, I have a plan," Xero's voice said, coming through the comms line. "We can keep Valcrinox shut up on Layer 10. Just requires you to use an Architect's Gate application. Rush to the entrance to the next Layer, seal it over, and then you'll have all the time you need—provided you keep renewing it and feeding it more energy."

Jace immediately changed the target of his Holy Hunt to the entrance to Layer 6 and began using Soul Tether to travel through the sky at his top speed—launching himself with Dark Energy Mines as he gained speed.

Void Stalker ensured he went unnoticed, and thus being in the skies was not a concern for him. On this Layer, at least, and at his current Potency.

Two cycles passed, and he kept his mind focused on thinking through possible scenarios in that virtual reality space inside his inner Cosmic System. Replaying the combat with the Potency 10 Astral Demon. Seeing every error, every flaw, every opening that he did not take advantage of. Training himself. Readying himself. *If they arrive before I seal it off,* Jace thought, *then I won't be able to benefit from Quinn's Skills.*

The cooldown for her Stratagems to be used on him, due to the depth of the Layers he was in, was lengthy. Still another few cycles away. And without those bonuses, Jace wasn't sure he could take on a Potency 10 demon, much less three of them.

He reached a large valley. It was idyllic, almost like a hidden paradise at the bottom of this sloping mountain range. The farthest west side of Layer 5. The river of Souls combined into a massive deluge that poured into the film leading to the next Layer down. A huge aperture.

And next to the entrance was another Demon Lord. One that dwarfed the prior one that Jace had fought, with deep blue scales tinged with white outlines. Easily the size of the enormous turtle creature that Jace had fought back on Regnum Mortis. An eye the size of a city block opened—deep blue and predatory—and tracked him.

Holy Hunt, Jace thought, focusing his intent on the closest Demon Lord, and sure enough, the golden line shot to the creature, outlining it. This also activated the (Provoking) Specialization, and the demon raised its bulk off of the valley floor, letting loose a tremendous roar that shook the air. *Well . . . shit.*

The demon opened its maw, and Jace instinctively pulled up Void Shield (Reflecting)—the green flames cascading around him. A glimmering teal light coalesced and surged forth, a blast so large that it encompassed the width of the valley and fast enough that Jace could barely react in time, putting up another Void Shield with the (Wall) Skill Evolution applied.

The screen of crackling green flames shot up and blocked the assault, but Jace saw his energy drain from near-full to just under thirty percent from blocking the single Talent. *We still have Emergency Battery*, he thought, knowing that enough time had passed to allow it to recharge back in his Universe. *Okay, you've got this.*

Damn right you do! Just another Demon Lord, Ollie said encouragingly. *Go get it!*

Jace was about to do just that, activating his suite of Skills and Talents that he had grown accustomed to activating pre-combat. He did not receive the notification about Shattered Limits being activated, and so he was sure he could take this thing on. Letting his Dark Energy Mine fade, he plummeted down, using several chained-together Soul Tethers to swing toward the huge dragon that stood up all the way.

It brought a massive claw across the sky, and Jace used a Void Step to get to the outside edge of the strike. But something odd caught him off guard. *A swipe like that should have some wind behind it*, he thought, knowing that there was a brief instant where the displaced air should have been replaced. Was . . . was that a fake?

To test, he threw his sword at the massive claw, and to his satisfaction, the weapon sailed right through it. *Some type of glamour*, Ollie noted. *Illusory.*

Where's the body then? Jace thought as his Holy Hunt outlined the entire illusory creature. He continued to fall and swing toward the bulk of the main body.

Using the drone. Jace saw as the HUD camera showed the drone zipping behind the dragon, then dipping into the thing's hide and revealing a more adequately sized Astral Demon, the same bulk as the Koris one that Jace had just killed. *Not too bad.*

Jace was about to reply, but his [Danger-Sense] went off, and he instinctively turned to face the threat—another Astral Demon, another in the same draconic shape—crashed down on him from above and to the side. His shield blocked the impact, but the trajectory took both of them down toward the ground. The claws that gripped around his torso squeezed down.

Jace used a Void Step to get out of the thing's grasp, right on its neck, and hacked down at the top of the skull. The thing's hide and scales began arcing with a deep green hue. Jace coiled his legs and jumped off the thing, using a Soul Tether to stay aloft as the entity flew down and did a tight circle.

The large, illusory dragon vanished, and the one that had just attacked Jace looked over to the now-revealed blue one. "Daksha," it said in a cordial way.

"Vremiv," the blue one rumbled back. "This is the Wraith. Kill it, split the Soul?"

"Sure," Vremiv, the green one, replied. It cackled and faced Jace, still flapping to stay aloft. "What do you say, little Valiant Psykinetic user?"

I think you shouldn't talk when you're going to fight, Jace thought. *Banter is a waste.* He dropped down and, in that brief instant, used Void Step, chaining them together and draining his energy to empty. The Emergency Battery kicked on, and he was able to use even more energy to get behind the blue one, Daksha.

Neither of the Astral Demons had been able to track him, his whole warp-skip travel having been performed so quickly that they had no way to keep up. Jace activated (Vengeful); feeling his guts roil and twist with a horrible cramp, as he also activated Raging Cleave (Rank 10) [Echoing Cleave]. The weapon ignited in his grip, and he swung with both hands, carving a clean slice through Daksha's scales, meat, and innards. The projected crimson blade of his Skill ensured the cut went through the body entirely, and a split-second later, a second cut followed up from the echo.

The demon lord recovered, mending itself with a deep blue glow of Psykinetics, but was obviously quite drained given their haggard appearance and heaving body. Jace's Hero's Arena burned and seared them, and he got ready to strike again.

But a beam of Psykinetics lanced toward him. With the warning from [Danger-Sense], Jace was able to manifest his Crusader's Bulwark in time to block the shot, which caused him to stagger back a few feet from the sheer force of the impact. But the golden flaming darts caused by (Retaliating) surged back to impact the green dragon demon, Vremiv. It let out a roar as it dove toward Jace, claws outstretched and mouth emitting a cloud of green energy.

Daksha turned to Jace with a swipe that he deftly jumped over, and he quickly moved forward, slashing into the hide he had cut through once with another Raging Cleave at maximum Rank. The Demon Lord let out a cry of anguish, and then tried to move back and away. Jace didn't let it.

He ran forward, chopping again with another Raging Cleave, slicing clean through her midsection horizontally, bisecting her body into two. The whitish Essence flew from her body as an explosion of Souls surged upward before joining the river running down to the next Layer.

The Souls blinded Jace with their numbers, and his [Danger-Sense] alerted him to the incoming strike. A quick Void Step ensured he dodged the blow, and as he turned to face the now-grounded demon dragon, he readied himself for a real fight. *Down to half energy*, he thought.

Vremiv paced slowly around the outside edge. "I should thank you, hero. You slew two of my three rivals on this Layer. But you cannot defeat me."

Again, [Danger-Sense] picked up something behind him, and Jace turned to interpose his shield. The dragon-creature had appeared behind him—somehow—and slashed at him with its claws. Jace got his shield in the way of one, but the other scored deep gashes across his armor and into his torso, sending him spinning.

Activating Holy Hunt, Ollie said in a slight panic. The golden hue outlined the one in front of Jace, and Ollie spoke with speed. *It can also use glamour-like Talents. This is the real one. No more tricking us!*

Jace activated (Dark Matter Binding) and got to his feet in time to meet the headlong charge of the Astral Demon Lord.

Chapter Twenty-Six

Sealing the Film

The dragon slammed into Jace's shield, the mouth crunching down on him from above and threatening to devour him whole.

Right where I want to be, Jace thought as he fired off a Templar's Smite (Cosmic), encompassing the whole Astral Demon's body, the gold and green flames surging up from below and scorching the thing's body.

A bead of green light appeared down the throat, and Jace used Void Step to get out of the jaws and atop the creature. A split-second later, the deep green laser shot out of the mouth, and the Astral Demon Lord Vremiv growled out, "Clever."

Jace tried stabbing down, but his weapon couldn't get through the dense scales that now brimmed with green hues. He saw one layer of Psykinetic Talent pop, and then, pulling back, stabbed down as he popped another—his Purifying Edge sundering the Talents. But this Demon Lord had a lot of defensive Talents at their disposal, or a massive reserve of energy.

Jace had to slide down the side of the thing as it rolled, trying to crush him with its bulk, landing deftly on his feet as he spun to face the foe that now clambered back to its feet. The burning flames of Valiant Psykinetics and the retextured Void still flickered inside the creature's mouth. It stay put at range and slammed its claws into the ground. "No more teleporting!"

A shockwave of deep green Psykinetic power surged through the ground, and Jace felt gravity increase ever-so-slightly. Testing, he tried to Void Step, but the Skill did not respond.

Ah, Ollie said with realization. *Localized teleportation and warping have been disabled due to a Talent. Good to know that there exists such a Talent.*

Shouldn't my being a higher Potency override that? Jace thought back.

Seems like Demon Lords can break the rules a bit. They get some amount of control over a Layer. Must be another reason why The Ancients want one Demon Lord per Layer—to ensure that only evil Souls are devoured for leveling up, but also to reshape the Layers. I would wager they looked very different in prior eons.

Jace kept his Bulwark in front of him as another green laser shot out and slammed into the defensive barrier. He could see the green Psykinetic power clash with his golden shield, and the shield began to slowly be eaten away. But the whole duration of the laser's continuous blast, his (Retaliating) Infusion continued to send bolts of gold flaming energy to strike at the Astral Demon Lord.

As Jace's shield was burned away by the potent beam, he was not just standing still—he was moving. Right toward his foe, dropping his sword as he pulled out some throwing knives from the TPSB, placed Dark Energy Mine on them, and threw them at the demon. They each clattered off of the scaled hide—but the detonation of dark, purple energy still went off and null-gravity asserted itself. The demon lord gripped the ground, staying put.

But it let Jace do something he wanted to try. He angled his shield just a bit so that he would take some injury from the green beam. It splashed his arm and seemed to go through the armor, making him queasy as his stomach twisted into knots. Then, the knots grew tighter, and he felt pain spread through him. Which activated Justice's Rebuke, and with (Bashing) also active, Jace used a quick Templar's Smite focused into a single point under the Astral Demon.

The golden inferno shot upward from a three-foot-wide point underneath it, and thanks to (Bashing) on the new Talent, the demon was bucked up—enough to break contact on the ground with its claws, and thanks to the lack of gravity, the thing was propelled upward. The concentration on its beam broke, and Jace took a breath of relief seeing his gambit pay off.

With his foe airborne and struggling to figure out how to fly with its wings while in zero gravity, Jace summoned his Divine Revenge back to his hand, activated the (Vengeful) Infusion, and threw his sword up at the creature. He felt the immense pain in his chest of the Talent activating, but the sword flew up in a straight shot to the eye—right where Jace had aimed at. The weapon sank deep into the aperture, eliciting a roaring scream of pain from the demon.

And then, while the sword was firmly affixed in the thing's skull, he used (Fulmination). The gold and green shockwave exploded right inside the thing's brain cavity, and the body went limp for a few seconds as some innate Talent reconstructed the thing.

Jace summoned the sword back to his hand and repeated his use of (Vengeful) and sword throw, scoring another blow into the same now-bloody socket, the weapon sinking even further into the skull. The thing twitched, but then his sword was ejected, and he quickly summoned it back to his grip.

The Astral Demon's wounds fully sealed over, and it regained its bearings as it tucked its wings in, then unfurled them with a mighty whoosh, finally figuring out how to navigate without gravity and utilizing the lift generated by the powerful strokes. It glared at Jace with a newly formed eye. "Die." Jace felt his chest tingle a bit, and he was confused for a moment. It seemed like the Astral Demon was just as confused, as its mouth dropped slightly. "What?!" it asked in outrage.

[Hey, boss!]
[The thing tried to shut down all your organs in one go!]
[Dumbass.]
[The demon, not you!]
[You got our wonderful, NICIF-EP organs now!]
[Kick its butt!]

Jace dismissed his Bulwark and used his Soul Tether to gain height. He had only twenty percent of his energy remaining, but that would be more than enough to deal with this demon. Activating Raging Cleave (Rank 10), he launched himself skyward and unleashed a two-handed strike, severing clean through the demon's midsection, which was followed up by several golden flaming explosions as the blade and its spectral projection cut through.

The demon writhed in pain before going limp, but then surged with a pale inner green light. "You force me to use it all!" it roared out as the body mended, and Jace was flung back, out of the air, and forced to use his Soul Tether to keep himself aloft.

The Astral Demon's form shifted and twisted as it must have utilized Souls to level up and increase its Potency. Huge spikes and spines grew out of its body—all over its form. The massive shape shrank down to a more sinuous design, and the wings elongated while flattening down—a form designed for speed and not bulk.

It shot forward under some unknown means of flight, and Jace barely twisted his body out of the way to dodge the headlong charge. But the spines along the back jutted up as if reacting to his presence, stabbing through the armor and into him, eliciting a yelp of pain as Jace could feel the sharp points digging into his body before being ripped out by the speed of the Astral Demon's passage.

He let himself drop down to the ground, landing lightly on his feet as (Dark Matter Binding) sealed over the wounds with a small geyser of purple energy. *Not enough damage for Shattered Limits*, he thought. *But I won't be hurt as much by the spikes thanks to Eidolon's Persistence.* He thanked his past self for taking the Class Expansion he did into <Eidolon>, which had come in clutch several times now.

The Astral Demon wheeled about and flew down to him, going for another flyby strike on the ground. But Jace re-manifested his Crusader's Bulwark, held his sword behind him and to the right, ready to strike, and took the charge head-on. His feet dug into the ground as he was pushed back, even with his (Grounding) Infusion. But the Astral Demon Lord was stunned briefly by the (Resonating) Infusion, and that gave Jace the opening to whip the shield to the side and deliver a vicious (Vengeful)-empowered strike.

Stab! Deep, directly into the eye socket again. The demon writhed and tried to pull back, but Jace dismissed his shield and latched his arms and legs around the thing's snout, holding the now-smaller mouth shut with sheer muscle and prosthetic power as he continued to stab his sword into the socket over and over, trying to flourish the blade inside each time to deal further damage to whatever internal organ was inside the skull.

He could feel massive strain on his arms and legs as the thing tried to open its mouth. The spikes and barbs on the demon's body angled toward Jace and shot at him, but he quickly used Void Shield (Rank 6) to manifest the green flame barrier around him. Each strike of the stabbing points drained his energy further and further, but Jace was able to stave off the assault as he continued to plunge his blade over and over.

Golden geysers of flame surged up with each stab, green flames licking deep and going inside as Void spread across the inside of the creature. Dark crimson nebula clouds dripped out around the wound in a miasmic torrent like a waterfall. And finally, with a grunt, the creature collapsed to the ground and turned to raw Essence.

Jace felt the warmth suffuse his body and checked his energy gauge. *Two percent? We cut it close.*

Yup, Ollie replied cautiously. *Do not do that again. Too risky.*

We won, didn't we?

Yes. And we now have a total of 6,000 Essence. Enough for one level.

Save it for the next Layer, Jace thought back. *We can get a Class Transmutation. I think we should pivot back to something defense oriented.*

An Astral System message appeared in the sky above Jace.

> [Mission Success: Consolidate control over Layer 5 to Demon Lord Kalec.]
> [Reward: Mythic (Gear) Infusion.]
> [Sender: The Ancients.]

Jace looked over at the now-placid river of Souls going down into the next Layer. *I need some time to recover. How much energy do I need to Gate of Architects over this?*

At least twenty percent. Give it about ten minutes.

Jace sat down and let out a slight sigh of relief. *At least we weren't also attacked by those Potency 10 demons. Pretty sure, right now, that would be a death sentence.*

Yroshnak coughed up blood as he wrenched the dripping crimson axe from the Astral Demon that served Valcrinox. The Demon Lord of Blood had amassed his forces to stop the three servants of the Demon Lord of Madness. And they had been victorious, but at a heavy cost.

Yroshnak looked out over the battlefield. *Sixty of mine for three of his?* He shook his head in disbelief. *I did not think that a few Potency would result in such a difference of power.* He looked up to the small drone that hovered above—invisible save for a tiny aperture on the bottom. "Well?"

The male voice of X replied, "I analyzed the combat data and am coming up with strategies. Thankfully, Astral Demons seem like apex predators—they come up with their methods and stick to them. But as thinking, rational beings, they can also shift that methodology."

Yroshnak sneered, "Anything useful you can tell me?"

X replied, oddly chipper and delighted, "Oh, no. But good news is that Wraith has finished Layer 5 and consolidated control up there! So, he's getting closer and closer to your Layer and being able to help out."

It needs to happen faster, the Demon Lord thought as he thudded over to the entrance to the next Layer down. He could not see through the opaque film but knew that the Demon Lord below would not hold Valcrinox's forces back for the sake of the upper Layers. "I need that Gate thing you mentioned to seal this off for now."

"I'm working on it."

Jace stood up and went to the film. "So, we are using the Architect's Gate on this?"

Yup! Ollie thought to him.

"Nope," Quinn's voice said over the comms.

"Why not?" Jace asked.

"That Demon Lord of Blood you fought in the arena—Yroshnak—he beat the three Potency 10 demons on their way up to you. That means that Valcrinox's remaining forces can almost all go up again. But Xero has a plan."

"I sure do!" Xero said, voice full of joy and almost glee. "I've figured out how to channel your Architect's Gate Skill through the voidlight tethers. Here, let me highlight the one you need to grab . . ."

Jace saw several silver threads appear in the sky above him. Then more. Dozens, thousands. "How many drones did you send out?" he asked.

"Xera's been at this for a while," Xero replied. "She has several billion drones out there in the Astral Verge—mostly in the first Layer trying to map out infinity. Not actually infinite, by the way, just really, really big. Found one edge of our reality on that Layer. But that's beside the point. Grab the green voidlight tether."

Jace looked for the green one and, spotting it high above him, used his Soul Tether to grapple his way through the air up to it. Grabbing it, he could feel the slight vibration of the string in his grip passing through his gauntlet entirely and against his palm. "Now what?"

"Just use the Skill on the line. I'll direct it!"

The Architect's Gate, Jace thought as he activated the Skill.

Yroshnak was staring. "Well?" he asked as he watched the film to Layer 9.

"Here it comes!" X replied.

Yroshnak frowned. "I don't see anything," he muttered.

"Try throwing something in."

Yroshnak picked up a small rock and tossed it to the film. As soon as it touched, it vanished—becoming nothing. Not ash or dust, but fully obliterating the object. Yet he could still see the pools of Souls slowly drifting into the film unimpeded. "What is this Psykinetic?"

"Trade secret," X replied. "It will prevent any Astral Demons from going up or down. Just make sure your underlings go through it."

Yroshnak let out a barking laugh. "And how long will this last?"

"I can re-manifest it regularly," X stated with pride in his voice. "I'll do the same thing to the film between Layers 9 and 10."

"And can Wraith pass through these barriers of nothingness?"

"Yup."

"I look forward to fighting alongside him," Yroshnak said as he slung his axe over his shoulder and went to check on his injured demon entourage.

Chapter Twenty-Seven

Layer 6

Tibalt finally, finally got to the Soul he had been trying to catch. A big one that he gobbled up and let join the mass within him. The simmering screams inside of him were like a calming chorus at this point and did not unsettle him in the slightest. It felt natural, almost, to be assailed by the voices begging, pleading for their release.

He had learned something about Souls. They came in different varieties. Almost like flavors. Some were big, some were small, some were absolutely fantastic to eat, and others were horrible to choke down. Generally, what he'd discovered was that the bigger they were, the more delicious they were. Sweet, tangy, a little bit of a tingling feeling that was intoxicating.

Tibalt had become less of a Dreamer Demon who would devour every Soul. Now, his eyes looked across the muck and swamps of Layer 6, seeking the Souls that swam through the mud. He chased them down, hunting the biggest ones, and sometimes had to dive into the murky waters to grab them.

Other demons had given him some trouble, but he had just slaughtered them with his Psykinetics—already powerful compared to the natives of the Layer.

His eyes caught movement from up above, and he ducked down into the mud, only letting his head be revealed. Another lesson he had learned was that some Layers, especially the deeper one went, had rules and restrictions. This Layer prevented flight unless the demon was of a higher Potency than the Layer itself. And so, Tibalt remained on the ground as he watched a higher Potency demon take to the skies and sail across the landscape.

Looking for something, no doubt. *Maybe*, Tibalt thought, *it is heading up from a lower Layer to get the bounty on Wraith.*

Tibalt wanted his revenge. He wanted to kill the Psykinetic user. But he knew he would need to either catch Wraith at a moment of weakness or be vastly superior. The man had been able to defeat a Potency 10 demon on his own—Tibalt knew he stood no chance on his own.

And so his plan was the same. Get to Potency 10, Layer 10, join with Valcrinox, work his way into the demon's faction while keeping control over himself and not being taken thrall. Faking it until Wraith arrived to fight the Demon Lord.

Then . . . I swoop in, kill the survivor, and rule. Tibalt swam away in the murk and muck, chasing down a juicy, huge Soul that he spotted making its way through the swamps.

Jace looked into the film that led down. *Okay, down we go.* He dropped into the film and felt the slight coating stick upon his body for a few seconds before letting him go. He plummeted down, and even though he used his Soul Tether, the line snapped, and he activated a Dark Energy Mine to negate gravity. That worked, and he hovered in midair above a huge swamp. The skies above were a solid murky brown that reflected the mud and muck below. Jace could see Souls streaming down from above and all around him before they landed in the mud and began swimming in various directions.

It is similar to Layer 4, Ollie said. *Each Soul has to find its way through the swamp until it finds a means to get down. Here, let me show you the map.* Jace saw the map appear in his HUD as Ollie explained further, *It is 2,500 miles across and 1,000 miles north to south. Smaller than the last Layer, which is the trend as we go deeper—they get more condensed. We are on the western edge, and the next Layer entrance is down far in the east. There are a few settlements on raised ground.*

Astral System messages appeared in Jace's vision.

[Mission: Consolidate control over Layer 6 to Demon Lord Ryun.]
[Reward: Mythic (Gear) Infusion.]
[Sender: The Ancients.]

[Congratulations on entering a new Layer!]
[You may choose to specialize your Class by performing a Class Transmutation!]
[Base Class = Bastion.]
[Options available:]
[Zealot—expand upon your offensive capabilities. Leads to further offensive Transmutations.]
[Guardian—expand upon your defensive capabilities. Leads to further defensive Transmutations.]
[Lightbringer—expand upon your support capabilities. Leads to further support Transmutations.]

Jace did not choose immediately as he thought he would, because an idea popped into his head. "We encountered an Astral Demon with a Talent to make illusions . . . does that type of thing fall under support?"

Let me query the System . . . yup! Ollie replied.

"Then maybe we should go with Lightbringer, just to make sure that I have some Talents that let me get around pesky Talents like that."

You sure?

"Pretty sure. I'm doing okay in combat."

Okay then!

[Class Transmutation Confirmed.]

"And we have a level up ready to go. Let's go ahead and use it."

Roger!

[You have leveled up!]
[You have chosen New Talent!]
[Talent Name: Revealing Light.]
[Effect: The user may activate this Talent to dismiss any Psykinetic Talent that augments reality in regard to perception (sight, smell, hearing, touch, taste).]

Name: Jace Seren (Potency 6)
Emotion [Class Level]: Valiant [Lightbringer 52]
Talent [Specialization]: Astral Adaptation, Astral Translation, Valiant Crusader's Might [Burning] [Vengeful] [Poised] [Unstoppable] [Bracing] [Voidbound], Crusader's Bastion [Retaliating] [Reinforcing] [Grounding] [Redoubt] [Spiked] [Resonating], Hero's Arena [Aura] [Incinerating] [Vexing] [Bolstering] [Suppressing] [Wrathbound], Indomitable Will [Zealous] [Intimidating] [Inviolable] [Enduring] [Ameliorating] [Dark Matter Binding], Templar's Smite [Spear] [Blast] [Lingering] [Challenging] [Inferno] [Cosmic], Holy Hunt [Marked] [Bursting] [Authoritative] [Provoking] [Inciting] [Branding], Purifying Edge [Cleansing] [Searing] [Purging] [Sanctifying] [Terminating] [Judging], Justice's Rebuke [Flaming] [Bashing], Revealing Light
Essence: 0
Infusions: x2 Mythic (Specialization), Mythic (Gear)
Gear: <TPSB>, (Convergent Edge) [Ruination 1] Divine Revenge, (Explorer's Embrace / Beacon) Paragon Armor, (Prosthetic Savant) Astral Appendages, (Draconic Sovereign) Arbiter's Sight, (Anathema) Astral Sleeve, (Reinforced) Psycrystal Lattice, (Pinnacle) NICIF-EP, (Restoring) Flame of Valor, Retribution Carbine (20 shots / battery)

"So, Demon Lord Ryun. Let's track him. Holy Hunt." Jace saw the golden line shoot off to his left—to the north. Checking against his map, he saw that it lined up with a settlement. And glancing down, he let his Dark Energy Mine fade and landed on top of the muck. *Nice. The (Lightfoot) Augmentation from way back on Nihilethelea lets me walk on top of this gunk.* He began sprinting across the surface.

Before he had gone even fifty feet, his [Danger-Sense] notified him of something in front of and below him. Drawing his Divine Revenge, he activated Crusader's Bastion and prepared for a fight. Placing a Dark Energy Mine on his chest, he waited until the danger got closer.

When it was right under him, he detonated the mine and pushed off the surface of the liquid—which, to his surprise, did not also begin to displace or float, as if his Skill had no effect on the rules of this part of reality.

A pair of jaws shot up out of the murk and snapped up at him—but he was just out of range. An Astral Demon that looked like a mix between Shhiv's species of Churkun, but instead of taking shark features and adding humanoid ones atop it, this thing was more like a crocodile-person. Still an Astral Demon, they must have partially gone down the refinement path of evolution, as they did look somewhat similar to the other humanoid demons on higher Layers.

But the monstrous features were quite apparent: scaled, leather skin that crackled with a bright, almost glaring pink energy of Psykinetic wrath bound within the flesh. A mouth that extended out, snoutlike and bristling with teeth that also crackled with the pink energy. The thing jumped out of the water, trying to bite onto Jace's foot.

Void Step, he thought as he warped himself just above and behind the thing. Stabbing down, he got it right through the head. The demon thrashed and tried to duck down into the water, but Jace just dismissed his Dark Energy Mine and dropped his hips down, tightening his thighs like a vice, repeating a familiar encounter from way back on Velenar Prime when his journey first started. He stabbed down into the head, neck, and back—over and over—as the demon tried to buck him off, snap its head around at him, or get at him in some way.

Jace was ruthless and squeezed with even more force—his powerful prosthetic thighs able to crush the creature beneath him, all the while his sword plunging into the thing's body cavity. The gold and green flames flickered and sizzled under the muck—still visible but dulled in the liquid morass.

Finally, the demon stilled and turned to Essence—the Souls inside them spreading through the mud in all directions. *How much?* Jace thought to Ollie as he stepped up atop the thick, sludge-consistency water.

900! Ollie replied. *And remember, 6,000 Essence for each level. We need 48,000 to reach 60, and then another 7,000 for level 61 and Potency 7!*

Jace kept following the golden line of his Holy Hunt, rushing toward the Demon Lord he wanted to meet with for intel on his marks.

Shhiv finished the last of the alterations to the array and wiped sweat from her brow. She pulled up her innate Cosmic System and sent off a message to Jace inquiring about how he was doing. The response came back a few minutes later as she was taking a water break in the break room off to the side of the Penrose Sphere's hangar bay.

[Hey honey.]
[I've been doing well.]
[Been leveling up pretty quickly, and my Potency is already 6!]
[I miss you.]
[Let's go somewhere nice on my next return visit.]
[Maybe Harkon Secundus?]
[We haven't been there since I proposed.]

Shhiv smiled with unrestrained glee and quickly sent a message back. "I'll get all the plans sorted! See you when you get back, my love. Send."

Xero walked into the break room, a very hands-on engineer, unlike Xera, who had utilized a bunch of robots and drones to do her work. He sighed as he sank into a chair opposite Shhiv. "Well, we are all ready for the expansion project to guard beneath the funnel."

Shhiv finished off her cup of water and nodded. "What's the next step?"

Xero leaned back and put one pair of arms behind his head, the other pair holding onto the table as he reclined in the chair. "Framework. It will need to be done quickly so we don't draw undue attention. Then, once the support structure is in place"—he snapped one pair of fingers behind his head—"bang, we get The Architect's Gate extended down and in place."

Shhiv leaned forward on the table. "What about the ground beneath? Is there a base to the Layer? Underground?"

Xero waved his hand dismissively. "There's a bedrock level, yes, that is some type of impenetrable substance. Not even Void could get through it. The framework is going to go all the way down to that." He sighed. "I tasked some drones to dig out the space we'll need. But this is going to be dangerous . . . we need others."

Shhiv heard the comms pick up, and Quinn spoke, "Everyone is on the call, Xero."

Greg's voice came over the comms. "I read the brief. Seems straightforward enough. Do we have a time for the operation figured out?"

"Yes," Xero replied. "We've got it all set up and ready to go. Three days from now." He looked at Shhiv. "We won't have Jace to help us out, so everyone will need to be on high alert. The starships, thanks to Shhiv's efforts, are ready to go and should be able to keep threats off of the work site—but Greg, Missy, Priam, Dee, Ree—you'll be a response force to specific locations if we notice an increase in demon activity."

Shhiv took a shaky breath. *I'll be as safe as can be*, she thought. *Greg's going to have his Skills on me, so even if I get hit, I won't really be hurt. It's going to be scary, though.*

Xero seemed to pick up on her discomfort and unease, as he cut the comms and leaned forward. "Hey. We can't do this without you. I'll keep you safe. Nothing is going to happen, I promise."

Shhiv was still concerned, but she knew that what he had described was necessary for the long-term safety of their Universe. For an eternal peace of a closed loop, where she and Jace could have a perfect existence for all time. "Okay. I'll be ready."

Chapter Twenty-Eight

Intel

Jace reached into his TPSB and pulled out the Retribution Carbine. It was fully charged, and he noted several Runes had been etched into the weapon by Shhiv—[Interaction] [Penetrating] [Ruination 1] [Accuracy 1] [Explosive 1]. *Always keeping an eye out for me*, he thought with a slight smile. Flicking the safety off, Jace took aim at the Astral Demon rapidly approaching.

He had seen the massive demon flying across the skies toward him. Not as large as the dragon, but easily the size of the Zifran he had fought on Harkon Secundus. It was arcing through the air without wings and, according to Ollie's intel on the Layer, had to be a Potency above him to overcome the Layer's inherent limitations.

The demon was akin to a bird of prey—some type of raptor—with a sharp, jagged beak, long claws that almost dragged along the surface of the swamp beneath it, a vibrant tuft of feathers along the neck that then gave way to leathery hide, and a flared tail made of some fleshy membrane that seemed to help with navigation and steering during flight.

Raising the weapon on his shoulder, Jace activated the (Vengeful) Infusion, feeling a deep pain in his stomach as he gritted his teeth. The weapon glowed with a brighter golden shine, and Jace let loose with a charged shot from the weapon. The laser shot out at the speed of light, slammed into the demon, and left behind gaping wound in the body that flickered with a golden flame that slowly burned it.

The thing roared, and Jace manifested his Crusader's Bastion, holding it in front of him with his left arm while keeping the gun upright with his right. A lance of Psykinetic energy slammed into his shield, and then an idea struck Jace. He willed the shield to alter form slightly—creating a small groove on the side he could rest the barrel of the firearm into it. Now, with a palisade in front of him protecting him from the bolts of energy that slammed into his redoubt, he was able to fire back.

Another charged shot, and a smaller explosion that left a searing wound on the demon. It kept approaching, and Jace fired off another two shots, draining the battery. Quickly ejecting it, he put the battery and the gun into the TPSB, drawing his sword in the same, smooth motion. The weapon ignited with the gold and green flames as the miasmic crimson dripped down the length.

The demon made a passing run at him, sharp talons lashing down. Jace blocked with the shield and returned a strike with the sword, scoring a deep wound that almost cut clean through the appendage. The creature let out a shriek and pulled up, flying high into the sky above.

Detonate, Jace thought as he activated the Dark Energy Mine on his torso. Curling his legs under him, he leaped skyward, using his Soul Tether to get more height as he ascended at a speed rivaling the demon's travel skyward. Jace had to use another few Soul Tether midair grapples to reorient himself, but he got up next to the thing and launched himself at it—stabbing deep into the underside and wrenching the sword back and forth.

The demon let out a screech, and more claws surged out of its stomach, cutting and slashing at Jace. He only blocked a few, parried one, and then was struck by several more that scraped against his armor. But one claw hooked him around the shoulder, and he was yanked up as the demon continued to ascend.

Raging Cleave (Rank 10), Jace thought as he slashed into the creature with a vertical uppercut. The phantasmal projection of the sword continued up through the body, cutting the thing clean in half and causing the lower half to fall away abruptly—the top half with the wings continuing skyward with Jace forced along for the ride by the claw that was now tearing into his shoulder. The talon pierced the armor and dug under his shoulder blade, eliciting a yelp of pain from the Dreamer.

The demon didn't seem to mind its lost lower body as it quickly whipped itself in the air and flung Jace, spinning from the momentum. Quickly firing off the Soul Tether, he arrested his momentum and caught his bearings as the demon wheeled around and shot right at him.

Jace put his sword directly in front of himself, letting it float there, tip facing the demon that approached, and when it was a few feet away, he kicked with all of his might—deactivating his Dark Energy Mine as he did so—and used Void Step to warp above the creature.

The sword, propelled far harder by the kick than his throw would have allowed for, skewered the demon right through the beak and planted itself somewhere in the middle of the body—giving off gold explosions as it buried deep. Jace landed atop the now-streaking-to-the-ground demon, holding on tight and summoning Divine Revenge back to his grip. Then, putting two hands on the hilt, he stabbed down—right between the wings of the creature.

It went limp and turned to ash and dust—Souls spilling out and falling to the murky mire below and Essence suffusing Jace's body. A quick trio of Soul Tethers helped to lower him back to the swamp's surface. *That wasn't too bad*, he thought.

And another 1,000 Essence, Ollie commented. *Well on our way to another level up.*

Jace followed the golden trail of the Holy Hunt that guided him over the marshes. He was able to travel quickly, thanks to being able to run atop the muck and thickened liquid, and sprinting atop the dark waters was an odd experience, as he felt the slight tension of the surface under his foot that threatened to break and send him tumbling into the muck—but it never did.

A half cycle passed before he arrived at a dirt platform. It slowly rose out of the bog and elevated higher until the dirt met large stone palisades, huge fences that had tiny gaps in between the slats.

"Hold there!" a feminine voice shouted from above.

Jace looked up to see an Astral Demon—refined path for sure, given that he could barely tell she was not like one of the species from up on Layer 1, especially with the heavy metal armor covering her body. "I'm Wraith—here to meet Ryun. Can you tell . . . them I'm here?"

The voice shouted back, "You a Dreamer? Demon?"

"Dreamer," Jace shouted back up. *Void Step*, he thought as he warped atop the wall next to her. "I'm not a threat, promise."

She wheeled to her left to face him, beginning to draw a weapon, but Jace just tapped his torso and some golden flames surged from the gaps between his armor pieces. Her hand fell off the hilt of the hand ax on her hip, strapped with some type of leathery hide. "Ah . . . gold flame Psykinetics." She nodded. "Definitely not a threat to us, then." She pointed into the center of the stone-palisade-lined settlement. "He's there."

Atop the walling, Jace could see more of the locale. Buildings were made from more of the odd stone palisades with mud shoved in between the slats. The walls were sparsely manned, with a few other Astral Demons around the small village that glanced up at the sudden arrival of a new visitor.

Jace jumped down to the dirt below and walked along the golden path, entering one of the buildings by pushing aside a leathery cloth that stood in for a door.

There were reeds piled up in one corner, and an Astral Demon that looked very humanoid but with a few small spikes and horns poking out of their skin stirred from their spot on the hay pile. "Fwasit?" they asked.

Jace just crossed his arms and stood expectantly. "Demon Lord Ryun?" he asked.

"Thassme," Ryun slurred out as he stood up, stretching. "Whose are you?"

"I'm Wraith. Ancients sent me."

That seemed to immediately jolt Ryun to a wakeful state, and his four eyes snapped onto Jace. "Ah. Sorry 'bout that. I enjoy a good nap." He yawned and walked across the room—past Jace—and to a small stone table that was propped up on a few rocks. "Sorry about the accommodations. This place is temporary."

Jace walked over next to him. "Tell me about the targets I'm going for on this Layer."

Ryun's fists—all four of them—gripped tightly, and he would've been white-knuckled if not for his pale brown skin. "They are all here," he said, pointing to an Astral System screen that only he could see.

"Hey, can't see it. Show me the map."

"Oh . . . shit, sorry." Ryun made some alteration, and Jace could see a map of the Layer that matched up to Ollie's—with some other notations such as Vault locations. "This place here," he said as he tapped a large fortification directly in the center of the Layer. "This is called The Solid Place. Big city, same type of stone as the buildings here and walls around us." He sniffed a little, wiping his nose with one forearm before continuing. "Demons drove me out, along with my friends here. Some of us got killed." He went silent at that, as if contemplative.

This one does not seem very lordly like the others we have encountered, Ollie observed.

Yeah. Makes me wonder . . . Jace spoke softly, "Did you prior leader die, by chance?"

Ryun nodded somberly, and Jace could have sworn he saw a tear in the demon's eye before he turned away. "Yeah. My best friend. Died getting the rest of us out. He told me to carry on after him."

Jace felt a pang of sympathy for the demon. "Right. Condolences. Tell me about the target I'm killing."

Ryun just said a name. "Gar. Just Gar. Got a whole bunch of demons together, declared himself Demon Lord, and took over The Solid Place." Ryun huffed with anger and pent-up aggression. He looked over at Jace, and there was a sadistic gleam in his eyes. "Gar is mostly refined, with a splash of monstrous evolution—like me. Powerful Psykinetic user."

Jace internally scoffed. *I haven't fought any Psykinetic user that has made me really worried*, he thought. But aloud, he said, "I'll get right on it. Might get a Vault first, though."

"Fair enough." Ryun walked over to the hay pile and laid back down on it. "If you wouldn't mind." He pointed to the flap door.

Jace left the building, and Ollie spoke in his mind. *I feel sorry for the guy. Kicked out of his home and having to live rough like this.*

Well, the sooner we beat a Vault, the sooner we'll go and clear out his home. I just hope we don't have to then escort him and his group over there. That would be a pain in the ass. Jace used his Soul Tether to ascend, getting over the wall, and used Holy Hunt to zero in on the Vault close by. He began sprinting across the mud and murk, using Void Stalker as he headed to current goal.

Tibalt reached the odd stone construction in the middle of the Layer. A massive walled fortification that felt wholly out of place. He could not see any entrance and began circling to the southern edge. The sounds from the inside let him know exactly what was within. Astral Demons.

Reaching the southernmost side, he saw a section of the wall that had been pulled down—a type of drawbridge-style entry into the solid city. *Finally getting out of this muck*, Tibalt thought as he stepped up onto the stone and sighed in relief.

"Hey. You." He looked up to see another demon—this one a humanoid-crocodile-shark mix; tall stature with a long snout, horns, and spikes growing from their scaled hide. "Yeah. You."

Tibalt sneered, "What about me?"

"You looking for a Demon Lord to serve? We got ourselves a good one. Gar."

"No," Tibalt replied as he looked past the gate guard and into the empty stone city. "Where is everyone? The only non-swamp place I've been to, you would think its full up." He felt genuine curiosity overwhelm his hunger and desire to rip and tear this demon apart—taking his accumulated Souls and his Essence.

"We drove them out," the demon replied. "Gar rules now."

Tibalt grinned a vicious, evil grin. "Thank you." He activated his Psykinetic claws and surged forward, gripping the demon by the snout and ripping the head clean off with a vicious scream of victory. The Souls began to pour out of the neck hole, and Tibalt put his mouth to it and gobbled them up—also feeling the soothing heat of Essence race through him as the screams from within stormed even louder in his ears.

"Hey!" Tibalt dropped the now-vanishing corpse as he stalked forward to the next victim. Another demon who was inside of the city. "Fucking Dreamer Demon!" the figure shouted as they pulled out a large mace.

Tibalt ran forward, dodging the mace at the last second before unleashing a vicious heel kick that caught the demon on the side, crushing bones and organs inside its body. He followed up with a vicious stab to the head—burying his claws inside the brain as he rent and tore the skull asunder. More Souls poured out, and he gobbled them up as he siphoned the Essence.

He could hear more coming. Much more. Ten or twenty. Too many for him to take on. Instead, Tibalt retreated to the swamp, sinking into the murk and muck as he moved off to the side of the walls. Hoping for more victims. Easy prey.

Chapter Twenty-Nine

The Sunken Vault

Jace continued to blitz his way across the landscape. He encountered a few more of the crocodile-like demons, but they were extremely easy for him to deal with in small, one-on-one encounters. He baited them in, jumped up, got on top of them, and stabbed them until they died. It was clean, efficient, and brutal.

This slaughter of demons ended up netting him a good 3,600 Essence, putting him just 500 Essence shy of the 6,000 requirement to level up.

Progression is starting to slow down, he thought. *I need more large-scale fights and less of these small one-on-one fights.*

We could always just openly broadcast your location onto the Astral System. Let everyone who wants that bounty know right where you are.

Jace frowned. *That doesn't seem very smart. Can we limit it to this Layer alone?*

There are different messaging apparatus for each Layer. But someone could . . . effectively copy and paste the announcement I make to other Layer's messaging platforms. Forget my idea. It was just an idea, but thinking it through out loud, not quite as smart.

I think we could do it, Jace thought back. *Just need a place where they can only come from one location.* He looked at the map, and an idea crossed his mind. *We can hit the Vault, go up a Layer, and then broadcast a signal. Get a bunch on that Layer to come after me. Then, once we have acquired a bunch of Essence, head back down to clear out The Solid Place for our Mission.*

Sounds like a plan. I will start to figure out what the message should look like.

Jace stopped in his travel as the golden line shot straight down into the mud and muck. *Void Removal (Rank 1)*, he thought as he pictured all of the mud being forced aside. But nothing happened. *Damn. Should've figured.* He took a deep breath and then plunged into the surface of the muddy water.

Visibility was nil save for the golden line that he followed. He went down and could feel the cold, seeping squishiness of the mud and water flowing all over him under the armor. It was disgusting, and he was thankful he could not smell anything while submerged.

Then, he breached some inner surface. Getting past all of the mud, he pushed into a large clear-water space. *Was there an ocean hidden under the surface the whole time?* he thought.

Querying . . . seems like pockets of this Layer have hidden reservoirs.

Jace was grateful for the clear waters. He looked around and could see arcing stone around the sides that gracefully met at a hole that he had just swum through—about five feet across. Beneath him was a tunnel that doubtless led to a Vault.

But something felt off. He couldn't put his finger on it, and nothing in his [Danger-Sense] was activating—but he couldn't shake the feeling that he was being watched. *Revealing Light*, he thought as he activated the newly acquired Talent. A pulsing shockwave of bright white energy surged out from him.

On the cavern wall to his left, he could now clearly see an Astral Demon that had camouflaged itself against the wall. It was limned in white light and seemed to have noticed him—as it slowly turned its head to track him.

Oh. Interesting. Some type of Talent that allows for chameleonlike camouflaging. Neat!

Jace activated his Talents and Skills, but the thing just continued to track him. It did not make a move towards hostility in any way, and Jace swam his way down to the tunnel that led to the Vault—keeping a wary eye on the thing the whole time.

When he reached the tunnel itself, then the astral demon moved. It swam up through the hole that Jace had entered from. *Weird*, Ollie commented. *Wonder what that was about.*

Not sure, Jace thought back. *But I'm happy to be full on energy when we enter this Vault.* Jace swam down until he found the familiar Vault door, and as he touched it, he was sucked through and into the dry interior of the area. Water dripped from him, and he shook his head slightly to get the water out of the helmet of the armor.

An Astral System message appeared in his vision. A familiar sight.

[Vault Challenge—Activated.]
[Show your endurance.]

The world warped around Jace, and he found himself armorless, gearless save for some undergarments, standing on a pedestal with a pair of pillars on either side of him. Chains were wrapped around the pillars and then wrapped around his wrists. He was in an empty white room, devoid of other features save the grey pillars and silvery chains.

Oh, interesting. This is a type of weight setup called Hercules Pillars. You need to hold them.

Jace gripped the chains, which quickly fell to either side. He could feel the strain on his shoulders where the joints of his prosthetics met with his torso—all now one piece thanks to the various Gear and Relics he had acquired thus far. The weight wasn't horrible—and he was able to hold it with little effort.

[Calculating appropriate weight . . .]
[Weight edited: 3,000 lbs. per arm.]

Jace gritted his teeth and had to heft with all of his might as the pillars suddenly became much denser. He could feel the strain and tension across his body and closed his eyes as he tried to focus on his breathing. The pressure kept building up in his shoulders and back, and he felt a deep soreness spread across his prosthetic muscles.

Then, he had an idea. *Don't heal me,* he thought to the NICIF. Then, Jace used the (Vengeful) Infusion over and over again, feeling the intense pain build up in his stomach. But through almost squeezed-shut eyes, he looked at his HUD and waited until he saw the health indicator dip below half. He was shaking and panting with exertion.

Shattered Limits (Rank 19), he thought, as he had injured himself enough to activate the Skill. The pillars felt like nothing, and he quickly pulled them up to their starting positions.

> [Calculating appropriate weight . . .]
> [Weight edited: 300,000 lbs. per arm.]

Oh, come on! Jace thought as the pillars pulled both directions, and he let out a grunt of pain as he engaged his whole body.

<u>*Looks like the Vault knows that you used a Skill that amplified your physical traits by x100, and so it is compensating to keep the challenge consistent. By the way, the weight is about equivalent to a blue whale from Earth—before they went extinct.*</u>

How long do I have to hold this?

<u>*No idea.*</u>

Jace felt the chain slipping slightly on his right arm, but the NICIF came to the rescue and altered his skin to be rougher and covered with small protrusions that hooked onto the chains and kept them firmly affixed.

Jace lost track of time, just watching as his energy drained. He could feel the breaking point coming on and finally let the two pillars go—they thundered to the ground with a tremendous crash that shattered the floor—the

NICIF returning his skin to normal so that he wouldn't be losing a limb from the spiked protrusions snagging on the released chains.

Jace crouched down and sucked in deep breaths as he just let his arms hang there. *Now you can heal me*, he thought to the NICIF. The Vault returned all around him, as did his Gear and Equipment—including the TPSB. Immediately, Jace reached into it, pulled out a pile of survival meals, and sat down as he tore through one after another—gobbling down the food as the NICIF set to work on repairing his muscles, torn prosthetic tissue, and internal damage he had self-inflicted.

When he was full and the NICIF notified him he was fully mended, Jace stood up and grabbed the Relic crystal floating above the pedestal.

[You have acquired a Relic of the Ancients.]
[Relic Capacity Detected.]
[Relic converted to Relic Upgrade Matrix.]

What to use this one on? he thought as he held it.

Armor, since you did the sword last time, Ollie stated.

[Relic Equipped.]
[Hero's Plate.]
[Amplifies depth of emotion related to the Valiance Emotion Source. Interacts with Psykinetics. Additionally, the armor is reinforced by depth of emotion.]

More defenses the more heroic I act. Good.

Take a breath!

Jace took a big inhale of air before he was sucked out of the Vault and floating in the water of the hallway outside of the door. Turning around, he headed back up the small tunnel, toward the underwater cave that would lead him to the surface.

Tibalt had successfully been picking off the demons in the fortified settlement until they finally had enough of losing perimeter guards and lifted the drawbridge gateway up. Unfortunately for them, he had already snuck his way inside before they made that decision.

And he had been stalking them since he got inside. Waiting until one went off on their own, slaughtering them, and then making his way across the entire settlement to strike again. Over and over, only taking breaks to find a place to sleep off in a distant, forgotten corner. Despite being a Dreamer Demon, he was still a mortal, and needed rest.

As he slept, fitful nightmares embraced him. The Souls in him ensured his rest was tumultuous, and he tossed and turned throughout the cycle as he tried to let his mind recover. But the voices were too much, and he consumed them all in a singular level-up burst.

[You have reached the next Potency.]
[Choose your path: monstrous or refined.]

"Monstrous," he whispered. The Souls in his chest all vanished, leaving him in a blissful silence that he knew he could actually sleep through. But before that was the pain of changing. Pain he had experienced several times now, having roughly split his evolution path along both tracks of refinement and monstrosity.

His skin cracked, muscles expanding and flexing as he envisioned the strongest creature in his Universe, shaping his evolution along the inspiration of that monstrosity. The deadliest of all predators who once threatened all of their existence and creation.

Tibalt's limbs lengthened as his body grew tauter and gaunter, sallow cheeks and hollowed stomach giving him a gangly appearance. Far away, one might mistake him for a tall Vanguard. But up close, he was a monster—his skin shifted to a deep crimson hide that was flecked with shimmering white scales that denoted an improved natural defense.

His claws shimmered and elongated, becoming all the deadlier. Tibalt would have let out a cackling howl of delight if he could—but he needed rest. Returning to a prone position as the pain faded, he closed his eyes and let sleep take him—the Souls no longer being a nuisance.

The Loud Ancient looked at the various monitors and tracking programs they were running. An alert caught his eye, and he turned sideways to more closely examine it. *Oh good!* He began relaying a message back before sending it off.

He was in charge of fulfilling their end of the bargain with Wraith. The Judgement Matrix was ready to go, but The Ancients had promised that they would contact the appropriate individuals in the Afterlives to notify them of X's plan. Thankfully, they were quite pleasant individuals—the most positive, joyous, and uplifting mirror of the sometimes-misery of the Universes on the opposite side of reality.

X had reached out again and informed The Ancients of the updated plans in regard to Wraith taking a vessel and a storage device, which was a far wiser plan than creating a permanent tunnel. But ultimately, the Loud Ancient did not care too much one way or the other. Because they were almost done.

Just one more clear-through of the Mantle of Burden, he thought. *Then we can merge and head to join The Council! Well, after we onboard the new Ancients and hand over the reins—including making introductions with our new on-call Bearer.* That was the most soothing thought of them all for the two Ancients. They would have an immortal and quite powerful Dreamer who could go into each Layer and reset them with relative ease.

Provided he survives, that is. But backups were well-prepared.

Another notification popped into the Loud Ancient's monitor, and he frowned. *Huh . . . Void and Dark Matter entwined . . . but in the Layers?* He immediately pulled up all known individuals who had harnessed that power—a very small list, thankfully. *Oh, X, you rascal,* he thought.

Pulling up the Astral System's interface, the Loud Ancient quickly did an audio call. "Hey there, X."

A masculine voice responded, "X here. You must be The Ancient."

"One of them," the Loud One replied. "But . . . uhm . . . you're not a female."

"My sister is out of commission. I took over for the time being."

Did I miss an alert on that? The Loud Ancient quickly went through his message queues and frowned. *No, I definitely didn't. Huh. Something about their Cosmic System prevents Astral System alerts from going out . . . neat.*

The male voice continued, "How can I help you?"

"Just checking if you used Void and Dark Matter to seal up the entrance from Layer 9 to Layer 10."

"Yup, that was me channeling Wraith's power."

"Ah. Well . . . okay . . . I understand why you did it, since Valcrinox's forces are almost ready to push away the call of the depths . . . but this is going to disrupt the Astral Verge's ecosystem."

The voice came back with concern laced throughout. "Oh, crap. Did I mess something up?"

"Not really, just can't keep it there forever."

The tone was filled with relief. "Oh, good. It should be for a short time. Just until Wraith gets to Potency 10 and can actually stand a chance against Valcrinox's forces."

"Understood. Thank you for the information. If you will indulge me—how did you keep Astral System notifications from going out?" the Loud Ancient asked.

"Ah . . ." X trailed off for a moment before returning with a confident and calm tone. "I have been making some tweaks in our Cosmic System—ensuring that the two remain separate. When we eventually isolate ourselves in our closed loop, we don't want anyone except a handful of our Signers to be Dreamers."

That is fair, I suppose. If everyone learned of the Astral Verge, they may try to break their way into the Verge for whatever reason. Mortals are so irrational. The Loud Ancient nodded. "Well, thanks for the heads up! Next time you make changes to the Astral Verge, just let us know."

"Will do! Sorry, I just took over, so I'm still figuring out some notes I was left."

The Loud Ancient, normally a very carefree person, felt a slight twinge of concern. "Well, best wishes to your out-of-commission fellow."

"She'll be fine," X replied. "We were around before you lot tore holes in our Universes."

That long? Interesting. He sighed, "Well, I apologize on behalf of my predecessors. It was an unfortunate accident. But, in a way, it was also a blessing—giving Souls the chance to see the realms of pure delight in the Afterlives."

X's voice sounded firm. "Well . . . I guess that is one way to think of it. Goodbye." The audio feed went silent.

The Loud Ancient sighed and felt authentic remorse for the actions of his trans-reality species. *Once we are on The Council,* he thought, *we can change things so this doesn't happen again.*

Chapter Thirty

A Brief Respite

Jace left the tunnel and was immediately alerted by [Danger-Sense] as dozens of projectiles headed his way. Almost reflexively, he activated Void Shield—and the green flames surged around him as the Skill manifested.

Psykinetic Talents pummeled him from all directions, and he could not see past the storm of projectiles. Beams, crackling arcs of electricity, flaming bolts, icy spears—all of them flew into him and were negated thanks to his shield. But that drained his energy rapidly.

It gave Jace enough time to use Crusader's Bastion, placing the shield in front of himself and retreating to the tunnel entrance proper, effectively blocking off all harm thanks to the shield blocking the entrance. More Psykinetic Talents slammed into his Bastion, and thanks to the (Retaliating) Infusion, the gold flame bolts shot back to strike the attackers.

After a few seconds of fruitless Psykinetic assault, the incoming attacks faded, and Jace could see through the still-clear water. Ollie was able to use his sight to tag each of them, painting them with a red arrow indicating their position and number. *Thirty?* he thought. *And my Shattered Limits isn't online?*

Must be because your Void Skills are now in play, so the calculation is taking that into account. Ollie sounded just as frustrated. *Well, you are safe here for now. And can always Void Step out of here. But this is a nice killing field.*

Jace was irritated at the ambush, but Ollie had a good point—these demons had come to him and would be easy to slaughter in the enclosed space. *We have the Emergency Battery still; time to go all out.* He used Void Beam (Rank 1) [Horizon-Splitter].

The entire world before him erupted in green flames that surged forth. They consumed the water, utterly annihilating the substance as mud and muck rushed in from above only to be destroyed as well. The Astral Demons in the chamber were obliterated, the blue of the Souls in them surging out in an explosion as they dropped to the stone floor and seeped down through the Layer's base. White Essence surged out, pooling in the air before floating to him and suffusing him with warmth.

With his energy zeroed out, Jace automatically drew on the Emergency Battery, refilling his energy to full, which kept him healthy and hale. The green flames vanished, and the mud began to fill the room. Jace used Void Step to get out of the chamber—the walls of which had kept intact—and another to get out above the muck and mud, using his Soul Tether to hold himself aloft above the murky depths.

The substance of the Layer itself must not be matter or subject to Void's power, Ollie reasoned.

Jace saw beams of light under the turbulent liquid and brought his Crusader's Bastion to bear, angling it to block the now-cascading-up-to-him projectiles. Each one that thudded into the shield seemed to tear away at the surface of the defensive barricade, and he had to keep reinforcing it with more energy. A few shots found their way around his defenses and slammed into his legs, causing intense pain that felt like he was being cut into by some serrated carver.

Dropping down, Jace activated Void Shield and prepared for attacks. But, to his frustration, the Astral Demons kept at a distance and just pelted him. He could get his Crusader's Bastion in the way of most shots, but a few hit his Void Shield and drained his energy. *Void Step*, Jace thought as he warped behind one of the demons.

Swinging his sword down in a vertical chop, he sliced clean through the creature—but it healed itself with some Talent that worked against his damage-over-time effects. But, ultimately, Jace had far too many of such persistent harm Skills, Talents, and Specializations active; the regeneration couldn't keep up, and the thing collapsed into the murk before dissipating.

Jace looked at the next demon, used Void Step to immediately get above and behind it, and repeated the feat. Each time, his energy dropped. But they were effectively guaranteed one-shot kills thanks to the stacking burns, bleeding nebula, and annihilating power of retextured green-flame Void. Within seconds, he had slaughtered the entire bunch and soaked up even more Essence.

Easy, he thought as he sheathed the sword and let his Skills and Talents fade. *And we still have twenty percent of my energy left over.*

It was very easy. The build is coming together, Ollie said with delight. *And we are now at 42,000 Essence total! That is seven levels' worth.*

Well, may as well use all of it. Let's do it. Jace began moving toward The Solid Place on his map in his HUD while the Astral System screens flickered in front of him.

[You have leveled up!]
[You have chosen Specialization of Existing Talent!]
[Talent Name: Revealing Light.]
[Specialization Name: Burdening.]
[Effect: Those affected by Revealing Light move slower as heavy light drags upon them.]
[Specialization Name: Limning.]
[Effect: The linked Talent effect lasts for an entire cycle.]
[Specialization Name: Fracturing.]
[Effect: The linked Talent reduces a foe's defenses.]
[Specialization Name: Potent.]
[Effect: The linked Talent temporarily blinds foes that rely on sight.]
[Specialization Name: Perilous.]
[Effect: The linked Talent ignites a searing damage-over-time effect on affected targets.]
[Specialization Name: Linking.]
[Effect: Enables all other Talents to apply Revealing Light.]
[Talent Name: Justice's Rebuke.]

[Specialization Name: Holy.]
[Effect: When the linked Talent is activated, the user's weapons and Talents deal additional damage in the form of searing radiance.]

Name: Jace Seren (Potency 6)
Emotion [Class Level]: Valiant [Lightbringer 59]
Talent [Specialization]: Astral Adaptation, Astral Translation, Valiant Crusader's Might [Burning] [Vengeful] [Poised] [Unstoppable] [Bracing] [Voidbound], Crusader's Bastion [Retaliating] [Reinforcing] [Grounding] [Redoubt] [Spiked] [Resonating], Hero's Arena [Aura] [Incinerating] [Vexing] [Bolstering] [Suppressing] [Wrathbound], Indomitable Will [Zealous] [Intimidating] [Inviolable] [Enduring] [Ameliorating] [Dark Matter Binding], Templar's Smite [Spear] [Blast] [Lingering] [Challenging] [Inferno] [Cosmic], Holy Hunt [Marked] [Bursting] [Authoritative] [Provoking] [Inciting] [Branding], Purifying Edge [Cleansing] [Searing] [Purging] [Sanctifying] [Terminating] [Judging], Justice's Rebuke [Flaming] [Bashing] [Holy], Revealing Light [Burdening] [Limning] [Fracturing] [Potent] [Perilous] [Linking]
Essence: 0
Infusions: x2 Mythic (Specialization), Mythic (Gear)
Gear: <TPSB>, (Convergent Edge) [Ruination 1] Divine Revenge, (Explorer's Embrace / Beacon) Hero's Plate, (Prosthetic Savant) Astral Appendages, (Draconic Sovereign) Arbiter's Sight, (Anathema) Astral Sleeve, (Reinforced) Psycrystal Lattice, (Pinnacle) NICIF-EP, (Restoring) Flame of Valor, Retribution Carbine (20 shots / battery)

Wow, Ollie said. *That Revealing Light applying to anything else you hit? That is going to really amplify your effectiveness.*

Jace nodded. *Yeah. Good thing we are building out a solid path of progression. Level 59, only 41 more to go.*

And even then, you do not need to reach level 100—just Potency 10.

Jace chuckled as he ran across the swamp. *I'm going to make damned sure that I can take on Valcrinox in Layer 10. I'm capping out my progression.*

And who knows? Maybe something special happens at level 100 that is restricted knowledge. Can you search the Astral System and see what the highest-level Dreamer has been?

Checking now . . . Oh, wow! Ollie said with some shock, *no Dreamer has reached level 51 or higher. Seems that it just gets too perilous. I can see why; without The Cosmic System and the dozens of amplifying Skills you have going on in the background passively, it would be tricky to survive.*

We didn't encounter anyone else from another Universe with a System, Jace observed. *I thought that might be a possibility.*

There were other Systems, but most were far, far beneath The Cosmic System in terms of sheer power. Not even worth alerting you. The equivalent of Tier 1 or 2 Aspirants.

Jace let out a barking laugh. *Yeah, you're right—no need to notify me of people like that who don't pose a threat.*

He continued racing off across the mud and bog of the swamp. The travel went quickly as he followed Holy Hunt toward the Demon Lord's location—his Holy Hunt focused on the Demon Lord Gar.

Tibalt had slaughtered all but thirty Astral Demons that had holed themselves up in the centermost building—afraid of the "marsh stalker" as he'd heard them call him.

He wanted to break down the doors. To rip them apart, claw into them, steal their Souls and suck down their Essence. But he had reached Potency 7, and the depths called to him. With loping strides, he went to the main entrance and activated the lever that dropped the bridge door contraption into the muck.

He dove into the murky mire and began swimming toward the next Layer but paused as he heard something in the distance. *Shink-plap shink-plap.* Poking his head up just enough for his eyes to see, he observed a Dreamer running across the top of the marshy waters, their armor making a jostling sound.

He recognized the person despite the changed armor. *Wraith*, he thought with a vile sense of disgust and repulsion. *The bastard.* He kept his distance, slowly moving away as Wraith moved into the castle-like fortification of stone. Backing up ever further, he recoiled in horror as he saw an enormous explosion of green flames that expanded up to the skies above—utterly annihilating everything it touched.

The same power he had used on Tibalt's grand armada. The same purging power, but he could see it now. *It must be because I am strong enough*, he thought, *that I can view whatever used to be invisible.*

He felt a stirring in his chest. A hunger. And something told him that he should see what a blast like that took out of Wraith. Slowly, he swam closer. Crawling his way up onto the stone drawbridge, his jaw dropped in shock—the entire central building he had been fruitlessly bashing himself against, trying to gain entrance, and the back wall of the entire defensive fortification—was gone. Just vanished.

He saw Wraith on his knees, seeming to suck in breaths. *My chance!* Tibalt thought as he activated his ranged Psykinetic Talent, Highlord's Wrath. The sphere of dripping crimson energy surged into his clawed hands, and he launched the projectile forward.

But Wraith reached his hand up and vanished—the Talent splashing harmlessly against the surface. "No!" Tibalt howled into the sky. "I had him!"

Jace had drained all of his remaining energy to use Void Beam [Horizon-Splitter], taking out the Demon Lord. And, since he now had enough Essence to level up, he wanted to do it in safety. He reached up, grabbed the voidlight tether, and traveled nearly instantly back to the tether room on the Penrose Sphere.

"How much Essence are we at?" he asked as he sucked in deep breaths—very tired due to his lack of energy, and only not rendered unconscious thanks to Indomitable Will's (Enduring) Specialization.

Ollie pulled out of his head, and Jace suffered the wicked headache that accompanied the action. He didn't have enough energy for Dark Matter Mending, and so had to grit his teeth and bear the pain. "Oh! Sorry!" Ollie said. "I probably should have waited a bit."

Jace saw his energy tick up to the requisite amount and activated the Skill, mending the headache instantly. "It's fine. How much Essence?"

"27,000," Ollie declared proudly. "A nice chunk. Thankfully, all those demons had holed up in a single location. Made for easy work!"

"No kidding," Jace replied. Then, an Astral System message flicked across his vision.

> [Mission Success: Consolidate control over Layer 6 to Demon Lord Ryun.]
> [Reward: Mythic (Gear) Infusion.]
> [Sender: The Ancients.]

"Just one more Mythic Infusion," Jace said. "Then, we get a Divine one and can see what something like that earns us."

"Want to spend all of the Essence right now?" Ollie asked as he swam in little circles.

Jace thought on that for a moment. "How much does Shhiv have?"

Ollie looked at him, dumbstruck, for a moment. "Really?! Why ask?"

Jace was taken aback by the sudden turn in demeanor. "I just wanted to see how much she had."

Ollie crossed his arms and bobbed in place—his sign of distress or dismay. "She can get Essence over time later. The focus is you, getting stronger, to deal with our Astral Verge problem permanently." He pinched the bridge of his little snout. "Just . . . do not worry about her, okay?"

"Okay," Jace replied, feeling like he had just been admonished by his dad.

Ollie sighed and floated in lazy little circles. "It is okay. You just got sentimental . . . and maybe I overreacted a bit to a simple question. She has 4,000 Essence and is saving up to do a single big burst."

Jace nodded. "Thanks. I wasn't intending on giving her any of mine." He frowned. "Give me a bit more credit. I know I'm not Quinn levels of smart, but I know that I come first." He grinned, thinking about being the only Potency 10 Dreamer except for his wife. "Besides, I can get her plenty of Essence once I'm the top of the top."

"Fair enough," Ollie replied with a slight chuckle. "Again . . . sorry. I must have been a bit testy because I missed our Universe." He smiled and clapped his little paws together. "I'm going to see Josie!" he blinked out of existence with a brief pop.

Jace activated his internal Cosmic System and located Shiliv in their apartment. Using the warp network, he arrived behind her, dismissing his gear to the TPSB leaving just a bracer around his wrist, and grabbed her from behind.

She giggled as he nibbled on her neck. "You're back!"

"Mm-hmm," Jace replied. "You wanted to get out of here, right?"

"Yeah! I talked to Hualong. She said she'd host us! Really wants to pick your brain about the Astral Verge."

Jace nodded. "Then what are we waiting for?"

She wriggled out of his grip, turned around, put a hand on his chest, and pointed to the hygiene station. "You stink."

Jace laughed, "I've been swimming around a swamp."

"Smells like it. Go on!" She gave him a firm shove.

Chapter Thirty-One

Talking About Souls

Jace exited the portal that led to and from The Cosmic Corridor to Harkon Secundus—the world where his Anathema prosthetics had come from and one of the few worlds in his Universe where Soul-based magic existed. A magic known as cultivation.

He had Shhiv's hand in his, and to his surprise, the top of the temple mount was full of people. They were sitting at dozens of tables, sipping from fine cups of tea and being attended to by Civilian-marked species from across the whole of The Cosmic System.

The mountain was breathtaking at the top of the Blossom Peaks. An enormous stone platform, made of intricately laid and carved stone tablets that depicted swirling flower petals of pinks and purples on a green and blue breeze. Small veins of cerulean dashed through to create differentiation between the various portions of the design. Behind them, the portal they had come through, and further past that, a temple. A temple high upon the mountain, with a long set of stairs leading to the main complex.

An attendant walked up to Jace and Shhiv. "Hi! Welcome to Hualong's Blossom Sky Garden. Table for two?"

Jace quickly replied, "No, thank you. I'm here to see Hualong personally."

The attendant shrugged, their customer service demeanor dropping almost instantly. "Oh. Alright. Good luck." He took back up a position at a small podium near the portal entrance.

Jace led Shhiv around the portal and they walked up the steps. She squeezed his hand. "Less than a year ago you flew us up to the top."

"We didn't fly," Jace replied with a slight chuckle. "I grappled us up there."

She squeezed his hand tightly. "I know, you goof." She leaned over and gave his cheek a little lick—the closest thing she could get to a kiss thanks to her physiology. "This is a lot of steps." She glanced sideways at him. "Want to race up?"

Jace smirked, "I'll give you a three second head start."

Shhiv let his hand go and began sprinting up the steps, faster than Jace had expected as she was almost at the top by the time three seconds had passed. He could have won if he wanted to by using Void Step, but he elected to not cheat with a Skill and instead sprinted at full speed up the steps—the few hikers going from the tea garden below up to the heights of the mountain left breathless as his travel caused a localized disruption of the air itself.

He got to the top a half second after Shhiv, and she was barely huffing at all. "I won!" she said with elation.

Jace just grinned like an idiot at her joy. "Yeah. Good job."

She looked back at him. "I wonder if I could beat you in lifting?"

Jace's mind flashed back to the Vault that had him holding up those pillars and shook his head. "Sorry, hon. I think I still win in that."

She gave a slight pouty face but shrugged, grabbed his hand, and the two went inside the large facility. An enormous stone temple, carved into the mountain just below the peak where Jace had proposed to Shhiv. There was a huge stone dais on the far end where Hualong, the local Cosmic System administrator—a Divine Beast—sat. Her sinuous form was coiled in on itself, and she was observing several people who were seated on cushions, seemingly meditating.

Jace and Shhiv quieted their movement, and he used Void Stalker (Group) to ensure they did not disrupt any of the people on the cushions. He got up next to Hualong before dropping the Skill. "Long time no see."

Hualong looked over at Jace and Shhiv, cracking a slight, soft smile. "Ah," she said softly. "Welcome. Please, head to the top of the temple—I will be with you shortly."

Jace nodded and used Void Stalker (Group) once more to quietly exit with Shhiv, and the two went up the small set of side stairs to the very top of the temple. There were a few tourists looking out over the vast world of Harkon Secundus with its flying mountains and gorgeous ocean of trees expanding out almost endlessly below. But they were behind railings that had been carved from the rock face itself.

Jace walked over to an attendant at a small stone gateway, dropping his Skill. "Hi. Hualong told me to come up here."

The attendant—a Oslia, just like Priam—looked him up and down. "Ah. Yes. One moment." He turned, grabbed a well-concealed handle, and pulled—the stone sliding ponderously upon some hidden rail mechanism and revealing the very top of the mountain.

The small, flat stone underneath the cherry blossom tree had been prepared already. Large, squishy cushions in front of a low table with a tea set and several ornate dishes were set up. Shhiv went over to one and plopped down on it, and Jace trundled down next to her.

A glimmer of starlight appeared next to the duo, and with a series of two pops, Ollie and Josie showed up—both spectral otters holding little paws in the air. And both were wearing little hats. Ollie had a wide-brimmed cowboy hat on his head, and Josie had a small beret. "Oh, Harkon Secundus," Ollie said, glancing over at Jace. "A nice little reprieve."

Shhiv looked up and stifled a giggle. "Where have you two been?"

"We did an Earth world tour," Josie said. "Lots of countries have re-established their pre–corpo war identities. My favorite place was called France. Very funny sounding people; an ancient language that was almost forgotten post–corpo war but has found a resurgence under the Star Council's efforts to preserve cultural heritage."

Ollie reached a small paw and tipped his hat. "And we went to the Great Plains of North America. The Star Council used their resources to clone native populations of animals as well as terraform less populated areas as nature preserves."

Jace replied, "I'd like to visit Earth some day now that it's not all corpo hellscape."

Shhiv squeezed his hand. "We can go right after this."

There was a tremendous whoosh of air as Hualong flew up from below the cliff in front of them, her massive form floating in the air above them as tourists oohed and aahed. "Excellent. Give me a moment here," she muttered. Her body was circled by flower petals that swirled faster and faster, and then compressed before surging to the table and taking the shape of a humanoid woman next to the duo. A plant-person. "There we are," Hualong said as she picked up the tea kettle and turned a knob on the bottom before setting it back down. "Thank you for accepting my invitation."

"No problem," Jace replied as he made to grab for one of the tea cakes, but Shhiv gently smacked his hand.

"You wait until the tea is served before you eat, hon."

Jace sheepishly pulled his hand back. "Sorry. Never learned that."

Hualong stifled a slight laugh. "Ah, yes. The child of the streets who became one of the strongest entities in our creation. Feel free to ignore customs." She leaned forward, and a few of the pink flower petals cascaded from her form and onto the table before vanishing into nothingness. "I am sure you saw those who were meditating below."

"I did," Jace replied. "Are they doing what I did? Going into The Cosmic System's depths to get Stardust?"

She smiled softly. "To an extent, yes. Mostly Aspirants, but a handful of Civilians. Not just that, though. Meditation allows one to calm the raging storm of their thoughts and find an inner peace. It is a spiritual experience."

Her glowing light-blue eyes in this form narrowed slightly. "And you know quite a bit about Souls, now, don't you?"

Jace sighed and nodded. "Yes. I've seen streams of them. Freed them from demons holding onto them. What did you want to know?"

Hualong sat back and took a deep breath before beginning, prodding Jace with all sorts of questions about what he had seen, experienced, and done. With a quick glance to Ollie for permission and the Wayfinder doing something to localized space to sequester them off from the tourists, Jace shared his experiences—only stopping when Ollie advised him that he should not reveal a specific detail or other.

When he finished, Hualong let out a slight scoff. "The Architects, always so high and mighty with their technology."

Ollie replied, "Why do you say that?"

Hualong grunted slightly, and the flower petal shape took on subtle draconic features of her full-sized form as her lips tightened. "A little history lesson on our Universe. The first three worlds progressed along technological, magitech, and then magic. Formulaic magic, I should add—like what you would find on most worlds in our Universe before they pursued magitech or forsook magic for technology." She took a sip of her tea, then continued, "The next ten included mine, Harkon Secundus."

Shhiv spoke, "You said the first three, then the next ten—I'm guessing you mean with species becoming sentient?"

Hualong nodded. "Yes. It was after the second 'wave' of sentience—not an actual wave of energy, mind you, just a grouping of planetary bodies and their resident species in a close span of time—that Oblivion formed, and The Architects put their Cosmic System in place."

Jace replied, "You were around when it was all a closed loop, no Souls going to the Astral Verge."

"Yes," Hualong said softly. "For a world of cultivation like mine, Soul-based magic being how we develop ourselves, the Astral Verge opening contributed to the downfall of our world. The Arbiter tried to stave it off and come up with means to trap Souls so they could possibly be reincarnated—but those efforts were fruitless." She looked at Jace with a hard stare. "Do you know what exactly a Soul is?"

"Kind of," Jace replied. "People are a mind, body, and soul. The mind is knowledge and experience, body is the physical form, and soul is glue that holds it together."

"Indeed," Hualong replied. "But when the body dies, the mind retreats into the soul. All your life, your experiences, who you are . . . and in the case of a cultivator, their power and Soul-based magic." She raised a quizzical brow. "Your and Shhiv's innate Cosmic Systems are tied to your Souls, so even if you were to die and somehow be reborn, you would have your innate System still."

"Good to know," Shhiv replied. "Not that we plan on dying ever. That's what immortality is for."

Hualong chuckled. "Yes, System-granted immortality avoids the pesky re-sleeving issue that The Architects had to deal with. But the important detail to consider here is that Astral Demons can consume Souls." She leaned forward, and her tone dropped to one of serious conversations spoken of in huddled groups, as if afraid of who might overhear. "What happens when an Astral Demon consumes a Soul of a powerful cultivator? Or an Ascendant? One who has imprinted The Cosmic System into their very being and made it a part of them?" She shook her head. "I don't know what would happen, but I would imagine it gives that demon the means to use that Cosmic System or draw upon that cultivated Soul's magical power."

Jace had not thought of Souls in that way so far—he'd been thinking of it as the currency of Astral Demons and nothing else. People he wanted to save and help get to judgement in the Nethershift. Hence the whole entire point of working for The Ancients to clear out the Demon Lords who consumed Souls regardless of their status of being judged. But now, he was being presented with the idea that some Souls might be more powerful than others.

"I don't think it matters much," Ollie replied. "We've had our hands on a couple of Souls—and they all looked the same."

Hualong shook her head. "I doubt that an artificial construct such as yourself could evaluate a Soul. Nor you, Wraith. Neither of you possess the necessary skill. I do." She looked over to Ollie. "The Cosmic System does not have the capability. But this Karma Judgement Matrix sounds like it can do what I can do innately. Please, put me in contact with X."

Ollie's eyes went black and Xero's voice came through his mouth. "Go for X!"

Hualong frowned. "You are not X. X is a woman."

"Ah, well, she's out of commission," Xero replied. "I'm her substitute for now. Wraith and Shhiv can vouch for me!"

Hualong looked at Shhiv, and she nodded. "He's really sweet and kind," Shhiv said.

"Very well," Hualong stated. "I want to come to this Penrose Sphere for a brief time and see if I am capable of judging the Souls of those who are collected there as this Karma Judgement Matrix can."

"Sure. We'll need Jace there also to be able to look at Karma Coefficients. Want me to warp the lot of you?"

Hualong nodded. "Sounds good to me." She looked at Jace and Shhiv. "Shall we?"

Shhiv looked down at the tea, now cool and chill thanks to the breeze atop the mountain, and then at the small biscuits and snacks. "Let me take a few for the road."

The group was warped a few moments later, appearing in a large room on the Penrose Sphere. Xero was standing, shrouded in a black overlay that only revealed his purple eyes, and he was in front of a massive chamber. A huge tube, filled with light blue Souls. "I've been ensuring no more Souls go through to the Astral Verge."

Jace could see the numbers above every single one of the Souls, knowing which ones were going to be judged harshly or redeemed.

Hualong walked forward, the flower petal form leaving small wisps behind her. "Wraith, choose one with a Karma Coefficient of zero, positive, and negative." She looked to Xero. "And please sequester those three in separate chambers."

Jace walked up and pointed out three to her specifications, and Xero quickly tapped a few buttons on a floating screen only he could see. The three Souls vanished from the main tube and popped up in small, singular tubes that were mounted along the wall. Hualong walked over to the first one. "Wraith, which is this?"

"The positive one," Jace replied.

She pressed her hand to the tube. "Hmm . . . I can sense the Soul . . . yes . . ."

"Well?" Xero asked impatiently but excitedly. "What do you sense?"

Hualong shot him a glare. "I know the Soul is native to our Universe . . . and is not a cultivator." She moved to the next one. "Which is this?"

"Negative," Jace replied.

She placed her hand to the tube. "I can sense the Soul . . . this one did not cultivate, either." She looked to Xero. "I cannot substitute my capability to examine and identify information about Souls. I am sorry, I thought I could be of some help."

Xero shrugged. "It is okay. Thanks for trying to help out. Appreciate it."

"Back to Harkon Secundus?" Shhiv asked.

Hualong nodded. "Yes, please. But I think our tea has concluded. Thank you both for visiting, and you, Wraith, for filling me in on what the Astral Verge is all about. I wish I could have been of more help. You are always welcome to visit and meditate or have some tea." She warped away in a flash of pixelated pink light.

Xero dropped his shadowy shroud and sighed. "Well . . . back to the drawing boards. I was kind of hoping we had a workaround to the Karma Judgement Matrix from The Ancients. But at least we learned a bit more about Souls." He looked at the mass of light blue swimming about in the tube. "Some are bigger, some are smaller. Not sure why—but I'll ask Hualong later. For now, you two have a bit more vacation time."

"How long on The Architect's Gate blocking off Layer 10?" Jace asked.

"Oh . . . yeah, we should have you re-update that," Xero said. With a quick snap of his fingers, the group were in the voidlight tether room. But not Jace's voidlight tether—this room had millions of tethers. Xero muttered to himself as he tapped his wrist pad. "Let's see . . . ah, this one."

One of the silver-white tethers turned green, and Jace walked up to it, grabbing onto it, and used The Architect's Gate to channel his Skill through the drone attached to that line.

"And done!" Xero said with a smile. "Good stuff. Okay, enjoy your vacation, you two!"

Jace and Shhiv were warped back to their apartment, and Shhiv leaned into Jace. "Let's go check out Earth! Do a little tour."

Ollie and Josie both popped into existence next to the duo. "We'll show you around. We figured out all the neat places to visit."

Chapter Thirty-Two

The Bronze Forest

Jace woke up and gave Shhiv a hug. "Morning," he said softly.

She wriggled around in his grip and returned the hug. "Yesterday was fun."

"Yeah—" Jace was going to say more, but he was cut off when Quinn's voice came over the comms.

"Alright, lovers. Get up, we have work to do."

Shhiv groaned, "Give me five minutes!"

Quinn sounded slightly irritated. "Xero is waiting with the rest of the Signers for the expansion. And I've already bought you two an hour. Come on! Get up!"

Jace sighed and gave Shhiv a kiss before slipping out of the water cube with her a step behind. "Well, if you're going to work, I'm heading back down." Jace activated his TPSB and pulled out his Gear and Equipment, quickly outfitting himself with his usual loadout.

Shhiv did the same and put on a skintight suit with a pair of coveralls over the top. "Well . . . here we go. Be safe."

"You, too," Jace said softly as he gave her another kiss.

"I'll be safe. I have Greg and Priam, who will keep me nice and protected." Shhiv vanished with a pop from the subspace warping.

Ollie popped into space next to Jace. "We have 27,000 Essence. Enough for 4 levels and Potency 7. Ready to level up?"

"Yeah, let's do it."

[You have leveled up!]
[You have chosen Specialization of Existing Talent!]
[Talent Name: Purifying Edge.]
[Specialization Name: Revealing.]
[Effect: When the linked Talent is used on a target, any sundered Talents that cause a glamour, illusion, or similar effect are disabled until a cycle passes.]
[Talent Name: Templar's Smite.]
[Specialization Name: Gaze.]
[Effect: The user's (Spear) Infusion range is overridden to line-of-sight.]
[Talent Name: Valiant Crusader's Might.]
[Specialization Name: Lightbound.]
[Effect: The user's attacks and Psykinetics strike fear into Astral Demons who witness the effect or are affected.]
[Talent Name: Crusader's Bastion.]
[Specialization Name: Glorious.]
[Effect: The user's (Retaliating) Infusion deals increased damage.]

Name: Jace Seren (Potency 7)
Emotion [Class Level]: Valiant [Lightbringer 63]
Talent [Specialization]: Astral Adaptation, Astral Translation, Valiant Crusader's Might [Burning] [Vengeful] [Poised] [Unstoppable] [Bracing] [Voidbound] [Lightbound], Crusader's Bastion [Retaliating] [Reinforcing] [Grounding] [Redoubt] [Spiked] [Resonating] [Glorious], Hero's Arena [Aura] [Incinerating] [Vexing] [Bolstering] [Suppressing] [Wrathbound], Indomitable Will [Zealous] [Intimidating] [Inviolable] [Enduring] [Ameliorating] [Dark Matter Binding], Templar's Smite [Spear] [Blast] [Lingering] [Challenging] [Inferno] [Cosmic] [Gaze], Holy Hunt [Marked] [Bursting] [Authoritative] [Provoking] [Inciting] [Branding], Purifying Edge [Cleansing]

[Searing] [Purging] [Sanctifying] [Terminating] [Judging] [Revealing], Justice's Rebuke [Flaming] [Bashing] [Holy], Revealing Light [Burdening] [Limning] [Fracturing] [Potent] [Perilous] [Linking]
Essence: 0
Infusions: x2 Mythic (Specialization), x2 Mythic (Gear)
Gear: <TPSB>, (Convergent Edge) [Ruination 1] Divine Revenge, (Explorer's Embrace / Beacon) Hero's Plate, (Prosthetic Savant) Astral Appendages, (Draconic Sovereign) Arbiter's Sight, (Anathema) Astral Sleeve, (Reinforced) Psycrystal Lattice, (Pinnacle) NICIF-EP, (Restoring) Flame of Valor, Retribution Carbine (20 shots / battery)

Once more, Jace fell to the floor as he felt pain rip through his body. A new type of affliction—this time instead of feeling his insides melt, he could feel his entire body freezing over and the deep, penetrating aches that come with submersion into icy depths.

But, just as quickly as it started and came upon him, it ended. The warmth returned to his body, and he stood up, shaking his head momentarily.

Ollie flew into his head, activating Verge Protocol, and spoke. *Looks like the support-focused Class Transmutation can amplify existing Talents or their Specializations. That may make it worth going higher up in a support focused class.*

"Good to know," Jace gasped out as he caught his breath. "Okay . . . voidlight tether room." The world warped around him, and Jace stood up all the way, grabbing onto his Voidlight Tether and traveling back to The Solid Place he had departed from.

He was not alone, however, as the Demon Lord Ryun was standing in the center of the area with his underlings. He jumped slightly as Jace appeared. "Oh! Wraith. Sorry, you scared me there." He gestured to the still-missing wall. "Umm . . . was this you?"

"Yeah, sorry," Jace replied. "I got a bit carried away."

"Hehe," Ryun laughed nervously. "Yeah, um . . . we'll figure it out. Thanks."

"No problem." Jace turned to leave and used his Soul Tether to get above the walls and headed east to the descent of the next Layer. *Void Stalker*, he thought as he activated the Skill and went undetected thanks to being a higher Potency than the demons on the Layer.

Valcrinox was infuriated. The Ancients had been giving him the runaround and only told him that Layer 10 had been sealed off temporarily by someone calling themselves X. The same nothingness that reportedly covered one of the Universes up above on Layer 1.

He was trapped. Trapped in a single spot on Layer 10 where he could not escape from. He did not have the means to get enough Universal Matter to create a Universe of his own—or attempt the feat, at least. That alone would necessitate him going up to Layer 1. If not for the nothingness covering the entrance to the next Layer above, he could go and get the requisite Universal Matter right now.

But no. Instead, he was holed up on his throne. It was maddening, and he let out a laugh of sheer insanity as the Layer shook in response to the Demon Lord of Endless Madness's frustration and irritation.

Tibalt was angry. Angry that Wraith had escaped him in a weakened state. His chance for revenge, stolen away by the sudden disappearing act of the Dreamer. And so, Tibalt left. He went to the next Layer.

Layer 7 was something gorgeous and awe-inspiring, making Tibalt pause as he soaked it all in. Huge, rolling hills interspersed with mountains. Massive trees that left miles of open space underneath their canopy—the gold and red leaves causing the whole environment to feel like it was in a perpetual sunset. The skies above reflected this, as they were a deep orange—well, the few places he could see the sky, at least. The tree canopies shrouded most of it from view.

But the ground below was a different story entirely. Withered, black grass expanded across the ground save for the rocky outcroppings of the mountainous areas. Each tree was like a beacon of life while the ground beneath them was a representation of death.

Tibalt looked for Souls and could see them dripping down onto the treetops, then trickling down the branches, to the trunks, and then down to the roots below. He went to a tree and tried to put a claw on it to ascend, but pulled his clawed hand back as he hissed in pain. It was as if he had just dipped his hand into a highly caustic acid. Shaking it, he frowned. *No easy Soul harvest, then*, he thought as he began going around the base of a tree, carefully plucking Souls as they traveled down.

To his surprise, he came across an Astral Demon doing the same thing. A demon who looked like they had gone down the evolutionary path of refinement. But a demon who did not take any offensive or hostile action toward him. Just looked at him, gave Tibalt a brief nod of acknowledgement, and then continued to pluck Souls from the trees and place them into jars, a small pile of which were next to her on the ground.

Tibalt wasted no time—he immediately moved over to them and tried to rip them asunder. To tear them apart. But they used some Psykinetic Talent that bludgeoned him with force and sent him flying away—rolling to a stop in the dead, lifeless dirt. He shook his head and stood up with a growl.

"I would not advise that," the refined demon said with a little sigh. "You are outmatched."

Tibalt harnessed his Psykinetic wrath and used his Talent to form a massive sphere of energy above himself. Throwing it forward, he let out a whoop of delight and glee as it splashed against the Astral Demon. Then, that joy turned to dismay as the figure stood, uninjured, surrounded by a shining, crystalline barrier.

"Just leave me alone, and I'll leave you alone, okay?"

Tibalt frowned, knowing he did not have an easy target in that person, and instead wheeled about and ran toward another tree, harvesting in earnest but keeping a wary eye on the Astral Demon.

Jace reached the film covering the entrance to the next Layer. Jumping in, he fell into a gorgeous gold forest and landed on the deep, black ground.

> [Congratulations on entering a new Layer!]
> [You may choose to specialize your Class by performing a Class Transmutation!]
> [Base Class = Lightbringer.]
> [Options available:]
> [Zealot—expand upon your offensive capabilities. Leads to further offensive Transmutations.]
> [Guardian—expand upon your defensive capabilities. Leads to further defensive Transmutations.]
> [Archangel—expand upon your support capabilities. Leads to further support Transmutations.]

<u>*What do you want to bet that Archangel will let you have access to some type of flight Talent?*</u> Ollie asked.

I think it's a safe bet, Jace thought back. *And now that we know that the support route can continue to empower other Specializations on other Talents . . . I think we should go with that.*

[Class Transmutation Confirmed.]

[Mission: Consolidate control over Layer 7 to Demon Lord Phytala.]
[Reward: Mythic (Essence Cache) Infusion.]
[Sender: The Ancients.]

Jace looked around, taking in the sights for a few moments before he spotted two Astral Demons. One of them looked like a lanky, walking wolf-monster. It glanced at him before scampering away. Jace would have given chase if not for the other Astral Demon.

A woman who walked over to him. She was similar to Esmerelda up on Layer 4 but was far more female and looked like one of the species he had encountered before. Very similar to Mizarion from the Star Council in appearance—she was tall, had slightly blue skin and green hair. Only two eyes, but he could see the small slits under them where other eyes once were. And she had no demonic features at all—no horns, scales, antlers—none of it.

"Ah . . . welcome, Wraith. I was expecting your arrival." She curtsied slightly. "I am Phytala, the Demon Lord of this Layer. Welcome."

"Thanks. What was that demon that ran off?" Jace asked.

"Dreamer Demon," she said bluntly. "Going to eat up Souls off of the trees." She gestured back to one of the massive trees, and Jace saw a bunch of Souls inside of jars.

"How do you know which ones to grab?" Jace asked.

"I don't," she replied as she walked back to the bunches of jars. "Not until I get my hands on them. If they are evil, then I eat them. If they are good, then I let them be and release them." As she said this, she grabbed one jar, uncapped it, reached in and grabbed a Soul, then held it up to eye level. "Evil."

Jace could see the Karma Coefficient over the blob of light blue and nodded. "Yeah, seems like it."

She smiled. “Relics of the Ancients are amazing, are they not? I do not have to wait for their judgement. But, I don’t have fancy eyes like you—I have to hold them.” She slurped down that Soul, then held her dainty palm up for him to see. Embedded in the skin were dozens of small crystals that looked like the Relics inside of the Vaults.

Jace looked around for any sign of an Astral Demon that was after him for the bounty, but the whole forest was placid and peaceful. “What’s wrong here? Who do I need to kill to let you get control of the Layer?”

She gestured to the black dirt below. “This is the problem. I don’t know what caused this. The Ancients are not answering my questions. Maybe you would have better luck.”

Might as well try. Ollie, mind trying to get in touch with them? Jace thought to his Wayfinder.

Accessing Astral System messaging, Ollie replied. *Huh, they just said, quote, “You are the bearer, solve it.”*

Jace shook his head and spoke, “No, they did not answer me, either. I’m supposed to figure it out. And I have an idea on how to do it. Holy Hunt.” He focused his Talent on whatever was causing the blight on the ground, and the golden line shot off to the west. “Give me a layout of the Layer,” Jace said. “I’ve got a general map, but anything specific I should know about?”

Phytala pointed over his shoulder. “Well, the entrance to the next Layer is to the west. There are a handful of sparse mountains along the way. You will find some Astral Demons lurking about the trees.”

Jace felt a little bit of dismay. “I need 57,000 Essence to reach Potency 8 and descend deeper. If there’s not a lot of demons on this Layer, I might have to do another plan and bait them to me on a higher Layer.”

Phytala frowned. “You should not discount the demons of this Layer so readily. Those that are here are potent. I believe each is worth a few thousand Essence.” She smiled. “We get much more . . . dense, I believe would be the right term, in terms of how much Essence comprises our forms, when we get to higher Potency."

That brought Jace a bit of relief, and he nodded. "Right, then I guess I'm off—" Jace was interrupted as he heard a titanic roar and looked to the source of the noise.

"Right on cue," Phytala said with a frown as she knelt and began gathering up her jars. "Have fun fighting that." She began walking away.

Jace drew his sword, manifested his Crusader's Bastion, and faced the lumbering form that emerged from behind an enormous tree.

Chapter Thirty-Three

Difficulty Spike

Jace had barely turned to put his shield between him and the figure, and it vanished from sight. Immediately, he used Revealing Light to remove whatever stealth capability it was using.

But it wasn't stealth. It was speed. As soon as [Danger-Sense] alerted him and before he could react at all, Jace was slammed to the ground, and something clawed down onto his chest—crushing his torso and forcing the breath out of him.

> [Foe that is vastly superior detected.]
> [Shattered Limits enabled.]

Immediately, Jace activated the Skill at full power with [Single-Minded Fury], feeling rage explode in him as he dropped the sword, grabbed onto the claw, and was lifted up into the air. The NICIF along with his (Dark Matter Binding) set to healing him, and he could take in a breath for a split-second before the creature swung him into one of the trees. Jace crashed through the surface and was embedded a foot into the growth.

Void Shield, he thought as he activated the blazing green barrier that manifested around him. The demon—a quadrupedal catlike creature comprised of plated fungal growth, moss-lined shoulders and claws, and lashing spiked tentacles—launched itself at him. Jace pulled his Bastion in front of him, summoned his sword to his grip, and shifted the shield so that he could point the sword outward.

The Astral Demon, body covered in lime green Psykinetic force, stopped its launch midair—and a concussive shockwave of its rapid travel hit Jace's shield. The thing backed away slightly with an odd, almost percussive growl that sounded like a snare drum being beaten on in rapid tempo. *Okay, fuck you and fuck this. Templar's Smite (Spear).*

The bolt of gold flames surged from Jace's eyes, a beam of holy, radiant blaze that slammed into the Astral Demon, who projected a shield in front of itself. A floating, bright green barrier that held steady before him and took all of Jace's wrath.

But it bought Jace the time to get out of the tree. <u>*Why not use Void Step?*</u> Ollie asked.

I need to gauge how strong it is, Jace thought back as he kept channeling the eye-beam of Templar's Smite while he got to an open spot below the canopy. *I need to draw this fight out a bit. Study it. Figure out how we can beat it. If this Layer is anything like the ones up above—more Astral Demons like this one will be aro—*

His thoughts were interrupted by his [Danger-Sense] going off, and he jumped to his left as a surge of spiked roots shot up out of the ground—coated in lime green Psykinetic power—and chased him. Down. Jace had to stop his Templar's Smite to focus on chopping through the encroaching roots, and the demon lunged at him with their empowered claws.

Claws that met Jace's Void Shield and drained its energy precipitously, to the point that Jace had to shut it off because a few more hits of that power and he would have to draw on the Emergency Battery.

<u>*This is a difficulty spike compared to higher Layers*</u>, Ollie observed. <u>*I am starting to track a few patterns. Just keep it going.*</u>

Jace had sliced through the roots and brought his Crusader's Bastion to block the next claw swipe. He caught the blow, and the (Glorious)(Retaliating) barrier caused a surge of flame that returned some of the potential damage back upon the Astral Demon. The thing used a Talent and summoned up another tendril of roots and wood that Jace had to cut through with his sword—keeping the Dreamer from focusing his attention on the demon itself.

Jace's Hero's Arena kept burning away at the thing, stacking damage over time from his various Specializations—so Jace knew it would just be a matter of time and holding out against the thing as long as he could. Cutting down the vine-tendril, Jace was able to refocus on the creature that slammed another claw into him. The force drove Jace to his knee, but he pushed his way back up and popped a Dark Energy Mine as he shoved up.

The cat-demon-plant began floating up, but vines that grew from its back like tentacles shot out and tethered it to the ground, keeping it from floating off. Jace's kick off the ground sent him airborne as well, and he used his Soul Tether to pull himself to the Astral Demon and was able to get a sword swing in—chopping through one of the vine-tendrils.

The creature spun, and the hard-to-discern vines that wrapped around its body unfurled and glowed bright green, slamming into Jace and sending him to his left, sailing up toward the canopy. But the demon did not chase the now-ascending Jace and instead waited on the ground—like a hunting hound that had run its prey up a tree and was waiting for it to tire and fall.

Jace felt the canopy of leaves behind him—a solid, almost metal lattice that had very little give to it. He was able to get his bearings and saw the thing below him. *Did you get the data you need?* he thought to Ollie.

I think so. I have figured out what I believe are its primary attacks. What have you learned?

It hits like a truck, Jace thought as he studied the creature down below, keeping a wary eye on his rapidly depleting energy. *It is an ambush predator and can use roots to trap its victims. Strong close-up defenses thanks to those tentacles and tendrils. It has a shield it can manifest to stop ranged attacks. But it did not want to get close to the tree.* He glanced down to the tree he had slammed into and saw the glimmering bronze-colored wood beginning to turn white on the black ground. *I think it might hurt them to touch the trees directly.*

I concur, but we would need to test that hypothesis, Ollie replied. *We need more combat samples to see if there is a pattern to its attacks.*

Jace pushed off the canopy, landed on the tree nearby, and ripped off a chunk of bark. It began to fade in its strong, bronze color. But Jace used a Void Step to warp behind the creature and stabbed the bark into it.

The cat-demon-plant let out a screaming roar of pain as it leaped forward away from the bark—vines whipping around to dislodge the improvised weapon.

Yup! The trees hurt them.

We have a solid defense then and can rest up whenever with the Wildercloth Tent, Jace thought. *Just have to be up in the trees. That means I can afford to go all-out.* He raised the sword. *Void Beam (Rank 3) [Limited Range].*

The green flames surged out, and the cat-demon-plant raised its Psykinetic barrier, which held for a few seconds before the sheer power of annihilating nothingness crashed through and bored a hole clean through the center of it.

The hole grew over as the demon regenerated, and Jace felt the worst case of déjà vu. *Just like the cheat death Skills that animals had on Harkon Secundus*, he thought with a bitter taste in his mouth. *I fucking hated those things.* He used a Void step to get close to the now-regenerating creature and chopped through the body with vicious swings that exploded with gold fury, spreading the green flame and the dripping miasma of crimson.

His energy drained lower and lower, but Jace held out and was able to outpace the thing's regeneration. It fought back, clawing at him and stabbing with Psykinetic-empowered tendrils—but could not hurt him. Not in any meaningful way, at least, that wasn't healed up by the NICIF and (Dark Matter Binding).

He killed the thing and watched as the body vanished in glimmers and sparkles, the white-grey Essence fusing into his body and the light blue of Souls shooting to one of the nearby trees. Jace immediately used his Soul

Tether grapple to get to the top of one of the trees and cut his way through the canopy to get up top.

The pure orange skies above were all that greeted him, along with a few small mountain tops poking out of the canopy. He let his Skills and Talents fade. "We should be safe up here," he muttered. "How much Essence?"

2,000! Ollie said excitedly. *They are really potent enemies, though. A single one of them was able to easily overpower you without your Shattered Limits.*

Jace watched as his energy refilled and spoke confidently, "Can you figure out the exact Rank I would need to be on an even level with them?"

(Rank 5) Shattered Limits with [Single-Minded Fury] should bring you to equal their speed and innate strength, Ollie thought back.

"That costs me less energy," Jace muttered. "Next time something triggers the condition for Shattered Limits, if it's one of those things, autoactivate at that Rank. We can save on the energy in case I need to fight off two at once or something like that."

Two at once, then you should be able to just do Rank 10. Looking back at the encounter, Rank 19 and [Shattered Limits] was overkill.

"Rather overkill than be dead," Jace replied. He leaned back on his hands against the slightly dense canopy that held him aloft. "Plus, I can always come up here to recover since it seems that the Astral Demons can't touch the trees."

I will task the drone with keeping a watch under the canopy from you. Ollie directed the drone down through the small gap Jace had cut.

Tibalt had seen the fight from a distance. *Wraith is still too strong*, he thought. *I keep going with my plan.* He moved further away toward the entrance to the next Layer as he continued to pick Souls off of the trees and shove them down.

Progress was slowing, and he knew he needed to start using the Essence he had been saving up. Thousands of it, from demons that had tried to fight him on higher Layers. Activating the Astral System's level-up interface, Tibalt quickly made his selections and felt his body go through the rapid changes of Dreamer-side-focused level-ups. He could feel his stature fix itself somewhat, back toward what his Vanguard species had as a baseline.

And he regained a bit of his sense of rationality. *I must be cautious about the other demons on this Layer*, he thought as he selected stealth-based Talents. *They are powerful, and while they aren't actively hunting me like they are for Wraith's bounty, if they spot me, they will probably attack me.*

He continued his hidden harvest, plucking Souls from the trees as they descended down the trunks and into the roots.

Jace's energy was full, and he scooted over to the hole in the canopy and dropped down, lowering himself with his Soul Tether until he landed on the dirt below. Keeping his shield out and the golden barrier held loosely at his side, he began following the golden line toward whatever was causing the ground to turn black.

I wonder what it could be? Jace thought. *And what this place looked like before the black ground happened.*

Perhaps it is a Demon Lord who went down a path of refinement for their evolution and chose to go into Talents that allowed it to manipulate the Layers themselves. Almost like terraforming it.

Seems possible, Jace thought. *We haven't encountered a refined-focused Demon Lord who did not discern Souls since Layer 2. They have definitely been leaning more monstrous thus far.*

Jace heard the familiar growling noise, and Ollie instantly activated Shattered Limits at (Rank 10) as a second growl joined the first.

Chapter Thirty-Four

The Blighted One

Jace saw the two creatures briefly before they performed a tandem attack. One of them stayed back, channeling green Psykinetic force into the ground, causing roots to shoot up and attack Jace—roots that he deftly dodged and then slammed with his (Spiked) Crusader's Bastion, destroying them while keeping his sword free.

The other cat-demon-plant charged forward and slammed a claw into Jace's right side, but he got the sword into the path and held the blow back. His wrist shook slightly from the effort of holding back the force of the blow, but it was enough that Jace was able to stave off the harm.

[Danger-Sense] went off, and he activated Void Shield as several vine-whips came around and slammed into him. Throwing caution to the wind because of his impenetrable defense, Jace moved into the gap between the demon's forelegs and stabbed once with his Divine Revenge, leaving it planted in the creature's chest, and then grabbed eight of the knives from his TPSB and jammed them into the creature's body as well.

Each dagger dripped the viscous crimson nebula of [Rending] and the green flame of Void Blade, which now, as retextured Psykinetics, meant that he could use any bladed weapon to apply the effects.

Using a Void Step, he warped above the Astral Demon, throwing another eight knives into the top of it before summoning his sword back and throwing that as well. All of the blades found their mark, and the cat-demon spun around to face him.

Detonate, Jace thought as he activated a Dark Energy Mine he had placed on himself. Floating in the air above, he summoned back Divine Revenge and threw the sword once more—but the weapon was batted out of the air by the demon cat that was staying back to provide ranged support. A vine-tendril had whipped out and smacked Jace's blade off course.

He summoned it back to himself as the demons swapped roles; the one that was injured and covered in multiple bleeds and burns—damage-over-time effects stacked up on one another—shed the knives with some regeneration and shot spikes of Psykinetic force up at Jace that slammed into his Void Shield and drained his energy.

The fresh one, who had previously been at range, jumped up and took a swipe at Jace with one of the massive claws. He was able to block it with Crusader's Bastion, but vine-tendrils grabbed onto him and pulled him down with the thing. *Void Step*, he thought as he warped right under the creature as it landed, stabbing up as he activated (Fulmination). The sword exploded with golden wrath, and he shoved the sword to his left as he threw the cat-demon off of himself.

As it landed, Jace threw his sword, then grabbed another eight daggers from the TPSB and flung them. The creature dodged a few, but more found their mark than missed, and the damage-over-time effects spread.

Now to play keep-away, Jace thought as he used his Soul Tether to ascend, summoning his sword back to his grip. Getting up to the canopy, he cut a hole and popped up top. The drone camera that had been studiously following him stayed put and showed the two Astral Demons move to one another as they used Psykinetic Talents to put out the damaging effects.

Well, they tried to; when it came to the Void Blade retextured as green flames, that could not be stopped, and Jace watched with satisfaction as they realized they could not stop the damage-over-time effect, panicked, and ran off. *Doesn't matter how far you go*, Jace thought. *Eventually you'll die, and the Essence will flow back to me.*

Jace let his Skills and Talents fade and waited, watching his energy fill up. Fifteen minutes passed, and he felt the warmth suffuse him as Essence flowed into his body. *And there we go.*

New tactic developed. Inflict the Void Blade effect and then retreat. It should make clearing out this Layer a lot easier!

I have to go recover the knives, he thought as he glanced down through the hole in the canopy. *Looks like we're down ten.*

I will ask Quinn to load more into your TPSB. That encounter only gave us 2,000 Essence. Looks like there is a range falloff for Essence collection.

Jace let his energy fill to full then jumped down through the hole in the canopy. He got the remaining throwing knives from the ground, stowed them in the TPSB, and kept traveling along the golden path. *Then no more of that strategy, we will have to develop another one. Kill them while they are close. But*—he glanced up to the canopy—*it is reaffirming having that fallback.*

Shhiv let out a sigh of frustration and shouted "I need cover over here!" as the automated turrets on the drones surrounding her continued to fire at the demon horde that had rushed to the mountain.

Greg appeared out of nowhere—some Skill he had that let him warp to marked allies—and used another Skill that gathered their attention. Deep, burnished bronze sparks crackled from his armor as his Psykinetic power of Resolve surged from him. He glanced back to Shhiv as he took hits from Astral Demons with no issue—all of his defensive Skills having made him an unstoppable juggernaut. "You good?" he asked.

Shhiv nodded. "They were just getting close, was all."

Dee's voice came over the comms in a loud whoop. "We're having so much fun over here! Oooh, Ree! There's a big one coming! Go shoot it!"

The Plorp's sister spoke over the comms. "Yeah! I'll get the head, you get the legs!"

Priam's voice cut through. "Hey, Xero, your shield popped. Come back to get it refreshed."

Shhiv glanced up at the top of the mountain where a temporary bunker had been constructed. A starship from another Universe was there with a mercenary company led by someone named Voor, who she had met earlier that cycle. Apparently, Voor had met Jace, and the two left on amicable terms.

Voor's voice came over the comms. "You've got incoming from quadrant C. Any chance you can redirect forces there?"

Xero replied, "Yup! Tasking some of the automatic starfighters!"

Shhiv was able to concentrate and finish the construction she was working on. A whole quadrant—effectively one-sixteenth of the mountain's perimeter—illuminated with a deep, burnished brown hue. A visual effect purely for their faction and the mercenaries led by Herdsman Voor. In reality, now they had a portion of the mountain covered with Void and Dark Matter intertwined. She pictured it like a window frame: the Dark Matter was the frame, the Void was the glass. All invisible to any except for the Dark Between Stars Signers.

"Done with quadrant A," Shhiv said as she looked up at the still-embroiled-in-battle Greg, the man swinging a laser sword with one arm and holding a huge sniper rifle that was more like a cannon in the other. "Moving to B." She got up, grabbed onto the drone above her as another flew under her feet and moved her around the base of the mountain perimeter.

Xero's voice came over the comms. "Just finished quadrant I. Moving to J."

Quinn's voice cut through the din. "Outer drones are picking up a few hordes coming our way. You will need to get over there, Voor."

"On it," the mercenary replied. "Sending one crew to hold that front."

Everything had been going pretty smoothly thus far in the expansion and fortification effort. The framework had been set up, and now they were installing the different components required. Shhiv didn't have any particular training for this type of work—she was a creative above all else—but her Skills from all her [Class] and [Advanced Class] choices had turned her into a better technician than Xero when it came to speed and quality.

She made it to the next quadrant and descended the scaffolding down to the bedrock layer. Drones brought her materials that were needed for the Void projectors, and she set to work with gusto; the light cerulean of her Determined Emotion Source poured from her as she did her tasks. *Plus*, she thought, *I have to go around afterward and do all of the Rune Carving.*

This was just the first layer of defenses. More would come after this perimeter was made and they did not need Ascendants and mercenaries along with thousands of drones and hundreds automated starfighters controlled by Wayfinders protecting their efforts.

Jace continued along the golden path lined out by the Holy Hunt toward his objective. He had been confronted by more of the cat-demon-plants and had bested them with relative ease now that he had seen the bulk of their Talents. *Strange*, he thought as he ran through the large gaps between the trees, *that despite leveling up on presumably different tracks and choosing different Talents, they end up operating similar to one another.*

Seems like Astral Demons can respec each time they evolve from an increase in Potency, Ollie replied. *They cannot go back and change refinement versus monstrous choices on their evolution, but they can re-customize themselves. Considering how monstrous these ones are, I would bet that they arrived here and the Demon Lord who is controlling or dominating them forces them to choose new Talents based upon what it deems as the most valuable in the environment.*

Jace nodded, thinking the explanation made clear enough sense. He traveled for a few cycles, not sleeping and only pausing to eat and drink up atop the canopy. More demons fell to his Talents, and by the time he reached a different part of the Layer where the terrain shifted, he killed twelve more of the cat-demon-plants, netting 24,000 Essence.

But as he skidded to a stop, he noted how different the area was around him. Dark, black cracks crawled their way up the large trunks around him, the canopy overhead withered and dull grey, the leaves and branches drooping down as the ground became an even darker black.

He could see four of the demon cats prowling around the base of a single, pure-black tree. And seated at the top of the tree, in a hole carved out high up, was an Astral Demon who looked just as refined as the one that Jace was trying to cede control over the Layer to.

Their voice creaked across the open space. "Ah . . . the Wraith." They leaned forward from their perch. "You are here to defeat me?"

Jace summoned sword to hand and activated his go-to Skills and Talents, watching as the Shattered Limits notification popped up in his vision. The drone that was following him shot up to provide an aerial view, and Jace saw another four of the demon cats behind the rotten tree, out of his line of sight. *There's a lot*, he thought as he raised his sword. *But they can't expect this. Void Beam (Rank 1) [Horizon-Splitter].*

The green flame of Void surged out and consumed the entirety of creation before him. All of reality before Jace—the tree, the Astral Demon in the tree, the demon cats—all of them were consumed by the Void retextured as Psykinetic flame. Jace's ultimate weapon. Inexorable, unstoppable annihilation.

And he watched with dismay as the surging flames vanished in a blink. The figure up in the tree laughed and clapped their hands together as Jace automatically drew on the Emergency Battery and refilled to full. "Fascinating Psykinetic Talent, that," they shouted. "Too bad for you, I specialized in countering Psykinetics. Now, pets . . . go rend him limb from limb."

Jace felt panic set in as his shield vanished, the golden flames around his sword vanished, all his Talents were deactivated forcefully. Even his Skills from his innate Cosmic System were wiped out in an instant.

This looks bad, Ollie said with fear tinging his voice.

Chapter Thirty-Five

Don't Get Cocky

Jace's panic turned to a grim resolve as he knew he had to survive. That thought, survive, had driven him onward to this point. Surviving for Shhiv. For Chroma. For all of the people that he had killed and wanted to bring back.

Ollie, he thought as he glanced behind himself to one of the trees that was partially healthy, *what did they do to shut down my Talents and Skills?*

<u>*Similar to your Purifying Edge*</u>, Ollie replied. <u>*Or Arbiter's Anathema. You can reactivate, but it will cost extra energy.*</u>

Jace turned and used two Void Steps to get to the tree and a third to get into the branches above. If not for his instantaneous warping, he would have been destroyed by the eight cat-demon-plants that now stalked the bottom of the tree. Off in the distance, thanks to the drone, Jace could see the Demon Lord that was spreading the black corruption descend their tree and walk toward him.

Once they touch the tree, they can probably negate the feature that hurts these demons. Jace went through his various Skills and Talents rapidly, choosing which ones were key to have active and which ones he could neglect. Thankfully, Astral Adaptation and Astral Translation seemed like they were not able to be turned off.

Valiant Crusader's Might, Crusader's Bastion, Hero's Arena, Indomitable Will, Purifying Edge, Swordmage Stance (Rank 3) [Astral Annihilator], Dark Energy Mine (Rank 3), Cosmic Infusion (Rank 10) [Innervating],

Energy Cost Reduction (Rank 10) [Siphoning], Shattered Limits (Rank 19), Raging Cleave (Rank 10) [Echoing Cleave], Edge's Intuition (Rank 5) [Danger-Sense], Edge of Possibility (Rank 3), Eidolon's Persistence (Rank 5), Power Through (Rank 2).

Jace felt the world speed up around him as his body quickly repowered up with the bevy of Skills. Golden flames flared to life all around and within him as the green flames of retextured Void flickered throughout his armor. He watched as the Astral Demon got closer and made a decisive move. *Void Step*, he thought as he warped behind them and immediately impaled them through the chest.

They were protected by some type of Psykinetic shell, but Jace used Arbiter's Anathema to shut it off for the whole cycle and felt the blade stab deep. Immediately, he poured energy into the impaling edge, watching the flames erupt and consume the cocky Demon Lord wholly. As they crumpled away, Souls escaping and Essence suffusing Jace, the cat-demon-plants rushed him. All eight at once—four staying at a moderate range.

But Jace was ready for that. *I want this entire area to erupt with my Psykinetic power like the volcano tile back on Nihilethelea. Archmage's Admixture.* The once-per-day Skill surged down his feet, into the ground, and the black cracked open to reveal a surge of golden lava that flooded the entire area for a full mile around in all directions.

The demon cat creatures all yowled in pain and tried to find an escape—running past Jace toward the relatively safe area near the blackened tree—which seemed to stymy Jace's Skill. But he managed to get a few hacking slashes at the Astral Demons as they fled past him, carving deep and imparting his various damage-over-time effects.

As they got past, he threw his sword, drew daggers, and flung them over and over at the retreating cats. Stacking Void Blade, [Rending], and the multiple burning Psykinetic Infusions, he afflicted each one of the astral demons with at least three different damage-over-time effects.

Summoning his sword back to his sheath, Jace pulled out the Retribution Carbine from his TPSB, held it in his right arm, couched it on the shield, and fired off all twenty shots in blisteringly fast succession, swapping the battery just as quickly and firing off another twenty, followed by the last battery and a third volley of shots.

The demons had recovered, however, and manifested shields of Psykinetic force that blocked Jace's shots. Stowing the rifle and the batteries back in the TPSB, Jace sprinted forward and threw his sword repeatedly, each time slightly injuring himself with the (Vengeful) Infusion to instill greater force on the strike.

Revealing Light was applied to all the demons thanks to his earlier once-per-day Skill, causing yet another damage-over-time effect as a white light surrounded each of the demons. Jace reached the edge of his golden lava patch and stood there, activating (Beacon) on his armor to draw the hostiles in.

And they rushed him. Once they got into range of Hero's Arena, they had no choice at all in the matter, being driven on by his compulsion effects that forced them to go at him with everything they had. Blades of Psykinetic force, beams of energy, and tendrils of black roots all sprang forth to strike at Jace's interposed Crusader's Bastion.

The golden lava under Jace vanished, and through the drone HUD, he could see the refined Astral Demon he had killed rise from the blackened ground. "Surround him!" a wavering voice shouted.

Crap! As soon as you stabbed it, the Demon Lord used a Talent to make a duplicate and merge with the ground. It had to shed Essence to do that and drop its Souls.

Jace was surrounded by the demon cats, and they unleashed their assault. Jace swung his blade left, then right, interposing his shield in between him and his foes' strikes as best he could. But the assault was overwhelming, and he detonated his Dark Energy Mine, following it up with a rapid Dark Matter Dart (Rank 4) [Exploding] in a tight circle around himself. Jumping up as they detonated, the invisible matter shot him up into the sky and blew the now gravity-less Astral Demons off and to his sides.

But Jace felt gravity re-grip him and shot out his Soul Tether as he saw the Demon Lord, whose hands glowed with deep, auburn Psykinetic power.

Then, Jace saw his Bulwark vanish and knew he had to act immediately to prevent more of his Skills and Talents from being deactivated.

Void Step, he thought—but nothing happened. *Shit.*

<u>*Disabled for a minute*</u>, Ollie thought back.

Void Beam (Rank 3) [Limited Range], Jace thought as the Skill surged out and went directly for the Demon Lord—but once more, the green flames vanished, and Jace received a Cosmic System notification that he was locked from the Skill for a minute. *Fuck!*

<u>*Going against someone who can negate your Skills and Talents. Not fun being on the receiving end*</u>, Ollie commented.

Do something useful! Jace thought back as he felt panic rise.

<u>*He cannot disable your Gear, so you are safe up here. The cat-demon-plants don't have enough range to reach you this high, and that Astral Demon specialized in disabling.*</u>

Can't disable my gear? Jace smiled. *Also can't counter what he can't see. Ollie, can we pull up Dark Matter Blade from my old [Swordmage] Class?*

<u>*It is part of you. Let me go through some regression protocols . . .*</u>

Jace's weapon blazed with the dark-purple, and he instinctively knew it had vanished utterly. Cocking his arm back, he disguised the throw with a swing move on his Soul Tether.

The Astral Demon Lord didn't see it coming. The blade slammed into their chest, and they reached down to grab the invisible-to-them weapon. The purple covering faded as they negated the Skill—which Jace received a notification for—but he then activated (Fulmination). The explosion of golden flames from the Gear's effect did not seem like it could be disabled—just how Jace's Soul Tether was part of his prosthetics.

The Demon Lord exploded with golden flames, and the Essence floated up to Jace. All of the black on the ground vanished, the trees instantly recovering as the canopy sprouted up under Jace. But he dropped down, cut through, and summoned his sword to his grip as he received a single notification.

[All blocked Talents and {Skills} re-enabled.]

All the demons rushed Jace, and he simply activated Raging Cleave (Rank 10) [Echoing Cleave], turning to face them as let out a single horizontal slice that cut into the whole group of charging foes. The crimson line shot out from his slash and carried the force of the swing. All of them, cut into by the phantasmal crimson extension of the sword—and a split-second later, a second swipe right where the first had been. They all went tumbling to the ground in a heap, and Jace had every foe in a single location.

Void Beam (Rank 1) [Horizon-Splitter], he thought. The blast of green flame surged out, engulfing the lot and immediately incinerating them wholly. The light blue of Souls flew to the nearest tree that was a healthy bronze once more, and Jace kept upright as he scanned for any more foes—but totally tapped out of energy and extremely exhausted.

Thankfully, all looked quiet and still. The tree that the Demon Lord had been in began to mend itself, the holes in the top filling themselves in and the black slowly receding and fading away. Within a minute, Jace was back in a pristine forest. Using his Soul Tether, he got up to the canopy, cut a hole, and laid back on the supportive leaves.

That was close, he thought.

Yup, Ollie replied. *Going against someone who can disable Skills or Talents.*

Now I know what it must have felt like for Aspirants and Ascendants I beat who lost their Skills, Jace thought. *It must have been terrifying.*

Just goes to show us one thing.

What's that?

We cannot ever be too cocky.

Jace nodded. *True. Okay, what is our total Essence at?*

*46,000. We needed 57,000 to reach the next Potency.*

We should be able to hunt more of the demons on this Layer with Holy Hunt. Plus, the Vault.

> [Mission Success: Consolidate control over Layer 7 to Demon Lord Phytala.]
> [Reward: Mythic (Essence Cache) Infusion.]
> [Sender: The Ancients.]

Jace shot up to a sitting position. "That's five! We can make the Divine Infusion!"

*Heck yeah!*

Tibalt finished the painful process of going up in Potency. This time, he chose to follow the evolutionary path of refinement, wanting to diversify his Talents. As his body shifted and contorted, it became even more like his prior form back up on Layer 1 when this whole Dreamer Demon experience first started. But he was still obviously a demon with his gaunt appearance and lanky arms and legs. A spindly creature with wiry muscle that was extremely dangerous.

Going to the film leading down to the next Layer, the moment he was through, he was grabbed by firm hands. Instinctively, he tried to fight back—clawing, slashing with Psykinetic Talents. He was able to rip deeply into something fleshy behind him, and he was dropped. Spinning, he saw a giant of a demon—four massive hands, two of which held weaponry that would have required Tibalt to use both hands to wield effectively—covered in layers of hide and fur that his claws had been able to shred through.

Tibalt realized that this was a Dreamer Demon as they continued to huff, breathing through a gurgling wound in their neck that slowly began to close. But Tibalt lunged on them, ripping them apart—yanking the head off entirely as he scooped the Soul out of them and gobbled it down—the Essence in the body breaking down and infusing him as it left behind a corpse.

That's when Tibalt thought to take in his surroundings. A vast series of lakes that were placid and multiple colors. The Souls that came down from the Layer above gathered on hanging, spikelike pylons that jutted down. They coalesced like dripping water, and dropped into the lakes.

Between the lakes, dozens of bridges made of stone.

He heard movement from behind himself and, glancing back, saw a stone building along one of the bridges and built into the water on stilts above a bright red lake. A hulking figure appeared in the doorway, and Tibalt immediately made for the Dreamer Demon, ripping into them.

Jace looked at his options. *I can upgrade the five Mythic to one Divine . . . but what do I want? I can do Gear Alteration, Gear itself, Specialization, or an Essence Cache. What do you think, Ollie?*

I would say you do not choose Gear, just because you have Relics already, and I do not know how much better a Divine piece of Gear would be than a Relic. Gear Alteration might be extremely powerful, but Specialization has the same capacity for being amazing. Essence Cache would have to be a ton of Essence. Ollie sighed, *I cannot know for sure; the logs for that type of intel is beyond my reach.*

Try reaching out to The Ancients—see if you can ask them.

Querying . . . No, no response.

Jace frowned. *Well, we know that Layer 8 is going to be friendly because Yroshnak runs it, and it seemed like he had things well in hand on that Layer. Which means we might be starved for Essence.*

Let me try sending him a message . . . Hmm . . . Okay, this is odd.

What is? Jace thought back.

Ollie sounded slightly concerned, *I'm getting a request for our comm network. But X would have to approve it.*

Jace spoke softly, "Quinn? You listening?"

There was a moment of silence before the familiar female voice came on the line. "Yeah. Monitoring a lot of action right now, but I'm here."

"Can you ask X to let the Demon Lord Yroshnak onto the comms?"

"You . . . you want to add a Demon Lord to the comms?"

"He's good," Jace replied. "Wants to help out."

"I can patch him in—Xera gave me override permission on the comms since she knew Xero would be focused on other stuff—" She cursed, and something slammed in the background. "Son of a bitch! I told him not to go to that quadrant!"

Jace felt worry settle in his stomach. "Is something wrong?"

"Just a mercenary not doing what he was told," Quinn replied with frustration. "Which means my Stratagem doesn't go off at the same efficacy because he's not following my strategy. Idiot." She sighed, and her voice became almost monotone as she engaged her focus on her other tasks. "I'll patch Yroshnak through."

There was a slight crackle in Jace's ear, and then he heard a deep, rumbling, familiar voice from the Vault arena he fought. "Wraith."

"Yroshnak," Jace replied. "I had a question."

"I might be able to answer," the Demon Lord replied.

"I'm up on Layer 7 right now and working on getting a Vault dealt with, gathering up some Essence, and then I'll be on your Layer. But my concern is that there won't be enough Astral Demons for me to hunt on your Layer for Potency 9, to go deeper."

"Do not concern yourself with that," Yroshnak replied. "I may have consolidated control, but I still have some demons that I wish to cull from my ranks. The plan is that I will descend with you to help you overthrow Valcrinox. I will take his throne and rule justly over Layer 10, as The Ancients decree, sorting the Souls of the evil damned to each Demon Lord on higher Layers. But, to do that, I must raise a subordinate to my position on Layer 8. And that chosen subordinate has enemies, and others who are jealous they will not be chosen."

Jace nodded. "Well, I understand. So we won't be needing Essence from a Cache, for instance."

"No, you should not," Yroshnak replied.

"Good," Jace said with relief. "Then, follow-up question. I have a Divine rar—"

"You do?" Yroshnak asked, his voice changing to a tone of genuine surprise. "That is powerful."

"What would you suggest I use it on?"

"Gear Alteration," he replied almost instantly. "A Divine piece of gear rivals a Relic, but Gear Alteration means you can make a Relic all the more potent. You used a sword in our Vault encounter some time ago. I would suggest you use it on that."

"Thanks," Jace replied. "I'm going to get this Vault dealt with then, and you should see me on your Layer pretty soon here."

"I will be waiting." The line went silent.

Jace took a deep breath. *Okay Ollie, let's do it. Divine (Gear Alteration).* He pulled his sword out and set it next to him.

> [Using Infusion: Divine (Gear Alteration).]
> [Target Gear: (Convergent Edge) Divine Revenge.]
> [New Infusion: Ancient Reckoning.]
> [Effect: The (Ancient Reckoning) Infusion causes the weapon to temporarily remove Potency from the target struck, disabling Talents at random. If this brings an Astral Demon to Potency 0, they are utterly destroyed. Astral Demons regain 1 Potency per cycle. If this brings a Dreamer Demon to Potency 0, they are purified and immediately judged.]

The weapon shifted form, the tip elongating and the blade slimming itself down. The hilt split apart and formed a basket-style guard that glittered a shimmering, pure white like freshly fallen snow. An incomprehensible scribble scrawled across the length of the weapon, and the hilt flashed a deep black, offset from the blade's coloration.

Jace picked it up, and Ollie spoke. *That means with eleven hits, you could kill the strongest Astral Demon.*

Jace sheathed the weapon. *Yeah, that is really useful. Plus, I can just do six Raging Cleave with [Echoing Cleave], and deal with a whole cluster of demons.*

Oh, I had not considered to look into its functionality with Skills! Let me check . . . Tsk, bad news—the blade itself has to hit them. Not a Skill, Talent, or something else.

Jace frowned. *Well . . . for how powerful the effect is, I guess that limitation is understandable. Now. Holy Hunt.* He focused on the closest Vault on the Layer and saw the line shoot off to the west. *Convenient. Toward the exit to the next Layer.* He descended from the canopy and began running.

Chapter Thirty-Six

Revelations

Priam was exhausted, walking into the small bunker atop the mountain beneath their Universe's funnel. He collapsed into a bed and let out a small groan.

Dee was there also, along with her sister, Ree, and Missy. Greg was the only one of the Signers not present because he did not need to sleep, eat, or drink to stay alive.

Shhiv was there, and she was also laying on a bed, just recovering energy.

Priam sat up and tiredly plodded over to the small fabricator and used some Stardust to create food—delicious baked pies that had perfectly flaky crust and a juicy vegetable interior that was rich and decadent. A perfect high-protein snack. He began to eat it right there at the fabricator.

Shhiv walked over and tapped a second fabricator next to him, grabbing the bottle of weird yellowish liquid before gulping it down. She looked over at Priam, who glanced up at her. She put a hand on his shoulder. "Thanks for the barriers. Kept me nice and safe."

"Oh," Priam replied, mumbling a bit. "Not a problem. I'm just happy things are going so well."

The doors opened behind the two, and both looked back to see Xero walking into the bunker. He pulled gloves off of his hands and smiled. "We did it! All the quadrants, sealed off with Void and Dark Matter! Greg is mopping up some demons along with Voor's mercenaries and, of course, our starfighter's support."

Shhiv grinned and gently squeezed down on Priam's shoulder. "We did it. Universe safe forever."

Priam felt excitement and would have jumped for joy if not for his exhausted state. "I could use a nice, long vacation," he said with relief at their task being done.

Dee spoke up at that. "We should go to the beach!"

Xero chuckled and shook his head. "You lot can do that. But, yes, our Universe is even safer now. I still want to set up secondary defenses and backups—but our entire funnel, the mountain, all of it is hidden with Dark Matter and Void. It will be as if our Universe did not exist." He walked over to the fabricator and glanced down at Priam's snack. "Smells great. I need to try one."

Priam tapped the fabricator and handed The Architect the snack. "Here." As he handed it over, he thought, *Xero is a lot different than Xera. But they are fraternal twins . . . I wonder if Xero is more representative of what Xera used to be like before she changed from being alive for so long.* Priam shrugged and scarfed down the rest of his meal.

Ree and Dee both stood up, their chitin clacking on the metal floor as they walked over. "Are we good to head back in-Universe?" Dee asked.

Xero nodded and swallowed down a bite. "Oh yeah. Go for it. Just grab a voidlight tether to go up to the Penrose Sphere, and then you can warp yourself."

Dee grabbed Priam's hand and reached up to grip a voidlight tether. Priam felt the weird rush of being discorporated and then recorporated, followed by the warping back to their apartment. He sank into the huge leather chair that was his dad's prized possession. Dee shed herself from her chitin and moved her goopy form into a small cubby that hung off the side of the chair.

"We did good work," Priam said softly.

"Mm-hmm," Dee replied. "Blowing up demons with my sister was fun!"

"Maybe we can make it a bit of a date night thing?" Priam suggested.

"Oh, yeah. That would be neat!"

Jace sprinted along the forest floor. He was not hampered in his journey by any Astral Demons and soon enough arrived at a massive tree. One that was easily four-hundred feet across on a single side whose branches surged far higher than all of the surrounding ones. The golden path of his Holy Hunt took him up the tree, using his Soul Tether to ascend up to the top.

To his surprise, a creature was sitting at the top. An Astral Demon, judging by the fact that there was no Karma Coefficient above their head. Definitely one that had taken the monstrous path of evolution. It looked like a huge bird, an eagle with a wingspan of easily fifty feet. Spines went along the ridges of the wings and down the back while each feather slightly wriggled as small tendrils poked between them.

Or so he thought; as he prepared himself to strike, the thing spoke. "Dreamer, come to enjoy the view?"

Jace stopped, hand on hilt of the sword, and shook his head. "No."

"Ah, pity. It is a lovely view." It looked at him with a sidelong glance before turning away. "The Layers are fascinating. I have been traveling up and down them for eons. I have seen Bearers of the Mantle of Burden succeed and fail in trying to destroy my brethren."

"Who are you?" Jace asked with mounting curiosity budding up inside him.

The eagle-demon chuckled. "I was one of the first. Twenty of us, there were, now only two remain. Myself, and Valcrinox." The eye glared at Jace. "You slew one of them. Troxanir. I heard his death cry. Tell me, Dreamer, chosen of The Ancients . . . why do you do what you do?"

Give a little bit of information, Ollie said, *but not too much. Be cautious about it.*

Jace spoke in measure and very carefully chose his words. "I want to stop the cycle of Souls for my Universe."

"And you seek a Karma Judgement Matrix to do so. Smart. One could close off their Universe to the Astral Verge by destroying their singularity funnel. It has been done before . . . but Souls have a secret, young Dreamer." The head turned to fully look at Jace, and he felt like a very small, insignificant insect in comparison to the demon before him. "Souls decay. Without being cycled through judgement or flushed out of a Universe into the Astral Verge, the Soul eventually unravels. The good is lost, and all that is evil becomes a miasma. If enough of that happens, then the miasma becomes aware. Grows a consciousness."

Jace frowned. "Why tell me this?"

The eagle-demon turned away once more, staring off into the distance. "In the beginning, there was the Nethershift, were Universes, and are Afterlives. The Ancients arrived and made the Astral Verge and Soul Realm as a middle-ground between the Nethershift and each other layer of our reality. A transitory layer. Then, they contacted the Afterlives. Learned about the paradise that was that existence. Prodding the Universes, so full of this miasma I describe, resulted in the very fabric of reality tearing—forming the singularity funnels that let the miasma descend. It polluted the Astral Verge."

The figure turned to Jace once more and lowered its head to his level. "The first group of Astral Demons, my brethren, were formed from the foulest sludge of every Universe, granted consciousness. I, however, was different. I learned from The Ancients and have dedicated myself to simply observing and reporting. The Astral System sees much, but not all, that occurs on the Layers."

Jace wasn't quite blown away by the revelations being told to him—he had known most of this information from the tablets he had received in Vaults on Layer 1. But the fact that Souls would decay and turn into a miasma was new. "Again . . . why tell me this?"

"You should know that Valcrinox is the craftiest of my brethren. He has a Relic, a throne, that makes him nigh-invincible while sitting on it."

"Yeah, well, we'll see about that," Jace replied with confidence.

"You think your reality-nullifying power will overcome the odds? I would not be so confident." The eagle-demon stood up and extended its wings. "I wish you luck in doing what others have tried in the past. If you succeed, I am sure that Yroshnak will do a fine job ruling Layer 10. Until, eventually, he himself becomes corrupted and needs to be removed. Thus it has been, and will always be." The mighty wings flapped, and the Astral Demon took to the air, flying up through the ceiling of the Layer and vanishing.

Wow, good thing I got all of that! Ollie said with excitement. *Good information to hold onto.*

Jace nodded. "Plus, we know about this throne now. Whatever it is. We need more information about it so we can figure out how to counter it." Jace saw the golden line lead to a knot at the top of the tree, and running his fingers along the outside edge, he found a small section that was covered with vines that he could move aside. A small hole, big enough for him to wriggle through.

Poking his head inside, he saw the tree center had been hollowed out, and far, far down at the bottom, past the curled roots that had been pushed aside by some force, was a rocky tunnel that circled away. Shoving himself into the gap, he fell down, using a Dark Energy Mine at the last second to negate momentum from the fall before letting that deactivate and landing on the ground. He moved into the tunnel and saw the familiar sight of a Vault door.

Placing his hand on it, he was sucked through.

Xero had finished up with his side project and was taking a well-earned break. He was sitting in a lounge chair, reading up on some of the histories of new species that had joined The Cosmic System since his leaving the Universe proper. Xera's pod thrummed quietly next to him, and he occasionally commented, speaking to her, about the various revelations he uncovered.

A Cosmic System message flickered across his vision from Jace's Wayfinder.

> [I am sending you a transcript of a meeting we had with an interesting Astral Demon that has been around for a long, long time.]

Xero put the data pad he had been reading down and read through the transcript quickly, his cybernetic eyes able to easily transfer the information to his brain as he digested the information. *Interesting . . . perhaps this miasma is what contributes to re-sleeving over long periods of time failing. Almost like a buildup of a foulness in the body. Hmm.* He looked over to Xera's pod and quickly had it run a diagnostic.

But the diagnostic showed the same as before, and he sighed. He pulled up an audio feed with Hualong, who had provided great insights into Souls thus far. "Hey, do you have a minute?"

"I can spare the time," the soothing female voice replied.

He quickly explained what had been presented to him about Souls degrading to miasma and ended with ". . . I can't help but feel there is a piece of the puzzle we are missing."

Hualong was quiet for a few moments before responding. "I am aware of what we called corruption or decay of a Soul. There is a means to purge it. Mindful meditation, stripping away the darker parts of one's Soul. The Arbiter had a means to destroy those darker parts of the Soul."

Huh. The Arbiter's Anathema could do that? Xero thought. Soul-magic was something he barely understood before leaving his Universe behind, but now that he had a bit more knowledge of it, he had made alterations to The Cosmic System for easier incorporation. But the way that Soul-magic functioned with this miasma was entirely new to him. "We have some of Anathema's items, do we not?"

"I believe that Wraith had several."

Xero pulled up Jace's status screen and frowned. "It looks like they were all overridden by Relics he acquired."

"May I ask why? This Karma Judgement Matrix will be solving this issue for us."

Xero sighed. "But we don't have a plan for what to do with those judged as not deserving another chance. If we could . . . come up with a Soul scrubber . . . something that lets us wash the ones judged as evil, we could ensure that no Soul ever reaches that miasmic state to cause problems." He looked through Xera's inventory list and found something with Anathema as a name. "We have something called an Anathema Core . . . looks like it could be used to make Anathema objects once every few months."

Hualong's voice perked up at that. "Bring it and meet me at the Soul storage machine in that sphere world around Oblivion. I have an idea."

Xero reached into the TPS via his bracer and pulled the spherical, warm, grey object out. He saw that on one side there was a hole. Using the warp network, he appeared on the Penrose Sphere inside the Soul storage room. Hualong's body of flower petals blipped into place a moment later.

"Hold it up," she instructed.

Xero held it upright, and she reached her hand into the aperture. There was a deep silver glow, and then she pulled out a large metallic plate—a rectangle that was just like one of the data storage arrays.

“Put this into the Soul storage device,” she said with excitement.

Xero did as she said, and there was a dull flash of silver inside the containment cylinder. Then, the Souls inside glowed slightly brighter and became a brighter blue. “Did it work?”

“Looks like it,” she said with pride. “Living creatures must still purge their Soul the old-fashioned way—thoughtful meditation and cultivation of their Soul. But”—she touched a flower petal hand to the cylinder—“in their raw state, a Soul exposed to Anathema’s nullifying power seems to be completely cleansed.”

Xero looked at the spherical device he had set down further back in the room. It must be because he had something that could nullify a Soul entirely. *I would bet that the reason that the Anathema prosthetics worked on The Cosmic System is because the framework anchors itself inside a person. And that framework latched onto the Soul because it was immortal unless eaten by demons. There is so much about the nature of Souls I still don’t know.* Xero turned to face Hualong, “Teach me.”

“Pardon?”

“Everything you know about Souls. I need to know everything”—he gestured broadly to the room around them—“to ensure that our Universe is forever secure.”

“It would be my pleasure.”

Chapter Thirty-Seven

Fear, Manifest

Jace readied himself with his full suite of Skills and Talents, his weapon surging with green, gold, and crimson as the Bulwark manifested on his forearm, and Hero's Arena crackled to full power as it surged out in all directions. "Here we go," he said as he waited for the Astral System message.

> [Vault Challenge—Activated.]
> [Face your worst fear.]

The room vanished around Jace, and he was standing in a familiar place. The park where he used to take Chroma. It was the day of her death, and her birthday. He watched from a distance as the guard came up to past-him and told him about the time in the park being over. Jace wanted to tell his older self to go home another route—but he could not speak. Looking down, he could see his body—wrapped in grey tendrils. They muffled his mouth and just allowed him to watch.

He was pulled along after his past self, holding Chroma's hand. Then, the sound of squealing tires. Gunshots. Whooping and hollering as heavy music blared out as some of the street gangs that the megacorporations allowed to flourish sped down the road.

"Get into the alley!" he tried to shout, but he was muffled. He watched with wide-eyed horror as past-him grabbed Chroma, picked her up, and made for the alleyway. Time seemed to slow as he saw the vehicle collision, the metal plate protecting the underside of the vehicle skidding off, chopping clean through his shins.

Jace felt the pain red-hot just like he had when it actually happened. Tears came to his eyes unbidden as in even slower motion, he saw past-him fall to the ground. Chroma falling backward into the street and being slammed into by one of the out-of-control vehicles.

"No!" he tried to shout, his voice hoarse from seeing the miserable moment in his history. He watched Chroma's head slam into the brickwork as her body fell limp. Felt the despair as he saw her blood dripping down the cement and into the gutter. Watched past-him crawl over, bleeding from the stumps, to comfort, to save Chroma, only to wail out in agony and pain as she died practically in his arms.

Jace felt hollow. The pain in his shins faded as the entire world faded around him. He hated himself in that moment. Hated himself for listening to his mentor, his father, and taking Chroma out of the relative safety of the orphanage. *If she'd just been there, and I'd just visited, she could still be alive . . . if I wasn't blinded by my disgust for the megacorporations and what they'd done.*

He felt the familiar rage. That burning anger rise up in his chest, and the world shifted around him. He was back in New York City. Again, a silent watcher, wreathed in grey shrouds that did not allow him to speak, only watch. He watched himself fall from the skies, sword thrown down at the four Signers for the Nebula Alliance who had almost killed him with their mixture of Skills.

Jace watched as past-him landed, stalked over to the door, and obliterated it before utterly annihilating the people inside. Young women, all of whom tried to kill him, and the medic that kept them alive and brought them back from the brink. He watched with a feeling of justification as he slaughtered them all.

But, as past-him chased the medic down into the building, a pang of regret welled up in Jace. *She didn't actually hurt me in any way*, he thought. *Just like Priam back on Nihilethelea. She helped my enemies, but she herself was harmless.*

He felt that regret grow even more as past-him snapped her neck and dropped her to the ground. The world vanished around Jace . . . but that regret vanished as he knew he had made the right call. *Leaving her alive would have meant more intel the Nebula Alliance would have about what I could do.*

Then, once more, the world shifted. It was not a scene he was familiar with, though. He was sitting in a room, not encompassed by anything, and Ollie spoke in his mind. *Huh. That was weird. Lost contact with you for a bit there. What has been going on?*

I've been seeing the past, Jace replied in his mind.

In front of him, Shhiv appeared. She looked devastated, standing up and throwing the ring Jace had given her onto the table. "I'm done with you," she said with finality. "I don't need you to keep me safe anymore."

Jace felt a pain in his chest and tried to stand up, to say something—but the grey film wrapped itself around him as he tried to plead for her to stay. Not to abandon him. Not to leave him.

She continued as she turned around, "I never really wanted you." Then, she left.

Don't leave me, he thought. *Don't leave me alone. Everyone leaves me. I just want people to stay. Don't leave me!*

Silence answered him, and Jace broke down crying. He was alone again. No one alive. No one who cared. A mother who had abandoned him, no matter what her reason was. A father who raised him in secret but who never revealed who he was. The death of his best childhood friend, Verve. Chroma's death.

. . . *Please come back*, Jace thought.

> [Greatest fear faced.]
> [Challenge—faile—]

Oh no you do not! Ollie shouted in Jace's mind. *I am still here! I will always be here with my Ascendant. You cannot take me away from him! He is never alone, not anymore.* Ollie's voice calmed, and he spoke to Jace, not yelling out into the empty room. And, for the first time ever as far as Jace could recall, Ollie's words weren't perfectly selected and proper. They were casual. *Jace. I'm here for you. Friends forever, I'm with you for your whole immortal life. Even if others leave, I will never leave you. And Shhiv loves you, she is not leaving. You don't have to be afraid of being alone anymore because you are never alone.*

Jace felt a calm wash over him as Ollie spoke. *I . . . you're right. You're not going anywhere. Shhiv loves me. I have friends who won't abandon me . . . fuck this Vault. I'm afraid of being alone, but I'm never alone. Not anymore.*

[Greatest fear faced.]
[Challenge—ERROR.]
[Contacting administrator . . .]

The Vault returned around Jace, and he found himself sitting on the floor. He let his helmet recede and wiped his eyes clear as a pixelized cloud appeared next to him, and the Quiet Ancient stood there in their large, flowing robe with the hood pulled up to obscure their features. "I looked through the logs . . . you failed the Vault."

No he did not! Ollie shouted as the armor reverberated, and he was heard aloud. *He cannot fail when facing his worst fear because that worst fear cannot happen. He cannot be separated from me. No matter what!*

"Oh? Shall we test that and see if you pass the Vault after all?" The Ancient snapped their fingers.

Jace felt the splitting headache as Ollie was unmerged from him, and the otter let out a surprised yelp as he was pulled over next to The Ancient. "Ollie!" he shouted.

The Ancient looked at Ollie with amusement. "Seems like I can remove him from you."

Ollie crossed his arms and pouted. "No fair! You can't take me further than a hundred feet from Jace."

"Oh?" The room expanded around Jace, and The Ancient was moved far away—but seemed to struggle as Ollie reached the one-hundred-foot tether distance. "Hmm. Interesting."

"See?" Ollie said. "Jace is never alone!"

Jace stood up. "Give him back. Now." His voice was a guttural growl, and the familiar ember of rage crackled in his stomach as he glared at The Ancient.

The Ancient frowned. "I need you to understand something, Jace Seren of Universe 348: you will need all of your power to survive Valcrinox and his horde. That means everything you have been holding back." He looked at Ollie, who he still held by the scruff of the neck. "Sorry for this."

Jace felt despair wash over him as Ollie vanished. He let out a scream of rage and felt the familiar yet long-unused surge of hatred rise up in him as <Wrathblade> reactivated, the latent Class Expansion surging to the forefront as he used Void Step to close the distance and slash at The Ancient. "Where'd he go?!"

The Ancient stood still, and Jace's weapon passed through the pixelated cloud. "That's it, Jace Seren. Show me the powers you have suppressed."

Jace felt the anger, but also deep down felt—no, he knew—that this Ancient had just gotten rid of Ollie. Jace drew upon Wrath's Embrace as the red lightning crackled and surged from him. Intermixed with it were the flickering green flames of Void, which also bled through and dripped white-grey energy of the Ascended Power itself. Pulses of Dark Matter surged out in their deep, purple tones, spikes and darts that surged toward The Ancient and seemed to phase through him entirely. The golden flames of his Psykinetic power surged out and tried to consume The Ancient.

But the entity was unaffected and just stepped to the side and waved his hand. Ollie reappeared with a pop. "That was uncalled for!" Ollie shouted.

Jace still felt that anger, that unmitigated wrath, but he also felt relief. Dropping his sword he grabbed Ollie and hugged him tight. "Don't leave me alone," he whispered to his Wayfinder.

"I was here the whole time! The bastard just made me invisible and undetectable. Rude!" Ollie said with outrage.

The Ancient sighed. "I apologize for the subterfuge, but I had to see the depths of what you had access to. Your Wayfinder had kept them blocked from my scans." He crossed his arms. "I had to see a bit of everything to extrapolate."

"You could have just asked!" Jace shouted at him. "And not put me through that bullshit!"

The Ancient shook his head. "You are correct, but I also needed to see what would happen if you succumbed to your worst fear. Your Wayfinder is correct—he will never leave you. He cannot. He is as much a part of your Soul as you are. Such is the nature of The Cosmic System you carry within you—it is bound to the glue that binds your body and mind together."

He cleared his throat and continued, rapidly, "Cosmic Power in the form of Dark Matter and the associated Dark Energy. Ascended Power in the form of Void. Emotion Source of Valiance, making you into an archetypical hero in Astral Verge terms . . . I do think you might stand a chance at surviving against Valcrinox . . . but you cannot cut yourself off from your past." He pointed to the crystal floating above the dais. "Grab it."

Jace walked over and grabbed the crystal, which turned into a capsule in his grip.

> [You have acquired a Relic of the Ancients.]
> [Relic Capacity Detected.]
> [Relic converted to Relic Upgrade Matrix.]
> [ERROR—Administrator Override.]
> [Converting to Infusion.]
> [Infusion Acquired—Divine (Talent).]

"Divine Talent?" Jace asked, still feeling quite wary of The Ancient.

"Yes. Use it. It will help you in your fight against Valcrinox and other demons. You will never be able to apply Infusions to it, but it will prove quite useful.]

Jace activated the Infusion.

[Using Infusion: Divine (Talent).]
[Talent Name: Final Form.]
[Effect: The user may activate this Talent once per cycle. Automatically activates {Wrath's Embrace} and {Shattered Limits} at their highest {Rank} possible, and elevates them by imbuing them with raw Dark Matter, Dark Energy, Void, and Valiant Psykinetics. If facing against a single foe, [Single-Minded Fury] will be applied. Additionally, the user gains a temporary massive boost to all traits (physical, sensory, cognitive).]

Jace saw several Astral and Cosmic System screens all intermingle and play across each other before they seemed to merge and combine into a calm black with cerulean text—just like Shhiv's Psykinetic power manifestation. "What happened?"

Ollie looked him up and down. "Huh. Seems like the Talent lays the groundwork for doing what we did with The Cosmic System to The Astral System."

"Correct," The Ancient replied. "When you reach Potency 10, level 100, and have defeated Valcrinox—you will be able to join us in the Nethershift, where we will give you the Karma Judgement Matrix and aid you in permanently integrating your Astral System. And, since I know you care deeply for your wife, Shhiv Seren, I will offer you the means to perform the same process outside of the Nethershift . . . but only for one individual."

Jace looked at the Quiet One and frowned. "I . . . I don't know whether to thank you for the help or tell you to go fuck yourself for putting me through that psychological torment."

"It matters little. The results are what I care about. Goodbye for now, Jace." The Ancient vanished in a cloud of pixelization, and Jace was yanked backward out of the Vault and into the dirt tunnel below the tree.

He still had Ollie in his left arm, hugged tightly to his chest. The Wayfinder tapped his paws against Jace's armor. "You and me to the end of everything."

Jace nodded and began ascending the steps of the tunnel. *I'm never going to be alone, ever again.*

Chapter Thirty-Eight

Reaching Potency 8

We are 11,000 Essence short. Jace glanced at his status screen. *Holy Hunt,* he thought as he breached the top of the canopy and focused his intent on an Astral Demon that had consumed Souls of all types. The golden path shot down, and he cut a hole in the canopy before dropping down, using his Soul Tether to slow his descend and then sprinting along the path laid out before him.

Winding his way through the large trees that grew ever closer together, the brightness of the permanent orange sunset sky above faded as the shadows cast by the thicker canopy felt almost visceral and alive, writhing about as something hidden in the shade pushed them like an ebb and flow.

Jace came to a stop and prepared himself, activating his usual Skills and Talents. His shield blazed to life as he summoned his Divine Revenge to his hand, the gold flames igniting, mixed with the green as crimson nebula clouds dripped down. To his slight surprise, the crackling red of <Wrathblade> appeared as well as a slight purple glow of Dark Matter.

Oh. That is what the Ancient did. I was wondering what that new line of code would do.

Jace saw an Astral Demon come out of the tree line. It was like the other demon cats, but this one was lither and more elegant, in a way. Less like a tiger, more like a bobcat. And the fur was bristling with spikes like a porcupine—each spike glittering with bronze shards of Psykinetic energy. It let out a growl.

And Jace heard another growl echoed from the other side, then another. Taunting voices overlapping. Five in total.

"The Wraith."

"Easy kill."

"Hunt."

"Split the Soul?"

"It's mine!"

The one he had Holy Hunt active against leaped at him, and Jace swiftly turned and brought his sword across it. The spikes and spines reacted to his strike, forming a barrier—but the power of Jace's blow combined with the (Bracing) Infusion sent it flying into a tree trunk, where it let out a yelp of pain—the trees burning it as it fell to the ground.

That was the indicator for the others to jump in, and they all leaped into the radius of Jace's Hero's Arena—which, he now saw, was crackling not just with the golden and green flames, but also purple wisps of Dark Matter and the crimson lightning of his <Wrathblade> coursed throughout. The effects stacked up burning damage-over-time afflictions upon each of his foes, and they were drawn in thanks to the (Vexing) Infusion.

Time to try this out. Final Form.

[Error.]
[May only be activated at Potency 10.]

Jace frowned and blocked the first of the claw swipes from the cat-demons. Another one circled behind him, and he interposed his shield between himself and that one.

Pulling up an old classic. Permission to increase anger response?

Do it!

[Regressing Shattered Limits.]

[Wrath's Embrace available.]

Jace felt the familiar hatred blossom in his chest before exploding in a firestorm of wrath as the (Focused) variant surged to life, the crackling crimson coating his whole body with a film of rage. Ollie kicked his adrenaline glands into overdrive, and Jace felt nothing but sheer disgust and hatred for these demons.

Downside is that even at maximum Rank, Wrath's Embrace only does a x6 amplifier to traits and attacks whereas just one Rank of Shattered Limits is x10.

Jace could barely hear Ollie as a tempest rang around his ears. He was able to get his sword around to another of the demon cats and slashed across it—sending it flying even further than the last one—causing it to crash through the center of one of the trees and become lodged in the wood that seemed antithetical to their being.

The hatred flowed through him, and he could feel a desire to kill, to destroy, a familiar torrent of emotions that flowed through him before and seemed perfectly acceptable to use against these irredeemable creatures.

Oh, look at that one.

Jace looked back to the first one he had cut into and launched—the target of his Holy Hunt. It was covered in multiple different applications of the golden flame, the green flame of Void, and the crimson miasma. But, more interestingly, the form had become less monstrous as his weapon's new (Ancient Reckoning) Infusion had regressed the Astral Demon by a Potency.

Focus target! Ollie said.

Jace turned back to the assault he was still under by the other three, getting his shield in the way of one of them, his sword to parry the second—but the third got into his space and clawed at his chest—the Psykinetic-empowered cutting edges slicing into his armor and a few finding their way into the skin and muscle below. But Jace couldn't feel it thanks to Wrath's Embrace.

Detonate, he thought as he used the Dark Energy Mine he had placed on himself when he first lined up and activated everything he was used to using. The Astral Demons next to him were caught off guard, and Jace sent them flying as he used Void Step to warp next to the still-recovering demon who his Holy Hunt had marked.

Slicing down, again and again, he made a total of six more cuts. Each slice seemed to take away a part of the demon's body, slowly shaving off the outside edges of its form until finally, on the seventh strike in total, the now–Potency 0 demon lay on the ground. A weak Astral Demon, just like the ones from up on the first Layer.

Data gathered. Finish it off! Ollie said.

Jace stabbed the now-far-weaker demon through the chest and then turned around to face the remaining four demons—the fourth of which had wriggled out of the tree it had been smacked into. "Bring it on!" Jace shouted as he ran forward. Then, as he reached the three that were close together, he used Void Step, followed up by Raging Cleave, and sliced through all of them from behind. *(Fulmination)*, he thought, and the weapon's arc exploded with gold flame that surged out from the impact point.

Each one of the three had their Potency reduced by one, and Jace felt the reinvigorating rush of his inflicting of wounds upon these foes. As they turned to face him, he used another Void Step, got behind them, and repeated his Raging Cleave, this time also stacking [Echoing Cleave] to see if that applied the weapon's Infusion.

It did not, unfortunately—but now de-powered to Potency 5, the demons began to scatter.

Regressing another Skill. Use it!

Void Brand, Jace thought as he flung his sword at the now-charging-at-him demon he had flung into the tree and trapped briefly. With his other hand, he dismissed his Crusader's Bastion, pulled several throwing knives out of his TPSB, and flung them at each of the Astral Demons that was fleeing. The weapons hit but did not sink in. That did not matter though, as Jace had tagged them with Void Brand and would be able to track them no matter where they went on the same Layer.

The one who he had thrown his sword at dodged the weapon and got up next to Jace, leaping on him and tackling him to the ground. But Jace had two more throwing knives in his hands and flipped them in his grip as he stabbed into the demon that brought him to the dirt. It clawed at him, biting down and injuring him—but Jace felt no pain, and thanks to the [Dark Matter Binding] constantly healing him, he was more than able to return the blows with his dual knives.

Why not dodge with Void Step?

They need to suffer!

Yeah, okay, Wrath's Embrace is making you do dumb stuff.

Jace finished off the demon with several jabs that eventually caused it to expire, and he tossed it off of him as he stood up, put the throwing knives back into the TPSB, and summoned his sword to his grip. *We need to hunt them down!* He began chasing after one of the foes with Void Brand, watching the slight grey shape bobbing in front of him through the trees—literally through the trees, as the effect enabled him to track them anywhere.

Fine, but I am turning off Wrath's Embrace for now.

Jace felt the rage and anger fade, and the dull ache of the still-being-mended wounds kicked in. "Ouch," he muttered as he continued to chase his quarry. "What's that for?"

You fight dumb when you are angry, Ollie said matter-of-factly. *Maybe we hold off on using that unless we really need it but cannot use Shattered Limits.*

I thought that when I went from Class to Advanced Class I lost all of the old Skills that got merged up?

You did, but I have been tweaking The Cosmic System since it became innate to you. It took an extreme emotional state, similar to what you past felt when *you first acquired <Wrathblade>, and The Ancient was able to get you to that point. Now that I have seen the framework in that new light, I can regress Skills to an older version.*

Do I lose the newer, better one?

Nope. You cannot use them at the same time. No Dark Matter Cloak and Void Stalker at the same time—one or the other.

Fair enough. Jace got behind the first of his prey he had tracked, and thanks to his reduction of their Potency, they could not hope to outrun him. He sliced across the hind quarters and then used a Void Step to get in front of them, stabbing down into the head for the killing blow. *Now . . . rinse and repeat.*

He took off after the next one and repeated the process—letting them impale themselves on his thrust as he warped in front of them. All three lay slain, and he soaked up the Essence as their Souls escaped and flew to the trees to continue their journey.

56,000. 1,000 short.

Jace sighed, "I was hoping that would be it and we could head down to the next Layer." He activated Holy Hunt again, looking for an Astral Demon near the western entrance that led down to Layer 8. The golden path illuminated, and he ran that way.

Tibalt had been hunting. *There are two factions*, he had observed. *Those that work for this Yroshnak who plans to leave soon and descend, and another that seeks to destroy his chosen replacement.*

Naturally, Tibalt had been attacking Yroshnak's forces. Like a horrible monster in the lakes, he went from body of water to body of water. Souls were tasty, and he had access to many here. But he learned very quickly that these Astral Demons had been storing up their Souls. Most likely, he presumed, in preparation to descend with their master.

He was stalking yet another group. The stone paths that went in between the lakes made for easy tracking, and the only time that Tibalt risked discovery was when he got out of the water to cross the paths and sink into the next pool of placid peace.

Then, he saw his chance. One of the demons split off from the others, and Tibalt shadowed them. Like a crocodile stalking the prey on the shore, ready to pounce. As soon as he went behind one of the several structures dotted about the landscape, Tibalt came out of the water and crept up behind them.

Severing their necks was easy, and even though all of them were Potency 8 and had their fair amount of tricks up their sleeves, Tibalt was relentless and found his methodology quickly—cut a gash in the neck, shove his arm down the throat, and then use his other clawed hand to pierce their vital organs.

Even those with armor fell to the method he had been utilizing, and Tibalt felt the thrum of Souls in his chest grow ever greater. *Almost*, he thought. *Almost at enough for Potency 9 . . . and then only ten more levels. But I need to harvest as much as I can.*

The stream of Souls would be its densest on the next two Layers down. This Layer, while fun to hunt the souls as they dripped into the lakes like countless falling raindrops, had slippery little bastards. They had more maneuverability it seemed, as if they knew they were closer to the end of their journey and moved with more urgency.

He finished ripping this Astral Demon apart and consumed the Souls that surged from their torso, gobbling them up and feeling the swell of heat. He also incorporated their Essence, and then sank back into the lake as he swam to lurk behind his next target.

Finding another one of the Astral Demons was easy, and after a brief yet intense fight with one of the demon cats, he slew them and acquired the two thousand Essence. Ascending to the treetops, he cut his way to the top of the canopy and looked around for any sign of danger. *Ollie,* he thought. *Unmerge to keep an eye out.*

Ollie did so, and Jace quickly used Dark Matter Mending to stop the piercing headache. "Okay," Ollie said. "I'll task the drone with overwatch up here, and I'll dip below the leaves. You ready?"

Jace nodded. "I know this is going to hurt like a motherfucker . . . but let's do it."

[You have leveled up!]
[You have chosen Specialization of Existing Talent!]
[Talent Name: Justice's Rebuke.]
[Specialization Name: Plasmas.]
[Effect: When the linked Talent is activated, the user's weapons and Talents deal additional damage in the form of blasting heat.]
[Talent Name: Justice's Rebuke.]
[Specialization Name: Energizing.]
[Effect: When the linked Talent is activated, the user's weapons and Talents restore a small amount of energy.]
[Talent Name: Justice's Rebuke.]
[Specialization Name: Languishing.]
[Effect: When the linked Talent is activated, the user's weapons and Talents cause the target to feel a malaise that reduces their reaction time.]
[Talent Name: Valiant Crusader's Might.]
[Specialization Name: Rallying.]

[Effect: While active, the user's strikes inspire those designated as allies who can see the user, causing their weapons and Talents to strike with more force.]
[Talent Name: Crusader's Bastion.]
[Specialization Name: Hallowed.]
[Effect: While active, the user's presence inspires those designated as allies who can see the user, increasing their defensive qualities.]
[Talent Name: Hero's Arena.]
[Specialization Name: Crusading.]
[Effect: Those designated as allies in the Hero's Arena heal from a portion of the damage they inflict upon foes.]
[Talent Name: Hero's Arena.]
[Specialization Name: Reckoning.]
[Effect: Those designated as allies in the Hero's Arena who are attacked apply a mark to the creature who harmed them. The user gains combat efficacy amplification against foes marked.]
[Talent Name: Templar's Smite.]
[Specialization Name: Blinding.]
[Effect: When the linked Talent is used on a target, they are temporarily blinded.]

Name: Jace Seren (Potency 8)
Emotion [Class Level]: Valiant [Archangel 71]
Talent [Specialization]: Astral Adaptation, Astral Translation, Valiant Crusader's Might [Burning] [Vengeful] [Poised] [Unstoppable] [Bracing] [Voidbound] [Lightbound] [Rallying], Crusader's Bastion [Retaliating] [Reinforcing] [Grounding] [Redoubt] [Spiked] [Resonating] [Glorious] [Hallowed], Hero's Arena [Aura] [Incinerating] [Vexing] [Bolstering] [Suppressing] [Wrathbound] [Crusading] [Reckoning], Indomitable Will [Zealous] [Intimidating] [Inviolable] [Enduring] [Ameliorating] [Dark Matter Binding], Templar's Smite [Spear] [Blast] [Lingering] [Challenging] [Inferno] [Cosmic] [Gaze] [Blinding], Holy Hunt [Marked] [Bursting] [Authoritative] [Provoking] [Inciting] [Branding], Purifying Edge [Cleansing] [Searing] [Purging] [Sanctifying] [Terminating] [Judging] [Revealing], Justice's Rebuke [Flaming] [Bashing] [Holy] [Plasmas] [Energizing]

[Languishing], Revealing Light [Burdening] [Limning] [Fracturing] [Potent] [Perilous] [Linking], Final Form
Essence: 1,000
Infusions: None
Gear: <TPSB>, (Convergent Edge / Ancient Reckoning) Divine Revenge, (Explorer's Embrace / Beacon) Hero's Plate, (Prosthetic Savant) Astral Appendages, (Draconic Sovereign) Arbiter's Sight, (Anathema) Astral Sleeve, (Reinforced) Psycrystal Lattice, (Pinnacle) NICIF-EP, (Restoring) Flame of Valor, Retribution Carbine (20 shots / battery)

The agony was excruciating, and Jace would have screamed out if Ollie had not shut off his vocal chords in preparation for this moment. He suffered in silence as his body writhed under the skin, the Essence of slain demons being incorporated into his body and strengthening it even further—putting him closer to being on level with those Astral Demons who once far outclassed him.

A few seconds of horrific, piercing pain, and it all faded. He took a deep breath and stood up. *Ollie? I'm good now.*

The Wayfinder popped up through the canopy and merged with Jace. *Good. Ready for the next Layer?*

Oh yeah. Let's do it!

The drone returned to its station, keeping above Jace, and the Ascendant ran across the treetops until he reached the entrance. A large clearing with a ring of the same trees, but open to the sky. He could see the film covering the entrance to the next Layer, and next to it, seated on a root that jutted up, was the Demon Lord Phytala, who he had just consolidated control to.

Jace jumped down and landed nearby, walking over. "I stopped the blight spread . . . whatever that was."

She looked up to him from her jars with Souls and nodded. "I saw, hence the Mission being complete." She glanced over at the film, then back to Jace. "I wish you the best of luck, truly."

"No need for luck when I have skill," Jace replied as he walked over to the film.

She let out a slight chuckle. "Well . . . take care, regardless. I sincerely hope you end Valcrinox . . ." she trailed off as if she wished to add more but thought better of it and simply refocused her attention on the jar she was holding.

Jace gave her a brief nod of acknowledgment that she did not return, and so he jumped into the film to the next Layer.

Chapter Thirty-Nine

Meanwhile . . .

"How long until the defenses are finished?" Valcrinox shouted to his minions, lamenting his earlier decision to kill his underling that normally managed the minutiae of the Layer.

"We are almost done!" the demon under Valcrinox's command replied. "Just need to get the spikes set up."

"Good," Valcrinox said as he leaned back in the throne and looked up at the empty hooks on the walls and ceiling, thinking about other options for what he could do to reinforce the Layer against Wraith's advance.

Layer 10 was very small compared to every other Layer. Only one hundred miles from north to south and five hundred east to west, with the entrance from Layer 9 at the farthest western edge of the near-rectangular final Layer of the Astral Verge. His palace, his stronghold, his throne, was on the far eastern edge. And behind the throne room—the pathway to the Nethershift.

And he had been fortifying the whole expanse. In past eons, he had prepared defenses. But, as each Bearer of the Mantle of Burden was defeated, he grew lax. Now, he rushed to enhance the defenses. Every single foot of the Layer would be defended by his army. Small but powerful, with each singular Astral Demon a perfect blend of half monstrous, half refined—and all dedicated to Valcrinox wholly.

He was not called the Endless Madness for no reason, just as Layer 10 was not called the Fields of Madness just because he wanted it to be called that. The deepest point of the Astral Verge would make any who arrived and were not Potency 10 go utterly insane. It is why Valcrinox had so many hooks on the walls and ceilings of his throne room—the screams and wailing of those Dreamers was like a subtle song that constantly filled him with a sense of comfort.

And now, the lack of screaming was disquieting, and he dared not get up from his throne. The Relic that would ensure he could not lose. He was forced to sit there, not by any external power, but his own sense of desperation.

I need to survive.

Tibalt had just reached enough Souls, Essence, and stolen Universal Matter to reach the next Potency, and he had overstayed his welcome on the Layer. Yroshnak's forces knew that someone stalked them from the waters, and he had no other means of hunting reliably.

And so, Tibalt chose to spend all of his level-up materials. He made sure he was at the bottom of a lake and went through the painful evolution, choosing further refinement. *I'm not going to be a mindless beast*, he thought. *A beast cannot be emperor of the whole of the Astral Verge. I must be a perfect blend: monstrous and refined, with the framing of a Dreamer. The mindset of a Dreamer. The drive of an emperor.*

His body contorted and wracked with pain as his blood boiled in his skin. He howled, and the gurgling water churned around his mouth as the bubbles escaped up to the surface, carrying hollow screams of pain and misery.

But he felt his body contort and become more humanoid, less like a horrific monstrosity from the nightmares that a Vanguard told their child before sending them off to cryo-sleep. He could feel the raw Psykinetic energy crackling through his veins and broke the surface as the pain faded, making powerful strokes as he headed to the entrance to Layer 9. *So close*, he thought. *I'm almost there.*

Shhiv finished up the last of her modifications to the defensive structure. "And done," she said with relief as she leaned back. "The whole thing is done."

Xero joined her on the bench in the mountaintop bunker on the first Layer of the Astral Verge. He handed her a bottle of refreshing lemon-flavored water that she greedily slurped down. "Good job," he said. "Without your Class selection and your chosen build . . . well, I think it would have taken a lot longer." He rapped a knuckle on the bench as she finished off the bottle. "Now, we have a fully hidden Universe. Fully encased. No way for anything hostile to get in, and if they did somehow get past Void and Dark Matter, they have to deal with this tower."

Shhiv smiled. "Yeah, I'm really proud of what we did here." She thought back to all of the various bits and pieces of the project she had engaged with up until this point. It was a laborious few days, and she really missed Jace, a longing in her chest as she frowned, remembering the empty water-cube bed they shared. Working had staved off the feeling, but now with every project Xero had laid out completed . . . the feelings surged up, and she felt herself tear up a bit.

Xero seemed to pick up on her discomfort immediately and put a reassuring hand on her upper back. "Hey . . . you did good. Good enough to cry over, even."

She shook her head. "Not that . . . I miss my husband is all. It's been over a week now."

"He's alive," Xero replied. "Almost done with his tasks. I would bet he can come up and take a break once he is done with Layer 8."

Shhiv wiped her eyes. "Please tell me you have other projects. I need to stay busy."

"Oh, uhmm . . . " He began tapping his wrist pad. "Well, I suppose we could work on some megastructures. I mean, everything that I'd need your help with for the Penrose Sphere and the tower here is done. So . . . let me make a few calls." His eyes went black, and he began whispering into the air to his right.

Shhiv stood up as he engaged in hushed conversation with whomever he had called. One of the updates Xera had put in when she had access to the exterior of their Universe—she had improved The Cosmic System's bandwidth. Within the Universe, or directly outside of it such as in this tower beneath their singularity's funnel, they could do voice and video calls—not text alone like it was previously.

She pulled up her contact list and reached out to her old friend, Bev, who answered. "Hey, girl! It's been a while!"

"Hi, Bev. I need to get my mind off something—"

"Oh, not your man leaving you, I hope?"

Shhiv almost laughed at that comment. "No, Jace would never leave me. I just miss him, that's all."

"Oh, still on his business trip across the Universe?"

"Yes," Shhiv replied, confirming the cover story they had chosen to go with. "I need to take my mind off of it."

"I know a good club! Let's go there!"

"Sounds good."

Shhiv turned around as Xero stood up. "Well," he said as he stretched down to his toes and then stood upright. "We have a few contracts available if you just want to stay busy—Star Council and Nebula Alliance are requesting megastructure construction assistance. Plus, I know the Dark Between Stars"—he winked as he said the name of his faction—"also could use some help in making even more defensive augmentations. I know of this great idea called a Solarcraft, where we take an entire solar system and turn it into a giant warship, using the star as the power source and making a framework . . . it's a neat concept I'd like to see if we could pull off."

Shhiv raised an apprehensive brow. "Why do you need a giant warship?"

"Just to see if we could make it," Xero replied. "Plus, we could have it as a backup in case there is a breach in the Penrose Sphere—not that that is likely."

Shhiv sighed but nodded. "Yeah. Give me a bit of time off, and then I'll call you."

"Sounds good!" Xero walked over to the central tether spire—all of the voidlight tethers that went from the Penrose Sphere up above the singularity funnel and connected the automated starfighters and drones that were now stationed inside the tower save for those still out mapping the first Layer that were inside the single housing. Shhiv walked over behind him and grabbed the cord.

Greg and Missy were having a blast. Her build perfectly suited a supportive bruiser role, and the two of them tore through Astral Demons with glee.

"Heads up!" she shouted. Greg ducked as she unleashed a torrential downpour of icy Psykinetic energy that froze a group of demons in place—affixing their feet to the rocky ground.

"Great job, hon!" Greg shouted as he swung his laser sword, cutting through the pinned-in-place foes. Within seconds, the small horde had been defeated by the unstoppable juggernaut and his lovely spouse.

Greg and Missy had special leave from Xero—to be allowed outside the tower to harvest Essence. Already notified by The Ancients through their faction leader that in case Jace failed, they would be the backup Bearers of the Mantle of Burden.

But Greg had a personal grudge against demons. Troxanir had taken almost all of his family, friends, and loved ones when he sent a suicide bomber to wreck his and Missy's wedding. Jace would try to get the Souls back and reunite them all again . . . but Greg still had a bone to pick with all of Troxanir's kind.

Missy walked over and put a reassuring hand on his shoulder. "You have that look."

Greg shook his head. "Sorry. Just thinking."

"Don't," she replied as she cupped his helmeted chin. "You leave the thinking to me."

"Yes ma'am," he replied, not daring to argue back against the woman he loved. His attention drifted toward the Vault that Jace had cleared out and whose map data they had. "Potency 3 suggested is what it said when he tried it."

Missy shook her head. "Nope. We aren't risking it. You might be an unkillable beast, but for all we know, those Vaults are one-person challenges only."

Greg nodded. "Understood." He reverted back to his military mindset. "Ready to go to the next target?"

"Sure," Missy replied. She reached a hand up and grabbed the invisible drone—invisible save for the tiny blinking aperture on the bottom that was only visible if standing directly under it and looking straight up—which, thankfully, they easily could do because Xero had tasked it with following the duo.

Greg reached up and gripped the fist-sized drone, and the two whizzed off over the shifting landscape, on the hunt once more.

Priam sighed after the hospital visit concluded. Vials in hand, he headed to his home world of Fernaid and, walking through, ended up in one of the metropolitan centers that was thriving now that the gods were back in control. He was given high respect by those he passed, being the last of the Westerfold Clan. The last of those who could put gods to rest permanently.

Dee squeezed his hand. "I know it's weird, but this is for the best."

"I know," Priam replied. "It just feels odd, to have a bunch of kids and not even know any of them."

Dee stopped and knelt to his level, putting a soft, warm, chitinous hand on his cheek as her glowing red eyes in the goop stabilized on him. "You do not have to do this if you do not want to . . . but this world does have a need for god eaters. And I doubt you will want to come here every month to keep doing the job over and over."

"True . . . it is a bit of a pain," Priam replied. "I know it needs to be done, but it's never been done before. Oslia raise their kids—we don't have orphanages."

"Times change," Dee replied. "Circumstances change. Come on." She stood up and took his hand again.

Priam walked with her to the clinic that had been set up by the Star Council, one of the few pieces of technology that was allowed by the gods, the local administrators of The Cosmic System, to persist upon a predominantly magic world. Entering the cool, air-conditioned clinic, Priam walked up to the counter. "I have a delivery."

The attendant, another Oslia who looked quite a bit older than Priam, nodded and held out her hand. Priam handed her the box and the small slip that he had brought from the hospital. She scanned it, then looked at him. "Thank you, Westerfold. We have a handful of families who cannot have children because of . . . a complex bouquet of medical reasons. This will give them families."

Priam sighed with relief, knowing that his offspring would end up growing up the traditional Oslia way. "Thanks," he said as he turned and left with Dee. He squeezed her chitinous hand. "Thanks for being here."

"Of course, my little fuzzball," she said with delight.

Chapter Forty

Layer 8

Jace fell through the film and stopped his fall with a Soul Tether. The entire environment around him was serene and tranquil. Lakes of various hues spread off in all directions, all of uniform size, easily a square mile if not larger. Intersecting the lakes in square plots were a series of stone walkways, and built on pedestals out on the lakes were several buildings that seemed occupied.

Or perhaps were once occupied, as Jace descended to one of the walkways and saw no signs of life presently, but there may have once been such a thriving group of demons living there.

On the ceiling of the Layer, far above—a deep blue specked with silver dots—Jace could see the small pointed bottoms of the roots trickling down Souls that dropped into the various lakes before moving about and sinking deeper. *We should be getting the notification any second now,* Jace thought.

And, true to what he thought, the Astral System message appeared in his vision. He already knew exactly what he wanted.

[Congratulations on entering a new Layer!]
[You may choose to specialize your Class by performing a Class Transmutation!]
[Base Class = Archangel.]
[Options available:]
[Zealot—expand upon your offensive capabilities. Leads to further offensive Transmutations.]

[Guardian—expand upon your defensive capabilities. Leads to further defensive Transmutations.]
[Herald—expand upon your support capabilities. Leads to further support Transmutations.]

Let's go with Guardian, Jace thought. *I need stronger defenses, and I'm pretty set with my offensive capabilities.*

[Class Transmutation Confirmed.]

No Mission on this Layer, Ollie advised him. *Yroshnak already has control, minus the few dissidents that we are going to help him put down. Oh, speaking of which, he has given us names.*

Jace saw a series of names scrawl across his vision. "Easy enough. We have a target list."

Yup!

"Holy Hunt," Jace muttered as he focused on the first name. Activating Void Stalker, as it was energy neutral given his current regeneration rate, he ran across the stone pathways and headed to the west.

A few minutes of running passed, and he saw no sign of life. No Astral Demons, no Dreamers, just the gentle dripping of Souls falling like rain into the lakes. It was meditative, in a way, and peaceful. Jace felt his mind wandering and had to pinch himself to force his mind to focus.

Well, to keep our mind off boredom . . . turns out each Layer has some type of meaning behind it. Want to hear?

Sounds interesting, and I don't know how far we're going to be running.

Ollie spent the next several minutes explaining each Layer and what its environment meant or represented: Layer 1 depicted all of the emotions that any person might feel, and due to the large buildup of miasmic degrading Souls from pre-Ancient arrival, that first Layer was still inundated with the darker aspects of people and their actions.

The deeper Layers, however, were more meaningful to demons specifically, as if fostering and encouraging their growth down the refinement evolution path, guiding them on a journey. Layer 2 was a forest, and that represented the unknown and ever-shifting paths that a new person found themselves upon. With each turn, each decision made, a new path opened up with its own obstacles. But pushing through all the obstacles, one could continue onward.

Layer 3, the city, was meant to show and teach Astral Demons that there was community to be found among their peers. To show them the meaning of connection to another. The power that comes from making a sincere friend or close ally. And to hopefully foster their desire to continue to travel the depths of the Layers, together.

Layer 4, the desert, was meant to show a demon that there would always be parts of their endless lives that would be boring but not to give up, and continue to their destination regardless of circumstances. It also reinforced how being with other demons, being with others one cared for, would allow them to survive those periods of long, empty boredom without succumbing to base urges like eating unjudged Souls.

Layer 5, the snowy mountains, were meant to be a challenge to navigate. Something that could be done alone with great difficulty, but was much easier with others and preparations. To demonstrate to a demon that they needed to be ready for challenges that lay ahead, even if they were unsure about the nature of the challenge.

The next Layer also reflected this, to a degree. Layer 6, the swamp, was meant to show a demon that even despite the worst circumstances, there was still a hope. A chance for escape, to push on through the bad times to find the good, and instead of turning around and fleeing, to face the challenge head-on. Plus, having proper equipment would help along the journey. And being with others would reduce the overall malaise that would occur when surrounded by such a dreary environment.

Layer 7, the forest Jace had just come from, was to show the beauty that comes from letting something grow and expand. To show an Astral Demon that they were capable of sitting back and appreciating the beauty in reality, in a Soul, without interacting with it. That if they held their destructive urges in place, then they would see great beauty could arise from just being present.

Layer 8, the lakes that Jace now ran past, was meant to be a chance for quiet solitude to reflect on one's journey. The opportunity for the demon to take a breather before the hardest challenges they would face.

Layer 9 was a trial. A series of challenges. *This is where things get interesting*, Ollie said with some excitement. *There are different paths for these trials. A bunch of paths that are designed to test all mixes of monstrous and refined evolutionary paths, and then another path for Dreamers, and another series of mixes of paths for Dreamer Demons, also with the same number of possible options. Once we clear that Layer, there is an express lane, of sorts, to get around the trials to go to and from the layers.*

Interesting, Jace thought as he slowed down to take a right turn on one of the roads and continued following the line of the Holy Hunt Talent. *I wonder what our trial will be like?*

Considering you are the first Dreamer to reach this deep? No one knows. And anyone who does not fall along a certain path cannot look into other ones.

What about Layer 10?

The Fields of Madness. Originally just called The Fields—it's the thing that your ancient Greek civilization had some mythology about, the Elysian Fields, I think they called it. It was meant to represent the final renewal of an Astral Demon as they went to the Nethershift. A fresh start, like a newly sprouted spring meadow.

Seems like The Ancients knew they fucked up with making those funnels and made a way for demons to redeem themselves. Just like the one demon who was kind enough to pull me into a building when Valcrinox's army flew overhead on Layer 3.

I believe they may have done something similar in other realities, Ollie said with caution and a voice laced with suspicion. *If they knew about Souls degrading into miasma, then part of me believes that they have a secret mission that they complete—draining the miasma and filtering it. Almost like they are custodians, going from reality to reality to clean up messes left behind by whatever created everything.*

Jace frowned as the thought that he had killed a bunch of demons traveling their own path to redemption raced through his mind. But he quickly dismissed it. They acted far differently than the ones that had shown him some kindness, some humanity. *I hope that is the case. The whole demon redemption part, and that they can find whatever comes next.*

A whole cycle passed before Jace arrived at one of the buildings that was built out over the water. He could see a light source through a window, and shadows danced upon the distant wall. Drawing his sword, he moved closer and sent the invisible drone ahead to peer through the window. What he saw inside was a bit confusing.

He saw men and women, people from all different species—four specifically here that matched up with his target list, and one of whom was limned in the golden glow. But they were dressed in a mix of advanced armor and carried high-tech weaponry. They had Karma Coefficients above their heads, and all were in the negatives. *Dreamer Demons*, he thought. *If I'm the first Dreamer down this far.*

Yup, Ollie said. *Looks like they have some demonic characteristics.* He controlled the drone and sent it into the room, and Jace could see the small bumps and protrusions that jutted up, displacing the armor slightly in portions.

Jace activated his Talents—all of them—and went to the door. He raised his foot and kicked it in. Immediately, guns were drawn on him and Psykinetic-empowered lasers shot his way. He just interposed the Crusader's Bastion and waited for them to run out of charge. "I am here to stop you from whatever it is you're plotting against Yroshnak," he said with as much authority to his tone he could muster.

"It's the Wraith!"

"Shit, Yroshnak is working with the Wraith?!"

"It is just Wraith," Jace said as he walked into the room. The figures all began channeling Psykinetic Talents at him, and he simply activated Void Barrier and continued to weather the storm as he made slight cuts and nicks along the first of the four. He saw his energy draining rapidly but needed to see what the (Ancient Reckoning) Infusion did against a Dreamer Demon firsthand.

The effects were immediately apparent. The first cut, their bulk decreased, and they sounded slightly winded. Each additional cut reduced their mass until finally, they were standing there—no ammunition, and with a terrified look on their uncovered face. *One of the Gyanv*, Jace noted.

Then, they screamed out, their eyes burning with a shimmering cyan that quickly shifted to red, then purple, and flickered through the entire color spectrum before landing on a pure black. The black spread across their body, and they were annihilated utterly—Souls pouring out of their body and scurrying along the floor and walls to the window, where they leaped out into the lake below the building.

A huge System message appeared above the body.

[Judgement Rendered.]

The other Dreamer Demons all said an overlapping variant of the phrase "What the fuck?" with alarm and panic in their voices.

Jace just turned to them and brandished his sword. "You next," he said as he advanced on them.

Yroshnak walked to the building and heard the screaming from inside. Oddly enough, a torrent of Souls were scooting their way out of the windows and plopping into the lake. When the last scream was silenced, a figure appeared in the entryway. One that looked both familiar and foreign. "Ah, Wraith. Well met again, but in the flesh. New Relics."

Wraith looked the part of a Bearer of the Mantle of Burden. His body was alight with crimson lightning that crackled and blended with a billowing, nebulous, invisible force that seemed to push all air away from him. Gold and green flames mixed in a torrent around his weapon, and his large, lustrous gold shield covered with spikes finished off quite the imposing figure.

"Yroshnak," he said as he sheathed the sword, and the effects faded. He walked up to Yroshnak, who stood double his height, and held out a hand. "Thanks for wanting to help out."

Yroshnak looked down at the hand, quickly assessed the Astral System database, and clasped it gently, giving the hand a small shake before releasing it. "Welcome to Layer 8. I see you have dealt with some of the malefactors here."

"I did," Wraith replied as he looked back to the house and the final few Souls escaping it and going into the lakes. "They were judged. And I got a decent amount of Essence out of the whole deal."

"How much do you need?" Yroshnak asked.

"I need a total of 81,000 for Potency 9," Wraith replied. "I'm currently at, after those Dreamer Demons, 11,000."

I knew they were hoarding Souls, but to think a Dreamer Demon's Essence is that potent. Yroshnak had brought Dreamer Demons into his fold on one of his expeditions up the Layers. Those that seemed like they just wanted power but were more inclined to only consume evil Souls he gave them. And he could always use forces that could break the rules that Astral Demons had to follow about technology limitations. But he had never killed any Dreamer Demons himself.

He spoke softly, "Leaving you with 70,000 more you need. Well, an Astral Demon on this Layer and this Potency is worth only 3,000. And I do not have that many here who need culling to ensure my chosen replacement's position is uncontested and secure."

Wraith sighed with frustration. "You said there would be enough Essence here to do what we needed to do."

Yroshnak grimaced. "I thought we had enough of these malfeasants to more than accommodate. But it appears that your level-up currency requirement of Essence does not track with my Soul or Universal Matter requirements."

Wraith shook his head. "I'll hunt down the last eight targets. Let me guess, two more groups of four?"

"That is right," Yroshnak replied.

"I'll deal with them and then do my backup plan."

"Oh? Which is?"

"Go to a choke point and let every Astral Demon know exactly where I am."

Yroshnak grinned with glee, his bloodlust rising at the idea of such a slaughter. "That sounds like a fine plan."

Wraith turned away and began walking down the road. "I'll keep you in the loop." He took off running, and Yroshnak was genuinely impressed.

From a cybernetic and armored warrior fighting a mere shade of me in an arena to being an entity I actually fear a bit. Yroshnak chuckled as he walked into the lake and teleported—one of the benefits of his current position as solitary Demon Lord of the Layer. He emerged back at his large lodge and began making final preparations.

Soon . . . we descend. And I face my trials. I hope Wraith passes whatever the Dreamer's trials may hold.

Chapter Forty-One

The Difference Technology Makes

Jace followed the golden path of the Holy Hunt, beelining for his next group of targets. Thanks to the stone paths being consistent and similar to one another, he could sprint at full speed, and it only took him three cycles to traverse the nearly nine hundred miles of distance to reach his goal.

Another building constructed on stilts, more sounds from inside. But parked atop the building was a starship that seemed on high-alert—its turrets sweeping from side to side.

I do not think that it can detect you while you have Void Stalker active, Ollie stated.

Jace had the Skill active and moved along the path as he approached the building. Drawing his sword, he went up to the door while the drone coated in Dark Matter maneuvered to the window to give him a view of the inside.

Another four Dreamer Demons, who had cut a hole into the ceiling with a small tractor beam poking down from the ship above. Three of them were wary, weapons at the ready—laser sword in one hand and some type of slug thrower in the other.

Word must have spread, Jace thought. *The group we already dealt with must have sent a message to their sympathizers.* He took a breath and kicked the door down, bringing his Crusader's Bastion to bear.

And he heard a loud click of some hidden trap that was out of sight of his drone. *Shi—* Jace couldn't finish his thought as he was blasted backward by a massive, searing plasma explosion. He went tumbling end over end and splashed into the lake opposite the building's entrance.

"He's here!"

"Get him!"

"Firing up the cannons."

Jace got out of the water and saw the ship cannons turning on him. *That's inconvenient*, he thought as he used Void Shield and began moving to his right—blocking the explosive bullets from the slug throwers with his Crusader's Bastion.

Then, the ship fired its beam. A huge, cutting blade of laser and plasma that was persistent and cut a trail behind then into Jace. He saw his Void Shield drain precipitously and had to shut it off or risk being tapped dry and having to use the Emergency Battery. His golden barricade was able to take the full brunt of the laser, but that exposed his right side to the explosive barrage.

"Die!" one of the Dreamer Demons shouted out.

Jace could see the bullet coming as time slowed to a crawl. *Void Step*, he thought as he warped out of the laser's line of sight and to the side of the building. Rapidly ascending with his Soul Tether, he got over the top of the roof only to be greeted with a point defense turret that snapped on him. *Proximity detectors?* he thought as he got his shield in the way just in time to block a barrage of lasers.

"He's up here!" a voice yelled from somewhere inside the ship.

Void Step, Jace thought as he warped down and into the lake underneath the building. Pointing his hand straight up, he breached the surface and fired off a Void Beam (Rank 3) [Piercing]. The blast of white-grey Void tinged with green flames surged up through the center of the building and into the ship, cutting a hole right through it.

"Under the building?!"

"We took a hit! Ship reactor core is still good, but the boosters are disabled!"

Jace used another Void Step to get into the building proper and stabbed one of the Dreamer Demons through the back, skewering them through the torso and ripping his blade sideways as the golden flames exploded from the wound. They let out a scream and were sent flying into the wall with a crunch as their body crumpled.

The advanced armor they were wearing seemed to keep them alive, though, as it ejected a healing goop that covered the burns and quenched the Psykinetic golden flames. But not the green flames of Void or the crimson nebula of [Rending]. Jace knew they were as good as dead and focused his attention on the next one.

Who approached him wielding a laser sword. The weapon seemed to have no or little weight, as they approached like a fencer with stabs and thrusts, blading their stance but holding a pistol that could easily be brought to bear against Jace. The laser sword and gun surged with violet energy.

Ollie, regress to Dark Matter Blade.

Done!

Jace's weapon was coated with purple and, to his opponents, became invisible. Jace moved forward with his shield in front of him, and as the Dreamer Demon moved to the side, Jace caught them with his sword, slicing across their torso with a deep cut that spread the [Rending] effect.

And because of the blade's (Ancient Reckoning) Infusion, they were weakened even further, their movement slowing to Jace's perception.

Something shot him in the side, pain blossoming through his body as his ribs cracked as the explosive round punched through his armor before detonating. Glancing to his right, Jace saw another of the Dreamer Demons at the window as they squeezed off more rounds that slammed into his side.

Void Step, Jace thought as he warped behind them. But they seemed ready for that as their armor exploded in Jace's face. It sent him reeling back, and he fell down into the lake. Which was actually a blessing in disguise, as Jace saw the explosive bullets impact the surface, sink only slightly, then detonate—leaving him unaffected save for the shockwaves that really did not bother him.

(Dark Matter Binding) finished mending his wounds, and the NICIF in him had accelerated the repairs. *About forty percent of my energy left*, Jace thought. *That ship blast on my Void Shield was a lot.*

A deep glow appeared above Jace, and he instinctively used a Void Step to warp under the building. He saw, to his left, the water pierced through by a blisteringly powerful ship's laser.

Wow. That is a powerful weapon, Ollie commented. *Would be nice if we could imbue such a thing with Psykinetics, but I think it does not qualify as handheld.*

Jace ignored Ollie's commentary to focus on the present. He had two more hostiles to deal with. One in the ship, and one somewhere up above him. *Holy Hunt*, he thought as he focused on the one who had shot him in the side. The golden path went to his side, then up. *Moved into the building. Void Step.*

Jace warped into the room and immediately struck at his target, who was midway through trying to patch up their ally. They turned around and activated their laser sword in the way of the blow, blocking as the beam of hardened burning light surged and flared where it met Jace's Divine Retribution. The figure let out a shout and slapped their thigh, where a button was conveniently located.

The entire room exploded around Jace, and he felt excruciating pain all along his side where the armor had been weakened. The defensive encasement protected the rest of his body, but that specific area was not repaired by the NICIF yet. The entire building erupted in a massive shockwave that sent rubble flying.

The ship above us dropped cluster munitions, Ollie stated. *You are fine.*

Jace barely caught his breath as the NICIF repaired his shredded lung, and he activated Dark Matter Mending (Rank 4) instead of relying on the slow, continual healing of (Dark Matter Binding) and his Flame of Valor Relic in his chest. *It still fucking sucks*, Jace thought as he recovered his bearings. The Dreamer Demons he had injured and who had been afflicted with damage-over-time effects had seemingly expired, as he saw Souls drifting through the water below the blasted-to-rubble pile of rocks that he was perched on slightly above the surface of the water.

The ship above was hovering, and it began to turn and take aim at Jace with its large ship lasers. And he saw an ascension line that his prior target had used to ascend to the ship. *Void Step*, Jace thought as he warped up and into the ship.

He appeared in what looked like a small, cramped crew's quarters. Opening the door, he immediately grabbed the Dreamer Demon that had signaled the cluster bomb drop. Squeezing their neck, he slammed their helmet into the bulkhead and then summoned his sword from wherever it had ended up in the lake, stabbing it into the person and pinning them to the wall.

Jace let them dangle there as the damage-over-time burns and bleeds afflicted them and ensured their death. Moving up the spine of the ship, he ripped through the sealed doors like tissue paper and reached the cockpit, where one of the Dreamer Demons was seated. They turned and raised a slug thrower pistol, and Jace quickly grabbed the weapon, bending it into a useless bit of scrap before he summoned his sword to his grip and stabbed through them, into the instrument panel, and heard their gasp of pain.

Watch out for the self-destruct button, Ollie said.

Jace just used Void Step to warp down to the lake below and swam down. The huge *crack, bang!* from above caused him to wince a little, but the target list from Yroshnak updated, and the warmth of the Essence flowing down suffused Jace. *I need to get some tech from our Universe that qualifies for Psykinetics.*

I will do some research on the Astral Verge database. See what counts, and what does not. A few grenades imbued with your Psykinetic Talents and

Specializations could be really, really mean. Especially if we can figure out a way to have it function as a bladed weapon for other Skills. Oh, we got another 10,000 Essence. Seems like that is the standard amount for a Potency 8 Dreamer Demon.

Jace got out of the water and looked back at the smoldering wreck of the ship that had crashed into another nearby lake. *And I should probably use my Carbine to pick off the next group. No reason not to.* He activated Holy Hunt on the last group of targets and began running that way. *Let's level up. I have 21,000 Essence. How many levels does that get us?*

Two. 8,000 per level.

Okay. Let's get Indomitable Will some Specializations to ensure that it is really bulking out all of my defenses as best as it can. Hopefully this newest Class Transmutation is perfectly suited to it.

[You have leveled up!]
[You have chosen Specialization of Existing Talent!]
[Talent Name: Indomitable Will.]
[Specialization Name: Galvanizing.]
[Effect: When the user resists or shakes off a mental or emotional effect, all those designated as allies who can see the user become immune to the same effect. This lasts for up to a single cycle.]
[Talent Name: Indomitable Will.]
[Specialization Name: Spiteful.]
[Effect: When the user resists or shakes off a mental or emotional effect, they have a reduced chance of suffering an effect of a similar nature from the individual who afflicted them.]

Name: Jace Seren (Potency 8)
Emotion [Class Level]: Valiant [Guardian 73]
Talent [Specialization]: Astral Adaptation, Astral Translation, Valiant Crusader's Might [Burning] [Vengeful] [Poised] [Unstoppable] [Bracing] [Voidbound] [Lightbound] [Rallying], Crusader's Bastion [Retaliating] [Reinforcing] [Grounding] [Redoubt] [Spiked] [Resonating] [Glorious] [Hallowed], Hero's Arena [Aura] [Inciner-

ating] [Vexing] [Bolstering] [Suppressing] [Wrathbound] [Crusading] [Reckoning], Indomitable Will [Zealous] [Intimidating] [Inviolable] [Enduring] [Ameliorating] [Dark Matter Binding] [Galvanizing] [Spiteful], Templar's Smite [Spear] [Blast] [Lingering] [Challenging] [Inferno] [Cosmic] [Gaze] [Blinding], Holy Hunt [Marked] [Bursting] [Authoritative] [Provoking] [Inciting] [Branding], Purifying Edge [Cleansing] [Searing] [Purging] [Sanctifying] [Terminating] [Judging] [Revealing], Justice's Rebuke [Flaming] [Bashing] [Holy] [Plasmas] [Energizing] [Languishing], Revealing Light [Burdening] [Limning] [Fracturing] [Potent] [Perilous] [Linking], Final Form
Essence: 5,000
Infusions: None
Gear: <TPSB>, (Convergent Edge / Ancient Reckoning) Divine Revenge, (Explorer's Embrace / Beacon) Hero's Plate, (Prosthetic Savant) Astral Appendages, (Draconic Sovereign) Arbiter's Sight, (Anathema) Astral Sleeve, (Reinforced) Psycrystal Lattice, (Pinnacle) NICIF-EP, (Restoring) Flame of Valor, Retribution Carbine (20 shots / battery)

Shhiv paused her workout as Ollie's request came across her vision. *Oooh! Sounds fun!* She wrapped up her workout and headed down to the workshop. Entering it, she saw Ree hard at work on some of the cosmopanel screens, and the Plorp gave her a brief wave before resuming her task.

"No Missy?" Shhiv asked.

"Still hunting with her hubby," Ree replied. "Dee and I will be going down later this week to blast some demons. Want to come? Should be fun!"

"I'm good," Shhiv said as she kept a smile on her face but inside felt tremendous fear. She did not understand Dee and Ree's desire for explosions and mayhem, nor did she understand Greg and Missy's drive to grow stronger. *Just seems foolish*, she thought as she walked over to her work bench, *risking your life like that. I understand Jace having to do it since he's this whole chosen one and all that . . . but still . . . it's not for me. I'm happy being where I'm at. Immortal, and happy.*

She grabbed the housing, then paused. *A knife that explodes into other knives?* Quickly accessing her internal Cosmic System, she scrolled through the database until she found something similar that she could use as a starting point. A needle-grenade. A shell with several embedded needles that had an explosive core. Upon detonation, the needles would be flung in all directions—normally coated with poison or paralytics.

Tinkering with several iterations of the design, she pulled out the plasteel cube that was a very robust test space. Placing each prototype inside, she detonated the charge.

Ree came over. "What you working on?" she said with fascination. "I heard explosions!"

"Blade grenade," Shhiv replied as she grunted with frustration. "I can't get the blades to split apart properly. And their trajectories are wildly varying."

"Hmm . . ." Ree tapped her chitinous shell foot on the ground several times. "How big do the blades have to be?"

Shhiv pointed to her sketch showing a two-inch pattern. "This big at least for Jace's Swordmage stuff to work on it."

"Does . . . does it need to be blades? Or do his Skills work with other projectiles?"

Shhiv frowned. "I don't know, let me check his status screen." She pulled up her comms. "Hey, Quinn, can you pull up Jace's Astral System Status Screen?"

"Sure," Quinn replied as she finished munching down some snack. "What do you need exactly?"

"Jace's Talents—do they work with anything handheld?"

"Yeah. It's the Skills from his Cosmic System stuff that is limited to blades."

Shhiv nodded. "Thanks." She shut off the comms and looked at Ree. "Yup, has to be blades."

Ree's goop inside her chitinous shell shifted, and the expression on the mask-like face altered to one of scrunched-up confusion. "Hmm . . ."

Shhiv looked back at her designs and sketches, racking her brain. *Come on. I know there has to be a design that works.*

Ree walked away and came back with a tablet and stylus. She made some traces and then handed the tablet to Shhiv. The design was far different than Shhiv had thought of. Almost like a bouquet of flowers: a weighted stick that would ensure that the "flowers" of the blades would land on the ground, letting the projectiles explode outward. "Try this?" Ree asked.

Shhiv grabbed her tools and began tinkering as her Cosmic System overlaid the insights and designs her mind envisioned after Ree's idea. "How'd you come up with it?" Shhiv asked.

"Missy told me about a tradition on Earth when someone gets married. They turn around and throw a bunch of bundled-together flowers." Ree shrugged. "Missy was lamenting she didn't get to do it thanks to that bomb."

Shhiv felt a pang of sorrow and sympathy, but nodded. "Well, it is a good idea. Let's see if it works." She placed the jury-rigged, rough-draft version inside the plasteel cube, shut the door, and triggered the explosive manually.

To her delight, the charge went off and sent the blades flying in all directions, clattering against the plasteel confines. "Yes!" she shouted as she reached over and gave Ree a side hug. "Great idea! Now I just have to streamline it and put a bunch into Jace's TPSB."

"Happy to help," Ree said.

Ollie spoke in Jace's mind, _*Looks like Shhiv has cooked up something neat that works with your Psykinetics and Cosmic System Skills. Go ahead and grab one from the TPSB.*_

Jace reached into the TPSB and pulled out a small stick with a circular container on the top, almost like a ball sitting atop a stick. "Okay?"

*It is a blade grenade! Inside the shell are dozens of razor-sharp blades that qualify in length for your various Cosmic System Skills. And it is small enough that it is handheld for Psykinetics!*

Jace eyed up the next and final house full of Dreamer Demons on his target list. They did not have a ship up top, and he crept up to the window. *Let's try it then.* He activated Void Blade [Rending] and saw the green flame flicker along the shaft of the grenade and then almost hide inside the sphere portion. The same went for the crimson nebula of [Rending], though that seemed to drip down the shaft. And then, golden flames surged up as the item qualified as a weapon.

Then, a devious idea crossed his mind. *Ollie. Dark Matter Blade on this also.*

*Oooh. That is dastardly!*

The grenade was covered in a purple sheen, and Jace tossed it casually into the opening. The Dreamer Demons were on alert and began shouting among themselves and moving through the interior space as, to them, something made a loud clang noise.

Jace saw a Cosmic System message.

> [Grenade Detected.]

[Charge Active.]
[Detonate?]

Yes, he thought. A small bang was followed up by a *thwip* as curses and shouts followed. Looking through the drone's camera, Jace saw that the blades had burst out in all directions, and each Dreamer Demon had been impaled by one or more—spreading the golden and green fire, the crimson miasma, and the purple of Dark Matter.

And thanks to Purifying Edge and its various Specializations, those tiny blades shut down Talents temporarily. The damage was done, and even though Jace saw the Dreamer Demons pull the blades out of their bodies—it was too late. The damage-over-time affliction spread, and despite their panic and rush to use medical kits, Jace just had to wait.

A short while, as he watched them all die. Their bodies lingered, but the Souls escaped and surged out the window past Jace, dropping into the lake. Their Essence flowed to him.

Another 10,000, Ollie said.

An idea popped into Jace's head. *We are going to set up a trap... see if Shhiv can make landmine versions.*

Ollie chuckled, *That is a genius idea.*

Chapter Forty-Two

Come and Get Me!

"You're going to do what?" Xero asked.

Jace gripped the voidlight tether and traveled back to the Penrose Sphere, and then immediately entered the airlock and jumped through Oblivion. "I'm going to draw them all to me."

"I mean . . . if you need Essence that badly, I'm sure we can draw it from everyone else. Greg and Missy have been—"

"No," Jace replied as he landed atop the tower constructed of Starheart Steel and covered in Dark Matter and Void. Thanks to his innate Cosmic System, and the fact that he was empowered by those substances, he was able to easily pass through and enter Layer 1 of the Astral Verge. "They are working hard for it. What I need is one of those starfighters."

"I'll task one to you now, slaving it to Ollie's AI."

Yup! Got control of it. A starfighter—a sleek, two-winged craft with thrusters on the back, front, and top and bottom of both wings—surged from one of the hidden hangars as a screen of Void slipped up to allow it passage. The vehicle landed next to Jace before the cockpit opened. He clambered in, and thanks to Edge of Possibility, the moment his hands touched the controls, he was a master of the vehicle.

Jace took off, and the vehicle was easily able to surpass the speed of light as he blitzed across the entirety of Layer 1, arriving at the entrance to Layer 2 within a minute. "This thing is invisible and undetectable, right?"

"Correct," Xero replied. "It is covered in Dark Matter."

"Ollie, have it hover here," Jace ordered.

You got it! the Wayfinder replied in his head.

Jace opened the cockpit and leaped out, using a Dark Energy Mine as he fell and waiting to detonate it right as he got above the film leading down to Layer 2. Using his Soul Tether grapple line, he pulled himself to the small defensive bubble that covered the city of demons he had been unable to enter previously. Going over the top, he got to the outskirts of the city and began planting the mines in the now-rolling grassland.

Shhiv had made him thousands of the landmines—all of them with the same capability as the blade grenades. He spent an hour setting up a whole network of the objects, draining his energy to empty, using the Emergency Battery, and then draining it to half, again as he imbued each with his Skills and Talents.

Finally, he dropped Void Stalker, and Ollie put the announcement out into The Astral System on the public forums.

[This is Wraith.]
[I am outside of the entrance to Layer 2.]
[The same Wraith that Valcrinox has offered instant Potency 10 for the slaughter of.]
[Come and get me!]

Jace watched the city from a distance as hordes of demons began pouring out and met the first row of mines that exploded—shredding them with invisible blades that carried the burning Psykinetic power. *And now, the decoy.* Jace pulled a dummy that was dressed up just like him, put it into the ground, and activated Void Stalker as he used his Soul Tether to ascend. He watched from above as waves upon waves of Astral Demons came out of the city and encountered the minefield.

Eventually, several thousands of demons later, they became cautious in their headlong charge as some of the higher-Potency Astral Demons arrived. Jace could tell just by how monstrous or refined they were, none were above Potency 5. And all threw themselves into the meat grinder. Their desire for Jace's demise, the reward, pushing them onward.

It helped that all of the mines were completely undetectable thanks to Dark Matter, and even when the detonations happened, the blades seemed to appear out of the blue. It was almost sickening, in a way, but Jace knew that all of these demons had a choice. They did not have to go after him and complete some Mission given to them by a Demon Lord. They could have just stayed put or continued their journey down refinement and the Layers.

They choose their deaths, Jace thought as he saw all of the white-grey Essence surging up toward him.

Valcrinox cackled with delight as he saw the Astral System public message broadcast. *Seems like the Bearer of the Mantle finally reveals himself,* he thought with glee. *Come on, kill him! Kill him you stupid bastards! Sheer numbers, endless demons, overrun him!*

One of the demons had elected to not join the assault and instead provided a play-by-play update on the public forum. As Valcrinox continued to see the reports, he realized the gravity of the situation and what Wraith was really up to.

Immediately, he sent out an Astral System message. "Stop going for him, you idiots! He is farming you for your Essence! You are just making him stronger!"

Jace saw the demons back off, and he frowned. "Ollie?"

Valcrinox told them to back off, Ollie replied.

"Well . . . looks like we activate them." Jace activated the "scuttle" protocol—and the mines all grew small crawling appendages and began moving to the Astral Demons. To his satisfaction, the mines scattered themselves silently among the demon forces.

"And . . . detonate."

The entire Astral Demon horde was pierced with countless blades, each burning with gold and green flame, dripping crimson miasma, and coated with the purple of Dark Matter. The Souls escaped from the crumbling corpses as the bodies of the Astral Demons were torn asunder by the sheer number of blades, the Essence flowing up to Jace in an enormous river. Not a ton, because most of the Astral Demons were low Potency, but a good amount.

A grand total of . . . drumroll please!

"Just tell me," Jace said as he recalled the starfighter and clambered into it, zipping back to his Universe's concealed mountain and funnel, piloting the vehicle through the small blip in the Void barrier that allowed vehicles in and out.

70,000 Essence! Enough to hit Potency 9 with 5,000 left over.

Jace nodded as he got out of the starfighter and went to the central pylon at the heart of the structure. Grabbing the voidlight tether, he traveled up and arrived back in the tether chamber of the Penrose Sphere. Xero was standing there and looked enthused. "Well, that was quite a showing."

"Sure," Jace replied. "I suppose so."

"No, really. I'm going to task Shhiv with working on bulking up more of that."

"Why?" Jace asked. "We have Void."

"Right . . . but I'm thinking about what we can do to help other species in their eternal struggle against Astral Demons. We might be safe forever, but we can at least pass the knowledge along. How to empower ordinance with Psykinetics."

Ollie separated from Jace, and he quickly used Dark Matter Mending to fix the piercing headache as Ollie spoke. "Why do you think no other species has tried it?"

"They might have tried it before," Xero replied. "But they were probably much easier to detect. We know that anything handheld can be imbued with Psykinetics. Ship weapons are too big . . . but what's to stop, say, holding a missile? That is technically handheld, and could be thrown by someone strong enough."

Jace rubbed his temples. "I just . . . this whole Astral Verge is weird. I'm surprised we haven't been told off by The Ancients about some bullshit rule that was artificially imposed."

Xero chuckled. "Maybe other people were too afraid of stepping on their toes to really push the limits like we are? Or, maybe other species just are not as smart as we are."

Jace gestured broadly down to the black hole beneath them. "Countless Universes, and we are the first one to think up fucking landmines? I mean, I'm not going to look a gift horse in the mouth, but someone else has to have had the same idea. Psykinetic-empowered grenades, too. I've not seen those."

"To be fair," Ollie said, "you have not been spending a lot of time with Dreamers from other Universes. Just small interactions here and there. For all we know, they are using such technology, and we just have not seen it. Infinity is a big place."

"Not quite infinite," Xero replied. "But damned close to it. A probe finally reached the farthest western edge. Now it can go around the perimeter . . . if there is such a thing." He shrugged, "Regardless, take your last little bit of vacation . . . sounds like once you enter Layer 9, this trial you will have to go through won't let you bail out midway through."

"Thanks," Jace muttered as he warped to his apartment in Khrox.

Ollie popped into place next to him. "You sound aggravated. Why?"

Jace shook his head. "I'm not. Sorry. Did I come off that way to Xero?"

"You did," Ollie stated like a parent admonishing their child.

Jace sighed. "Just irritable. I think things will be a bit better when I get some time with Shhiv." He glanced at Ollie. "Alone time, if you don't mind."

"Way ahead of you!" Ollie popped out of existence again, and Jace headed downstairs.

Shhiv was sitting at her work bench, working at a speed that Jace couldn't even comprehend. On one side, piles of Stardust that she would grab, turn into raw materials in her grip, and then tinker with. A split-second later, a finished landmine slid across the table and into a small funnel that sucked it up, compressing it down in size—Jace instinctively knew it fed to the TPS.

He walked up behind her and gently wrapped his arms around her neck, giving her a light kiss on the cheek. "Hey, gorgeous."

She barely flinched or acknowledged his presence, and he just stood there, watching as her hands moved at speeds he was barely able to keep up with. A one-woman assembly line thanks to her Cosmic System Skills and selected build with Class and Advanced Class. It was a full five minutes before she came out of the trancelike state and sighed, leaning back into him. "Hey honey," she whispered as she gave his wrist a little nibble.

"I have a bit of leave time . . . what do we want to do?" he asked.

Shhiv stood up, stretched, and then pointed upstairs. "I need a good workout."

"The gym is downstairs, though," Jace said.

Shhiv's eyes glinted, and her face slipped into that sensual smile he loved so much. "Not the type of workout I was envisioning."

Valcrinox stewed on his throne. Hundreds of thousands of low-Potency Astral Demons—annihilated almost instantly. *They are using technology*, he thought. And once more, he cursed The Ancient's rules of the Layers that prevented Astral Demons from using technology.

One of his servants came running in. "Lord Valcrinox."

"Hmm?"

"The defenses are ready."

Valcrinox tapped his fingers along the arm rest of his Relic throne. "Well . . . we also need countermeasures for technological machinations that would amplify our foe's capabilities." He leaned forward. "I need one of you to defeat the Vault here on this Layer and acquire a Relic that deactivates all technology on this Layer."

"I . . . your will be done," the Astral Demon replied as they bowed and left.

Valcrinox leaned back in the throne and looked up at the still-empty hooks, craving the sound of screams and lamenting his lack of Universal Matter. *We are close*, he thought. *So close. Soon enough, I will have enough to attempt to create my own Universe.* He slammed his fist on the throne and let out a shout of hatred. *Curse you, Wraith. And curse these damned Ancients!*

Tibalt fell through the film and landed in a large square chamber. Souls were nowhere to be seen, but before him, he saw three tunnels with films over the top. His Astral Translation deciphered the different options. Dreamer, Dreamer Demon, Astral Demon. He made for the Dreamer film but, pressing his hand against it, found that it would not allow him entry. *I figured as much. Still, worth a try.*

He moved through the film that said Astral Demon and found himself in yet another chamber. Three more films, three more messages. Refinement, Mixed, Monstrous. Knowing he was mixed, he entered the center film.

And stepped out into a large circular chamber. A tube with a single floating white orb for light up above him, smooth polished stone all around, and a pedestal with a circle embedded that could accommodate a hand, claw, or other appendage. Glancing back, he saw the entrance was gone. *Point of no return*, he thought.

Facing the pedestal, Tibalt placed his hand on it.

[Monstrous 3, Refined 6.]
[Altering Trial . . .]

Tibalt watched as the walls shifted colors, and then the pedestal sank as a hallway beckoned him forward. Quite literally beckoning him, as a white glowing line the same color as the light source floating above surged in a continual pattern down the hall.

It is time to pass these trials and enter Layer 10. Tibalt strode forward with confidence as he activated his suite of Psykinetic Talents.

Chapter Forty-Three

The Layer 9 Trials

Jace laughed an exhausted laugh. He and Shhiv had not left the apartment in days—just indulging in each other's company. Going between romantic and sensual interludes to them watching movies from all across the Universe.

It was peaceful, quite enjoyable, and Jace was happy. Really, truly happy, and he did not want to leave.

But Ollie popped into existence just after Jace had exited the hygiene station and had his hair cut a bit shorter. "Hey. Yroshnak has his forces ready to descend. They are waiting on us."

Jace sighed and closed the door to the restroom as Ollie followed him. Jace plopped himself on the couch next to Shhiv and gave her a kiss on the cheek as she giggled at the attention. "Hey . . . I've gotta go and finish it," Jace whispered as he gently ran his hand through her hair and along the fin running atop her skull.

She sighed and hugged his arm. "I hate having you leave."

"The last time," Jace said. "I go down, beat Layer 9, beat Valcrinox, come back for the starfighter and the Soul container . . . we're almost done."

"For now," Shhiv muttered. "But The Ancients already said they'd call on you again."

Jace chuckled. "I'm so strong now, hon. And do you really think Greg is going to let me be the only Potency 10 Dreamer for our Universe? Him,

Missy, heck I even imagine Dee and Ree, maybe Priam—I would bet they will dip into the Astral Verge now and again to keep progressing." He stood up. "Plus, it sounds like it takes a long time for a Demon Lord to go corrupt and start eating unjudged Souls. I'm sure I won't be the only one who can do The Ancient's dirty work for them."

Shhiv sighed and sat up, hugging Jace's waist and burying her face in his chest. "Fine," she mumbled, muffled by his sculpted muscles. She looked up at him, and those deep, black eyes with the shimmer of cerulean sparkles inside transfixed Jace as she whispered, "Just come back safe."

"I will." Jace looked to Ollie. "Let's do the level up in the Penrose Sphere." He gently extricated himself from Shhiv's grip, gave her a delicate kiss on the forehead, and then warped through their Universe. Once he arrived in the voidlight tether room, he equipped all of his Gear from the TPSB storage. "Okay, Ollie, let's do it."

"Here we go! Get ready for some pain."

[You have leveled up!]
[You have chosen Specialization of Existing Talent!]
[Talent Name: Holy Hunt.]
[Specialization Name: Invigorating.]
[Effect: When the user strikes a marked target with the linked Talent, they restore a small amount of their health and mend injuries.]
[Talent Name: Holy Hunt.]
[Specialization Name: Bolstering.]
[Effect: The user gains an increased defensive boost against the designated target of the linked Talent.]
[Talent Name: Justice's Rebuke.]
[Specialization Name: Deflecting.]
[Effect: The linked Talent may now be activated in response to being attacked, instead of when they are harmed, at a lower efficacy.]
[Talent Name: Justice's Rebuke.]
[Specialization Name: Guarding.]
[Effect: When an ally within line of sight is injured, the user may activate the linked Talent at lowered efficacy.]

[Talent Name: Purifying Edge.]
[Specialization Name: Condensing.]
[Effect: When the linked Talent is used on a target, the user may take on afflictions and harm suffered by allies within line of sight.]
[Talent Name: Revealing Light.]
[Specialization Name: Redirecting.]
[Effect: Those affected by the linked Talent are drawn to the user.]
[Talent Name: Revealing Light.]
[Specialization Name: Identifying.]
[Effect: The linked Talent reveals weaknesses of those affected.]
[Talent Name: Crusader's Bastion.]
[Specialization Name: Aegis.]
[Effect: The user's linked Talent can become a shield that completely covers a full one-hundred-eighty-degree angle in a chosen direction.]

Name: Jace Seren (Potency 9)
Emotion [Class Level]: Valiant [Guardian 81]
Talent [Specialization]: Astral Adaptation, Astral Translation, Valiant Crusader's Might [Burning] [Vengeful] [Poised] [Unstoppable] [Bracing] [Voidbound] [Lightbound] [Rallying], Crusader's Bastion [Retaliating] [Reinforcing] [Grounding] [Redoubt] [Spiked] [Resonating] [Glorious] [Hallowed] [Aegis], Hero's Arena [Aura] [Incinerating] [Vexing] [Bolstering] [Suppressing] [Wrathbound] [Crusading] [Reckoning], Indomitable Will [Zealous] [Intimidating] [Inviolable] [Enduring] [Ameliorating] [Dark Matter Binding] [Galvanizing] [Spiteful], Templar's Smite [Spear] [Blast] [Lingering] [Challenging] [Inferno] [Cosmic] [Gaze] [Blinding], Holy Hunt [Marked] [Bursting] [Authoritative] [Provoking] [Inciting] [Branding] [Invigorating] [Bolstering], Purifying Edge [Cleansing] [Searing] [Purging] [Sanctifying] [Terminating] [Judging] [Revealing] [Condensing], Justice's Rebuke [Flaming] [Bashing] [Holy] [Plasmas] [Energizing] [Languishing] [Deflecting] [Guarding], Revealing Light [Burdening] [Limning] [Fracturing] [Potent] [Perilous] [Linking] [Redirecting] [Identifying], Final Form
Essence: 5,000
Infusions: None

Gear: <TPSB>, (Convergent Edge / Ancient Reckoning) Divine Revenge, (Explorer's Embrace / Beacon) Hero's Plate, (Prosthetic Savant) Astral Appendages, (Draconic Sovereign) Arbiter's Sight, (Anathema) Astral Sleeve, (Reinforced) Psycrystal Lattice, (Pinnacle) NICIF-EP, (Restoring) Flame of Valor, Retribution Carbine (20 shots / battery)

Jace gasped as he fell to the ground. His insides roiled and turned into knots, and it felt like he was being eaten alive as thousands of insects burrowed around under his skin. Instinctively, he tried scratching to get them out—but the armor prevented him from doing that, and he had to bear with the horrid pain and writhing under the surface.

But it faded, and he breathed in a deep gasp as he got up. "Always . . . sucks."

Ollie flew into his head. *Yup. But hey, it is done. And now we are on to the second-to-last stage!*

Jace nodded and grabbed his initial voidlight tether, traveling back to Layer 8 in a flash. "Ollie, tell Yroshnak we are on our way."

Jace sped across the breadth of Layer 8, and the landscape began to blur as he traveled faster than he ever had before. The miles practically zipped by, and he reached the large square lake that was dominated in the center by a circle, covered in a film. Yroshnak was standing in the water next to the film and looked over at Jace as he approached.

"Ah. Good. We have held off on leveling up, as we needed to keep the call of the depths farther away." Yroshnak looked to the fifty Astral Demons he had with him. "Do it."

All of them began to shift, and their forms writhed. Jace watched with morbid fascination as he saw the process of becoming a higher Potency for a demon in person for the first time. Bodies warped, distorted, and either shrank or grew in their monstrous or human appearance depending on their chosen path. Within a few seconds, all were huffing deep breaths and looked hale and hardy.

"Okay," Yroshnak said as he walked to the film. "Let's go." He hopped in, and the Astral Demons quickly followed.

Jace jumped in after them and felt the film cling to him for a few moments before he fell into a large circular chamber with three tunnels. One labeled for Dreamer, one for Astral Demons, and one for Dreamer Demons.

Yroshnak clapped him on the shoulder. "Good luck in your trials, Wraith." He cracked a smile. "Making history, being the first Dreamer to do this." Yroshnak headed into the Astral Demon door, and his forces were split between the Dreamer Demon and full demon doors.

Jace faced the door film that had the Dreamer name across the top, and drawing his sword, he walked forward, ready for the challenges he would face. Before he could go inside, an Astral System message appeared before him.

[Congratulations on entering a new Layer!]
[You may choose to specialize your Class by performing a Class Transmutation!]
[Base Class = Archangel.]
[Options available:]
[Zealot—expand upon your offensive capabilities. Leads to further offensive Transmutations.]
[Warder—expand upon your defensive capabilities. Leads to further defensive Transmutations.]
[Herald—expand upon your support capabilities. Leads to further support Transmutations.]

"Okay, let's go into Herald since we can use the level-ups to change the functionality of a Talent with Specializations."

[Class Transmutation Confirmed.]

He entered a smooth stone room that seemed to be carved from a singular piece of dredged-up rock. He could see his reflection faintly in the polished surface. Above him, a white light hovered—an orb that illuminated the space.

The door and film behind him had vanished, leaving Jace, the light, and the pedestal with a circular indentation in the center. *I would bet you put your hand in there*, Ollie said.

Jace put his hand down and felt an odd vibration in his palm. An Astral System message appeared in the air before him, the pink text on black background almost piercing him with how bright and offset it was.

[Welcome, Dreamer, to Layer 9.]
[Here, you will face a series of challenges.]
[They can range across a multitude of trials.]
[Each one defeated awards enough Essence to allow you to level up a single time.]
[Time moves slowly in the trials, and what may seem like decades is seconds in reality.]
[Warning: this is your last chance to turn back.]
[Once you start the trial, it cannot be canceled.]
[Remove your hand if you choose to retreat, and press down if you wish to proceed.]

Jace pushed his palm into the depression, and a white line thrummed to life above him in the ceiling, running from the floating white orb and down a hallway that appeared in the stone structure. The pedestal sank into the floor. "We're ready," Jace muttered as he walked down the path.

Tibalt gasped for air as he broke the surface. *Really? A vertical swim? What kind of challenge was that?* he thought as he clambered onto the small rocky outcropping. He shivered and wrapped his arms around his body as he curled up into a ball. *So cold.*

Then it hit him. It was getting colder. *Did I miss something? Some type of warming element in the depths?* He inhaled deeply and dove back into the waters, looking around in all directions. The chill from above grew stronger, and with growing horror, he saw a thin layer of ice begin to build.

I need to find an underwater source of air and heat, he thought as he swam for the bottom of the artificially manifested ocean. Down, down he went—his breath slowly being let out in brief little bursts to ensure he could keep descending.

And then, he found it. A ledge. Checking underneath, he saw a small pool, and poking his head up, he found an air pocket that he could suck breath within. The space was big enough for him to crawl into, and there was a small vent to some underground heat source that made the small enclosure comfortable.

He wanted to laugh at his triumph but did not know how long he would need to be in there—nor how long the air pocket would last him. And so he forced himself to breathe in a meditative fashion, just how he used to when worshipping at the temple. He could hear the Souls screaming inside of him, and that was enough of a distraction to prevent him from fully concentrating on his breathing.

Thankfully, the room reappeared around him as he fell a few inches onto the smooth, stone floor. *Another challenge defeated!* he thought with pride as Essence flowed into him from a hidden mechanism in the ceiling. He immediately spent it to level up, choosing a Talent that allowed him to survive without breath.

Moving forward, he found another pillar and pressed down in the recess.

Jace reached a chamber that was identical to the last one. Raising his left hand, he pushed down, and the pedestal vanished into the ground. The entire room shook around him, and he readied himself for whatever might come—firing off all of his Talents and Skills.

The new Crusader's Bastion was far larger and could easily cover his entire front half. All assault from that whole frontal arc could be blocked. The downside was that it seriously limited his offensive capabilities, as he could not shoot through the shield. And so, he willed it down to its usual tower shield size.

The walls of the room vanished, and Jace was standing in an infinite black space. An Astral System message appeared in his vision.

[Trial 1.]
[Defeat a god.]

Jumping into the deep end there, Ollie commented wryly.

The blackness fell away, and Jace found himself standing on a vast, icy tundra. Ancient Colosseum walls rose up around him but were shattered in several places and completely obliterated. Remnants of skeletons were strewn about of all different species. The skies above were a deep black streaked with crackling white lightning.

The wind howled around Jace, and his feet crunched on the ice as he walked toward the center of the arena, looking around for whatever foe he would be fighting. *Holy Hunt*, he thought as he focused on this god he had to fight. The golden path shot straight up into the sky, and Jace looked up as the glow outlined a massive flying bird-shaped creature.

A lightning bolt shot down, and thanks to Jace's reflexes, he was able to dodge it. The crack of it slamming into the ice followed up by a crackling as the sparks discharged into the now-shattered ground sent a slight chill down Jace's spine. *I have to go up there to fight it?* He eyed the storm clouds carefully. *If it's a god, it probably controls all of that.*

Another lightning bolt streaked down, and Jace deftly dodged. Switching his Crusader's Bastion to its Aegis configuration, he sheathed his sword and used his Soul Tether to ascend into the skies while keeping his shield held above his head. Bolts of lightning slammed into the protective barricade.

Do not fear electricity, Ollie commented. *Remember, your body is literally reinforced with Dark Matter. It is bound to you, as is your inherent resistance to electricity.*

Jace smiled. *I had forgotten.* He continued to ascend into the dark storm clouds. He could feel the crackling around him as the air vibrated with energy. A bolt of lightning struck him from the right—and while he felt the impact, there was very little pain, just a slight tensioning in his arm as his body was jolted.

He made a beeline for the entity outlined by his Holy Hunt—and the thing turned to fly at him. Jace readied himself, using (Vengeful) from his Valiant Crusader's Might; he felt the pang of pain in his guts but shrugged it off. The marked foe appeared: a huge wolf, its body covered in crackling lines of yellow, white, and blue. Two wings like an eagle jutted out to either side of the creature from the shoulders, and it let out a howl that mixed with the peal of thunder that echoed all around them.

Jace used Void Step and got right up in its face, unleashing a massive swing as he slashed down through the snout and cut it cleanly off. The creature yowled in pain and lashed out with thousands of bolts of lightning.

Dark Matter Shield (Rank 3), Ollie stated, and Jace saw the film of deep purple pop up around him, the intrinsic nature of Dark Matter negating the electricity wholly—and not costing Jace any energy. *Haha! Take that, you weird eagle-dog hybrid!*

Jace shoved his arm into the opening that the cut-off snout left behind and used a Templar's Smite (Blast), unleashing riotous golden flames that flickered with green and crimson. The blast exploded down the thing's body, and the backblast sent Jace tumbling backward. He had to use a Void Step to reorient himself and keep from falling too far as he shot out the Soul Tether to keep himself upright in the air.

The god survived, and its snout regrew. The thing opened its jaws, and a massive beam of crackling lightning shot out—impacting Jace's Dark Matter Shield with no effect. Jace just swung himself forward and slashed again—cutting into the thing's snout once more. It recoiled and swiped at him with a claw ablaze with light blue lightning—but Jace simply used Void Step, dodging and getting onto its spine, right next to the wings. Slashing at first one then the other, he cut clean through the joints where the wings met up with the shoulders, and the deity plummeted.

It let out a snarl as it turned around in midair, the wings regenerating as it tried to spin Jace off. But he knelt, grabbing on with a hand as the deity eventually stabilized and leveled out in its flight. Arcing beams of lightning continued to rain down on Jace to no effect, and he used the (Vengeful) Infusion once more before slamming his weapon tip-first into the body and using the (Fulminating) Augmentation. The weapon exploded with gold, crimson, and green as all of the force went directly down and into the wolf lightning deity.

It let out a gurgle and then fell limp, and Jace saw it vanish; the world went black, and he was standing in the stone chamber he had left from. Essence flowed up from the ground where the pedestal once stood, and it pooled at his feet before absorbing up into him. "How much was that?" he asked.

9,000 Essence, Ollie replied. *Puts us at 14,000. But, as the start screens said, we should be able to level up with every single trial completed.*

Then level up, but hold the status screen. No need to constantly have that flash up when I'm just adding a single new feature.

Fair enough!

[You have leveled up!]
[You have chosen Specialization of Existing Talent!]

[Talent Name: Valiant Crusader's Might.]
[Specialization Name: Inspiriting.]
[Effect: The linked Talent also empowers all those labeled as allies within line of sight.]

Jace followed the glowing white line as he walked into the next chamber.

Chapter Forty-Four

The Trials Continue

Tibalt finished cleaving the last of his foes in two, the blood and viscera spilling out over him as he was infused with Essence from the now-returning room around him. In front of him, the final doorway revealed itself, and he went through to find a massive circular chamber. Glancing to either side, he saw other tunnels—presumably for those who cleared Trials from the other two paths.

Additionally, to the right, there was another hallway that read above the door "Upper Layers." *Must be for those who pass the trial*, he thought, *and want to get back up.*

And before him, in the ground, was a massive circular pool covered with a pink film like every other Layer. He sat down, needing to rest and recover his energy before going deeper and meeting Valcrinox's forces. And as he sat there, he could see Souls dripping down from above in a constant, steady stream. Right into the center of the film.

Standing up, he moved around the film, trying to find a good angle to get at those delicious Souls. But they were out of reach, and despite trying to activate Demon Flight, the Talent would not function. Tibalt let out a growl of frustration and shuffled forward—not wanting to go into the film, but trying to eke out that last little bit of reach.

He felt an odd tingling sensation along his toes and, glancing down, recoiled in horror and backed away from the film. The front toes of his right foot had slid toward the film, and as he pulled back to the walls of the chamber, he saw that they had been completely removed. As if they were erased from existence.

What is this? he thought as he tried to activate his regeneration and saw, to his relief, the toes slowly grow back. Creeping forward to the film, he held a single, clawed finger out and dipped the nail into the film, watching it vanish. Pulling back, the nail spike was gone—as if it had never existed. Just erased from reality from midway down. *Why can't I go through?*

Then, he heard loud, thundering footsteps. Spinning to face the source of the noise, he saw a massive Astral Demon walk through the demon-only hall. "Hmph," the figure glanced at Tibalt and then walked to the wall, leaning against it as more demons followed after him. None made a move against Tibalt, and the imposing figure just stood there.

"Who are you?" Tibalt asked.

"Yroshnak, former Demon Lord of Layer 8." The figure looked to another hallway, then to the film, then across to Tibalt. "See anyone come out?"

"No," Tibalt said, knowing that this demon and his lackeys could defeat him by ganging up on him. He gestured to the film. "Something prevents my descent."

"Hmph." Yroshnak said nothing, but just stared at Tibalt.

"What do you know?" Tibalt growled as he stood up, reflexively brandishing his claws.

"The way is shut. You cannot proceed until the way is open, or you will perish."

Tibalt scowled and turned on his Astral System, sending a message to The Ancients. "This is not fair. Some external force prevents me from descending. I worked my way here. I demand to be let through! Send."

No response came to him, and he waited, impatiently, for any sign of his message being received. But nothing came.

Yroshnak shook his head. "Just wait until the Bearer of the Mantle arrives. They will deactivate the barrier."

Tibalt felt a twinge of fear trace through him. *That Wraith? He's taking the Trials?* Tibalt had to leave, to get to Valcrinox, to ally himself with someone powerful.

Thankfully, the Astral System message came through.

[We will disable the film.]

He did not know which Ancient sent the message, nor did he care. He dove into the film and passed through, falling into an endless field.

"Why'd you do that?!" the Loud Ancient said as he pushed his peer's door open.

"Hmm?"

"Letting the Dreamer Demon through the Void film!"

"Ah," the Quiet Ancient turned in his chair to face his companion. "The purpose of the Void and Dark Matter barrier that was temporarily placed was to stop Valcrinox's forces from rising up. Nothing about others descending."

"You're effectively sabotaging Wraith!"

"Am I?" the Quiet One turned to pull up an Astral System visual feed of Valcrinox on his throne. "You have seen the internal dialogue logs just as I have. Tibalt will backstab Valcrinox, thus making Wraith's task all the easier."

The Loud Ancient let out a sigh of frustration, "You really think giving Valcrinox another piece to add to his arsenal is helping Wraith out in the long run?"

"This Tibalt will betray Valcrinox for his own selfish desires. Such is the nature of all Dreamer Demons—power at any cost. Trust me."

"I . . . Fine."

Jace's booted, armored feet clacked on the floor, and he placed his hand into the depression on the pillar, shoving it down. As it descended, the Astral System message appeared in the air above him.

> [Trial 2.]
> [Rely on yourself.]

The room vanished around Jace, and he found himself standing in a small square arena. He recognized it immediately from a movie he had watched with Shhiv; ropes along the sides, a slightly padded floor, a crowd of faceless fans cheering on the sidelines—he was in a boxing ring.

His Gear vanished, leaving him standing there in just a basic set of workout clothes. "Ollie? You here?"

Yup. Just in your head. Seems like you will not be able to use any Skills or Talents while in here.

In front of Jace, a shadowy figure appeared before becoming solid darkness. A facsimile of Greg: the wide build, broad shoulders, sturdy legs, and a bearded face pulled back into a joyous grin. The shadow-Greg took up a boxer's stance, wordlessly, and began lightly hopping from foot to foot with a speed that belied his mass.

No Edge of Possibility to make me a pro boxer, Jace thought. He raised his fists in front of him, slightly angling his body and taking up a partial bladed stance. *But I'm not wholly unskilled at fighting unarmed.*

As part of his honeymoon with Shhiv, they had not just visited hundreds of worlds, but also engaged with the various unique cultures. And, with Shhiv being very into physical activities, they had their fair share of watching and even sparring with natives of varying locales. And all that information, all of those observations, were technically a part of Jace thanks to his innate Cosmic System, through his Edge of Possibility Skill, memorizing and committing those moves to muscle memory.

I may not have pro boxing abilities, Jace thought, *but I am ready for this.* He moved forward and released a vicious snap-kick with his leading left leg, striking shadow-Greg on the right. Shadow-Greg raised a knee, blocking the strike, then planted that foot down and unleashed a vicious combination of punches and elbows.

First came a right jab, which Jace moved back and away from. Greg then followed up with a left jab toward Jace's chest, which the latter deftly deflected with his forearm. Next came a kick at Jace's shin, and he quickly lifted that foot to avoid the strike. Dropping back down, Jace counterattacked with a right jab that shadow-Greg took in the chest, staggering back very minutely.

Jace recovered his posture and dodged to his right as shadow-Greg came in with another left jab. With Jace on the outside of shadow-Greg's body, he was able to unleash a vicious elbow right into the ribs—feeling the cracking underneath the impact as the force of his prosthetic-empowered body sent shadow-Greg staggering toward the ropes.

But the shadowy opponent recovered and used part of the momentum to kick out, and the blow caught Jace on the outer thigh, right above his left knee. He hissed in pain and backed off, circling to shadow-Greg's injured right side. His opponent was slightly bent over to the left, so Jace knew that he had inflicted a lasting injury on his opponent. *This really isn't fair,* Jace thought, *I have the NICIF to heal me up, bones that can't be broken, and prosthetic musculature.*

Yup. But do not get cocky.

Jace moved to shadow-Greg, throwing a left hook as a feint before following up with a vicious right knee. Shadow-Greg blocked the knee, ignoring the feint, and stepped into Jace's center as he unleashed a wicked headbutt. Jace felt his nose squish, and pain bloomed across his whole face.

But that brought shadow-Greg close, and Jace capitalized on that to wrap the leg he had kicked with around the back of the shadow's leg and push his weight forward with his other foot—taking them both to the ground. Jace squirmed around shadow-Greg's back as he fell, getting a lock in place with his arms and legs that began choking the man out.

Shadow-Greg punched at him, elbowed him, but Jace held firm and kept pulling until he heard a loud snap and the shadow-Greg went limp.

Jace's Gear reappeared on him, and the stone chamber returned. Essence flowed out of the depression that the pylon had sunk into, and he felt the warmth suffuse him. "Another nine thousand?" he asked as he used Dark Matter Mending to quickly fix his few aches and mend the pain in his face.

Yup! Ollie said. *Another level's worth.*

> [You have leveled up!]
> [You have chosen Specialization of Existing Talent!]
> [Talent Name: Hero's Arena.]
> [Specialization Name: Encouraging.]
> [Effect: The linked Talent also encourages allies in the Hero's Arena, granting their weapons and Talents a burning damage-over-time effect based upon the user's Emotion Source.]

"Good thing we're getting all of these upgrades that are focused on group combat," Jace commented as he moved down the hallway to the next chamber. "Especially since we will be working with Yroshnak and his demons on the next Layer."

Agreed, Ollie said. *A balanced build, which I think is the best route we could have taken. If we had others traveling with us, then perhaps going more specialized would have worked—similar to what Priam, Greg, and Dee did with their journeys back in The Cosmic System pre-Troxanir demise.*

Jace entered the next chamber and pushed his hand onto the pylon. It sank into the ground, and another Astral System message appeared.

> [Trial 3.]
> [Demonstrate your intelligence.]

As the room shifted and warped, Ollie chuckled in Jace's mind. *Seriously? I am an Artificial Intelligence! This is going to be easy!*

Jace was sitting in front of a board filled with pieces. He recognized the game, as post–corpo war, a bunch of people from all over the world were displaced and intermixed. A complex strategy game that he was always utterly destroyed at when played. *Shit*, he thought. *It's Go.*

Hey, you got me. And this game is easy!

Opposite Jace, a shadowy version of Quinn appeared. Her piercing, telescoping eyes narrowed in on the board, and she made the first move.

Somehow, Ollie made the sound of knuckles cracking in Jace's mind. *Let me have control over your body. This is going to be fun!*

Jace allowed Ollie to take over, becoming a passenger in his body just like when he had ceded temporary control over to the NICIF so he could be in his internal virtual reality while traveling. But this time, he watched as his Wayfinder faced off against one of the smartest people Jace knew. Someone who even Xera seemed to respect, given the lengths to which she went to acquire her for the Dark Between Stars.

He tried to soak in all of the moves that Ollie was making, watching as the white pieces were moved around the board and he captured several of shadow-Quinn's stones. The shadow-Quinn showed no emotion save for pure concentration, and despite her vast intelligence and what must have been an integral understanding of the game and all of its elements, she was up against a thousand year old Artificial Intelligence.

Jace was sure he would have lost already, but shadow-Quinn was able to stave off the end for quite a while. But, finally, Ollie made his last move, and the shadow-Quinn vanished as a point tally appeared next to them. *Not my best score*, Ollie commented.

The room returned around them, and Essence flooded into Jace as he regained control of his body and stood up. "Do you just play games while you're hanging out in me?"

I have a part of my processing dedicated to games, yes. Not just strategy—all types from all different cultures!

"Huh. Okay, well, good to know." Jace looked to the next hall that opened up in front of them. "Okay then. Another level up. Let's keep specializing."

> [You have leveled up!]
> [You have chosen Specialization of Existing Talent!]
> [Talent Name: Indomitable Will.]
> [Specialization Name: Ensnaring.]
> [Effect: When the user resists a mental or emotional effect of Psykinetics, the creature who attempted the affliction is temporarily stunned.]

Jace walked down the corridor and into the next chamber. "How many more do you think?" he asked.

I would imagine one per level we could obtain before going to Layer 10.

Jace put his hand on the pedestal and pressed the indentation.

Chapter Forty-Five

Ghost Ship

Tibalt landed in the stone depression that collected Souls before they flowed down a stone channel that led into the distance. He immediately scooped up a handful and began gobbling them down.

"Hey, you!" He turned to the source of the noise and saw an Astral Demon dressed in full plate armor and holding a halberd that crackled with green lightning.

"I have information! On Wraith! Take me to Valcrinox, and I'll tell him what I know."

The Astral Demon seemed to access a System screen as he glanced to his side and his eyes tracked something. Then, he nodded. "Very well. I'll send you with an escort."

With nothing to immediately threaten him, Tibalt took in the environment. He could see the walls of the Layer: a subtle yellow hue that slowly turned into a calming green as the walls of the Layer extended up to a bright blue ceiling that was the closest comparison he had seen to an actual sky on an agri-world back in his Universe. It was calming, and serene.

He had landed in a stone depression, but it was only thirty-feet wide before giving way to shin-high grass. He now knew why the place was named how it was—he heard the very grass itself screaming out in pain, as if the entire Layer was driven to insanity and couldn't help but cry out in agony. The screams were soothing to him and paralleled the screams and whimpers of Souls in his torso.

Fortifications had been erected—four towers raised up around the depression he fell into, with enormous cauldrons ready to be poured out—steam rising up from whatever superheated liquid was within. The small channel that ran out to the east in a straight line was paralleled on either side by a stone-lined path. A path that looked like it had also been fortified on either side.

The more he examined the environment, he realized that the entire distance from north to south that comprised this giant rectangle of a floor was only a few miles across. If they fortified the entire distance, then they could just attack from a range and on high and then fall back to the next fortification line. This was designed to bleed a larger opposing force. *Makes sense, considering how strong Wraith is.*

He was escorted by two Astral Demons and flew across the distance from the entry point into the Layer, following the channel of Souls. He looked to his escorts. "I need more Souls to grow in power enough to serve Valcrinox."

The one on his left grabbed his arm with a grip like an iron vice and yanked him down to the stone pathway along the channel of Souls. "Drink up."

Tibalt began gobbling them down, plunging his head into the river of condensed Souls and immediately leveling up. He would have laughed in joy if he did not want to waste a second slurping down the delicious morsels, and he saw an Astral System message as he selected yet another Talent.

[Maximum level in the Astral System achieved.]

Pulling his head up, he let out a cackling laugh that perhaps bordered on madness. But to him, it was a laugh of triumph. *I've done it!* he thought. *Potency 10, and the highest possible level I could obtain!*

Standing up, he wiped the slobber off of his mouth and took flight with his escort, heading to Valcrinox. His new "master" he would serve until the opportune moment to strike him down and take over. *Tibalt, Demon*

Emperor of the Astral Verge, he thought as a smile plastered itself across his ghoulish visage.

The pylon dropped down, and Jace saw the Astral System message appear in the air above him.

[Trial 4.]
[Protect the citadel.]

The world vanished around Jace, and he appeared atop the walls of a massive fortification. A vast alien world extended before him—lush with vegetation that had been clear-cut a half mile in the lead-up to the walled fortification. To either side, he heard the sound of people preparing for battle, and glancing sideways, he saw several people in bulky, futuristic armor preparing huge siege weapons and other defenses; turrets swiveling into place, small drones rolling along the top of the wall with what must have been barrels and belts of ammunition, and the shouts of encouragement to stand against the tide all intermingling into a chorus of preparation before a chaotic assault.

The fortification under Jace's feet was some type of roughed-up metal. He wouldn't slip around at all, and it provided good grip. Glancing over the edge of the raised lip of the wall that allowed for three-quarters cover, so a person could fire a weapon over without too much exposure, he saw that the wall had been covered with spikes that angled slightly down.

Behind him, he saw a sizable military complex of square buildings set against a substantial cliff wall. Atop the cliff was a large star ship that had a lift system that was lowering men and equipment down.

Then, he heard the roaring and skittering. Looking out to the line of the vegetation, he watched as a swarm of monstrous insects surged out from the foliage. They screeched, roared, and some even took flight.

Jace quickly grabbed his Retribution Carbine from his TPSB and began picking off the fliers with precise shots that each found their marks, the superheated beam of energy slicing through the joints where the wings connected to the bodies and sending the hostiles crashing into the earth. The loud bangs and booms of weapons going off around him were indicative of the troops on the wall firing on this horde of creatures, and the explosions in the mass of creatures ripped through the ranks as chunks of goopy bits and pieces scattered about.

Jace went through all twenty shots taking out each flier, then swapped batteries and continued to gun them down. A third swap to his final battery and he had eliminated sixty of the creatures. Putting the Carbine back into his TPSB, he moved over to one of the small carrying drones, grabbing a large machine gun that would need to be mounted—but he was able to lift it with ease. "Ammunition," Jace said to the small drone.

It seemed to understand the order as it moved behind Jace and fed a belt of ammunition into a slot on the side of the weapon. Jace instinctively knew how to use the heavy slug-throwing machine gun thanks to his Edge of Possibility, and he began firing down upon the advancing horde. Each bullet, thanks to the weapon being handheld, resulted in a burst of golden flames that scorched and scattered clusters of the insectoids. He swept the weapon back and forth along the front of the line, focusing fire on where the line of the charge bulged outward, showing the insects gaining some ground.

And the little droid seemed to follow his orders; as Jace reached the end of the ammunition feed and he turned to bark for more ammunition, the little droid was there and fed the next belt in. Jace re-racked the slide to feed in the next belt and continued to rain down death on the insectoid swarm.

"Breach!" someone shouted inside the walls behind him. Glancing back, he saw the ground crack open, and the insectoid creatures began surging up.

Shit, Jace thought. *Should I go down there and help out, or keep the main force held back?* He watched as armored men on the walls turned around and began firing on the bugs that emerged from the hole and saw they were losing ground as the insectoids broke into the encampment and started killing the support personnel. *Damnit.* Jace turned around and unleashed his weapon on the inside of the fort.

Every bullet found its mark, exploding one of the insects. The little drone slammed in another belt, and Jace shouted at it, "Wrap them around me!" The drone complied, and Jace felt the ammo belts looped over his shoulder in such a way that they would feed into the machine gun while he moved. Jumping down the thirty-foot distance, he landed inside the fort and shot the last few insects before he moved to the tunnel.

It was a smooth, bored-out entrance that insects poured out from, and Jace unloaded, emptying the entire belt of ammunition as the swarm surged toward him. Up close, they were even more disturbing—some type of blend between a spider and a cockroach, with huge pincers that clicked and looked like the primary offensive tool.

Jace ran out of ammunition and tossed the weapon aside, pulling his sword out and descending into the tunnel and carving a path of bloody retribution through the insects. They stood no chance against his Talents, and even entering the radius of his Hero's Arena killed the small skittering ones that looked like some type of scorpion mixed with an ant. He only had to bring his sword to bear against the larger spiderlike ones, and they were easily dispatched with a single swing.

He emerged from the tunnel less than a minute later in the middle of the assaulting force, and his [Danger-Sense] alerted him to every single incoming attacker. Like a mindless horde driven by some basic instinct, they threw themselves at him. The (Vexing) Infusion on his Hero's Arena ensured that they continued onward despite the burning aura surrounding him, and Jace looked for whatever might be commanding the forces.

Holy Hunt, he thought, theorizing that the insects had some type of queen or other controller. The golden path appeared in front of him and led to his left, into the foliage. He ran that directly, slicing through the larger foes that were not immediately incinerated, and reached a huge, disgusting, fleshy tube of a creature that looked like a grub. It was surrounded by enormous sapphire-colored beetles that had massive pincers.

Jace simply used a Templar's Smite (Blast) to annihilate the whole group in a single move. They ceased to be as the roiling golden flame surged over them.

The insect army seemed to lose cohesion a moment after that, and the groups that had reached the walls began skittering in varying directions as they sought to escape the pain rained down from above.

The walls of the room returned around Jace, and the Essence flooded up into him. "That wasn't too bad," he said as he felt the warmth suffuse his shins and travel up to his chest before fading.

Yup, Ollie said. *Having a machine gun made things a lot easier. I think I will send a message to Shhiv and see if she can augment your Retribution Carbine. Something like fusion battery for unlimited ammunition could be quite useful on Layer 10.*

Do it, Jace replied as he used the essence to level up.

[You have leveled up!]
[You have chosen Specialization of Existing Talent!]
[Talent Name: Templar's Smite.]
[Specialization Name: Rooting.]
[Effect: When the linked Talent is used on a target, they are temporarily rooted in place, unable to move.]

That's useful, Jace thought as he moved down the hallway to the next trial chamber. Checking his energy with a quick glance and seeing it was still at eighty percent capacity and slowly trickling up, he pushed the pedestal and watched it descend into the floor. "You think these challenges are universal? Or tailored to me?"

Seems like they are a bit of both, Ollie commented. *The board game challenge would have wrecked you, and I imagine if a Dreamer traveled down here in a time of peace and did not have a combat-focused build, then fighting a god would be impossible.*

[Trial 5.]
[Hijack the ship.]

The room fell away, and Jace was sitting in a small starfighter cockpit in the depths of space. Far ahead of him, in the upper gravity well of a massive gas giant, was a huge spaceship that was the largest stellar construction he had seen aside from the Penrose Ring when he went to assault Troxanir. A massive, bulbous construction that was bristling with armaments. A deep purple against the black of space and the light green of the gas giant planetoid.

Okay. Board a ship, hijack it. I need to get to the bridge. Holy Hunt. The golden path of light shot forward across the vast emptiness of space, and Jace moved the ship forward. Almost immediately, warning lights and notifications flashed as he saw the huge starship's guns turn to point at his little starfighter.

He took stock of the ship's weapons and found, to his surprise, that there were none. And there were no shields—unlike some of the starships he had seen, it looked like this one relied on heavy metal plating to protect its important components and keep the pilot alive. He was in a metal container, traveling extremely fast through space toward an equally unshielded vessel.

He saw rockets fly out of batteries on the starship in the distance and immediately began evasive maneuvers as he tried to disperse the heat trail that they were doubtless utilizing for their lock-on mechanism. *Ollie, any ideas?*

Use Void Removal and get rid of all artificially created heat in a huge area. Max Rank.

Oh, good idea. Void Removal (Rank 10). Jace felt his body go cold as the entirety of existence around him in a fifty-foot radius sphere of the ship suddenly went cold, becoming indiscernible from space around it. Yanking the control stick to the left, Jace did a tight turn before swinging back toward the large starship, and thankfully, the missiles did not seem to track after him at all, still on their prior trajectory.

They have point-defense turrets, Ollie observed.

Then another Void Removal and we get rid of all momentum caused by projectiles. Jace reactivated the Skill and saw his energy drain double in how quickly it progressed, but as they got into range of the huge starship and it fired, Jace saw the metal slugs traveling through the vast emptiness only to stop before reaching his starfighter. His vehicle still suffered some damage from running into the now-motionless slugs, but he made it to the starship without issue and brought his vehicle to a halt near one of the circular apertures with a keypad on the outside.

He popped the starfighter's cockpit open and used his Soul Tether to bring himself next to the ship, and instead of trying to hack into or open the vehicle, he simply used a Void Beam [Limited Range] to cut through the exterior of the vessel. The life support inside surged out past him, and he used his Soul Tether to pull himself in before a bulkhead slammed shut behind him—sealing up the gap.

He was inside one of several empty honeycomb construction compartments on the exterior of the ship. *They were smart with the design*, he thought as he drew his sword and manifested his Crusader's Bastion. Holding it in front of him, he used his sword to cut through the next doorway.

Indeed, Ollie observed. *Taking the important components and placing them deep inside and having the outside be full of openings where impacts may occur without causing lasting damage. A framework, surrounding the vessel, to provide extra protection. In an environment without shielding like what some vessels have, it is a good setup.*

Jace walked down the corridor and blocked the storm of bullets that flew out from the turrets embedded in the ceiling. With a simple sword throw, he dispatched them with ease and continued onward down the spine of the ship, following the Holy Hunt golden path as he went toward his destination of the bridge.

Oddly enough, there were no occupants, and he felt the disquiet of the silence permeate the environment like a thick fog. *They had life support*, he thought. *That means there should be life. Somewhere.*

Touch one of the panels on the left coming up, Ollie instructed. Jace walked over and did so, using the back of his sword hand to tap the panel. *Accessing . . . huh. Ghost ship. No crew, just automated. Get to the bridge.*

Jace headed down the spine further, traversing with caution despite his confidence to go faster. He wasn't taking any risks with an unmanned vessel, even if it was just part of a trial. And time wasn't an issue, as he knew no matter how long passed inside this place, only seconds would pass back in reality.

Eventually, he reached the bulkhead leading to the cockpit and cut his way through it with a quick series of three slashes—making a triangle-shaped hole, he stepped through. The bridge was quiet, and he sheathed his sword, dismissed his shield, and moved over to the captain's seat. The second he sat down, Edge of Possibility activated, and he instinctively knew which buttons to press to activate manual control. He took the helm and began typing in orders to the ship's subsystems to move the vessel out of the gravity well of the planet and head into deeper space.

As soon as the vehicle began to move, the room returned around Jace, and he was back inside of the trial chamber. Essence surged from the floor and flooded into his body. "That wasn't too bad," he said as he let his Skills and Talents fade, watching his energy trickle back up.

Not bad at all, Ollie replied.

[You have leveled up!]
[You have chosen Specialization of Existing Talent!]
[Talent Name: Holy Hunt.]
[Specialization Name: Coordinating.]
[Effect: When those designated as allies strike the target of Holy Hunt, the target suffers additional harm.]

"Onto the next one," Jace said as he walked down the hall and entered the next chamber.

Chapter Forty-Six

Supplication

Tibalt landed on the stone path that led to the horizon-encompassing, enormous building at the farthest eastern end of Layer 10. A massive black monolith that was covered with words that constantly shifted and twisted until it became a message he could read.

[Here lies the entrance to the Nethershift.]
[Souls will be judged.]
[Demons will be evaluated.]
[Dreamers will be blessed.]

The towering structure was flat and featureless otherwise, a massive level expanse of stone save for the two thirty-foot-tall rectangular doors that ponderously swung inward, revealing a massive, awe-inspiring, gemstone-crusted interior. The stone-grey channel of Souls continued forward before him and under another set of doors. But aside from the grey stone, the entirety of the floor was silver panels that were crusted with rubies and sapphires that ran along the crevices—embedded to be flush so that his clawed feet easily strode across the opulent expanse.

The walls were the same monolithic and firm black as the exterior structure was comprised of, and along the ceiling, Tibalt could see his own reflection in the polished black stone.

The two demons escorting him grabbed his shoulders, and one said, "We will be ensuring you do not try anything stupid."

Tibalt did not fight them at all on that, and they half-carried him to the inner doors before those swung inward. *Ah, this is what I expected from a Demon Lord of madness.*

The stone groove with the Souls ran down to a dais before going underneath that and vanishing from view. A huge, white stone square, and atop it was a throne of a deep, almost sickly yellow color with a rounded top that extended down in graceful arcs. The walls and ceilings were covered in spikes that were crusted over with dried viscera and blood.

Upon that throne sat the most imposing figure Tibalt had ever seen. A grey near-Vanguard with only two arms and legs, surprisingly. Their legs were covered with booted sabatons, and the torso was covered in some shimmering armor that was thin but obviously high-quality in its protective nature. Gauntlets that matched the leg armor adorned the figure, whose hands were resting on the throne's edges. In fact, the only sign that this was a demon and not a Dreamer was the upper body. Above the pectorals, tendrils sprouted off from the shoulders and collarbone of the muscled figure. The head had a large, gnashing mouth full of razor-sharp teeth, and the eyes were covered with some type of purple film that extended back over the top of the head. In addition, two wicked, sharp horns protruded up from the crown of the creature.

"Well now . . . Dreamer Demon." The voice that greeted Tibalt caused shivers to run down his spine. "You say you have information for me?"

Tibalt cleared his throat. "Yes . . . Lord Valcrinox."

"Share," the deep voice boomed out.

And almost instinctively, Tibalt complied. "Wraith is a Dreamer who utilized a power that annihilated matter . . ." He spent the next several minutes detailing his encounters with Wraith, from when they first met up on Layer 1 when Wraith helped protect his Universe to the recent encounter Tibalt had observed before fleeing. He ended with "I wish to help you kill him. Please, take me on in your service. Let me hide here, in your throne room, to ambush him."

"If he makes it this far," Valcrinox replied as he tapped the arm rest of his throne with his fingers, the gauntlets making a consistent, rhythmic clanking noise with each tap. "Give me everything you have."

"Souls? Essence?"

"Everything," Valcrinox replied.

"Of course." Tibalt swallowed his pride and was guided over by the shoulder. Valcrinox held out one of his hands, and Tibalt touched it, transferring everything he had—Infusions, Souls, Essence, and Universal Matter, despite him having very little of the last.

Valcrinox laughed a deep, bellowing laughter of delight. "You magnificent bastard! I needed a little more Universal Matter, and you have given it to me!" He cackled with pleasure, and the laughter veered on the edge of utter insanity. Tibalt felt his vision fog over and couldn't help but join in the laughter.

No, he thought as he pushed aside the enthralling force. *I have Talents to keep in control. I'll swear to you, then stab you in the back the moment I have the chance. Highlord's Resolve.* He felt the laughter fade and resumed his stony expression.

Valcrinox ceased laughing and glared at Tibalt. "I will allow you to remain in the antechamber to ambush Wraith from behind if he should make it this far. I doubt he will, though."

"He has others with him," Tibalt said.

"What?"

"Yroshnak from Layer 8, and his cohort."

Valcrinox's grip tightened on the armrest. "He seeks my throne, doubtless. Wraith is helping him. Or they are helping one another." Valcrinox nodded tersely. "Go to the antechamber and wait to ambush them as I said." Valcrinox's eyes shifted to the other two demons accompanying Tibalt. "Stay with him. In fact, recall a full squad of ten of our forces. We can bleed them on the way here, and then when they enter and I lure them in . . . you attack from behind."

The demons nodded, and Tibalt bowed slightly—as much as the hand holding the shoulder would let him—and he returned to the antechamber as the doors shut on their own behind him. *I'm in!* he thought with glee. The two demons split off—one of them staying with Tibalt and pointing him to a spot against the wall that, as long as someone wasn't looking backward after entering, would not be visible. A perfect ambush position. The demon took up a spot next to Tibalt while the second one went outside.

Soon . . . I'll get my revenge and take that throne. All will serve me.

[Trial 6.]
[Plead your case before The Council.]

The room fell away, and Jace found himself standing at the far end of a large rectangular table with a series of cloaked figures. They all looked at him, and their deep black hoods revealed no light and gave no clue as to their features, species, or the like.

However, he assumed it was some approximation of The Council of Ancients, considering the cloaks looked similar to those of the few Ancients he had spoken to thus far. "Hi," he said with a brief wave.

They all spoke at once, overlapping voices, feminine and masculine, robotic and organic, all together. "We are The Council of Ancients. You are Wraith, Jace Seren, from Universe 348 in Reality 768. You come to us to plead your case for having a closed loop once more. Explain your reasoning."

We're 768? Wow, that's a lot of realities. And Universes in those realities. The sheer enormity of what they had said hit Jace like a wave, and he was just shocked at the number of possible existences.

Hey. Focus up! Ollie said.

Jace cleared his throat and spoke, "I was given a mission. The Ancients, the precursor civilization that made The Cosmic System in my Universe, charged me with fulfilling their Grand Design. They want to return our Universe to how it was before Oblivion—erm, that singularity at the center of the Universe, was made. Before Souls escaped out."

He took a deep breath and continued, "If we close off the loop, then Souls in our Universe are going to be safe. We have Void to keep our Universe secure, and my wife, along with one of The Architects, has already built up defenses to keep it unharmed . . . hopefully forever."

"You seek isolation and safety," One of the voices, a synthetic female voice, said from his left.

"Yeah," Jace said as he turned to face that Ancient. "I started out just wanting to get my sister back. I still do; her Soul is in an afterlife, and she deserves a good, full life. She was my responsibility."

"And you think you should have the authority to remove her Soul from eternal bliss in an afterlife?" a masculine organic voice said from his right.

Jace turned to them, and he felt filled with conviction as he spoke. "She never experienced life. Not really. She deserves the best."

"Or," the female synthetic voice said, "you are trying to fix your own errors, and you feel responsible for her death."

"Yes," Jace whispered as he turned to face her. "I'm responsible for her death. And the deaths of hundreds of thousands of others. I want to fix my mistakes and give them all the lives back that I tore away from them."

"Then your intentions are selfish," another male voice said, this one more monotone and robotic.

"Yes and no," Jace replied as he spoke with resolve filling his tone. "I want redemption. I want my sister back. I want my dad back. I want everyone who was killed in the pursuit of a greater good to come back."

"You speak about what you want, but is it not true that your Ancients are the ones who came up with this Grand Design and desire a return to how your Universe was before The Ancients arrived?"

"Yes," Jace replied.

All of The Ancients spoke together again, their voices overlapping. "We have overseen the blossoming and deaths of realities time and time again. We have seen Universes torn asunder and stitched back together. We have seen creation die and return."

"And?" Jace said as they stopped.

The masculine voice spoke, "You are Bearer of the Mantle of Burden. Members of our kind have deemed you as worthy enough to fix the mistakes inherent in Reality 768's Astral System and Soulstream flow. As such, some accommodations can be made."

The female voice added, "The Council approves of your actions. The Ancients wish you luck in your endeavors."

The room vanished around Jace, and the Essence surged from the floor of the trial room. "Were we . . . actually talking to them?" he asked Ollie.

Maybe? I do not know, honestly. But it is fascinating to learn that our Universe is number 768.

"Doesn't matter much in the long run," Jace replied as he pulled up the Astral System interface to level up. "Our Universe will be closed off." He spoke calmly, but his words were filled with determination. "We do not share knowledge of our reality number with anyone else. I don't want Xero or Xera getting ideas."

I get it. You still do not fully trust them, which, given your experience with Xera, is understandable. This secret will remain with you and me.

"Good."

[You have leveled up!]
[You have chosen Specialization of Existing Talent!]
[Talent Name: Purifying Edge.]
[Specialization Name: Silencing.]
[Effect: When the linked Talent is used on a target, they are prevented from communicating for ten seconds—including accessing the Astral System's interface.]

Chapter Forty-Seven

Guilty

Jace placed his hand on the pedestal in the next trial chamber and pushed down. As it sank, he was confronted with yet another Astral System screen.

> [Trial 7.]
> [Judge.]

The room fell away once more, and Jace was seated on a chair with a table in front of him and a long, expansive hall ahead of him. There was a data pad sitting on the desk before him, and a line of people with plasteel bindings around their necks, down to their wrists, and around their ankles as they waited their turn.

A man, a human man, which was a pleasant surprise to Jace because he had not seen a full-on human like him since his visit back to Earth, spoke. "Step up!"

A pale, thin-skinned old man shuffled forward and took his spot at the small raised railing just below Jace's seat.

Oh, neat! We get to be judges. Look at what he did.

Jace looked down at the data pad and scrolled through the information presented. Everyone had been found guilty, but their circumstances varied, and his task was to dole out punishment to each of them. *A trial that is almost like an actual trial*, he thought, as he had seen them in movies he watched with Shhiv and had heard of them back on Earth as a bygone system of evaluating guilt.

The first case, this old man, had committed theft. He had stolen medication from a doctor and was found guilty of that act. But the documentation also revealed to Jace that his reason for doing it was based out of desperation. The man would have suffered greatly without the medication, barely being able to walk.

A few things to consider here, Ollie said as he examined the data pad through Jace's eyes. *First, if this guy has to steal to get the medicine he needs to live, then perhaps staying incarcerated where medical care is provided is a viable route to ensure he gets what he needs.*

But that might not be the trial's challenge, Jace thought back. *Will it accept any choice I make? Or is there some correct answer?*

Depends on the local jurisdiction and laws. Checking through that data pad—scroll down, please. Jace did so, and Ollie spoke. *Nope. It is just the information about the case. Each person was found guilty by a jury trial. You get to decide the punishment. I do not see anything about sentencing guidelines, either.*

Jace nodded and looked to the old man. "Would you be able to afford your medication if you were released on . . . what do they call it—"

Probation.

"Probation?" Jace asked.

The man was silent, and just looked ahead with dead eyes. *Ah. Seems like we only get the information put forward to us*, Ollie remarked.

Jace tried to tap on the man's name on the data pad for more information. Something about his income, or where he lived, or anything like that—but all he had was the name, the event that occurred, the reasoning behind the event happening, and then the guilty verdict. *He's old*, Jace thought. *And going by human standards, he doesn't have many years left. But it's about pain and not necessarily quality of life.* Jace looked up. "I sentence you to . . . one year in prison, one with end-of-life care."

The old man vanished in a glimmer of sparkles, and the next one walked forward. *Wait, we don't get any indication of if we made the right call?*

Does not seem like it, Ollie said. *Maybe no matter what we do, we cannot be wrong.*

Can you see any reason to why the trials we are facing are the way they are? he thought to Ollie.

The Wayfinder sighed with frustration. *I am not seeing a detectable pattern. My only guess is that you will be the overseeing System Administrator of our Universe's Cosmic System—maybe this is a way for The Ancients to see if you are the right person for the job.*

But I won't be doing this type of stuff!

You might have to at some point. Like if you had a rogue Wayfinder that tried breaking things for their own benefit. Ollie sounded dismayed at the idea, but it wasn't an unreasonable implication.

Jace read the next case's information, resigning himself to finishing the trial and just trying to be fair about judgement. A woman who had killed her husband. A husband who had abused her but whom she stayed with because she had nowhere else to go. *Self-defense*, Jace thought as he handed down the sentence. "No prison." She vanished in a glimmer.

"Next!" the bailiff shouted as a figure stepped up to the well.

Jace glanced up and was quite confused. He saw the person before him shift and alter shape—turning into Xera.

Oh, now that is a surprise, Ollie said with genuine shock. *That . . . huh . . . okay, do your job.*

Jace read through the data pad. *Xera'tal Pen'arkon. Responsible for the deaths of quintillions of creatures across millennia upon millennia.* There really was not any other option Jace saw. "Death seems like the only realistic punishment."

Xera vanished, and to Jace's surprise, the next person to step up shifted shape and turned into Greg. *Let's see . . . murder for hire, robbery, manslaughter . . .* He kept reading, and the list went on and on. *If any of this stuff is half true, then Greg has done some fucked up stuff.*

He was part of the military, and then a secret agent, and then a freelance Streetrunner. Lots of unsavory business.

I suppose. Still, the judgement that fits these crimes is "Life in prison."

Greg vanished, and Dee walked up to the well. Her list of crimes was extensive: hundreds of years of theft and property destruction. "Restitution," Jace stated. "Pay back everything you owe."

She vanished, and Jace saw the point of the trial, finally, as he saw himself walk up. *Should've known that was coming*, he thought as he looked through the data pad.

What he saw was a list of crimes that were varied and nuanced. Many, many different types, and the list kept going and going. The hundreds upon hundreds of thousands dead stood out the most drastically to Jace. "I . . ." he looked at himself, then at the data pad, then down at his hands as he set the data pad down. "If I was judging myself . . . and wasn't me . . . this would be damning."

Well, I think the trial will know if you go easy on yourself.

Jace nodded and swallowed, and he whispered, "Death."

The other him vanished, and Jace's consciousness flickered out.

He floated in an endless abyss. Darkness swallowed him from all sides. Endless black. A peaceful darkness that was all encompassing. Then, a swirl of colors—purples, pinks, greens, blues—as he felt himself falling.

Something grabbed him from above. He had no clue what it could be, what force had gripped him, but he saw the colors culminate into a bright white dot in front of him. He was shoved into the white, and like a goopy film, it coated him. Words in strange, archaic, and ancient languages appeared in front of him.

Then, he was falling again. Through a golden mist, through a silver cloud, and through a light blue sky before he landed in the middle of a gorgeous city park.

Chroma was swinging on a playground swing set, laughing as she played with other kids. "Chroma!" Jace shouted as he ran over to her.

She looked at him, smiled, waved, and kept swinging. "Come on! Push me higher!"

He felt at ease. At peace. And he ran over to push her.

But something gnawed at him. Glancing down to his chest, he saw a light, sparkling, dark purple. A deep feeling of longing hit him. A craving. A despair that washed over him as he saw a flash of dark, black eyes glittering with cerulean light. A whisper in his ear.

"Don't leave me alone."

He looked at Chroma, then looked back to the purple light that shone within. It switched hues, becoming a deep, crackling crimson. Then, a white-grey. Finally, a sparkling, flaming gold that surged up all around him.

Shhiv, he thought as the eyes flashed into his vision again, as he regained focus on her. The woman he loved. He looked at Chroma, and tore himself away as he turned and ran. He ran as fast as he could.

I have to get back, he thought as he sprinted as fast as he could. Faster than he ever had before. He had to return. To be with her. It was an all-encompassing need.

Then, a loud pop sounded off next to him, and he glanced sideways to see Ollie casually swimming through the air. "Ah, this is where you went."

He skidded to a stop, "What? Where am I?"

"Some bullshit The Ancients put in as part of the trial. You passed. Hold on a second, let me just . . ." Ollie flew into him.

Jace coughed as he sat up and sucked in a deep breath. The warmth of Essence suffused him as he looked around and saw the walls of the room.

Ollie spoke in his mind. *You passed the trial. But there was some—*

Jace cut him off as he stood up, "Where was I? Did I die?"

No. It was like an artificial recreation. They locked your consciousness inside a program. Took me two-hundred years to crack it.

"Two . . . two hundred?" Jace asked in disbelief.

Oh yeah. Took me a long time to untangle all of the code. I mean, there was more to it than that, but it was so technical that it would take me a whole year to explain it.

Jace didn't know what to feel. *So long* . . . He immediately panicked and began to speak, but Ollie cut him off.

Remember, it does not matter how long passes in these trials—only seconds actually pass in our reality. And even then, Shhiv is immortal. And I know she would wait for you.

"It . . . it was more than that," Jace said as he dry-swallowed, opened up his TPSB, and pulled out his water to drink. He was starving and grabbed survival meals as he scarfed them down. Swallowing, he continued. "I was willing to give up Chroma for Shhiv."

Makes sense. Chroma was a responsibility you took on. Shhiv was a choice. Many species would put their mate—or in more civilized cases, their spouse—before their blood related family. Aside from children, normally, but not always!

It made some sense to Jace, but it was also discomforting that the goal that had pushed him on from the beginning was now supplanted by something he already had, and now he was just going to try and rectify his mistakes. "She looked so happy," he whispered. "Am I . . . do I . . . should I really take her away from that?"

It will be their choice, Ollie said comfortingly. *Everyone will choose if they want to come back or not. If she wants to stay, then she will.*

"I need to move," Jace muttered as he stood up. "I can't think about this." He pulled up the Astral System screen and quickly made his choices.

> [You have leveled up!]
> [You have chosen Specialization of Existing Talent!]
> [Talent Name: Justice's Rebuke.]
> [Specialization Name: Castigating.]
> [Effect: When the linked Talent is activated, the user's weapons and Talents deal additional damage in the form of sonic waves.]

Keep moving, Jace thought as he pushed on to the next chamber. *Survive for Shhiv.*

Chapter Forty-Eight

The End of the Trials

Shhiv pored over the schematics. "And you're sure it'll work like that?"

Xero nodded from across the table as he took a sip of hot chocolate. "Oh yeah. It'll work. See, we just have to put the insulation coil over here, and then make sure the housing is made of Graded-Z shielding, which we can whip up easily enough. And even then, the cancer isn't an issue with Jace's innate NICIF to fix things up. The bigger issue is the heat distribution. Hence the coil to insulate the reaction."

Shhiv rubbed her temples. Despite her Skills, she was still having trouble comprehending Xero's design. "Can you just . . . make a step-by-step version? A checklist I can follow? Preferably with pictures of each step?"

"Yeah," Xero replied with a chuckle. "I should have you sit down at one of the education terminals and get a few doses of knowledge downloaded." His eyes flicked up to her. "Since you are going to be Ms. Tech Support once Jace takes over as Administrator."

Shhiv shook her head. "I don't want that job."

"Then how about Head Engineer?" Xero asked as he took another sip of the hot chocolate, licking his lips as the goopy liquid clung to his mouth.

Shhiv tapped her toe. "What will it entail?"

"Just fixing things. Which you already do. It's not like Xera and the rest of my species are going to be gone. We'll be around in a pinch if needed."

Xero tapped the stylus he had in his left hand to his temple. "I should ask Quinn if she wants to step into the Tech Support role."

"I've been meaning to ask," Shhiv said softly. "Why are The Architects so willing to just let go of control over everything?"

"We're a precursor civilization," Xero replied solemnly as his voice took on a serious tone. "Part of being one of the first sentient species is to seed other worlds with life and guide them. Then, to recede. Keep an eye on things but not interfere unless as a last resort." He sighed, and then his jovial nature kicked back in. "Instead, we'll be entrusting it all to the Wayfinders, and, of course, Jace, as the watcher of the administrators." He leaned back and took another sip of his hot chocolate. "Plus, we get to retire. Endless . . . whatever we want to do."

Shhiv nodded. "Makes sense. Did you have someone tell you to do the world seeding stuff?"

Xero chuckled. "No. No entities revealed themselves and told us to do it. We just decided, as a whole, that we should foster growth across the stars, create a framework for those civilizations to grow without destroying themselves while still leaving them mostly to their devices. I like to think of it as absentee parenting. We are responsible, we are around to help if things go horribly wrong, but we let the young species make mistakes and suffer the consequences. Hopefully, they learn. Hence why Cosmogenic Merging has the requisite of hitting a population threshold based on a complex equation that correlates to world size. That demonstrates that a species is stable enough to be considered an adult, to use my earlier example. And sometimes, we interfere when circumstance conspires to end that chance—like Xera removing the inhabitants of Poltor Six from their world when their star died earlier than anticipated."

It sounds very altruistic but also a bit careless, Shhiv thought. But, ultimately, she had her answer, and she smiled. "Thanks for indulging. Send me the instructions when you can, and I'll make Jace's weapon upgrades."

Jace entered the next chamber and pressed down on the pedestal.

[Trial 8.]
[Kill them all.]

The room fell away around Jace, and he stood in an enormous throne room. Four hundred feet long and half as wide, with dozens of men and women who were engaged in an elegant series of dances. Music echoed through the room from an orchestra at the far end, and a couple sat upon a pair of chairs as they looked out upon the dancing guests.

Really? Killing a whole bunch of party-goers? Jace thought as he pulled his weapon and it ignited with radiant golden flames.

It is an easy task, Ollie said in his mind.

Jace moved to the servant next to the door and grimaced. "Sorry," he muttered as he brought Divine Revenge up and slashed at the man's neck. But the figure moved their hand up and caught the blade, turning to Jace as his eyes flashed a pure white and stayed that way. He opened his mouth, and a geyser of flames shot out right into Jace's face.

Jace pulled back, slicing the figure in the process, and he heard the music stop. Glancing to his right, he saw that every person in the room had turned to look at him, and their eyes had flashed to white as well. *Huh. Wonder what they are?* he thought as he took up a position in the doorway he had appeared in. Manifesting his Crusader's Bastion, he placed it in front of him as the entire room erupted with flames.

Jace activated (Aegis) and watched as the shield completely cut off the room in front of him that became white-hot. The ambient heat rose even more, and Jace squeezed himself against the wall before he finally relented and used Void Shield to protect himself. The relief from the heat was almost instant, and he sighed as he pushed his way into the room. *Raging Cleave (Rank 10)*, he thought as he swung in a horizontal sweep that covered the entire first quarter of the room's length. People fell, and the flames grew less intense. Taking another step forward and using another Raging Cleave at maximum (Rank), he cut down another swathe. Continuing that way, he made it to the end of the room and cleaved through the last group.

All of the corpses were on the ground, slowly being consumed by the gold and green flame, crimson miasma, and wriggling toward each other. *Oh, I bet they're going to merge or something like that.*

Jace began hacking away at the bodies on the ground closest to him, but he saw his prediction come true as the corpses all merged into an amalgamated monstrosity of torsos, legs, and arms. The entire room became sweltering, but Jace was protected thanks to his Void Shield. "Ollie, we can wait in the trial rooms, right?"

Yup!

"Good. Void Beam [Horizon-Splitter]." Jace watched as the entirety of the room was completely obliterated along with everything within it. Only the area to his left, right, and behind him was left intact, and a vast, empty blackness was all he saw beyond where he stood.

The room returned around him, and the Essence surged up from below and imbued him with warmth that traveled up his legs and his spine. He doubled over as Void Shield deactivated and prevented Emergency Battery from autoactivating as he let his energy naturally refill. It would take a while, but thanks to the time dilation, they were not in a rush.

We should just do that on any fight coming up, Ollie commented. *Since we can just wait it out.*

Sure, Jace thought as he caught his breath and watched the energy slowly refill. *Now to level up.*

[You have leveled up!]
[You have chosen Specialization of Existing Talent!]

[Talent Name: Revealing Light.]
[Specialization Name: Shrouding.]
[Effect: The (Potent) Infusion applies a vision-degrading effect that slowly lessens in severity after the initial blindness ends.]

He walked through to the next chamber and sat as he waited for his energy to return. "Ollie, can we talk to other people back in our Universe with the whole time-dilation thing?"

Yup. It is weird how that works; I am still trying to figure it out.

"Get Quinn on the comms."

Just a second!

A few moments passed before Quinn's voice came over the comms. "Go for Quinn."

"Hey. I need you to have the Stratagems ready to go on me."

"What trigger condition?" Quinn asked.

"I'd say when I feel like I am in over my head. Can you do that?"

"Sure. I'll tie it to an emotional state." She was silent for a few seconds. "And done!"

Jace glanced up above him and saw the small drone still hovering there, the gold Celestial Observer of Quinn's Skill and now the small hourglass next to it representing her Stratagems being ready to go. "Thanks. How are things up there?"

"Doing well. Seems like Xero wants me to be Tech Support for the whole Cosmic System. Stepping into a Xera-like role."

"You're the smartest computer person I know," Jace replied. "If you want the job, it's yours."

"Oh? You giving out jobs now?" she asked as a playful jab.

"I mean, I will be the System Administrator once I'm all done here. That means I can hire and fire."

Quinn chuckled, "Alright. I'll keep that in mind, boss." The word was filled with a slightly bitter tone, but the overall implication was one of amusement and that she was playing up the word overtly. "Otherwise, everything else is going well. Universe is all sealed off, Greg and Missy are out with Dee, Priam, and Ree fighting Astral Demons—"

"Why?" Jace asked.

"They are a bit jealous. Or bored. Honestly, I'm not quite sure why Priam is doing it—I bet that Dee and Ree wanted to blow stuff up without consequence while Greg and Missy want revenge against Troxanir's distant cousins or some shit like that. Priam probably is just along for the ride to keep them all safe."

Jace sighed, feeling a mix of relief and tension. "Well, Priam and Greg together are basically invincible with the whole damage-redirect and healing-plus-shields combination. Having the ladies all as damage dealers . . . They should be safe." He glanced at his almost-full energy. "I've gotta go. I think I'm almost done with these Layer 9 trials. At least, I hope I am."

"Good luck," Quinn replied as the comms then went silent.

Jace took a deep breath and pressed the next pillar's indentation, watching it sink down into the floor.

[Trial 9.]
[Combat Challenge: Overridden due to {Void Beam} being observed as a cheat {Skill}.]
[Substitute Challenge: Endure.]

The walls fell away around Jace, and he found himself standing on a tiny platform, barely large enough for both feet to stand on. It was unbalanced as well, and he had to quickly find his center before he breathed a little sigh of relief and could take in where he was. In all directions—up, down, and all around, he was surrounded by roiling, turbulent waves that hissed and spat at him. *Acid*, he thought.

Just to test if he could use his Gear to cheat the situation, he fired a Soul Tether up, but it did not emerge from his arm, and he frowned. *Nope. I just have to keep my balance.*

It said endure, Ollie stated. *I would bet that things are going to change further.*

True to Ollie's words, after a tense five minutes, the edges of the platform Jace was standing on vanished, leaving him wobbling and barely keeping his balance.

[Let us, boss!]
[We can take over and have perfect balance.]

"Go ahead," Jace muttered. He felt his legs become rock-steady beneath him, and another five minutes passed as the acid-liquid-wave walls began moving in, getting closer and flicking acid toward him. A rapid Void Shield protected him from the splatter, and he continued to let the NICIF keep control of his body.

Yet more of the platform under his feet fell out, but the NICIF expertly shimmied to balance on a single leg, maintaining a perfect balance.

The acid kept spitting onto Jace, and he saw his energy drain little by little. "How is someone without an innate System supposed to survive this?" he asked.

Ollie replied, *Maybe they are not meant to. Or only extraordinary individuals can do it.*

The walls of liquid acid got even closer, and Jace saw the sloshing liquid hit ever more frequently as his energy continued to drain and get closer and closer to empty.

Then, the walls returned around him. Essence poured up from below and filled him with warmth. Jace reasserted control over his body. "Thanks, NICIF."

[No problem!]

"Maybe we should hold onto the Essence this time," Jace commented. "Save our level up for when we get to the next Layer. Dip down, get the Class Transmutation, and then come up and level up here on Layer 9 if we can."

Decent idea. But, counterpoint, what if we cannot get back from Layer 10 like you think?

Jace thought on that. "I mean . . . fair enough, I guess."

[You have leveled up!]
[You have chosen New Talent!]
[Talent Name: Herald's Healing.]
[Effect: The user may activate this Talent to cure all wounds, afflictions, and other negative effects on a target creature within one-hundred feet and line-of-sight. May be used on self.]

Why a healing Talent? Ollie asked.

We will have allies on Layer 10, Jace thought back. *Demons, sure, but ones that follow Yroshnak. We need to keep him alive to take over Layer 10 as the new Demon Lord of the Layer. If he dies, then we probably have to waste time finding a replacement.*

Ah. Fair enough!

Jace walked on to the next trial chamber. Another pedestal stood before him, and he pressed it.

[Trial 10.]
[Strategize.]

The world fell away once more, and Jace stood inside a room. In front of him, he saw a long rectangular table. Around the table were shrouded figures: humanoid, but with something off about each of them.

I recognize this! It is the map of Layer 10 that Xera's probes were able to map out!

Jace saw the top-down depiction of the Layer as Ollie overlaid Xera's scans. A two mile north-to-south expanse and a fifty-mile expanse from east to west. The film that covered the entrance to the Layer was at the farthest eastern end, and he could see the entire layout of fortifications and defenses.

One of the shrouded figures became defined, and Jace saw the Loud Ancient standing there. "Hi! Figured we would give you a bit of a sneak preview of what awaits you!" He pointed to the map. "I cannot help you strategize at all, as that would violate the rules I have to follow. But I can at least explain what you are looking at!"

Jace walked around the table. "I talked to a Council of your species," he said.

At this, The Ancient turned to face him, but his face was shrouded by the hood. The tone, however, was miniscule and tiny, like he had shrunken into himself. "Oh," he barely whispered. "Well . . . how did the talk go?"

"The conversation was fine," Jace replied. "They asked some weird questions. Mostly about my reasons for doing what I'm doing."

"Ah. Well . . . Trials are different for each person. Tailored, if you will. But The Council actually spending a moment of their time on a non-Ancient?" He shrugged, and his voice became slightly more chipper. "Well, it's not unheard of. But it is weird that a Bearer of the Mantle of Burden was given an audience for a Trial."

Jace looked down at the battlefield board again. "Any chance you can bring Yroshnak in here to theorize and strategize?"

"Sure!" the Loud Ancient replied.

One of the shadowy figures around the room was replaced by the imposing frame of Yroshnak. He looked around with curiosity, then his eyes settled on Jace. "Ah, still doing your Trials, I see."

"The last one!" The Ancient replied.

Jace pointed to the map, which showed the entry point as being surrounded by fortifications. "They are expecting an assault. Looks like their defenses are pretty nasty."

Yroshnak peered down at the table and nodded. "Indeed. Valcrinox has only one hundred demons at his command while I have my forty. We are outnumbered."

But not outgunned! Ollie said, his voice reverberating out of Jace's armor. *Wraith has a neat weapon in his arsenal. Benefit of being a Dreamer? Technology!*

Jace reached into the TPSB and pulled out the Retribution Carbine—but it had been upgraded. The design was sleek and smooth, with a small shark fin that ran along the top, a stylized bit of extra flair that told Jace exactly who made it. He set the weapon down on the table and pulled out a blade grenade, and the land mines. "We have lots of tools at our disposal. The land mines can be turned invisible and undetectable. I can drop them through the film; they can skitter to the defenses at the entrance and then detonate them. Take out the defenders before they can do anything about it."

Yroshnak nodded. "That gets us in, but then look at all of these fortifications we have to work our way through." He traced a line with a large finger, dragging it along the length of the road that ran down the center of the Layer. "On both sides, with more defenses and emplacements. They will retreat as we overrun their positions."

Jace grabbed the blade grenade and tossed it up and down in his hand. "This should help with that. Plus, I can shoot them down as they retreat. And I've been picking up a lot of Specializations around supporting others—just stay close to me."

Yroshnak grinned and looked up at Jace. "Been preparing for it, eh?"

Jace nodded, but Ollie spoke. *Yup. We are more than prepared.*

"Then the landmine plan is sound to begin," Yroshnak said. "And we can slowly advance while staying together. By chance, do you have a means to heal—"

"Just picked up a Talent for that," Jace replied.

"Excellent." Yroshnak walked to the far end of the table where a massive stone structure stood. "The entrance to the Vault on the Layer and the Nethershift portal. More importantly, it is where Valcrinox will be on his throne." He looked up at Jace. "A powerful Relic." He looked to The Ancient. "Isn't that right?"

The Loud Ancient shook his head. "I cannot tell you the specifics. All I can say is that the Relic from Layer 10 is potent. And the Vault is currently unavailable, having recently been conquered."

"Damn," Yroshnak muttered. "I was hoping to hold him in the throne room, and then send you, Wraith, to defeat the Vault and acquire a Relic to even the playing field."

Jace held up his sword. "This touches him, he loses Potency."

Yroshnak's eyes went wide at that. "Well . . . that is something. Hopefully his Relic does not prevent that from happening." Yroshnak looked back to the map. "I think we have a solid plan. Slow and steady. We keep you protected, you heal us up. And"—he grinned—"shoot the fuckers out of the sky."

The Ancient looked to Jace. "All done?"

"Yes," Jace replied.

Yroshnak vanished, but The Ancient was still there. "I am going to provoke your last Class Transmutation here, before you descend further and reach Potency 10. This is the home stretch." His voice almost became pleading. "I hope you succeed. If not . . . we have backups."

"My friends," Jace said softly. "I won't fail . . . but they are a good backup. Greg, Dee, Priam—they alone are formidable. Ree and Missy added into the mix? I would bet all five are going to be unstoppable."

The Ancient chuckled, "Very well. When you return, you will get the Essence, and your prompt. See you in the Nethershift beyond the throne."

The Ancient vanished, the room went black, and Jace found himself back in the chamber with the pedestal. Essence flooded into his legs, up his body, and shot to the top of his head. *10,000 Essence,* Ollie said. *Puts you at 15,000 Total. And it will take 10,000 for your next level-up, which will mean Potency 10.*

[Congratulations on entering a new Layer!]
[You may choose to specialize your Class by performing a Class Transmutation!]
[As you have reached Potency 10, your prior selections will be examined, and a hybrid Class Transmutation will be applied!]
[Prior selections: Offense x3, Defense x2, Support x2.]
[Calculating final Class Transmutation . . .]
[Designation: Hero.]

Valcrinox grinned as one of his Astral Demons came into the room at full speed, falling prone at the throne while holding a glowing silver crystal. "My Lord! I have it!"

"Bring it to me," Valcrinox ordered.

His underling brought it up to him and rapidly spoke as he handed the Relic over. "The object will disable all technology within the palace."

Valcrinox frowned. "I said for the whole Layer, did I not?"

"The Relic did not allow for that, my lord," the demon replied sheepishly as they retreated down the steps and stood a respectful distance away.

Valcrinox placed the item into his chest and willed the flesh to grow over it. "You have done well. Now, this Wraith will meet his end. And we will make our Universe."

The demon bowed and left, shutting the doors behind them.

Valcrinox was thankful to the Dreamer Demon who had joined his ranks. The Universal Matter necessary to create the Universe was provided by his generous gift for service. And now, Valcrinox had it all compressed into a single point. Ready to blossom up on the first Layer to create a whole Universe. One that he could immediately make himself the one ruler of. *Not just a Demon Lord . . . a god. A singular ruler who is completely impossible to counteract or contradict. I will be absolute.*

He laughed a mad, cackling cry as he waited for his foe to come to him and meet his demise.

Chapter Forty-Nine

The Fields of Madness

Jace shook his head when he saw the title of the new Class Transmutation pop onto his Status Screen and then fade away. "Really? Just 'Hero'?"

It is apt, Ollie commented. *If you had gone more into offensive, defensive, or support focus, it would have been different. Want me to show you the list of permutations?*

"I'm good," Jace replied as he looked at the hallway leading onward—covered in a bright white film. "Okay . . . last time for intense pain. Let's level up." He laid down on the floor. "Hit it."

Here we go!

[You have leveled up!]
[You have chosen Specialization of Existing Talent!]
[Talent Name: Hero's Arena.]
[Specialization Name: Perfected.]
[Effect: Combines and amplifies all other Specializations of the linked Talent.]
[All Specializations being combined:]
[Aura—The linked Talent is constantly active, and will only affect those that the user desires.]
[Incinerating—The damage inflicted also stacks a damage-over-time effect.]
[Vexing—Those in the Hero's Arena who suffer damage are driven toward the user.]

[Bolstering—Those in the Hero's Arena designated as allies (including the user) gain a defensive boost.]
[Suppressing—Those in the Hero's Arena who suffer damage must spend twice the energy as normal to activate Talents.]
[Wrathbound—Incorporates the user's {Aura of Wrath} at maximum {Rank}, extending the radius to match that of the linked Talent, and with all {Skill Evolutions} applied.]
[Crusading—Those designated as allies in the Hero's Arena heal from a portion of the damage they inflict upon foes.]
[Reckoning—Those designated as allies in the Hero's Arena who are attacked apply a mark to the creature who harmed them. The user gains combat efficacy amplification against foes marked.]
[Encouraging—The linked Talent also encourages allies in the Hero's Arena, granting their weapons and Talents a burning damage-over-time effect based upon the user's Emotion Source.]

Name: Jace Seren (Potency 10)
Emotion [Class Level]: Valiant [Hero 91]
Talent [Specialization]: Astral Adaptation, Astral Translation, Valiant Crusader's Might [Burning] [Vengeful] [Poised] [Unstoppable] [Bracing] [Voidbound] [Lightbound] [Rallying] [Inspiriting], Crusader's Bastion [Retaliating] [Reinforcing] [Grounding] [Redoubt] [Spiked] [Resonating] [Glorious] [Hallowed] [Aegis], Hero's Arena (Perfected), Indomitable Will [Zealous] [Intimidating] [Inviolable] [Enduring] [Ameliorating] [Dark Matter Binding] [Galvanizing] [Spiteful] [Ensnaring], Templar's Smite [Spear] [Blast] [Lingering] [Challenging] [Inferno] [Cosmic] [Gaze] [Blinding] [Rooting], Holy Hunt [Marked] [Bursting] [Authoritative] [Provoking] [Inciting] [Branding] [Invigorating] [Bolstering] [Coordinating], Purifying Edge [Cleansing] [Searing] [Purging] [Sanctifying] [Terminating] [Judging] [Revealing] [Condensing] [Silencing], Justice's Rebuke [Flaming] [Bashing] [Holy] [Plasmas] [Energizing] [Languishing] [Deflecting] [Guarding] [Castigating], Revealing Light [Burdening] [Limning] [Fracturing] [Potent] [Perilous] [Linking] [Redirecting] [Identifying] [Shrouding], Final Form, Herald's Healing
Essence: 5,000

Infusions: None
Gear: <TPSB>, (Convergent Edge / Ancient Reckoning) Divine Revenge, (Explorer's Embrace / Beacon) Hero's Plate, (Prosthetic Savant) Astral Appendages, (Draconic Sovereign) Arbiter's Sight, (Anathema) Astral Sleeve, (Reinforced) Psycrystal Lattice, (Pinnacle) NICIF-EP, (Restoring) Flame of Valor, Retribution Auto-Carbine

White-hot pain engulfed Jace's entire existence. He could feel every single nerve light up, a glowing agony just as if he had been fully submerged into molten metal and cut open as to allow the glowing-hot liquid to flow through his whole body. He wanted to scream, but no air met his lungs.

Existence was torment, and he lost all sense of what was going on around him—even the stone floor he had laid down on was lost in the blistering fire that engulfed his body.

And then it stopped. He was left, gasping, on the floor of the trial chamber.

Wow, Ollie muttered in his mind, *that was really violent thrashing there.*

Jace's head was pounding, and he tried to sit up, but dizziness overtook him, and he laid back down, taking deep breaths to recover. "I . . . whew . . ."

[Hey, boss!]
[Looks like your prosthetics are really pushing the limits of what is possible strength-wise!]
[Plus, seems like we got a bit faster at processing, and our efficiency for repairs and maintenance increased!]
[Woohoo!]

Jace would've chuckled if he could, but he was still struggling to take deeper breaths. Ollie commented, *Since you have just upgraded to the maximum possible Potency for a Dreamer, it only makes sense that you will need some time to recover.*

"Mind . . . just keeping watch . . . while I nap?"

Sure. Ollie pulled out of Jace's head and swam in little circles above him as Jace let himself surrender to the bliss of unconscious sleep.

Yroshnak glanced sideways as Wraith walked out of the white film-covered hallway. The Dreamer glanced around briefly as if taking in the area, then looked to Yroshnak. "You ready?" he asked.

Yroshnak grinned and grabbed his axe. "Just waiting on you. Give us a moment to level up . . . and then it is time to go." He looked back at his demon cohort, giving them a brief nod, and then he initialized his final level-up.

He gritted his teeth as the horrific pain shot all through his body, and he selected the path of refinement as his body compressed—keeping all of its strength but gaining agility and empowered Psykinetic prowess. Then, just as quickly as it started, it stopped, and he let out a gasp of relief.

Wraith chuckled, "I didn't know demons went through the same thing, the whole painful Potency increase."

Yroshnak got his breath back and stood up straight. "It is painful, but now . . . we are ready."

Wraith walked to the edge of the film, raised his hand, and Yroshnak saw a brief shimmer over the entrance to Layer 10. Then, Wraith knelt and began pulling small discs with little legs on the bottom out of his bracer. Hundreds of them. As he waved his hand over them, they vanished, and he made a throwing motion as if he was tossing the small discs into the film.

"Those are the landmines you mentioned?" Yroshnak asked.

"Mm-hmm," Wraith replied. "I'll use all of them I have. We give them a few moments to get into position, and then we go do—"

He was cut off as an Astral Demon flew up through the hole. Before it could gain its bearings, Yroshnak surged forward with two of his fellow demons, and they all imbued their weapons with Psykinetic might. Yroshnak could also see the flickering golden flames upon his weapon. *Must be Wraith's Talents to empower us,* he thought as he carved into Valcrinox's demon.

The demon let out a screech as a Talent attempted to paralyze the whole lot of them—and as Yroshnak mentally utilized a recovery Talent, he realized he was not affected. Wraith drew his blade and quickly bisected the demon, then decapitated it, and then a third, blisteringly fast strike to slash it through once more. The demon withered away. "You have a Talent to protect our minds?" Yroshnak asked.

"Indomitable Will with the (Galvanizing) Infusion," Wraith replied as he resumed turning the discs invisible and tossing them into the film. He glanced over at Yroshnak, and the helmet covered the expression, but not the sounds of satisfaction in his tone. "Good to see it pay off, finally."

Yroshnak waved to his demons to stand along the edges of the film, just in case another of Valcrinox's demons flew through. None did, though. And Wraith finally stood up. "We're set."

"Then we go in!" Yroshnak activated his full set of Talents as his body was covered in a shimmering, blood red, liquid barrier. His weapon, still empowered, glowed an even brighter crimson. And he felt stronger. More agile, more precise. "Down to victory!"

Jace watched the Astral Demons jump down and waited until they had all jumped through before jumping down after them. *How much did that one demon give us?*

5,000, Ollie replied. *Enough with your current 5,000 to get another level.*

We only have to kill another sixteen of Valcrinox's demons to max out?

Yup!

Jace took in the tenth Layer of the Astral Verge. The first sense that struck him was the noise—the world was screaming around him. It was quiet, almost like someone was on the opposite side of an apartment and screaming for help, begging for mercy, or just scared out of their mind. Peppered among the screams were laughs of utter madness, cackling and crying intermixed with chants. Thankfully, the mental effect of the Layer had no hold on him—but Jace could only imagine what would happen to someone who was not Potency 10 nor had Talents keeping their mind safe.

The scent was odd as well; it smelled like a fresh spring day with a new rainfall and the slight, earthy aroma of muddy ground. But underneath that was a sulfuric rot; subtle, but enough to make the entire experience entirely unsavory.

Grassland extended all around, interspersed by the fortifications that were erected from a monolithic black stone. Four towers surrounded the stone depression that Yroshnak's Astral Demons had jumped through.

And the moment Jace saw Valcrinox's forces atop the towers begin to pour the steaming-hot cauldrons of whatever foul liquid they planned to use as they brought ranged weaponry in the form of spikes and spines launching from their hides and covered with Psykinetic power—he detonated the landmines.

All eight hundred that Shhiv was able to make in the weird time-space distortion detonated atop the towers, absolutely shredding the sixteen Astral Demons. They were studded with the Dark Matter, Void, and Psykinetic-infused knives that had launched out of the mines, and as Jace landed in the stone bowl where Souls trickled down into, Yroshnak glanced at him with a confused expression.

"What hit them?"

Jace let the Dark Matter and Void fade from the blades embedded in the mines. "Just that," he said as he reached into the TPSB and pulled out the new, upgraded Retribution Auto-Carbine. He placed the shoulder slot around his pauldron and held onto the handle along the exterior with his right hand, gripping the trigger mount with his left. "Let's go."

They moved as a unit, Yroshnak's demons staying within the visible aura of Jace's Hero's Arena and therefore gaining all of the benefits of his numerous ally-empowering Specializations. In the distance, atop a tower, he could see another four Astral Demons, who were some mix between refined and monstrous, condensing large spheres of Psykinetic force and launching them.

Yroshnak stepped forward and swung his axe like a baseball bat, slicing clean through one Talent as it burst into crackling energy that pierced and singed him. *Herald's Healing*, Jace thought as he saw the white glow surround the Demon Lord and cure his wounds. Then, he aimed the viewfinder at the first of the Astral Demons on the tower and squeezed the trigger.

An enormous beam of light shot out—gold and green flames twisting around the solid beam—as he moved the blast across the four demons, cutting them clean in two as they exploded with gold and green fire.

Oh, wow, Shhiv and Xero outdid themselves, Ollie stated.

Jace felt the weapon begin to warm up in his grip, and he let the trigger go as the Carbine cooled. "That was badass," he said with glee.

Yroshnak, still facing forward, waved the demons ahead. "Let us advance!"

As they continued running, Jace received the Essence from the demons he had shot off their perches. *Another 20,000. We are at 110,000 and we only needed 90,000 to max out. We should consider stopping and leveling up.*

We don't have a time constraint, Jace thought. *Let's get to the fortress, and we can hole up outside and I can level up and recover energy. Task the drone to scout.*

Roger!

Jace was blasted from his left and rolled with the blow. Coming up with the Carbine raised, he unleashed the beam of blistering fury at an Astral Demon that had hidden in the grass and shot a lance of Psykinetic energy at him. The same demon manifested a barrier that deflected the laser, and Jace released the trigger as he drew his sword with his left hand. "Yroshnak, got a few to lend here?"

The demons accompanying the former ruler of Layer 8 ran over to Jace and took up a defensive position in front of him—wielding shields and spears that bristled with Psykinetic power. Another one next to Jace raised their clawed hands, and a sphere of energy manifested in their grip and surged forward to slam into the barrier. Jace followed up with a laser blast directly into the demon's shield, and it cracked under the combined assault as the sphere and laser both hit the demon and destroyed them.

Ollie, keep an Essence tally, and tell me at the end.

Okay, will do!

Jace sheathed his sword, and the group continued moving. From tower to tower, bunker to bunker, the only difference in their strategy was that for the bunkers, Jace set the Carbine down, pulled out blade grenades, and ran forward with his Crusader's Bastion protecting him from the hail of Psykinetic powers. Once he got close enough, he activated and tossed the items inside—the loud bang and dozens of pings of blade off stone followed by the oozing, white Essence that surged out of the small apertures to him were all Jace needed to see to know that he had killed the demons inside.

"Keep on moving!" Yroshnak shouted as he led the charge further and further into Layer 10. Energy stores began depleting, however, as some of the Astral Demons had their Talents disrupted and broken by the assault of Valcrinox's forces. But they were well-trained, and the ones who had low energy fell to the rear while others went up front—keeping a balance of defensive Talents to protect the group and offensive Psykinetic bolts, spheres, and beams that would shoot out at the foes on their fortifications.

This is kind of a pathetic defense, Ollie commented. *Technology really does make things unfair.*

Yeah, Jace thought back as he squeezed the trigger again and lasered through another four demons on a tower. *This is a bit too easy.*

<u>*Oh, now you have jinxed it.*</u>

Valcrinox watched the Astral System screen intently. A top-down view of Layer 10, where he could see every single entity moving as small dots. His forces were being destroyed before they could retreat to the next set of fortifications to join others stationed there. Bleeding their enemies dry was not working.

"Time for plan B," Valcrinox said aloud. "Everyone, fall back. We will activate the Citadel."

He watched as the command went out across his localized network, and the demons retreated—some were picked off by ranged attacks, but he saw as the dots all got closer to the fortification, and then entered.

Time to use my secret weapon, Valcrinox thought as he pulled up another Astral System screen. A last resort, given to the ruler of Layer 10 by The Ancients, to protect the entrance to the Nethershift from an overwhelming force that may seek to claim or destroy the hard work that The Ancients had accomplished.

A large overlay appeared in front of him, and he took the phantasmal control stick in his hands. An image of the Layer, from the top of the citadel, appeared with targeting reticles. He could see Wraith, finally, having a firsthand visual of the hero. They disgusted Valcrinox, and he thumbed the trigger.

Jace saw the huge, black citadel in the distance. Something moved at the top, and then began to shift sideways, the structure unfolding to reveal some hidden compartment. That, combined with all of the demons having fled back to the fortress and abandoning the defenses, let Jace know all that he needed to about what was coming.

"Everyone! To me!"

The demons all moved to him, and Yroshnak looked at him. "What is coming?"

Void Shield (Rank 6) [Wall], Jace thought as he manifested the white-grey wall of Void—but green flames licked all along it. Additionally, he swapped to the (Aegis) Infusion and braced the shield in front of him. "Get behind me!" he shouted.

A dot appeared at the hidden aperture of the fortress in the distance. A pale yellow dot that flickered with orange and grew in size.

Kaboom!

A huge shockwave emanated from the now fully revealed defensive fortification, some massive, Rune-covered cannon. Jace braced himself and sucked in a deep breath as everything went quiet for a split-second before the Void Shield was impacted by the yellow-orange ray of raw Psykinetic power.

He saw his energy drain to zero from Void Shield holding off the strike, and it popped. The Emergency Battery was instantly drawn upon to fill him back to the top on energy, but the beam continued its path and hit his Crusader's Bastion, fracturing and splintering off to the sides as he held firm. But the golden flames began to flicker, and the hardlight construct protecting them all began to shatter and chip away.

Ollie's voice emanated from the armor, *Quick! Place your limbs on Wraith and give him your energy! He has a {Skill} that lets you do that!*

Jace felt dozens of hands on him as energy poured into him, and the hardlight shield regained its hardness and even expanded a little in size. Thanks to his (Siphoning) Skill Evolution acquired so long ago for his Energy Cost Reduction Skill, they were able to hold and outlast the laser.

It faded away, and Jace felt his arms shaking as he let out the held-in breath in an explosive sigh of relief. Raising the laser Carbine on his shoulder, he took aim at the defensive installment and shot. The laser, intertwined with gold flames of his Psykinetic power and the green flames of retextured Void, slammed into the weapon, and it flickered before fading away—disintegrated by Void and annihilated utterly.

"Not bad," Yroshnak said as he pulled his hand off of Jace's upper back. "You good?"

Jace nodded. "I'm . . . Just give me a minute to catch my breath."

"We get to the building, hold them in the doors, and you can recover then." Yroshnak moved forward, and his demons followed, with Jace close behind but letting them take the lead. He was stumbling just a bit but quickly regained his footing as he caught his breath again.

They reached the doors of the structure, and the Astral Demons set up a perimeter, going down either side of the building to find that it met the edges of the Layer, and going up, it also met the roof of the space. Yroshnak spoke softly as Jace jogged up, "There is but one entrance. This door. We can try to break it down. But your ability to destroy matter is our best way to get in."

Jace nodded and squatted down. "Let me rest, level up, and we go in."

"We cannot take too long," Yroshnak replied. "The Vault is inside of that citadel, and if it resets, Valcrinox can send a minion in and acquire something to turn the tides."

Jace looked up at the giant turret that hung far above them. "I thought demons could not use technology?"

“Not technology,” Yroshnak replied. “Just a tube for focusing Psykinetic energy. All the ambient energy in the Layer. Do you hear the screams anymore?”

Jace closed his eyes and focused on his sense of hearing, and to his surprise, Yroshnak was right—there were no screams of horror. “Nope.”

“That blast took all of it. I am surprised we survived. That energy transfer . . . Skill, is handy.”

Jace frowned under the helmet. “Yeah, well, I also have something else pretty neat.” He reached into the TPSB and pulled out his (Restful) Wildercloth Tent and began setting it up along the side of the building.

“We do not have that long,” Yroshnak said.

Jace set the tent up and pointed at it. “One hour out here, a full night’s rest in there.”

Yroshnak’s mouth split to reveal a toothy grin. “Oh . . . then by all means, we can hold them for an hour at the single door if they try to get out.”

Jace crawled into the tent and used the small strings and clips to get it sealed up. Laying back, he put all of his nonessential Gear into the TPSB. “Ollie.”

Hmm?

“Can you stay merged and just monitor things outside with the drone?”

Sure, can do.

“And record a message for me.”

Chapter Fifty

The Last Level-Up

Shhiv was just about to go to bed when she received a message through The Cosmic System. A video message. As she opened it up, her heart skipped a beat because she saw her husband, laying back and smiling without his helmet.

"Hey, Shhiv. I'm just outside the last Demon Lord's . . . castle? Fort? Something like that. This is the last hurdle before the end." He sighed, and a look of frustration crossed his face. "I wish I could hug you and give you a kiss before doing what I'm about to do. I am going to survive. I will survive for you. But if something—" He grimaced and shook his head. "No. I'm not even going to mention it because it won't happen. Just . . . I love you, Shhiv. So much. I started this journey, the whole Aspirant-to-Ascendant path, to try and get Chroma back. Surviving for her. To fix my mistakes. But now? I'm surviving for you."

Shhiv felt a tension in her chest. A conflicted feeling. She wanted to help, to do something to assist him. But she couldn't do a single damned thing. Except send back a message. She set her cosmopanel up and activated the camera as she sat down. "Jace . . . You are going to beat the heck out of that Demon Lord and do what you need to. I'll be here, waiting, when you get back. I love you so much. You're my everything." She could feel herself tearing up, and wiped the corner of her eyes. "Just come back to me."

She got up, stopped the recording, and sent it to her beloved. "Josie?" she asked quietly.

Her Wayfinder popped into existence next to her. "Yes?" she asked softly.

"Can you do something to help me fall asleep? I don't think I'll be able to do it while thinking about what Jace is facing now."

"Alright. Go to bed."

Shhiv went to the water cube and stripped down, entering the room that was designed to look like the Starlit Sea—the black emptiness speckled with glimmering starlight. She went over to the side of the room that had a bit more gravity, which functioned as a sort of means to keep them from floating around too much during sleep. "Thanks, Josie." *And be careful, Jace.*

Jace got up, cracked open some survival meals from his TPSB, and scarfed down the food along with plenty of water. He watched Shhiv's message as he ate and felt a deep warmth settle in his chest. *I'll get back to you*, he thought as he finished his meal and washed it all down. "Ollie, time for the last level-ups."

Yup! I did some digging, it looks like most of it will be compressing and condensing down existing Talents and Specializations, just like it did with Hero's Arena, minus Templar's Smite because of its multiple modes. Oh, and our grand total Essence right now is 150,000. So you will have a lot left over.

Okay then. Let's do it. And transfer the Essence using the voidlight tether up to Xero. He can distribute it to whoever needs it most.

[You have leveled up!]
[You have chosen Specialization of Existing Talent!]
[Talent Name: Valiant Crusader's Might.]
[Specialization Name: Perfected.]

[Effect: Combines and amplifies all other Specializations of the linked Talent.]
[All Specializations being combined:]
[Vengeful—The user may injure themselves to deliver a Psykinetic-empowered strike.]
[Burning—The user's offensive capabilities leave a lingering flame of Psykinetic energy that continues to harm those struck.]
[Poised—The user's offensive capabilities will naturally find their way around defenses.]
[Unstoppable—The user's offensive capabilities cannot be negated or nullified. Blocking, Parrying, or other defensive maneuvers may still apply.]
[Bracing—The user's attacks and Psykinetics have increased capability to force movement.]
[Voidbound—Incorporates the user's {Void Blade} at maximum {Rank} and with all {Skill Evolutions} applied.]
[Lightbound—The user's attacks and Psykinetics strike fear into Astral Demons who witness the effect or are affected.]
[Rallying—While active, the user's strikes inspires those designated as allies who can see the user, causing their weapons and Talents to strike with more force.]
[Inspiriting—The linked Talent also empowers all those labeled as allies within line of sight.]
[Talent Name: Crusader's Bastion.]
[Specialization Name: Perfected.]
[Effect: Combines and amplifies all other Specializations of the linked Talent.]
[All Specializations being combined:]
[Retaliating—When blocking a Psykinetic Talent, the user retaliates with a spike of Psykinetic energy.]
[Reinforcing—The user gains a defensive boost while Crusader's Bastion is active.]
[Grounding—When active, the user is resistant to forced movement.]
[Redoubt—The user's defensive boost from (Reinforcing) is amplified even further if the user does not move outside of a ten-foot radius upon engaging in combat. Resets upon moving.]

[Spiked—The linked Talent functions as a weapon. Obtains all offensive Talent benefits.]
[Resonating—The linked Talent causes a temporary stunning effect to apply to those who strike the shield.]
[Glorious—The user's (Retaliating) Infusion deals increased damage.]
[Hallowed—While active, the user's presence inspires those designated as allies who can see the user, increasing their defensive qualities.]
[Aegis—The user's linked Talent can become a shield that completely covers a full one-hundred-eighty-degree angle in a chosen direction.]
[Talent Name: Indomitable Will.]
[Specialization Name: Perfected.]
[Effect: Combines and amplifies all other Specializations of the linked Talent.]
[All Specializations being combined:]
[Zealous—The user's depth of emotion can affect others around them, instilling them with a deeper connection to their emotion source.]
[Intimidating—The user's depth of emotion fills them with authority, causing their social interactions with lesser-Potency figures to have more favorable outcomes.]
[Inviolable—For the purpose of this Talent's baseline effect of mental and emotional resistance, treat the user's depth of emotion as maximum at all times.]
[Enduring—The user will not pass out due to exhaustion from depleting energy.]
[Ameliorating—The user cannot be incapacitated by mental or emotional effects.]
[Dark Matter Binding—Warning: Not linked to Talent by default, must be manually activated alongside Talent. Incorporates the user's {Dark Matter Mending} at maximum {Rank} and with all {Skill Evolutions} applied.]
[Galvanizing—When the user resists or shakes off a mental or emotional effect, all those designated as allies who can see the user become immune to the same effect. This lasts for up to a single cycle.]

[Spiteful—When the user resists or shakes off a mental or emotional effect, they have a reduced chance to suffer an effect of a similar nature from the individual who afflicted them.]
[Ensnaring—When the user resists a mental or emotional effect of Psykinetics, the creature who attempted the affliction is temporarily stunned.]
[Talent Name: Holy Hunt.]
[Specialization Name: Perfected.]
[Effect: Combines and amplifies all other Specializations of the linked Talent.]
[All Specializations being combined:]
[Marked—When the linked Talent is used on a target that can suffer harm or injury, the user inflicts additional injury.]
[Bursting—When the Marked target suffers harm or injury, that additional injury is afflicted to those surrounding them.]
[Authoritative—When the linked Talent is used on a target, they deal reduced damage to the user.]
[Provoking—When the target of the linked Talent sees the user, they are compelled to attack the user.]
[Inciting—The user gains a movement speed boost when moving toward their target.]
[Branding—Incorporates the user's {Void Brand} at maximum {Rank}, applying the {Skill} to the marked target.]
[Invigorating—When the user strikes a marked target with the linked Talent, they restore a small amount of their health and mend injuries.]
[Bolstering—The user gains an increased defensive boost against the designated target of the linked Talent.]
[Coordinating—When those designated as allies strike the target of Holy Hunt, the target suffers additional harm.]
[Talent Name: Purifying Edge.]
[Specialization Name: Perfected.]
[Effect: Combines and amplifies all other Specializations of the linked Talent.]
[All Specializations being combined:]
[Cleansing—In addition to defensive Talents, the user's weapon temporarily sunders support Talents, shutting them off.]

[Searing—When the linked Talent is used on a target, they take damage from your Psykinetics.]
[Purging—When the linked Talent is used on a target, it temporarily sunders offensive Talents, shutting them off.]
[Sanctifying—When a Talent is shut off, reactivating it costs double the energy unless five seconds pass in the interim.]
[Terminating—In addition to defensive Talents, the user's weapon temporarily sunders offensive Talents, shutting them off.]
[Judging—When the linked Talent is used on a target, they take additional damage equal to the number of unjudged Souls they have.]
[Revealing—When the linked Talent is used on a target, any sundered Talents that cause a glamour, illusion, or similar effect are disabled until a cycle passes.]
[Condensing—When the linked Talent is used on a target, the user may take on afflictions and harm suffered by allies within line of sight.]
[Silencing—When the linked Talent is used on a target, they are prevented from communicating for ten seconds—including accessing the Astral System's interface.]
[Talent Name: Justice's Rebuke.]
[Specialization Name: Perfected.]
[Effect: Combines and amplifies all other Specializations of the linked Talent.]
[All Specializations being combined:]
[Flaming—When the linked Talent is activated, the additional damage inflicted is in the form of a damage-over-time effect. Stacks with (Burning) from Valiant Crusader's Might, (Lingering) from Templar's Smite, and (Inferno) from Templar's Smite.]
[Bashing—When the linked Talent is activated, the user's weapons and Talents gain the ability to blow foes back with concussive force.]
[Holy—When the linked Talent is activated, the user's weapons and Talents deal additional damage in the form of searing radiance.]
[Plasmas—When the linked Talent is activated, the user's weapons and Talents deal additional damage in the form of blasting heat.]
[Energizing—When the linked Talent is activated, the user's weapons and Talents restore a small amount of energy.]

[Languishing—When the linked Talent is activated, the user's weapons and Talents cause the target to feel a malaise that reduces their reaction time.]
[Deflecting—The linked Talent may now be activated in response to being attacked, instead of when they are harmed, at a lower efficacy.]
[Guarding—When an ally within line of sight is injured, the user may activate the linked Talent at lowered efficacy.]
[Castigating—When the linked Talent is activated, the user's weapons and Talents deal additional damage in the form of sonic waves.]
[Talent Name: Revealing Light.]
[Specialization Name: Perfected.]
[Effect: Combines and amplifies all other Specializations of the linked Talent.]
[All Specializations being combined:]
[Burdening—Those affected by Revealing Light move slower as heavy light drags upon them.]
[Limning—The Revealing Light effect lasts for an entire cycle.]
[Fracturing—The linked Talent reduces a foe's defenses.]
[Potent—The linked Talent temporarily blinds foes that rely on sight.]
[Perilous—The linked Talent ignites a searing damage-over-time effect on affected targets.]
[Linking—Enables all other Talents to apply Revealing Light.]
[Redirecting—Those affected by the linked Talent are drawn to the user.]
[Identifying—The linked Talent reveals weaknesses of those affected.]
[Shrouding—The (Potent) Infusion applies a vision-degrading effect that slowly lessens in severity after the initial blindness ends.]
[You have chosen Specialization of Existing Talent!]
[Talent Name: Final Form.]
[Specialization Name: Hero's Ultimatum.]
[Effect: The user's next strike deactivates Final Form and drains all available energy to cause devastating harm.]
[You have chosen Specialization of Existing Talent!]
[Talent Name: Final Form.]
[Specialization Name: Hero's Salvation.]

[Effect: Upon activating the linked Talent, the user's energy fills completely, and they are cured of all wounds.]

Name: Jace Seren (Potency 10)
Emotion [Class Level]: Valiant [Hero 100]
Talent [Specialization]: Astral Adaptation, Astral Translation, Valiant Crusader's Might (Perfected), Crusader's Bastion (Perfected), Hero's Arena (Perfected), Indomitable Will (Perfected), Templar's Smite [Spear] [Blast] [Lingering] [Challenging] [Inferno] [Cosmic] [Gaze] [Blinding] [Rooting], Holy Hunt (Perfected), Purifying Edge (Perfected), Justice's Rebuke (Perfected), Revealing Light (Perfected), Final Form (Hero's Ultimatum, Hero's Salvation), Herald's Healing
Essence: 0
Infusions: None
Gear: <TPSB>, (Convergent Edge / Ancient Reckoning) Divine Revenge, (Explorer's Embrace / Beacon) Hero's Plate, (Prosthetic Savant) Astral Appendages, (Draconic Sovereign) Arbiter's Sight, (Anathema) Astral Sleeve, (Reinforced) Psycrystal Lattice, (Pinnacle) NICIF-EP, (Restoring) Flame of Valor, Retribution Auto-Carbine

Jace sat up, got his helmet back on, and exited the tent. Yroshnak was standing there, expectantly, as his demons stood around on guard and facing the doorway leading to the citadel in a half-circle formation. "Ah, good, you're finally awake."

Jace nodded. "Yeah. Level 100 and ready to kill this Demon Lord."

Yroshnak nodded. "More mines and blade grenades?"

"I've got a lot of them left. The grenades, I mean." Jace began pulling them out, but as he walked to the door, they sparked and then melted in his hands—becoming slag. "The fuck?"

Must be some type of effect of the fortress, Ollie said in his mind. *Some type of technology-disabling barrier. That means your TPSB is going to be off-limits, along with everything in it.*

What about the NICIF?

[We'll be good, boss!]
[Technically we are not technology alone thanks to all The Cosmic System integration and other stuff.]
[Those Potency-up, painful moments?]
[Yeah, sorry, that was us a bit—we were changing and adapting as well.]
[All of your body—prosthetics and us included—are fully Astral Verge adapted!]

Jace sighed with relief and looked to Yroshnak before walking over to join the Demon Lord. "No technology inside." He reached into his TPSB—now being further away, it worked just fine—and pulled out throwing knives that he put on a bandolier that he wrapped around his chest.

"Then we do this the demon way. The way it has always been done." Yroshnak brandished his axe and gestured to the door. "Will you do the honors?"

Jace smiled and raised his hand. "Here we go. Time to secure the Astral Verge."

Chapter Fifty-One

Breaching the Citadel

Jace activated Void Beam at (Rank 3) with [Limited Range] applied. The white-grey beam of Void surged out, retextured to others' vision with the green flames, as a hole was cut clean through the doorway.

Yroshnak's demons rushed in, and Jace heard the sounds of combat pick up. The Demon Lord himself stood outside and held a hand up for Jace to wait. "We both are valuable," he said with grim resolve. "They are disposable."

Jace knew the truth of the statement, but it still felt antithetical to him to just wait there for others to fight. He felt that flaring, golden surge in his chest as his Emotion Source ignited and pushed him to acts worthy of Valiance, of being a heroic figure. Jace had his sword out, and the blade ignited with even brighter gold, green, and crimson that flowed and flickered around each other. *Crusader's Bastion*, he thought as he manifested the shield onto his forearm at its tower-shield size to allow him mobility and excellent defenses. The spikes on the front flickered and crackled with golden sparks.

All around him, a storm of gold and green flames exploded to life as Hero's Arena reached its maximum output, the tendrils of crimson flickers from the innate Aura of Wrath surging around him. "I'm not waiting," Jace said, and despite Yroshnak's protestation, he went into the hole and was immediately surrounded by sounds of combat.

Astral Demons fighting other demons in close quarters—spikes and spines stabbing into each other, flickering flashes of Psykinetics arcing across the space with riotous reports. Screams of combat and guttural growls of exertion permeated the air, and Jace saw that the Astral Demons that were fighting on his side looked like they were losing due to sheer numbers.

However, the tides began to turn the second Jace walked in, as his Hero's Aura surged to fill out the space; Astral Demons arrayed against him, Valcrinox's forces, becoming burned and seared by his multiple damage-over-time effects that stacked upon each other. The Astral Demons on Jace's side were all suffused with his Psykinetic power as golden flames wreathed their weapons as they hacked into Valcrinox's forces with renewed vigor, their blows leaving yet more flames that spread across their foes.

A pulse came from behind Jace, and he turned as he raised his shield to block the incoming attack. But it never came. Instead, a peal like a loud bell sounded and filled the entire room with vibrations that shook his teeth.

Some type of mental effect, Ollie stated with confidence. *Too bad for them, you are kitted out against that.*

Jace saw some of the surrounding demons on his side momentarily succumb to the effect, starting to stagger over, but thanks to his Indomitable Will's (Galvanizing) Infusion, thanks to Jace resisting it, his allies also became immune, and they renewed their assault.

Turning, Jace saw a squad of Astral Demons at the farthest end of the room standing in front of another massive set of double doors. They launched spears and bolts of Psykinetic energy that would have slammed into the Astral Demons on Jace's side. But he quickly used Void Step in rapid succession, getting in the way of each strike and blocking the blow with his shield. He followed that up with another Void Step and a Raging Cleave–empowered strike as he sliced clean through the four demons comprising the ranged unit.

Two of them managed to duck the blow while two were cut in half but began to mend—swapping to melee weapons. Jace used his tower shield to cover his left side and harried the two on his right with constant swings and chops that kept them on the back foot.

I need to reserve my energy for Valcrinox, he thought.

Tibalt was on the outside edge of the room, concealed within one of the nooks in the wall. He could see the chaos unfolding before him, and his heart quivered in anticipation of his goals coming to fruition. He just had to wait, watch, and then strike at Wraith's weakest.

The demons that fought on Valcrinox's side had been winning until Wraith entered, and Tibalt had to scrabble to another alcove to hide in as the glowing, golden aura filled with crackling flames almost reached him. Activating a Talent that he had acquired specifically to hide, Tibalt kept quiet, watching and calculating.

Wraith fought against four demons at once and was holding his own just fine against them. He suffered occasional injuries, but Tibalt saw that the weapons either bounced off of him, or when they did cut deep and then pull back to reveal a goopy, black liquid, the black liquid would vanish from sight, and the wounds would seal over with a gout of green flame.

He planned out his build, Tibalt thought as he kept watching. *A blend of self-empowering, survival, defensive, and offensive Talents. I must wait until the last possible moment.* He brushed his hand against the weapon he had found in Valcrinox's armory—a powerful firearm that he could use thanks to being a Dreamer Demon. A firearm that, according to his Astral System readout, was a Relic earned by a prior Bearer of the Mantle of Burden who tried to defeat the Demon Lord of Madness.

A weapon that could, perhaps, kill Wraith. But only if the opportune moment arose. And Tibalt needed Wraith to kill Valcrinox first.

Another figure entering caught his attention, and he saw a massive hulking monster of a man—an Astral Demon, for sure, but a seemingly perfectly blend of monstrous and refined evolution paths. For some reason, Tibalt felt anger toward him, and his hand itched to grip the pistol and draw it.

That Astral Demon surged with a bloody red aura and let out a bellowing war cry. The goopy red aura fell around all of the Astral Demons that were fighting on his side, and he joined the fray on the opposite side of the room from Tibalt.

Wraith, however, did not seem affected. *Must be some type of empower—*

Tibalt's thoughts were cut off as a massive golden-and-green explosion shook the center of the room. When it cleared, Wraith stood, alone, at the doors to Valcrinox. He shouted out, "Yroshnak! Numbers?"

"Support!"

Tibalt watched as Wraith blinked out of existence and reappeared in the middle of the fray. Then, he watched with fascination as Wraith began pointing with his sword at this Yroshnak's demons, and they were surrounded with a white light that mended them.

We can't have healing, now. Not like that. Antithetical Hypocrisy, Tibalt thought as he activated a Talent that would disable another Talent he saw being used for a minute.

Wraith shouted in frustration, "I can't heal anymore!"

Tibalt cackled and kept watching, identifying every single Talent that Wraith was using and quietly firing off his Talent to shut them down, one at a time.

<u>*Another one down*</u>, Ollie said with worry entering his voice. <u>*A demon in here is disabling your Talents for one-minute intervals.*</u>

Can they get to my Skills? Jace asked.

Nope. Looks like those are too ingrained into you for their Talent.

Jace nodded and swapped his now-gone Crusader's Bulwark for his old friend, the Dark Matter Shield at (Rank 2). The familiar purple barrier manifested on his arm, and he also activated Dark Matter Blade at its maximum rank with [Rending] applied. Moving back into the fray, he began hacking and cutting away at the Astral Demons.

He suffered wounds and watched as his health display continued to slowly drop down before being offset by the NICIF and his (Dark Matter Binding), but his energy was falling at the same rate in compensation to fuel the Infusion. The fight was going decently, as their side had lost as many as they had killed.

But there were still dozens of Valcrinox's demons to go. Jace thought to Ollie, *Regress Shattered Limits.*

Coming up!

Wrath's Embrace, Jace thought as the billowing crimson sparks surged around him as lightning stormed at its maximum (Rank). He let out a scream of utter rage as the flames of gold billowed even higher and with more intensity before he launched himself across the room—a crimson blur as he cut into the demons facing off against Yroshnak's forces. He did not stop to kill one at a time; instead, he scored a hit against each with the edge of his blade, inflicting them with the slowing effect of Dark Matter Blade, and the micro-singularities, and the [Rending] bleed.

His headlong rush took him behind the opposing group, and he identified one of the demons at the center of the group. *Holy Hunt,* he thought, focusing on them as they became surrounded with the limning golden glow. Jace then launched Dark Matter Dart (Rank 4) [Exploding] into the cluster—but with three of the nine focused on that marked target.

The darts sank and drilled into their targets before detonating—spreading the golden flames and triggering the (Bursting) Infusion on Holy Hunt with each shockwave, causing another burst of the golden radiance that scoured across the demons' now-dwindling numbers.

But Jace saw his energy was still slowly slipping down, and demons turned to rush him—because to them, he had no weapon or shield. Jace grinned under the helmet as he easily dispatched the trio that rushed to him; one stabbed clean through the head, another whose head he bashed in with the leading edge of the shield, and a third that he sliced through as he ripped the blade out of the one he had stabbed.

The fight dragged on, as Valcrinox's forces were quite hardy. Jace kept fighting, healing, and supporting while trying to keep a level eye on his energy, never letting it dip below thirty percent. *No Emergency Battery*, he thought. *Final Form can fix me up when I need it, but that's once a day. How long does it last?*

A minute.

Jace let his energy dip down to twenty percent, and by the time the combat had concluded, only ten of Yroshnak's starting forty demons were left alive. All were wounded and breathing heavily . . . but they did it. Valcrinox's forces had been defeated. Yroshnak let out a victory shout, and his demons followed up.

Jace walked over to him, glancing at the next set of double doors that led to the ruler of the Layer. "Think we can wait to recover and then rush him?"

"I would say yes, but I do not know the capabilities of this citadel. We could retreat outsid—" Yroshnak was cut off as a loud voice bellowed out. He growled, "Valcrinox," as the voice overlapped his own.

"Well done. You've done me a favor, killing off my minions. Less to deal with." There was a mad cackle that reverberated. "The longer you stay here, the stronger my control grows. Even you, Yroshnak, will succumb eventually. Instead, I challenge you! Face me!"

Yroshnak frowned and looked to Jace. "He is correct; the longer we stay here, the more likely we are to be thralled by him. We could retreat to Layer

9 to rest and recuperate . . . or." He put a hand on Jace, and Jace felt the warmth of energy transfer to him. "We can do this."

The other Astral Demons came over and transferred energy to Jace, filling him to full. Yroshnak pulled his hand away and looked exhausted. All of his troops did as well. "Go and end this, Wraith. Fulfill the Mantle of Burden's Mission."

Jace took the outstretched arm and gave him a firm handshake. "I will." He turned to face the door and waited out the timer on his last few locked-out Talents. When they had returned to him, he reactivated them all—Crusader's Bastion, Hero's Arena, Holy Hunt with a target of Valcrinox, and Purifying Edge.

Here we go, Ollie said. *We should activate Quinn's Stratagems since they last so long.*

Right. Okay . . . I'm feeling like I'm in over my head.

With the command phrase thought, Quinn's Skills all activated in rapid succession, each buff giving a quick description before the readout compressed down. A message from Quinn also popped up after the readouts finished.

[Mobility—Stratagem-marked allies have their movement speed doubled.]
[Obliteration—Stratagem-marked allies increase outgoing damage by x2.]
[Bulwark—Stratagem-marked allies reduce incoming damage by 50%.]
[Grounded—Stratagem-marked allies cannot be moved against their will.]
[Resolved—Stratagem-marked allies cannot be subjected to mind-altering, -reading, or -influencing effects.]
[Chaos Strike—Stratagem-marked allies' damage is altered to that of the target's least-resistant variety.]
[Shattered Views—Stratagem-marked allies are shrouded by illusory duplicates that partially overlap with their real body.]

[Slip Away—Stratagem-marked allies are incredibly difficult to detect.]
[Skip—Stratagem-marked allies are able to teleport a single time within the time limit, with a maximum distance of 100 feet.]
[Time Lock—Stratagem-marked allies may lock themselves into a temporary stasis, making themself invulnerable but unable to move or be interacted with.]
[Hey. It's go-time if you're seeing this. I pre-loaded every Skill into this, and with the weird Layer dilation, it all should last five minutes. Good thing I dumped so many Ranks into Stratagem! Here are your orders to trigger Grand Tactics and Tactician's Orders—kill Valcrinox. Coordinator's Critical Gaze and Warning System will activate once you get line of sight, if you don't already have it.]
[We have been through a lot. Thank you for forgiving me all that time ago back on Velenar Prime. Go kick some ass, and make sure you come back to give me the Tech Support role Xera used to have! If you die, I'm sending Greg to go yank you out of whatever pit of hell you fell into!]

Jace chuckled a little bit at the last part of her message as he put a foot to the door and pushed it open. The ominous stone entrance swept inward, and he walked forward to face off against the Demon Lord of Madness.

Chapter Fifty-Two

Unburdened

Jace entered the enormous chamber to see nothing but a pale, yellow, almost pastel-like barrier in front of him. The golden line of Holy Hunt led right into the barrier. He frowned as he walked up and tapped it with Purifying Edge on his blade, dismissing the Talent and revealing the room as a whole.

The stone groove carrying Souls ran underneath a throne with a sickly yellow hue that seemed to leech into the surrounding environment and made Jace feel queasy just because of the horrible color alone. The walls and ceilings to either side and above were covered in old blood that was the color of rust and gave the room a scent of pungent iron.

Atop the throne, Valcrinox sat. A Demon Lord who was just a few heads taller than Jace. He looked shockingly humanoid and had armor on most of his body, save for his chest, which pulsated with a glimmering, silvery crystal of a Relic from a Vault. The head was naught but gnashing teeth and an odd purple film that covered where the eyes would be.

"Wraith," the voice said. "Welcome to your death."

Jace didn't exchange words. He had a Mission to complete, and he wanted to finish it. *Void Beam (Rank 3) [Limited Range]*, he thought as he unleashed the blast of grey-white energy infused with the green retextured flames. The beam flashed forward but sputtered out before it got even a third of the way to the throne.

"Like this? My throne?" Valcrinox rapped his knuckles on the arm rest. "A Relic that completely shuts down Psykinetics."

Ollie, Jace thought. *Turn off the Void retexture if we can.*

I cannot do that, Ollie replied with a little bit of anxiety. *We need to get him away from his throne to hit him with Talents.*

Jace raised his hand, and Valcrinox let out a barking laugh. But Jace used a Skill, one he had used to great effect when he first fought for his life against a Black Hole Conclave Signer who had taken his arm. *Dark Matter Dart (Rank 4) [Exploding].* The small purple darts flickered forward—the golden Psykinetic power fading from them as Valcrinox kept laughing.

But the laugh cut off as the darts drilled into him and exploded with the shockwaves of Dark Matter—like a grenade going off inside of a person's body. Valcrinox erupted only to pull himself back together.

Void Step, Jace thought as he got up to Valcrinox and cut down with his sword. All of his Talents were suppressed, but the blistering light of deep purple from Dark Matter Blade still covered the weapon along with the [Rending] Skill Evolution. He carved a deep gash into Valcrinox's still-reforming torso.

The Astral Demon Lord let out a scream of rage, and Jace felt pressure trying to force him to be moved—but he stood still thanks to Quinn's Skills and continued to hack into Valcrinox's body over and over again, the Demon Lord screaming out in pain.

But then those screams turned to laughter, and Jace took a step back as he wrapped himself in a Dark Matter Shield (Rank 3), expecting some assault.

"Impressive," Valcrinox said from all around him as the throne in front of Jace and the partially reforming demon vanished. "But did you think we were really in reality?"

Jace felt the floor fall away, and he was floating in blackness as he was surrounded by dozens of duplicates of the Demon Lord of Madness, each holding a wickedly sharp weapon covered in glittering yellow sparks that let out small screams as they flickered in their grips.

Artificial construct, or a mindscape, Ollie stated.

Good thing I have one use of this—Arbiter's Anathema. He fired off the Skill, and thanks to being Potency 10, anything his Potency or lower could be countered for a whole cycle. In this case, whatever reality-warping effect he was being subjected to was instantly shut down. The blackness fell away, and Jace was standing back on the dais as Valcrinox reformed. He kept hacking down into the still-regenerating Demon Lord.

"How!" the chunks screamed out.

Jace threw his sword behind him and began grabbing Valcrinox's chunks of writhing flesh, throwing them across the room as he made sure to get all of the bits and pieces off of the throne. Then, for good measure, he activated Ruination Razor as he summoned his sword back to his grip—the weapon ignited with crimson crackling fury as he sundered the throne.

His energy drained to zero as he was flung back from the force of the explosion, going flying through the air and into the wall—embedded on one of the meat hooks. He felt the air escape him as his lungs were punctured and heard Valcrinox's scream of frustration as the chunks finished reforming to create the figure.

"What have you done?!"

Bang! Jace felt his [Danger-Sense] kick in, and he immediately used Quinn's Time Lock. A massive burning bullet bounced off of him. And he saw a Dreamer Demon standing behind Valcrinox with a very low Karma Coefficient.

Fuck! Tibalt thought as he saw the round rebound off of Wraith. He squeezed the trigger another two times, watching the rounds just ricochet off of him harmlessly.

Valcrinox turned to face him—now fully reformed and looking furious. "Give me that," he said as he tried to grab the weapon from Tibalt.

But Tibalt dodged the strike and placed the barrel under Valcrinox's chin. "Die," he growled as he pulled the trigger.

Valcrinox's head vanished in a bloody mist, but the body grabbed onto Tibalt, and the Dreamer Demon screamed out in frustration as he activated all of his offensive and defensive Talents, trying to get away from the iron, vicelike grip. "I will be Demon Emperor of the Astral Verge!" he screamed as he dropped the gun and began tearing at Valcrinox with his Psykinetic-empowered claws.

"Too bad," Valcrinox's voice said from seemingly all around. Tibalt felt himself weakening and saw his body slowly returning to its Vanguard, pre-demon form. "You are a demon, on my Layer! I control all demons who are lesser than me!"

That's what you think! Highlord's Resolve! Tibalt activated the first Talent he ever acquired as a Dreamer when he initially entered the Astral Verge—a means to insulate himself from anyone's control.

But Valcrinox just laughed and brushed away the defenses. "That might have worked if you were a pure Dreamer. Now, give me your power!"

Tibalt screamed as everything was drained from him and he was left a shallow husk, his vision going black.

Jace let the Time Lock deactivate, and he managed to free himself from the meat hook with a Soul Tether that got him a decent distance away as he hung from the ceiling. His energy was empty, and he was tired as he sucked in deep breaths. Valcrinox was reforming. *No time to waste*, he thought as he dropped down. *Final Form (Hero's Salvation)!*

Jace gasped as he was flooded with energy and his body fully regenerated. The world exploded around him with a mix of colors: the purple of his Dark Matter—fractal shapes that danced within the crimson sparkles and bleeding nebula clouds that was the home to countless golden flames that sparked and ignited to a roaring inferno. The white-grey of Void billowed out as the green flames ignited and swirled around him in a fiery vortex.

Finally, all of the various empowering Skills and Talents combined, and he brought his sword to bear as he activated Crusader's Bastion. The shield was crackling with all of the same hues before settling on a solid white, and the sword glowed with the same bright cleansing power.

Divine Revenge peeled off a bunch of his Potency, Ollie said, going into a rapid breakdown of what had happened to that weird demon. *Valcrinox sucked out the Potency from another demon—sort of like a self-healing Talent that requires sacrifice.*

The Demon Lord of Madness turned to Jace with that Relic in his hand, and he crushed it, containing the explosion within his palm before he dropped the slagged piece of metal onto the ground to leave a small molten puddle. "You destroyed my throne!"

Jace wasted no time. *Void Step [Burst]*. He warped, leaving behind a white-grey and green shockwave as he blitzed to place behind Valcrinox, slashing down into the entity's back and leaving a white brand that exploded, launching the Demon Lord forward.

He spun with the launch and came up on his feet, his hands warping and shifting along with his arms as he became more monstrous. Sharp bone scythes extended from his elbows and were covered with the crackling yellow Psykinetic power. "I will not die!" Valcrinox rushed forward.

Jace blocked the scythe that came in from his left side, catching the yellow blade as he had the NICIF reconfigure his legs and the armor to allow for the bladed protrusions of his Steelstalker Sabatons from the past and shifted the soles of his feet to that of draconic claws like he had so long ago with his Dragonclaw Devastation Legs. His lower extremities ignited with the same white power as his sword, and as he blocked the scythe coming in from the right with his sword, he kicked both legs up and stabbed them into Valcrinox's chest—causing small explosions of pure white as he staggered back—and Jace landed on his feet.

Void Beam (Rank 3) [Limited Range], Jace thought as he launched the beam to Valcrinox. But he must have had something akin to Jace's [Danger-Sense], as he dropped to his chest and dodged the beam before launching himself up at Jace. Jace caught one of the strikes from the dual upward-angle slashes with a leg blade and caught the other on his shield as he stabbed down with his sword.

Valcrinox's body warped and grew more spikes that thrummed with energy to catch Jace's weapon, and he twisted his body. Jace let the sword go, and as Valcrinox turned to launch it, Jace quickly drew one of his throwing daggers and stabbed it down into the Demon Lord's eye. *Detonate*, he thought as he triggered the Dark Energy Mine he had placed on it. Grabbing the spike on the top of the head, he yanked up to launch Valcrinox skyward, kicking against the scythe he had blocked at the same time.

Valcrinox went flying up and reoriented himself as he launched a series of arcing beams that traversed in odd directions, winding around Jace's defenses. *Aegis*, he thought as he curled himself against the floor and covered himself with the fully encompassing barrier. The yellow bolts and crackling lightning surged into the barricade before fading—and the golden flames of (Retaliating) launched back up at the Demon Lord, striking him and inflicting yet further injury.

Curling his legs under him, Jace launched himself skyward and up to Valcrinox, who had hit the ceiling and rooted himself with his legs dug into the stonework and wrapped around the meat hooks. The scythes flashed out, and Jace lost an arm—an arm infused with NICIF that was able to teleport right back to him thanks to the (Restoring) Infusion. He activated (Vengeful) from his Valiant Crusader's Might and felt his weapon thrumming with power as the white exploded with a pure golden flame.

He did not feel the pain, thanks to Final Form giving him the damage-ignoring effects of Wrath's Embrace. Swinging with a mighty blow, he slammed the blade into Valcrinox's scythe that managed to block—shattering it entirely to the surprise of the Demon Lord as the weapon sank into his chest.

The other scythe came up, and Jace barely ducked the blow as he was pushed away, floating down. Valcrinox launched himself at Jace, but Jace just used a Void Step to warp up to the ceiling and pushed off to launch himself at the enemy with his blade extended point down, stabbing into the entity and slamming both of them into the floor. Jace followed up with a vicious kick that sent the figure spinning across the room and another Void Step to get behind the demon and kick him into the ceiling yet again.

This time, he used Quinn's Skip Stratagem to get up to where Valcrinox was flying and used the force of the fling to empower his stab to cut even deeper. The Demon Lord let out a scream of rage as his whole body twisted upon the blade—snapping in unnatural directions as he grabbed both sides of Jace's head and squeezed, the scythe blade pivoting to his forearm while his other hand had regenerated.

Void Step, Jace thought—but nothing happened as he felt the pressure mounting on his skull as the armor bent inward. *Void Beam [Limited Range]*, he thought as he had the Skill fire from just above his right shoulder and through Valcrinox's wrists—severing them with nothingness. The Demon Lord looked weakened, and as Jace's Dark Energy Mine faded, sending both to the ground, the Demon Lord landed and made for the doors.

Yroshnak stood in the doorway, axe at the ready, and Valcrinox stopped before reversing course to meet the tip of Jace's sword. "I cannot, no, I will not die here!" the Demon Lord of Madness screamed. His body erupted in yellow as armor encrusted itself around him. "I'll use everything! Every bit of Universal Matter! I can get more to make my Universe!"

Jace slashed at the Demon Lord, trying to cut him off mid-speech, but his weapon hit an impossibly hard stone that deflected his swing. *Matter? Good thing I have the opposite. Void Beam (Rank 3) [Limited Range]*, he thought. The white-grey and green flame beam shot out from just over his shoulder, ruining Valcrinox's defenses.

It was enough of an opening. Jace saw the exposed torso with the crystal Relic embedded within. *Ruination Razor, (Hero's Ultimatum).* His energy drained to zero, and he let out a war cry as he stabbed forward with all of his strength. The crystal shattered, his blade sank deep, and then the world exploded in front of him, a glorious white flame that surged upward as Valcrinox screamed. All of the consolidating Universal Matter—Stardust, but brown instead of a silvery-blue—fell to the ground in piles that filled up the room. Valcrinox turned to ash, the white Essence of his defeat flooding to Jace and suffusing him with warmth.

He sat down in the pile of dirt and let out a laugh of relief. *Good job!* Ollie said with excitement. *We did it!*

Yroshnak looked around. "Well . . . thank you, Wraith." He pointed past Jace, past the dais, to a bright white hallway. "That is the Nethershift. I believe The Ancients await."

Jace nodded and, after catching his breath, stood up. He looked to where that weird demon had been, digging its way out of the dirt. He recognized the person. "Highlord Tibalt," he said with a deep disgust.

The man, a hollow shell of the former military tactician he once was, glared at Jace. "Wraith!" he tried to stand, but fell back down into the dirt. "Curse you! I was so close to ruling it all!"

Jace walked over to him and ruthlessly stabbed him through the chest with his sword. He watched as the Karma Coefficient hovering above him began revolving. Tibalt screamed out as his body exploded with a crimson, then a violet, and finally a deep red before he went limp.

[Judgement Rendered.]

Chapter Fifty-Three

Nethershift

Jace pushed himself up and off the dirt pile. He held out a hand and shook Yroshnak's. "Don't go evil," Jace said solemnly. "I'll come back and stop you if you do."

Yroshnak chuckled. "Just send a message every now and again to remind me how powerful you are—that should always keep me in check. Say, every five hundred years?"

Jace nodded. "Sounds like a deal. Until the next time we meet, then. I'll be flying a starship through to do a pick-up run, so you'll briefly see me pop by. Maybe make this please a bit less dreary, also. I heard it is supposed to be really nice."

"I will fix it up when I instill my control. Take care, Wraith, Bearer of the Mantle of Burden." Yroshnak moved to the front antechamber and began bringing his Astral Demons into the room and started to evenly distribute the Universal Matter.

Jace turned and made for the white tunnel behind the throne's dais. It was completely smooth, and he walked down it as a white light at the farthest end seemed to beckon him forward. A small groove ran along the ground below him, and he saw the light blue of Souls traveling down the same path.

Must be the light at the end of the tunnel some people who experience near-death have reported, Ollie said.

Jace nodded in agreement as the hallway continued onward. Then, it angled down—and he slipped. Activating a Dark Energy Mine just in case, he slipped down the now-circular tube of white before he ended up popping out of a wall.

The sight that greeted him was awe-inspiring and completely rendered him speechless. An enormous expanse of space that was akin to the Starlit Sea of The Cosmic System's interior workings. Instead of glittering, golden stars, he saw dozens of colors of sparkling celestial bodies. Coursing comets, meteoric masses of molten rock, hurling through the infinite expanse. Huge gas giants, slowly swirling in place—some with rings, some without. Stars, burning away in the vast emptiness of space.

Jace stood up. He was standing on a single white-stone pathway that extended from the tube in the wall behind him, and glancing back, he saw that the tunnel of white still persisted, but now angled the opposite direction, as if he could slide back down and reach Layer 10. But aside from the sides of the tunnel, nothing but more space greeted him.

The white path went forward before meeting stairs, and he walked up them—the stream of Souls climbing alongside him in a small groove along the stairs that made for a ramp. And reaching the top, he found a very humorous and completely out-of-place sight. He saw a single-story house with a small fountain out front that the Souls flowed into. Some vanished into the drain while others exploded upwards in a geyser of glittering sparkles before flying off into the vast emptiness of space.

Jace walked up to the quaint, cottage-like house and knocked on the broad, red wooden door. The cool brown tones of the building offset the coloration nicely, and he turned back to face the door as it opened.

A familiar robed figure stood there. But, until they spoke, he wasn't sure which one it was. "I . . . hi there, again." Jace let his helmet recede.

The figure pulled their hood back to reveal the human façade of the Quiet Ancient. "Wraith . . . Jace Seren . . . Bearer of the Mantle of Burden." He bowed slightly at his waist. "You have done us a great service. Please, come in."

He stepped back a few feet, and Jace followed him inside. The house was very cozy, with a small kitchen splitting off to one side with homey wooden chairs and a slightly rickety table. A small living room and lounge were on the opposite side of the entrance, and a corridor leading back seemed to go to other rooms.

The other Ancient walked out, and Jace's mind couldn't comprehend their form—just a blurring mass of pixels that spoke. "Oh, crap! Sorry, let me just—" Then, Jace's vision was able to see the Loud Ancient. "Hey there, Jace!"

The Quiet Ancient rolled his eyes and led Jace over to the small lounge, taking a seat on a couch and pointing to a recliner across from him. Jace sat down as the Loud Ancient joined them. The Quiet One spoke, "You have completed our task. As such, we will follow the accord we made. First, you will be imbued with the Astral System—permanently. Much like The Cosmic System you already bear, it will imprint on your Soul. This has no side effects aside from the fact that you will feel your Emotion Source push you to heroic acts when the need calls for it."

"I'm fine with that," Jace replied.

"And!" the Loud Ancient followed up. "We will also give you a one-time thing called a 'Binding' which will let you do the same for your spouse!"

Jace smiled. "Good. I don't think anyone except myself, my wife, and my few other Signers will be accessing the Astral Verge, ever."

"And," the Loud Ancient said, "we have the Karma Judgement Matrix ready to go!"

Jace glanced at the small window, where he could see the fountain out front. "The fountain, I'm guessing?"

"Yup!" the Loud One replied.

The Quiet One spoke softly, "The look is purely cosmetic." He waved his hand, and a cloud of pixels appeared before Jace before an object formed in his lap. A cube that was pure black. "It will automatically integrate into the object that X has been working on."

The Loud One interrupted, "Oh yeah! And that way around Soul Miasma is genius, by the way. We are definitely taking some of that knowledge with us to the Council when our turn to leave comes up!"

Jace leaned forward as he put the Karma Judgement Matrix into the TPSB. "I have a few questions, if you'll allow me to ask them."

"One more detail," the Loud Ancient said. "We have spoken to the various rulers of the afterlives. You have full permission to go and offer people the chance to return to your home Universe. They have already sorted out who is who—only those from your Universe will be able to see you, so there won't be any mix-ups."

"Indeed. Some vessel you need to take?" the Quiet One asked.

Actually, Ollie said over the armor's reverberating feature, *we can pull the object out of the TPSB and fly there from here. We will have to go back up through the Verge manually, though.*

The Loud Ancient nodded enthusiastically. "Sounds fun! Anyways, go ahead and ask your questions!"

"We aren't living in some type of simulation, are we?" Jace asked. "Just because of the whole pixelization thing."

"Oh!" the Loud One laughed. "That is sort of like a safety precaution. If you saw what we really looked like, or how our amazing powers actually manifested—your mind would melt."

"Good to know," Jace muttered. "Next question . . . what drew you to pick me as the Bearer?"

The Quiet One replied, "You cleared a Vault well before you should have been able to. Once that happened, we dug a bit deeper into your Astral Verge profile. Learning you had an innate System that rivaled the power of a Universe-controlling deity? You were our best bet in the moment. We have dozens of backups just in case . . . thankfully, we did not need them."

"Last question, for now," Jace said as he leaned forward a bit. "I am fine with being your Bearer of the Mantle of Burden if you need the job done in the future. I know I'm capable, and the faster it is dealt with, the better for everyone. But when you do leave, will your replacements keep our deal in place?"

"Of course," the Quiet Ancient replied.

I have a question, Ollie said. *Where do The Ancients come from?*

The Loud One replied rapidly, "We are a trans-reality species that comes from what we believe is the first reality ever created! We completely mastered our reality and began exploring for other ones. It's been going on for a long, long time. Think of us like a precursor civilization, but for trans-reality beings."

The Quiet One looked at his fellow, slight annoyance on his face, but turned back to Jace as his expression softened. "That is about the sum of what we can share. Suffice to say, we are benevolent. Opening the Astral Verge and pulling the Soul Miasma from your Universes was a necessary evil. To fulfill a greater good."

Jace heard Xera's voice echoing those words in the back of his mind, and he frowned. "I do not mind being your asset in the whole Mantle thing . . . but I am not under your control. Got it? I make my own decisions. I control my fate."

"As you should," the Quiet Ancient replied. He stood up and bowed at the waist. "Thank you, Jace Seren."

The Loud Ancient stood up and held out a small capsule that looked like a pill. "Swallow this for your Astral System integration and soul binding." He held up his other hand with another. "And this is for your wife."

Jace held the second one tightly and made sure he put it into a protective hip pouch instead of into the TPSB—not wanting to risk anything happening to it. Then, he grabbed the first one and swallowed it.

His vision went black, and he saw pink text on the black screens of the Astral System flickering across his darkened vision.

[Astral System Soul Bind Protocol—Initiated.]
[In Progress . . .]
[. . .]
[. . .]
[Completed!]

Jace's vision came back. "That's it? No fighting for my life against the depths of a System?"

The Ancients both laughed—the Loud One riotously as he held his sides, the Quiet One with a lighter chuckle. The Quiet One recovered and replied, "No? That is . . . well, a flaw in design, if you had to deal with that to soul-bind a System."

It is fixed now, Ollie said out loud. *That was just while it was not in its best shape.*

"Ah, that makes sense," the Loud One said as he recovered from his giggle fits. "Now . . . I think you have some afterlives to visit . . . and a sister to save."

The Ancients escorted Jace out of their house, and the Loud One waved. "Feel free to visit if you want! You are always welcome. And when our replacements arrive, we'll let you know to come and say hi and introduce yourself."

The Quiet Ancient just gave a brief nod and said, "Farewell . . . for now." Then, the door shut.

Jace turned out to face the vast emptiness. Reaching into the TPSB, he felt something big. "Umm . . . Ollie? How do I get this thing out of there?"

Oh. One second. Just turn your wrist out to your side so your forearm is facing in front of you . . . and a little bit higher of an angle.

Jace followed his instructions, and he saw a thin metal pole fly out before unfurling to become a one-person starship, just like the ones he had seen on the Penrose Sphere. But this one was covered in Runes and had a massive cylinder strapped to the top that thrummed with a vibrant blue light.

Jace went over to the vehicle and popped the cockpit, slipping in and feeling a slight crunch of paper under his rump. He pulled the sheet out and read it.

[To the love of my life,]
[If you are reading this, then you did it! And you are hopefully on the way to get your sister and everyone else you care about.]
[I wanted you to know that I love you. I look forward to being a big sister to Chroma and helping her become the best person possible (we will definitely get her into good eating and gym habits, since I know you aren't as knowledgeable about that stuff. I've been researching human children's diets, also! We'll get her spice tolerance up so that she can eat ghantos-pepper-spiced food with me while we laugh at your wimpy palette!).]
[Joking aside . . . Just make sure you always have time for me. I feel stupid writing that, but I wanted to write it.]
[Okay. Love you. See you soon.]
[Shhiv Seren.]

Jace folded the letter and put it into the same protected pouch as the pill for Shhiv's Astral System soul binding. He took the controls of the vehicle and lifted off. "Okay, Holy Hunt . . . show me where Chroma Seren is."

The golden path shot out in front of him and then arced to one of the distant planetoids. Jace slammed the takeoff button and felt the vehicle thrum to life under him as it lifted up and shot forward—carrying him to his final goal. The person he had started this whole entire Aspirant-to-Ascendant-to-Dreamer journey to save.

I'm coming to get you, sis.

Chapter Fifty-Four

Reunion

Jace pushed the starship to its maximum speed, watching the whole swirl of countless eternities in the vast openness of space expand out before him.

A voice came over the comms: the Loud Ancient. “Oh, by the way! You are technically in the Soul Realm. You shouldn’t have any threats to worry about. And the various Afterlife rulers know you are coming, so just be polite! Okay, talk to you later. Bye!” The comms went silent.

“Ollie,” Jace said as he tapped the autopilot button as the vessel shot toward the golden path to Chroma. “Pull up the comms for our Universe.”

Will do. There is a bit of a delay thanks to the voidlight tether being so far along now.

Jace heard the comms crackle for a moment before Quinn’s voice came through. “Go for Quinn.”

Jace practically beamed with excitement as he felt a flutter in his chest. “I did it! I’m on my way to get Chroma!”

Quinn’s voice practically exploded over the comms. “Holy shit! Great news! I’ll tell everyone. Shhiv’s been bugging me—” She was cut off as if someone pulled her aside, and Quinn’s voice of protestation faded away.

“You made it?!” Shhiv asked with panic and elation in her voice. “I’ve been watching your status screen here with Quinn the whole time!”

Jace laughed and felt some tears at the corners of his eyes. "I made it. Valcrinox gone. Matrix acquired . . . and I got your letter."

Shhiv's voice became sheepish, and she mumbled, "Yeah . . ."

Her voice was pulled away and Quinn came back. "Hands off, fish."

More distant, Jace heard "Don't call me a fish!" almost said in a friendly manner, but still with an underlying tone of being pissed off. "Love you, Jace! I'll see you when you're home!"

Quinn's voice came back full force, and she was all-business. "Okay. Judgement Matrix inside the TPSB you said?"

"That's right," Jace said.

"I'll let Xero know."

Xero received the message from Quinn and immediately tapped his wrist pad, opening the TPS and the connected TPSB, pulling out the strange cube-shaped device. He glanced up as he saw a pixelized cloud appear in front of him, and one of The Ancients, hooded and robed, stood there.

"Ah, you have received it in your Universe," the Quiet One said.

Xero walked over to the Soul container and began configuring the front panels. "I got your schematics and already integrated them. Now we just need to install it."

"I am here to ensure it is installed correctly," the Quiet One muttered as he walked closer. "To ensure there is no error."

"Thanks for the oversight," Xero said as he began to connect the glimmering, pixelized cube into the interface slot. He watched with glee as the black-colored cube flared a deep purple, and then a silvery white before finally settling to a cool silver steel. “Are we good now?” he asked as he made to walk to the cloning chamber. “I’d like to get my sister back.”

The Quiet Ancient walked with him. “You intend to keep your Universe sealed off, yes?”

“Oh yeah,” Xero replied as he walked into the cloning bay and began cycling through until he reached the template he had designed for Xera. “We already built up a Void and Dark Matter tower beneath our Universe’s funnel in Oblivion. Should be nice and safe.”

“My kind will call on Wraith to fulfill the Mantle of Burden in the future.”

“I’m well aware.”

The Quiet Ancient walked over to loom over the tube holding Xera’s now quickly forming clone. “This is someone special?”

Xero ran his hand along the tube. “My sister. She helped me make The Cosmic System.”

The Quiet Ancient nodded, then looked up to Xero, his eyes glowing a deep purple as he looked into Xero’s. “A good design. Good framework.” He raised his hand, and a small data pad just like Xero’s usual one appeared in his grip. “This has upgrades. Balancing changes, alterations, permutations to the algorithms for calculations.”

Xero gently took the data pad from him. “Why give us this?”

The Quiet Ancient looked down, and his face disappeared from view for a moment as he spoke softly. “Because I support your isolation stance. I . . . do not agree with much of what my species has done. I support it, because the greater good must be done and soul miasma must be purged. But I think everyone would be safer if they stuck to their own Universes. Their own realities.”

“I agree,” Xero said in response as he watched Xera’s body quickly age-up from childhood to young adulthood.

"Thank you for lending us your asset."

Xero looked up, and his visage darkened. "No. Wraith—sorry, you know his real name—Jace chose to help you and take on that Mantle of Burden all on his own. I had nothing to do with it. As far as I know, Xera didn't either." He ran his hand along the tube with his now-finished-growing-sister's body. "He'll be taking over as the System Administrator."

"I didn't think him the type."

Xero chuckled, "The Wayfinders will be running things. But always have an organic at the helm."

The Quiet Ancient laughed a short, barking laugh. "Good, you learned the AI lesson early on."

"It caused the first apocalypse on our home world. We learned quickly."

"Well . . . take care. I may contact you in the future." The Ancient vanished in a cloud of shimmering pixels.

Xero tapped his data pad and activated the intra-Universe warp network, pulling Xera's current life-support and stasis pod into the space next to her new body. Then, he grabbed the lever. A single moment of hesitation flickered across his mind before he yanked the life support lever and shut down her vital functions, instantly killing her.

Come on back, Xera. Time for our fresh start.

He saw the light-blue light flicker and vanish up, getting sucked into Oblivion, and then watched as it shot back up the voidlight tethers leading to the Soul Storage. Running into that room next to the cloning chambers, Xero saw her slightly purple-hued Soul spin in place before being sucked down into the Karma Judgement Matrix and then shooting out to the tubes in the wall.

Running back to the cloning chamber, he waited, his hearts beating rapidly. The cloned body jerked for a moment before Xera's eyes opened. She reached up and tapped the release pad, and she sat up. Her eyes met Xero's, and they were filled with tears of joy as she embraced him.

"It worked," she whispered through the tears. "I don't feel the fraying edges of my mind anymore."

Xero was crying with happiness at the return of his sister. His long-lost sibling. He ran a hand along the top of her shoulders. "I told you we'd be together again."

Xera's body shook as she cried, and Xero just held her tight.

Jace was anxious and eager. He wanted to get there faster but could only watch as the large planetoid slowly grew in size until, finally, he got close enough to make out some of the structures on the surface. The entire world was something Ollie called a "Gaia" world; a perfect paradise with all the resources one could need.

The entire upper atmosphere was covered in a slight shimmering haze of silvery light, and as Jace's vehicle sank down through it, he saw a new System message—one that was a white box with black text on it.

> [Welcome to Prismari.]
> [You are not a Soul.]
> [OVERRIDE.]
> [Welcome, envoy of Universe 348.]
> [All willing Souls, from all afterlives, who desire to return to their home reality, are in the location that will be tagged in the following message.]
> [Please go there, and only there.]
> [Thank you for visiting.]

Another System screen came up, and Jace guided the starfighter down through the silvery clouds to be greeted with a sight that paralleled the most gorgeous worlds in his Universe. A vast paradise extended before him. A world that was covered in lush, rolling, green fields. In places, the green gave way to golds and silvers. Vast, pure-blue oceans slowly lapped away at bronze-colored sandy beaches. Mountains that were as magnificent as they were terrifying given their heights pierced into the silvery haze of clouds up above.

And on the horizon, as he descended, a city. What looked like a perfect recreation of his home when he escaped the boarding school. A pure version of what could have been—the city he grew up in. No corporations running the streets, no huge logos on buildings as the greasy smog wafted through the air. No acid rain that would irritate the skin of the street folk.

As he flew across the landscape, he glanced down out of the starfighter's cockpit windows and saw all manner of shimmering, sparkling shapes—people of species innumerable, animals and creatures that were regal and seemed primal.

He flew over the city and saw a familiar sight, and he felt his heart skip a beat. The park he used to take Chroma to. The familiar pastel-colored rubber pads that were under the various pieces of gym equipment were glaring in comparison to the neat black streets and grey sidewalk. No gates around the park like when he lived in New Jersey with Chroma, but instead, it was open to everyone—and he saw children playing as their parents watched and chatted idly with each other. People who looked like people—humans specifically—but were covered in sparkling energy.

He landed at the edge of the park and slowly got out of the starfighter cockpit, hands and legs shaking as he saw her. "Chroma," he whispered.

His dead sister; her dark brown hair with the single cluster of light-blue neon highlights, dressed in her small jumpsuit with her name on the front, swinging on the swings and laughing. Jace ran forward. "Chroma!" he shouted.

She looked up and tilted her head sideways slightly. "Jace?"

Fuck! NICIF, make me look like I used to. Skin color, hair, all that stuff!

[On it, boss!]

Jace saw Chroma's face broaden into a smile as she waved for him to come over. "Come push me higher!"

Jace got to her and dismissed his Gear into the TPSB, leaving him in just lounge-about clothes. He grabbed her from the swing and hugged her tightly, feeling the tears roll down his cheeks as he wept for joy. "I got you back," he whispered as he ran a hand through her hair. "I'm so sorry, Chroma."

"Sorry for what?" she asked, muffled against his chest as she struggled to break free.

Just leave it be for now, Ollie said. He pulled out of Jace's head, causing the massive headache, and he floated in front of Chroma. "Hi there! I'm Oliver, but you, little missy, can call me Ollie."

Chroma managed to wriggle her head free of Jace's hug and giggled. "You're a cute furry snake."

"I'm an otter," he said with pride. "And I'm Jace's best friend."

"Can I pet you?"

"You may," Ollie said.

Jace felt someone tap his shoulder and glanced back to see a well-dressed man in a business jacket. But there was something off about him. He looked like the other people around, but he had a charisma that seemed to exude from him. "You must be Wraith."

Jace let Chroma go, and she grabbed Ollie, who distracted her for a moment—but Jace kept a hand holding Chroma's hand. "Yes, that's me."

The gentleman smiled broadly. "The Ancients told me you would be coming by. Everyone who wants to go back, from any afterlife, is ready. Shall I begin boarding them into your Soul storage container?"

Jace nodded. "Please . . . and thank you for keeping her safe."

The man chuckled. "My entire existence, Wraith, has been to safeguard Souls and keep them happy. The Afterlives are all connected, you see, and each afterlife is a pure mirror of what could have been." His smile softened. "But, kiddo, let me tell you something secret." He leaned in and whispered to Jace, "Paradise can be achieved within a Universe as well. Just requires you to make sure the bad Souls get sorted out."

Jace nodded. "We have that covered. Karma Judgement Matrix, and some means of cleaning up Souls."

"Soul Scrubbing? Not unheard of." The man glanced at Chroma, who had quieted and was listening to the conversation, holding Ollie in her arms as he poked his head up under her chin. "Now, if you'll excuse me, I'll start onboarding your passengers." He looked up to Jace. "They are your responsibility to deliver."

"Nothing will stop me from delivering them," Jace said.

The man nodded and turned away, and Jace watched as he raised his hand and all of the people around them except for Chroma turned into glimmering, silver shimmers that consolidated down to the light blue of Souls. They all then surged to the container atop his starship. And as the man waved his hands above him, Jace saw countless Souls fly to the container from all directions in the skies above.

Chroma squeezed Jace's hand, pulling him back to her. "Are we going home?"

Jace picked her up and gave her a tight hug. "We are, sis."

The man walked over for a moment and looked at Chroma, then to Jace. "If she wishes to depart back to your Universe, she must enter the vessel with the rest." He gestured to the container.

Jace hugged Chroma. "We are going to see some amazing places, Chroma."

"Prettier than here?"

Jace nodded. "Yeah." He reluctantly let her go, and the man gently reached down, tapping her on the head. Her body vanished in a glimmer of silver as her light-blue Soul coalesced and zipped into the container. Turning to the man, Jace nodded resolutely. "I'll get them back."

"I don't doubt it. Now, I was told every few thousand years you would be visiting just in case more decided to go back. Is that still the plan?"

"It is," Jace replied.

"Good. Then I will utilize the Astral System to contact you." He chuckled, "I may not be a part of it, but I can send messages through it." He vanished in a brilliant golden glow.

Ollie swam little happy circles around Jace. "Let's go home!"

Jace went to the starship and got back into the cockpit. Strapping himself in, he closed the canopy and took off, rocketing straight up. *Okay Holy Hunt—take us home.*

Flying back through the Soul Realm seemed to take very little time. Jace blitzed by The Ancient's small cottage into the white tube that angled down sharply but also seemed to expand to accommodate the starfighter. He emerged in the throne room of Layer 10, still covered in small dirt piles, and saw Yroshnak wave briefly before Jace jetted out of there and across the much more idyllic-looking Layer 10.

Through the film and up to Layer 9, then through a tunnel leading up to Layer 8. He did not stop to look at what had changed about each one—his focus was singular, and his command of the vessel masterful. It took less than a cycle to reach the first Layer of the Astral Verge.

A communication line opened up, and he heard a somewhat familiar voice he had not heard in a long time. "This is Grand Coordinator Brok. Wraith? Any chance—"

"No," Jace replied as he turned off the comms. *I'm not beholden to anyone now . . . I will do what I want, when I want. And Chroma is first on that priority list.* He reached the huge, white-grey tower of Void and flew the starfighter into the docking bay. Then, he exited out of an upper tube that led him into the singularity and up to the Penrose Sphere.

Landing in the docking bay next to the Soul Storage, he got out of the cockpit and saw both Xero and Xera—the latter looking much better than before, with a more hale complexion and a broad grin across her face—running up. "You have the Souls?" Xera asked.

Jace nodded. "Chroma first."

Xero tapped his wrist pad, and a series of drones flew over, connecting tubes and cables from the large cylinder strapped to the starfighter. Xera grabbed his hand and pulled him into the adjoining room, where he watched the Souls flood through and into a storage container. She began pointing at various instruments. "First, they go through the Soul Scrubber that Hualong helped us design—all the evil things they did, all the bad impulses, gone. Then, they get put into the holding cell where their Soul is placed into a queue. Into the Karma Judgement Matrix, where they are judged, and then—"

"Hold up," Jace said briefly. "The Soul Scrubber getting rid of evil . . . are you brainwashing Souls as they go through?"

Xera shook her head. "No. It's for Souls that have been stagnant for a long time. It gets rid of the miasma that builds up and can cause a lot of fucked up shit." She covered her mouth. "Whoops. Don't know how many kids are in the tube. My bad." She pointed to the Karma Judgement Matrix embedded at the bottom of the Soul repository tube. "The miasma is like a bad karma amplifier. If they did really bad things in life and didn't try to balance their karmic scale, then the Karma Judgement Matrix would judge them, and they'd be sent down into the Astral Verge. Maybe they make it down to the Afterlives, or not, who knows? Maybe that journey would change them for the better."

Xero walked up behind them. "Then, once they are in the queue, they get a cloning vat where their consciousness can design their body to their specifications."

"You're not going to have kids come back in adult bodies, are you?"

Xero chuckled and shook his head. "No, we put in limitations, of course. Come on, let's go greet your sister." Xero led Jace with Xera trailing into the cloning room, and Jace saw Chroma's body in the tube. He put his hand on the glass as Xero spoke. "She is making any final alterations she desires."

"Like what?" Jace asked as concern washed over him.

"Minor physical modifications—eye color, hair color, that type of stuff."

The tube opened, and Jace held his breath as Chroma's eyes flickered open. She looked over at him and smiled. "Hey, Jace . . ." Then, her eyes seemed to register Xero and Xera, and her face beamed with enthusiasm. "Aliens are real?!"

Chapter Fifty-Five

Endings

"And that is all, Your Grace," Grand Coordinator Brok said as his mandibles clacked out the last syllable.

Hive Queen Phrakal scoffed, "No matter. If one possible ally does not wish to assist, then that is fine. The Vanguard Empire was the only real threat, and they are now contained to their Universe." She clicked her mandibles. "Any word on the mountain that vanished along with its Universe funnel?"

"No, Your Grace." Brok knew better than to tell her that they had lost four expeditionary vessels that just vanished upon entering the region that the mountain had previously existed in. *We aren't throwing away more lives for a stupid desire to find and possess whatever technology exists there.*

The Queen waved her hand, dismissing him. Brok went back to his station deep in the bowels of their flagship, and he began setting up more diplomatic envoys for newly discovered Universes. *The Gyanv Alliance Coalition will grow*, he thought. *We will unite everyone on the first Layer of the Astral Verge, no matter how big or endless it is. United in cause, to stop the Astral Demons for good.*

Yroshnak finished his speech over the Astral Verge Demon–only communication relay. “And thus it shall be,” he stated. “Demon Lords will remain.” He dismissed the attending Astral Demons save for the Demon Lords of each layer. “Now that we have only those who make decisions present . . . here is how distribution will work . . .”

Yroshnak spent the next several cycles delving into the exacting specifications of how they would be distributing the judged Souls from the top-down. As he concluded the meeting, Malphitria of the third Layer spoke. “I will need some of your higher-Potency forces to assist with a few lingering Dreamer Demons who are overstaying their welcome.”

Yroshnak looked out over his new throne room in the citadel before the Nethershift and gestured to two of his demons, who nodded and headed out of the building. “I am sending two of my best to assist.”

Phytala, of the seventh Layer, spoke up next. “I have a pilgrim who has gone down the path of refinement alone. They have met Wraith, and even helped him out. As such, if I can have Souls of the judged to pass on to him, we can see if there is any truth to this idea that a pure-refinement-path Demon can become a person.”

“I have a lot of Universal Matter on hand,” Yroshnak said. “I will send most of it to you, Phytala, and you, Ryun, as those who reach Potency 6 will then be able to use it.”

“A wise decision,” Ryun said. “I could use an enforcer or two of yours to help clean up the Layer. We still have some monstrous path demons who are resisting my decisions.”

“I will help,” Yroshnak said. He saw a large shape fly through the double doors. One he had not seen in a long, long time. “I must go. Contact me if it is urgent.” He stopped the call and stood up as he walked down the dais. Approaching the large, bird-shaped Astral Demon, he bowed deeply. “Rickard,” he said solemnly. “To what do I owe the pleasure.”

The eldest of all Astral Demons, the firstborn of the first wave and the last of that group to survive, dipped his large, beak-shaped head. “I simply wished to see how you were settling in on my way through.”

Yroshnak gestured back to the still-messy throne room, where some of his demonic horde were pulling the spikes off of the walls. “It will take a while to restore this place to its former glory.”

“You are capable enough, no doubt.” The massive demon lowered his eye to Yroshnak’s level. “Now then . . . about this Wraith. Tell me what you thought of him.”

“A mighty warrior and a truly heroic soul.”

Rickard nodded. “As I suspected and sensed. Good. Then my aid to him was not misplaced.”

Yroshnak felt a pit in his stomach. “You . . . you met him?”

“On Layer 7,” Rickard replied. “I told him of the Relic throne of my younger brother.”

Yroshnak felt relief. “Ah, well, just informing him and not forming a pact was kind of you.”

Rickard looked at the tunnel leading past the Demon Lord of Layer 10. “I will go, I think. To visit The Ancients.”

As the massive bird demon walked past Yroshnak, he couldn’t help but ask one more question. “What exactly is your role in all of this?”

Rickard looked back with a somber expression. “Reality is ever changing, ever fluctuating, young demon . . . One day, you will realize that this existence is not all there is to reality. There is something we all were destined to do. Even the mightiest of Astral Demons can go through the Nethershift for judgement.” He looked back to the tunnel. “I am the last of my kind. The first wave of Astral Demons. The only one who resisted the darkest urges of my being. I wonder . . . will I be judged kindly?” He chuckled as he flew down the white tunnel.

Yroshnak simply raised a hand. “I hope you are found worthy of whatever lies beyond.” He then looked out to the now-green, verdant fields of Layer 10. “But my time is a long ways away. There is work to be done.”

Jace popped into existence in his apartment with Chroma popping in next to him a split second later. He scooped her up as Ollie flew little laps around their heads. Chroma's hand glowed with the brown C of the Civilian marker.

"I liked the alien lady," Chroma said as she gently kicked her legs back and forth. "She was nice."

And that is exactly why I'm going to keep you far away from her manipulating bullshit, Jace thought as he smiled and looked over at Ollie. "Did we end up converting—"

"Way ahead of you!" Ollie flew in front of Jace and pointed at a door. "This one is set up."

Jace looked at it, puzzled. "This door wasn't here before."

"I added extensions," Quinn said over the comms. "Easy enough with our Stardust reserves."

"Our?" Jace asked.

"Who are you talking to?" Chroma asked with curiosity.

"Your Auntie Quinn," Jace said with a wry smile.

Quinn appeared with a pop in the hallway next to them. "Hi there, Chroma. I'm Quinn." She glared at Jace. "I am not an auntie. But I am happy to be your pal." She tapped the door and it slid open. "The room is yours."

Chroma wriggled out of Jace's grasp and ran into the room before loudly complaining, "It's just an empty white room!"

Jace chuckled, and Quinn rolled her eyes as she stepped inside and tapped the panel that adjusted itself to waist height for adults—just about as tall as Chroma's head. "You get to design it."

Chroma looked at Jace. "I have my own room?"

Jace squatted and nodded; he couldn't keep the grin off of his face. "Yeah. This is your room. And when you are all settled in, we are going to go get you a whole bunch of clothes, and go out to eat. Whatever you want—we'll get it . . . I finally finished that gig. We're set for life."

Chroma giggled with delight and began tapping the panel.

There was another pop, and Shhiv grabbed Jace from behind, pulling him up. "You got back and didn't immediately tell me?!"

Jace turned around in her grip and gave her a kiss on the cheek. "I'm sorry, but—"

"No buts!" Shhiv said as she pulled him out of the way and knelt next to Chroma. "Hey there."

Chroma looked sideways at Shhiv, and her eyes went wide. "You're even more alien-looking than that Xera lady!"

Shhiv giggled. "Yeah. I'm called a Churkun. And I'm your big brother's wife." She held out her hand. "I'm Shhiv."

Chroma shook the hand. "I'm Chroma," she said with confidence. "Does that make you—"

"Your big sister," Shhiv said with a smile. "We're going to have so much fun." She leaned her head against Jace's shoulder. "As a family."

"Okay!" Chroma kept tapping the console as Shhiv stood up and joined Jace and Quinn just outside the room in the hallway.

Quinn chuckled, "We've got a weird thing going on here." She gestured between the three of them. "Remember when I was trying to get into your pants for the Star Council? That was weird."

Jace shook his head at the recollection of her trying to be romantically interested in him. "That was weird . . . You can be as involved with our family as you want. Whether you want to be a big sister also, an auntie, whatever. You've more than enough to make up for what you did back on Velenar Prime."

"I'll get the whole crew together for a little get-together," Quinn said as she disappeared with a pop.

"I'm done!" Chroma said.

Jace looked into her room and felt his senses assaulted by the bright neon pink and blue. It was a little girl's dream bedroom, complete with a cosmo-screen embedded into the ceiling, tons of stuffed animals on a massive bed that was designed like one of the Webwalker pods, and with chromed-out walls that reflected the bright neon lights. "It's all yours," Jace said. He wrapped an arm around Shhiv's waist and leaned against her, feeling her return the gesture and pull him tight.

"Ready to go shopping?" Shhiv asked.

"Yeah," Chroma said. "I want something that is sparkly."

Xera and Xero stood in the tower overlooking Khrox. He tapped the console in front of him and then looked back out at the infinite expanse. "All done," he said. "Administrative controls have been transferred to Jace Seren."

Xera finished tapping a screen as well, her whole demeanor back to what she used to be—bright-eyed, inquisitive, enthusiastic, and a delight to be around. No more the dark, brooding person he had first seen when she had pulled him into the virtual reality to recover. "And I just finished transferring Tech Support permissions away. Looks like Jace has assigned Quinn. I figured as much." She sighed and went to sit down on the couch, tenting her hands. "Now we focus on getting the rest of our species through therapy and into new bodies."

Xero sighed and walked over to her. "We'll get them through it." He put a hand under her chin and smiled down at her. "We have our perfect Universe. Forever safe. A closed loop again . . . you did great, sis."

She smiled and grabbed his hand gently before playfully tossing it to the side. "What do we do now?" she asked.

"I would love to design some games," Xero said as he looked back out to the city. "A virtual reality where Civilians can train up to eventually tackle the Aspirant challenge."

"Always wanting to improve the lives of the species in our Universe," Xera said with a slight giggle. "You are a one-track mind, you know that?"

"What about you?" Xero asked as he looked back at her.

"I think I want to work on my people skills a bit. I might work with Doctor Restra and try to do something with therapy through technology. Like an accelerated VR therapy experience."

Xero smiled. "First things first. Let's get the rest of our species back."

Felicity Seren reached her apartment and began to walk up the stairs, only to hear a voice from behind her on the street. "Fifi?"

She wheeled around and dropped her cosmopanel, the device clattering on the ground as she gasped. "Arthur?"

Her husband, killed in the corpo wars—or so she thought—was standing in front of her. His broad smile, short-cut brown hair, and piercing brown eyes made her legs weak, and she gripped the side of the building to steady herself.

He came over to her and gave her a big hug. "I'm back," he said softly. "I'm alive again."

"How?!" Felicity said, fully confused and in shock.

"Our boy," Arthur said as he began choking up a bit. "Our boy . . . our Jace . . . he saved me. Dozens—no, trillions. Countless people." He pulled back and put a hand behind Felicity's neck, pulling her in for a kiss that she returned happily.

They separated, and Felicity shook her head. "What do you mean?"

Arthur looked at the apartment door. "Mind if I come in and we can talk?" He reached down and grabbed her cosmopanel from the ground, handing it to her.

Felicity took him by the arm and entered the hallway. Going to the elevator at the end, she entered with him, tapped the button for her floor, and ascended. "How?"

"Jace went through hell and got back with everyone who died." Arthur smiled. "I got a nice little information download when I woke up. This whole Cosmic System is pretty neat." He looked at her and squeezed her hand. "Death doesn't matter anymore. If you die, and you were a good person—I was told that guidelines are going to be sent out soon—then you come back." He squeezed her hand. "We get another go of things, Fifi."

Felicity felt her breath catch in her chest as they reached her floor. She floated more than walked over to the door to her apartment, tapping her cosmopanel to it as they both entered. Once the door was shut, she set her few items down on the table in the entrance hall and turned to look at Arthur. "Tell me everything."

Arthur nodded, and she guided him to a small living room. They sat on the couch, and he began going over everything that happened after he was marked as KIA in the corpo war. His finding out about Jace, getting him from the boarding school, and his death. Then, his weird time in a liminal space before finding himself in a paradise-version of New York City.

"And then I was given the chance to come back," he finished as he squeezed her hand. "And I had to come back to you."

Felicity had sobbed during the story, and now she was out of tears to cry. "And . . . oh God, I fucked things up so badly with our son." She wanted to cry more but could not.

Arthur brushed her cheek gently. "Hey . . . no, you did the best you could."

There was a knock at the front door, and Arthur got up. "I'll get it."

Felicity was quiet, and felt her heart beating rapidly as she took it all in. From the hallway she heard a familiar voice, and stood up immediately. "Jace?" she whispered.

Her son, her boy, came into the room with Arthur right behind him. Jace looked like the spitting image of his father, except for the slightly bronzer skin and the piercing, celestial eyes. "Mom," he said tersely.

Arthur pushed past him. "That's your mother there," he said. "And if you want to get to know me as your dad . . . you have to accept that we are a package deal, her and I." He grabbed Felicity's hand.

Jace sighed, pinched the bridge of his nose with one hand, and tersely nodded. "Mom," he said softly. "I . . . I'll be back in a second." He vanished with a pop and then reappeared a second later with a metal, rectangular plate in one hand and a small credit stick in the other. "You should read this."

Felicity grabbed the metal plate and read the message pressed into it from her husband. She had to sit down as her legs were shaking again, and she numbly looked at the credit stick in Jace's hand. "We . . . I didn't . . . oh God . . . "

Jace walked in front of her and knelt, taking the plate from her as it vanished, sucked into a bracelet on his wrist. "I . . . I forgive you. You kept Dad's gift safe for me, you never opened it . . . but I wish you had. Then, maybe, we could have had a better life." He looked to Arthur, who had sat next to Felicity, then back to her. "Mom . . . I forgive you." He sighed and stood up. "Chroma, however, never knew you. And by your own admission in the past, she was meant to be a bargaining chip to work your way up the megacorp ladder . . . I will tell her everything when she is old enough to understand why you did what you did. Then, and only then, will I allow you to meet her. If she wants a relationship with you . . . that's her call."

Felicity felt her heart drop, but understood. "I have to suffer the consequences of my actions." She nodded solemnly and squeezed Arthur's hand. "Thank you, Jace, for bringing my husb—your dad back."

Jace looked to his dad. "I'll talk to you soon." He then vanished with a pop.

Arthur sighed, "I think we should just give him some space." He squeezed Felicity's hand. "He'll come around a bit more, I think."

Felicity just nodded silently. *At least I have you*, she thought.

Greg and Missy got back home via the voidlight tether, warping to their apartment as they took turns in the hygiene station—washing off all of the blood and guts from their bodies.

Getting revenge was great, and Greg was about to go and fabricate some raw food to cook up into a delicious meal when he got a message from Jace. Opening up the comms, Greg spoke softly, "Hey man, what's up?"

"Got Missy with you?"

"Mm-hmm," Greg replied.

"Good. Get together, put on your wedding outfits—we're doing a take two."

Greg blinked a few times and then turned on his heel. "Missy! Hurry up and get that fine ass into that wedding dress!"

She poked her head out of the bathroom. "Sorry?"

"We're getting married again!"

Missy's grin widened as much as it possibly could, and she quickly dipped back into the restroom, coming back with immaculate hair and makeup. "Hurry up!" she said as she rushed to the bedroom and began changing with the help of her Wayfinder.

Greg quickly got ready, and the two looked their best possible. He was so ready to see everyone again. The world shimmered around them, and they were warped to The Cosmic Corridor in front of a portal Greg knew well enough. Stepping into the black space that led to the console and selecting a destination, Greg chose the option for London, England, and he and Missy walked through.

There were cheers and shouts, and Greg was taken aback as he saw the entirety of St. Paul's Cathedral towering in the background, covered in glimmering neon lights and with a huge banner stretching across the front entrance that said "Bhastal Wedding" across it in glittering green letters.

The entirety of the churchyard seemed to be closed off for the private event, and Greg saw everyone they had lost at the wedding to the bomb that went off under the venue. He shoved down the tears and squeezed Missy's arm tightly with his as he heard her gently crying.

Jace walked over, dressed up in a nice suit with Shhiv, arm in arm. "I hope you don't mind," he said as he gestured to the cathedral. "I know you are a religious man, and figured this would be a good place."

"It's England, not Scotland . . . but it'll do," Greg managed to get out.

"You should see Chroma! She's going to be a flower girl," Shhiv said. "Figured you wouldn't mind," she whispered.

"I don't," Missy whispered.

Greg led her into the cathedral and up the steps to the altar of the historical site that he could never have rented out for such an event. He looked over at his teary-eyed bride and felt such rapturous joy and, glancing back, saw that all of the crowd following in—all of his vast extended family—had filtered to their seats.

Jace and the other Dark Between Stars Signers were sitting in the front row, and off on the farthest edge of that row, Greg saw the two aliens, Xero and Xera.

He turned back to the front as a priest dressed in immaculate robes entered the room from a side chamber. "I understand that your first time was interrupted," the man said softly. "Shall we do this from the top-down?"

"Yes," Greg said. He glanced back to Jace. *Thanks for this.*

Dee cackled with delight as she and her sister Ree sat on the oceans of Pirthimalin, one of the resort worlds that they had visited a few times. She watched as Priam built a sandcastle with Chroma and was laughing at the disagreement they were having on how to build the front-most section.

Quinn was next to them, working on a tablet as she reclined in a beach chair. "Always working," Ree said as she glanced over at the woman.

"I'm focused on fun also," Quinn retorted.

Dee ignored their idle conversation and kept her eyes on her precious little fluff ball. Priam had taken to the role of being a fun uncle right away and was reading Chroma a bedtime story almost every night. Dee had taken on the role of a fun auntie and was barely able to sneak Chroma away a few times to show her how fun it could be to lockpick, even smuggling the girl a small set to practice with at home.

Priam walked over to her with a frustrated look on his face and plopped down next to Dee. “She won’t listen to me,” he grumbled as he crossed his arms. “I told her we needed wetter sand. See?” he gestured as Chroma tried to put a new, small tower on the sandcastle and knocked over a large chunk of it.

Dee chuckled and rubbed his head with her chitinous shell hand. “She’s a little rebel, that one. Can’t wait until she can choose Aspirant and decides to follow in her brother’s path.”

Priam leaned against her, and she let her goop seep out of her chitin to rest a bit on his upper shoulder, leaning on him in a way. “That’s a few years away.”

Dee watched as Jace and Shhiv breached the waves off in the cool, crystalline ocean waters in the distance. “Yeah . . . she’s got a ways to go.”

Quinn sat up. “Shit. You three mind helping out for a minute?”

Dee bolted upright as her goop sucked back into her chitinous shell. “Where-to?” she asked, knowing that Quinn asking for her help meant she got to blow something up.

“We’ve got a rogue asteroid on a collision course for a high-population world. I’d rather not warp everyone off-world and have it destroyed.”

“On it!” Dee looked at Priam and ruffled his fur on his head again. “Ree and I got this. Come on.” Ree stood up, and both Plorps warped into the void of space.

Dee saw the enormous asteroid in the distance, hurtling toward a planet. She looked to her sister, and both shared the same thought. *Time to blow shit up!*

Quinn finished dinner with her parents and said her goodbyes as she left their apartment. Once she was outside and the door had shut, she warped to Xera's tower and walked into the main battle station room.

Greeting the various Wayfinders that were floating about, she checked all of the logs and ensured things were running buttery smooth. Satisfied nothing was wrong, she turned to her investments and stock portfolios. In addition, she pulled up the trade inventory and began setting up deals and exchanges.

Rare resources from various worlds, objects factions needed, and more. The Universe was more-or-less at peace. *Let's take a look at those few on my radar*, she thought as she pulled up a screen with three worlds she had been monitoring. All of them were not at the threshold for Cosmogenic Merging, but they were also on the verge of total war. *Magic, magitech, technology . . . how quaint.*

Opening up the comms, she spoke to the Dark Between Stars Signers. "Anyone want to go and stop a few world wars from happening? Priam, got a magic world that needs some intervention."

"Ohh!" his voice came back. "Can we pull the whole 'god from on high' routine again?"

"I don't mind, as long as you do not do a mass healing Skill across the whole world this time."

He made a grumpy, frustrated sound but ultimately acquiesced with a small "Okay."

Greg and Missy replied next, with Greg saying, "Give us the job."

"Tech or magitech?" Quinn asked.

“Tech,” Missy replied.

Quinn tapped off the orders and instructions. “Sent. Jace, Shhiv? Wanna deal with magitech?”

“I’ll handle it,” Jace said. “Shhiv’s watching Chroma.”

Quinn nodded. “Okay. That’s all for now. See you all for game night later.” She shut off the comms and leaned back in the chair.

Xera walked in from the main part of the apartment that was still her residence, though now she had another bedroom that Xero occupied. “Hey there, Tech Support.”

Quinn glanced over to her. “Hey. Coming to game night?”

“I’d love to,” Xera replied with a genuine smile on her face. Not forced, not manipulated. “It’s been nice the past few months.”

Quinn nodded. *Already six months*, she thought as she sank into the comfy chair. Life had become nice and predictable, with a little bit of action here and there. But Quinn got to do what she always wanted—be a Webwalker and sit behind the scenes, supporting others.

And she wasn’t just a solo act anymore. She had a found family. Yes, she had real family . . . but she also had others she cared about now. She flipped open her thermos and took a sip of coffee, feeling the buzz whir through her circuitry of the bionic implants as the chemicals were accelerated.

Glancing over at Xera, she raised a curious eyebrow. “Going to let me win tonight?”

“Absolutely not,” Xera replied.

"And that's the story of the great mage, Asher," Priam said softly as he closed the book. "He lived happily ever after."

Chroma had just fallen asleep, and Priam always made sure to finish the chapter before he quietly got up and padded his way outside the room. Heading to Jace and Shhiv's living room, he found the couple sitting on their couch. "Hey," Priam said softly. "She's asleep now."

"Thanks," Jace said as he paused the film and glanced over at Priam. "Same time tomorrow?"

"Actually . . . do you mind us talking?" Priam asked.

"Sure, I don't mind. Shhiv, you good giving us a minute?" She nodded and stood up, squeezing past Priam down the corridor and vanishing into the restroom.

Priam sat on the farthest edge of the couch and sighed. "I . . . I'm grateful for the trust we have." He looked to Jace. "I just wanted to say that I'm happy you trust me so much."

Jace looked perplexed. "You're welcome?"

"I mean . . ." Priam fidgeted with the book in his hands. "I . . . remember way back when we met? During the Dungeon Run?"

"Yeah, you tried to help a group capture me." Jace shrugged. "What about it?"

"I . . . one of the reasons I wanted to stick with you is because you reminded me of my big brother." Priam sighed. "He didn't come back."

Jace sat up. "Shit, why didn't you say something earlier?"

"I didn't know how to say it," Priam replied. "And . . . well . . . I was too nervous to ask you if you could check the Soul Storage thing to see if maybe he was just waiting his turn."

Jace stood up. "You want to know if he's out there . . . or if . . ." Jace trailed off, implication well understood.

Priam nodded. "I want to go with you on your next visit to the Afterlives. Maybe talk to someone and see if they know if he's there and just chose not to come back . . . the same with my dad."

Jace nodded and walked over, placing a comforting hand on Priam's shoulder. "Of course. Anything for you."

Priam looked up into the kind, compassionate face and nodded. "Thanks, Jace."

"Let's go check now." The world warped around the two, and Priam was standing next to Jace in front of the starship with the soul canister attached to the top. "Hop in the back." Jace popped the canopy, and gave Priam a boost up before clambering in himself.

Priam clicked the harness into place as Jace closed the canopy and the vehicle blasted out into Oblivion. Down through the singularity, into the Astral Verge, and began racing across the Layers. The duo made great time; less than an hour to the Nethershift. They flew through the open doors, over a throne, down a tunnel, and past a weird, floating cottage in the middle of a gorgeous view. "This is incredible," he muttered.

"I'd recommend closing your eyes," Jace replied.

Priam shut them, and felt the acceleration increase, then slow to a stop. "What happened?" he asked, eyes still closed.

"Just asking for directions." The vehicle kept moving, and then Priam felt it land on something. "Okay, you can open your eyes."

Priam opened them and found that they were on a huge, desert planetoid. They had landed on a large plateau, and it was covered in magnificent houses of Fernaid design. He unbuckled and got out of the harness. Jace popped the canopy, and Priam scrabbled down the outside as he saw familiar figures approaching. "Dad! Big brother!" He ran into their embrace and cried tears of sheer joy. "You're alive!"

"Not quite," his father replied, the soft, stern and warm tones bringing Priam back to the past.

Priam kept clutching to his father, and heard Jace's footsteps on the hardened crust of sand that his own footsteps didn't impact. "I can take you all back to our universe, and new bodies, if you want."

Priam's felt his father's chest rumble with a chuckle. "Thanks, mister. But we are where we should be."

"But Dad—"

"Seems like you visited us just fine," his big brother said, cutting him off. "We'll just do more visits."

Priam pulled away from his dad and looked back to Jace, who gave a little thumbs up. Priam then turned back to his family. "Sure . . . you won't get to meet my partner though."

Both other Oslia smiled at that. "Look at you, little guy," his big brother said. "Come on, tell us about her."

Shhiv dropped Chroma off at the pool for her lessons with some of the other kids. It had been a year since Jace had rescued everyone who wanted to come back from the Afterlives. And now, life had fallen into a wonderful routine with just a few occasional changes that would pop up.

Shhiv had fallen in love with Chroma, who she now fully considered her little sister. They were a perfect little found family, her, Jace, Chroma, and their weird aunts and uncles: Quinn, Greg and Missy, Dee and Priam, Ree, and Xero with Xera. Xera, however, was kept at a slightly farther distance from Chroma due to Jace's lingering bad feelings about her interactions with him in the past. After all, trust was a hard commodity to recover once broken.

They had weekly board game nights, group vacations to various worlds all across the Universe. It was a blissful life, a peaceful existence that was everything Shhiv could have ever wanted.

But Shhiv valued this time most of all. Her daily time alone with Jace. She warped back to their apartment and went into the living room, finding him already dressed up in his swim trunks and waiting. "Ready to go?" he asked her.

She nodded as she grabbed her change of clothes from the TPSB bracelet on her wrist, and the two of them warped to the Harkon Secundus portal. Stepping through, Jace picked her up and used his Soul Tether to whisk them across the vast distance at blistering speeds until they reached the huge lake region dominated by the cultivating leviathans.

She cracked her knuckles and grinned as she eyed some of the medium-sized ones that were still as big as trucks. "They are expecting us, right?" she asked with a glint to her eyes.

Jace was stretching a bit but nodded. "Yup. Go for it, honey."

Shhiv grinned and dove into the depths, sinking down toward the bottom and facing off against a Leviathan that dipped its head in a sign of respect. She activated her Skills and Talents as it did the same, and she engaged in a wrestling match with the powerful, cultivating creature. Not being combat focused in her build, she struggled a bit—but Jace was always on standby, keeping a close watch on her and not directly getting involved unless he saw her really having a hard time. Then, he would come to her rescue.

She wasn't ashamed to admit it to herself, but she sometimes threw the fight so that she would be rescued by her handsome man. The person who she entrusted her everything to. This time, though, she wanted to win, and so she was able to bait out a tail whip from the Leviathan before getting around behind the neck and choking the thing out to unconsciousness.

The task complete, she swam up and breached the surface, only for Jace to swoop by on his Soul Tether and grab her from the surf. She giggled with delight. "That was a good workout!"

"Wrestling building-sized leviathans is about the maximum for you without weapons, I think," Jace said as he gently set them both down on one of the floating rocks. He reached into the TPSB and pulled out a blanket, setting it down as they both sat and watched the huge creatures fighting in the waters below.

Shhiv was taking in deep, huffing breaths as she watched the visceral display of strength. Lifting weights had gotten boring, and she wanted a challenge. As she was not a combat-focused build in The Cosmic System or her now-internalized Astral System, she had a good challenge with the giant Leviathans.

She looked over at Jace, watching the sun glisten off of his perfect body. Scooting over, she put a hand on his cheek. "Hey . . . why don't we ever warp directly here?"

Jace shrugged and looked over at her. "I like the trip." He smiled. "Why? Did you want to go back home already?"

Shhiv laughed and shook her head. "No. I want to rest up a bit and then go for a round two. We still have a few hours before we need to pick up Chroma."

"We can always ask Priam to pick her up," Jace replied. "If you want to do something else."

"What did you have in mind?" Shhiv asked suggestively.

Jace grinned and turned to her, leaning into her and kissing her deeply as he gently laid her down.

This is it...I'm finally here, the Refined Pilgrim thought as he saw the huge stone doors leading to the Nethershift. Astral Demons stood guard, but gave him nods of respect, and he knew he would be safe. The Pilgrim entered the antechamber and stopped for a moment, tracing his hand along the wall. A bas relief that showed the whole history of the Astral System. It ended at the inner set of doors, which led to a throne that was currently unoccupied, leaving him alone.

A deep tunnel of white led back, and he felt called to it, but paused before going. *I must pay my respects.* He went to the foot of the dais and knelt. *System, dump out all of the Universal Matter I have left.* Piles of rocks and dirt appeared around him, and he stood up. He had to take a step back in shock as he saw a figure on the throne.

"Ah . . . welcome, Refined one. I am Yroshnak, Demon Lord of Blood. You have come a long way."

The Refined Pilgrim bowed at his waist. "I hope giving you the rest of my Universal Matter is the right thing to do. I have already purged the evil Souls entrusted to me by the different Demon Lords of the Layers I have traversed through."

"Excellent." Yroshnak gestured to the tunnel behind him. "Please . . . go through and find whatever awaits." He cracked a broad smile. "If you can come back, tell us what happened. You're the first to be fully Refined, with no good Soul consumption."

"I will," the Refined Pilgrim replied. He stepped around the dais and instinctively ducked as he heard a loud roaring noise overhead – engines firing at full blast. He *barely* saw the tail-end of a rocket engine. "What was that?" he asked.

"Ah, the Bearer of the Mantle. Going on another journey." Yroshnak chuckled. "Don't you worry about that. On you go."

The Refined Pilgrim nodded, swallowed, and went into the tunnel. As he walked, the corridor shifted from bright, white stone to black, then finally gave way to the gorgeous void filled with the planets of the afterlives. Stepping up the stairs, he approached the cottage with the fountain in front of it. To his surprise, the starship that had raced overhead had landed, and he spotted a familiar figure next to it. "Excuse me!"

The piercing, cosmic eyes looked at him. "Yes?"

The Refined Pilgrim walked over, and saw a small, blue-furred creature *pop* into existence next to the armored figure. "I . . . I met you, and helped you, a long time ago. Up on Layer 3."

The figure's gaze narrowed, then widened. "Oh . . . shit. Good job on getting here." He held out his hand, "Jace Seren, Bearer of the Mantle of Burden."

The Refined Pilgrim took the offered hand and shook. "My name is Eric."

Jace smiled, "So, Eric, you stayed Refined the whole way down, eh?"

"Oh yes. The temptations were great, but I persevered." Eric let the hand go and looked at the cottage. "What's in there?"

"The Ancients," Jace replied, crossing his arms. "I stop by every once in a while."

"What . . . what do I do?"

"Knock, maybe?"

Eric looked at the cottage door. "Then I guess it's my time." He looked back to Jace. "Have a good life."

"Best of luck with whatever comes next," Jace said as he hoisted himself into the starship and rocketed away.

Eric approached the door and knocked. A hooded, veiled figure opened the door. "Yes?"

"I . . . um . . . I finished my journey."

The voice of the Ancient sounded *elated*. "Excellent. Then join us, worthy one."

Ollie swam about the Starlit Sea with Josie. The two Wayfinders had integrated their code, the AI equivalent of a marriage, and were inseparable from their Ascendants. Two immortal, completely incorruptible AI constructs who could keep an eye on the inner workings of The Cosmic System on behalf of the System Administrator—Jace—and his Support Administrator—Shhiv.

Ollie looked over to Josie. The otter form had grown on him, and he found the cute pictures that Josie constantly sent him over their private messaging network of the creatures from Earth's Webnet so adorable. The otters floating, paws clasped, as they drifted through the river.

Josie swam over to him as she deactivated a node she was working on. "You okay?" she asked.

"I am," Ollie replied. "Just thinking about how lucky we are." He grabbed her paw gently. "What's next on our to-do list?"

"Well, we have the party coming up. I think the whole Star Council and Nebula Alliance-led coalitions are going to be there. It should be a blast!"

Ollie raised a paw to rub his temple. "We will need to get some other Wayfinders to handle asset protection and risk manage—"

"Already done," Josie said as she swam around Ollie in tight little circles, leaving behind starry blue nebula clouds in their wake. "You and I are going to have fun and focus on us."

Ollie chuckled and swam in circles opposite her, barely passing by her in an intricate dance as they both just enjoyed the quiet of each other's company in the ocean of shimmering starlight.

Jace ran his hand through Shhiv's hair and along the fin atop her skull, giving her a little scratch as she sighed, resting on his chest. He quickly scanned through the few Cosmic and Astral System messages he had—all of them of little consequence—and dismissed them for one of the extra Wayfinders Ollie had assigned to him to handle.

He looked down at the still-snoozing Shhiv, both suspended in the liquid starlight pool of their bedroom. "You okay if I slip out for a minute?" he asked her.

She nodded very slightly. "Sure," she mumbled.

Jace warped himself across the Universe, using The Cosmic System to launch himself across space within an instant. He stood in a familiar field. Lush grassland rose up all around him. The gritty dirt beneath his feet was a lingering reminder, and the multiple celestial bodies across the almost-painted sky brought him back to the moment his journey first started.

"Ollie," he said softly.

The Wayfinder appeared with a telltale *pop*, floating in lazy little circles around Jace's head. "Back to Velenar Prime?"

Jace nodded as he walked to the very place he had impressed Xera and every other faction leader with his defeating of the Vyrknadine so long ago. "Remember when we first met? You thought I was going to die and were such an asshole."

Ollie grumbled, "I was . . . but you proved me wrong."

Jace nodded and stood up. "I know," he whispered as he looked at his Wayfinder, then up at the gorgeous moons and the silent skies as a distant thundercloud roared with violent fury. "Thank you for being with me."

Ollie flew over and wrapped himself around Jace's neck as the new System Administrator reached a hand up to scratch his head. "What's going on?" Ollie asked. "You're not sentimental normally."

Jace smiled softly. "Chroma's sixteen, Ollie. She wants to take her Aspirant Trial. Greg, Priam, and Dee have all agreed to watch her and keep her safe . . . but I won't lie, I'm scared."

Ollie sighed. "Every creature must make their choice. Is her Karma Coefficient in the positive?"

"Yeah," Jace replied, as he had ensured she had followed The Architect's Guide to Positive Karma, with footnotes by Hualong, Herald of the Blossom Peaks, to the letter. "She is well up in the positive . . . but I can still worry." He looked down at Ollie. "Can we make sure she gets an amazing Wayfinder?"

"I will get Valerie," Ollie said. "She reset herself back when Quinn dismissed her. She's fresh, but experienced!" His voice shifted a bit to one that was almost apologetic. "That makes more sense to me than you, I bet."

Jace chuckled and scratched his best friend's head. "Together forever, and never alone . . . thanks for always being there."

Ollie made an almost purring noise. "Friends forever."

Jace just stood there, in the moment, with his Wayfinder as he heard the distant howl of a Vyrknadine. He chuckled for a brief moment as he recalled the visceral fear he had felt so long ago contrasted to how he felt now. Completely invincible, and the strongest entity in his Universe.

"Thanks," he whispered. "You can head back. I'm going to go back to Shhiv."

Ollie gave a thumbs up and vanished with a pop.

Jace warped himself back home, hopped into the hygiene station, and then went back to the bed-cube of water in the representation of the Starlit Sea. He curled up around Shhiv and felt her push back into him.

"I love you," he whispered to her.

"I know," she replied.

Made in the USA
Coppell, TX
21 January 2026

68950138R00272